Lyn Andrews

The House on Lonely Street

headline

First published in Great Britain in 2001 by
HEADLINE PUBLISHING GROUP

First published in this paperback edition in 2016 by
HEADLINE PUBLISHING GROUP

1

Cataloguing in Publication Data is available from the British Library

ISBN 978 1 4722 3773 6

Typeset in Janson by Avon DataSet Ltd, Bidford-on-Avon, Warwickshire

Printed and bound by CPI Group (UK) Ltd, Croydon, CR0 4YY

MIX
Paper from
responsible sources
FSC® C104740

HEADLINE PUBLISHING GROUP
An Hachette UK Company
Carmelite House
50 Victoria Embankment
London EC4Y 0DZ

www.headline.co.uk
www.hachette.co.uk

L ... . Her
fa ... onths
o ... Frank
M ... ught
u ... rying
p ... lets –
tw ... t few
y ... d her
fi ... since
w

th ... nt on
M ... ck on .

P

'

'

'

"

' ... king
c

By Lyn Andrews

Maggie May
The Leaving Of Liverpool
Liverpool Lou
The Sisters O'Donnell
The White Empress
Ellan Vannin
Mist Over The Mersey
Mersey Blues
Liverpool Songbird
Liverpool Lamplight
Where The Mersey Flows
From This Day Forth
When Tomorrow Dawns
Angels Of Mercy
The Ties That Bind
Take These Broken Wings
My Sister's Child
The House On Lonely Street
Love And A Promise
A Wing And A Prayer
When Daylight Comes
Across A Summer Sea
A Mother's Love
Friends Forever
Every Mother's Son
Far From Home
Days Of Hope
A Daughter's Journey
A Secret In The Family
To Love And To Cherish
Beyond A Misty Shore
Sunlight On The Mersey
Liverpool Angels
Heart And Home

For Michael and Concepta (Ceppie) Guinan:
Ceppie for lending me her name and becoming a
new but valued friend; Michael and the children,
Keven, Michelle and Damien, for making us feel part
of a truly close and happy family.

Lyn Andrews
January 2001

Chapter One

Dublin 1911

'WHY DO YOU have to be so nasty to them, Da? It's not their fault.' Katherine Donovan's blue eyes met her father's cold, flint-grey ones without flinching. She had never before commented on the way he treated his customers, though many was the time she'd pressed her lips tightly together in mute anger and cast darting, fury-filled glances at him. It was the poorest of the poor who came, filled with abject desperation, to the Harp and Shamrock, to pledge or sell whatever would raise a few shillings, for her da was a pawnbroker. He was also a money-lender, and his rates were nothing short of extortion. But people were grateful for the cash and didn't protest or argue. Most of them didn't really understand what they were agreeing to, for in the heart of the slums of Dublin, few could read or write.

'I'll stand no more talk like that from you, you bold rossi,'

1

her father growled back. His tone was chilly and bitter. 'And anyway, for your information, they're all eejits and idlers.'

Now that she'd started, Katherine plunged on, determined to have her say for once. 'They *can't* help it. They're not eejits, there *isn't* any work.'

He snorted derisively. 'There's plenty of work for those who want it. They can't pay their rent or feed their families because they're all going on strike by the minute. But more often than not they've the price of a pint of porter or a packet of Woodbines.'

She turned away from him as he slammed out of the kitchen. What was the use? There wasn't a drop of kindness in him. She would make no apology for challenging him, he deserved none. At heart she'd known there would be no satisfactory reply. He'd been like this for as long as she could remember: cold, unbending and relentlessly strict.

'Don't let him break your spirit, Katherine, I made that mistake,' her mam had once urged, and as she'd grown older she'd understood: her father was a cruel, twisted man. Many people were afraid of him and none had a good word for him, and she had suffered because of it. In all her years at school she'd been taunted and shunned. It had been the same with the kids in the street. They'd never let her join their games and she'd often gone home in tears, to no comfort from her da. Gradually she'd become used to it. She never spoke to those who called her names, she just learned to hold her head up defiantly.

She could remember quite clearly the only time Mam had ever stood up to him, a week before she'd died. It had been over what poor Joe Healy owed. He'd shouted down Joe's excuses and pleadings and actually struck the pale, stooped man twice before Mam had intervened.

'Leave him, Albert, for the love of God! Don't go taking the debt out of his poor, half-crippled body.'

'You mind your tongue, woman, or it's *your* body I'll go taking the debt from,' he'd bawled at her.

Now, up to her elbows in greasy water as she washed the dishes in the scullery sink, Katherine let her mind wander back over those years. Her poor, poor mam. A slave would have had a better life. She'd worked ceaselessly from dawn to dusk every day, including Sundays. By the time Da got up the breakfast was ready, the tea wet and the room warm. After that it was washing, polishing, scrubbing. More meals to cook, bread to make, socks and stockings to be darned; the list was endless. She had never been strong, either in body or personality. Her mam had had miscarriage after miscarriage before she'd been born. That in itself had been a disappointment for her da. He had wanted a son and after Katherine there were no other children. It was Da who insisted that she should always use her full name. Kate, Katie, Kath, Kit: none of these derivatives was permitted. She was 'Katherine' to everybody. Her da always said it separated her from the illiterate rabble they lived amongst.

Mam must have loved him once, she mused, otherwise she would never have married him. How long had it been before she'd realised she'd committed herself for life to a bully? She wrung out the dishcloth and hung it over the single tap, then, taking up the tea towel, she began to dry the dishes. She'd been close to her mam and as she'd grown older she had begun to understand just how she was suffering.

Nothing ever pleased Da. Nothing either she or Mam did was right. Much as she'd loved and missed her mam she would never wish her back here to this existence, in this slum, even though they had a comfortable home, good food, decent clothes and occasional treats like a few sweets. Of course she'd never been allowed to choose what kind of sweets. Da just gave her the small paper bag and she'd been grateful for that.

She hated this part of the city. Oh, the public buildings and parks were magnificent and were well maintained, and she'd often stared into the windows of Switzer's and Brown Thomas in Grafton Street, especially near Christmas. It didn't cost anything to look or wish. The streets with their rows of once-stately Georgian houses, now referred to as tenements, were home to thousands of people. Whole families lived in one or two rooms. Dark, damp cellars with no heating housed the truly destitute. The stone steps leading up to the front doors were all worn and cracked. The doors themselves, warped, their paint peeling – if there was any paint left on them – were left wide open all year, rain or shine. The fanlights above them were glassless or had jagged, fly-blown shards that time and the elements had not quite succeeded in dislodging. You couldn't see clearly into the halls, but maybe that was a blessing.

Her work finished for the day, Katherine took off her apron and went through to the living room. She permitted herself a cynical smile as her father hastily got up from the table, cramming notes and coins into the old tea caddy. With his back turned deliberately towards her, he fumbled under the big, heavy basket that held the turf.

She knew where he kept his money. She'd never touch it, he knew that.

'Are you going out, Da?' she asked, although she was certain of the answer.

'I am so. Isn't it Wednesday and don't I always go out?'

Katherine nodded. He didn't drink in any of the local pubs, he would be ostracised, at best, by the other patrons. He took a tram out to Dollymount. In a quiet, respectable pub with a snug he would have three pints of porter and a small Jameson's. Well, it suited her fine because she was going out herself to a public meeting in Beresford Place at which Mr George Bernard Shaw, amongst other illustrious people, was going to speak. Dublin was in turmoil as one after the other the city's industries were closed down by strike action. She felt great sympathy for the strikers, many of whose wives and mothers were amongst her father's customers. He was always giving out about them, berating and ridiculing them, and they could say nothing because they needed the money so badly.

When he'd gone out, she put on a jacket and her hat, a straw boater with a blue and white striped ribbon. As she gazed at her reflection in the mirror she felt overdressed for walking through the streets of decrepit houses, but to abandon the hat in favour of a shawl seemed somehow hypocritical. She sighed heavily. She was eighteen years old and she hated her life. Not one single aspect of it could she point out as satisfying. Many of the girls she'd been at school with were married now, and some even had children. She wondered: would she ever meet someone and fall in love? If she did, she'd have a war on her hands because she knew no local lad would ever come up to Da's expectations.

She'd gone as far as the corner, ignoring the looks of contempt cast by the groups of thin, anxious women whose lined and wrinkled faces were pale with ill-nourishment. Their barefoot children, rickety bodies clothed in what were little better than rags, played in the gutter, faces and limbs already so dirty that the extra grime made little difference. Some of the older ones stared at her and put out their tongues and made monkey-like faces at her. This too she ignored although inwardly their animosity cut deeply. If only there was *something*, *anything*, she could do to help them. But any help she offered would be refused. They wouldn't take charity handouts from Donovan's daughter.

'Katherine! Katherine, will ye wait for me!'

At the sound of the child's voice she stopped and turned around. She smiled. This was the exception to the rule. This was the one who braved the wrath of the others. Eight-year-old Concepta Healy, or 'Ceppi' as she was known, was like her shadow. She followed her everywhere. Da wouldn't have the child over the doorstep, so Ceppi always waited by the corner.

'Are ye going on a nice outing with the good hat on ye and all?'

Katherine took the grubby hands in hers. 'Well, I don't know if it will be a nice outing. It's a meeting.' She brushed back the strands of Ceppi's tangled copper-coloured hair. 'Isn't this desperate. It's like a furze bush.'

'Sure, we've no comb or brush. Didn't our Annie and Sally break them in the fight they had over them?'

Katherine smiled. 'Never mind, I'll buy you a hairbrush.'

Ceppi shrugged nonchalantly. 'Oh, I'm not troubled at all. Anyway, me mam would take it offen me.'

Katherine nodded and looked into the grey-green eyes that always seemed to be too huge for the pale, pinched little face.

'Will ye bring me on the outing too? I don't care what it is, really I don't.'

Katherine thought about it. There would be crowds of people and also the police and perhaps even the military. If things started to go wrong . . . well, she was a bit apprehensive herself if the truth be told.

'Please? Please? No one will miss me, no one cares. Except maybe me da.'

Katherine relented. Poor Joe Healy. He was a pleasant man who bore his many afflictions with patience and cheerfulness, despite the fact that Lily Healy did nothing for her husband, nor for her eight children, who were left to fend for themselves. Ceppi was the youngest. Joe Healy had been born with what everyone referred to as a crooked backbone. Walking was not easy and in his latter years he'd been crippled with arthritis. He had also contracted consumption to add to his misery. He got little sympathy from his wife: she'd once yelled at him she was sure he'd got the consumption to spite her. Everyone said he'd never see Christmas, but seemingly the child didn't know this or was putting a very brave face on it.

'Come on then, Ceppi, keep tight hold of my hand.'

The child grinned. 'Will you bring me on a tram?'

Katherine nodded. 'I will so, we're going up to Beresford Place, to a meeting. A big, important meeting.'

'Sure, what's a meeting? Have I been brought to one before?'

Katherine's explanation lasted until they boarded the tram.

Beresford Place was packed, the crowd thickest at the jumble of half-derelict buildings that used to be the Northumberland Commercial and Family Hotel. The twilight of a day that had taken a long time leaving the sky had finally been blanketed by a heavy darkness. At intervals the flaming, pitch-soaked torches men had attached to the walls of buildings illuminated faces and forms, all pale, all etched with hunger and anxiety. And yet, in their eyes there was a spark of determination and hope.

A double line of grim-faced police officers from both the Royal Irish Constabulary and the Dublin City Constabulary blocked their way to the nearest rank of the crowd. Katherine tapped the shoulder of the officer next to her. 'Would you excuse me, sir? I want to get through.'

The constable looked down at her. 'Now why should a respectable girl like you want to come here and join this mob of reprobates?'

Katherine looked up at him warily. He wasn't very old and he was quite good-looking. 'You're RIC?'

'I am so, I'm a Kerry man.' He had an accent as thick as butter.

'I didn't think it would be like this, not as crowded, but seeing as we're here we might as well stay.'

'Would ye look at all the polis,' Ceppi said in amazement. As long as she was with Katherine she wasn't afraid of them. Katherine was chatting in a friendly way to this one. She sensed the excitement. 'Oh, please let's stay!' she urged.

Katherine agreed warily, unable to resist the child's enthusiasm.

'On your own head be it then,' agreed the policeman, 'but if there's trouble get yourselves home immediately. I'll look out for you. Mind yourself now.'

As they joined the main body of the crowd Ceppi tugged at Katherine's skirt. 'Wasn't the polis man a sort of . . .?'

'A decent class of a man. But I'm still worried you won't be able to see anything and you might get crushed.'

'I won't! I won't be after letting them walk on me!' Small and thin as Ceppi was, Katherine knew the child could give as good as she got. She'd always had to, just to exist.

The press of bodies increased as more people joined the crowd. The night air became oppressive and it was difficult to hear all that was being said by the speakers. What she *had* heard she agreed with. Their leader, Big Jim Larkin, had demanded a fair day's pay for a fair day's work and an overtime rate of ninepence an hour. He'd demanded that there be no discrimination against union members. He'd already put a stop to stevedores paying the dockers in pubs and exacting a drink for it. There would be no more restrictive practices.

She looked around at the sea of uplifted faces. The torch-light made some of them look grotesque but there was something else too, a dawning recognition, and resolve to fight for that 'decent day's pay'.

There was some sort of scuffle going on in the crowd behind them and Katherine began to feel very anxious. 'Come on, Ceppi. I think we'd better go home. I'll buy you a hot pie to eat on the way,' she added, forestalling the child's complaints.

With an effort and the aid of the policeman from Kerry they got through the crowd, and they were even more fortunate to get a tram. The driver told her he was on his way back to Nelson's Pillar in Sackville Street. 'That'll be me lot,' he said. 'We're going on strike and the back of me hand to Mr William Martin Murphy and his Dublin Tramway Company.'

They walked quickly to the O'Connell monument and then along the Quays, noting how many people were out on the streets. As promised, Katherine bought Ceppi a pie which the child crammed greedily into her mouth.

As they turned the corner they both stopped. There seemed to be some sort of commotion going on around the Harp and Shamrock. The street lighting was dim: just one single gaslight struggled feebly against the darkness, creating deep shadows. A figure emerged from the mêlée by the shop and Katherine recognised it as Ceppi's brother, Con.

'What's wrong, Con? What's going on?'

Con looked wild and distraught, his eyes wide with some sort of panic. 'Ah, God, isn't it me da and your da and the men from the houses,' he panted.

'What men? What's the matter?'

'Me da . . . me da's dead and it was *your* da what did it!'

Katherine was stunned. 'No! No! In the name of God, he couldn't, he . . .' For a second she was stuck for words.

'And now the men are after murderin' *him*.'

'Oh, Jesus!' Katherine's hands went to her cheeks. It couldn't be true. It *couldn't*! Her da couldn't have killed poor Joe Healy.

'Come back with me now, Ceppi,' Con demanded, catching hold of his sister's arm.

She shook it off. 'What'll I do?' she asked, looking up at Katherine wide-eyed and bewildered.

Katherine felt ill. Her imagination was running wild. They'd come for her next! she thought in panic. 'Ceppi, go with Con,' she urged. 'Go back with him.'

The little girl stood firm. 'No! I will not! I'm staying with you!' Her confusion seemed to have been replaced by a blind obstinacy.

'Ceppi, please?'

'No!'

It was useless and time wasn't on her side. She caught the child's hand. 'Run! We've got to run, Ceppi. Run for our lives!' They both tore out of the small circle of gaslight back into the darkness.

Con watched them disappear, then turned and walked unsteadily away.

Chapter Two

———◆———

THEY WERE BOTH panting and shaking by the time they reached the corner of the street. There was a patch of scrubby land there where two of the old houses had finally collapsed from neglect. The streetlamp had suffered a similar fate to the houses and no one had bothered to replace it. They were both grateful for the darkness. Katherine leaned against the soot-blackened bricks of the wall of the corner house. It just *couldn't* be true. It *couldn't* be. Oh, she knew her da's temper well enough from experience, but to *kill* someone and that someone as near to a cripple as Joe Healy had been . . . Joe'd never have dared start an argument with anyone, let alone defend himself.

'Oh, God, Ceppi! Why would he do it? He knew your da's a sick man! Maybe it isn't true?' She held tightly to the shred of hope that it was all a misunderstanding, that it had been exaggerated. Things often were and the more people gossiped, the more fictional the accounts became.

The child looked up at Katherine's pale, tear-stained face into eyes that were full of horror and disbelief. But it *must* be true, she thought wildly, Con wouldn't make up something like that. It was too terrible. She was afraid, very afraid, because she knew it took a lot to get Katherine into a state like this.

'What'll we do now?' The child's voice was hoarse with fear.

'I don't know, Ceppi. I can't think straight. Give me a few minutes while I try to think.' Katherine slid down the wall until she was resting on her heels. She covered her face with her hands. She'd never been so terrified in all her life.

Ceppi crouched down beside her, her large grey-green eyes filled with dread. She was frightened, but she'd make herself stay silent for Katherine.

Finally she could bear it no longer. 'Will I go back to see . . . to make sure it's true?' Her voice was thin and shaky.

'They'll make you stay. Maybe it's right that you do stay.'

Defiance rose in Ceppi's eyes. 'It's not right and I won't stay. I *won't*.'

'Ceppi, I . . . I can't look out for you.'

'That doesn't matter, I . . . I'll go!'

Before Katherine could stop her she'd turned and was lost in the darkness.

Katherine wrapped her arms around her body and began to rock to and fro. She felt sick and cold and shocked. If what Con had said were true she had no one to turn to. No one to give her strength or protect her. Maybe it would be best if she were to go on running by herself? Ceppi would be upset but she'd have to go home and a home was more than she could offer at this minute . . . No, the child doted on her, she couldn't just abandon her. She began to pray but the words were disjointed. She couldn't remember the prayers she'd learned at her mother's knee. Don't let it be true, Lord! The words went round and round in her head, and she seemed powerless to silence them. If life had been miserable before at least it had been secure and stable, but now . . . Frozen with terror, she peered into the darkness for Ceppi.

There was still a small crowd of people around Ceppi's house, neighbours mostly, but then the child caught sight of Father Flynn's white clerical collar. She stopped. She didn't want to get too close in case her mam saw her and told her to get inside the house and she'd *have* to go, Father Flynn would see to that, and then what kind of a life would she have? Ignored, left to fend for herself, frequently bawled at and belted too. No, Katherine had been the one person to offer her any real kindness and she'd go to the ends of the earth with her. She caught sight of a figure detaching itself from the crowd and starting to walk up the street. It was her oldest brother, Liam. She rushed up to him. 'Will ye tell me what's going on? Our Con said Da's dead, murdered!'

Liam Healy was sixteen, a tall thin lad with the same mop of red hair all the Healys had. 'He is so and if the lads had had their way they'd be killing that bastard Donovan, but didn't the Father arrive and tell them all to stop. He sent Matt Farrelly for the polis and Joe O'Shaughnessy for the ambulance. Still, Donovan's hurt bad. I hope the bastard dies, he'll go straight to hell.'

The tears had welled up in Ceppi's eyes and her lower lip trembled. 'Oh, God!'

Liam looked down into her face. 'Where have you been that you didn't know?'

'Mind your own business!'

'Talk like that again to me and I'll clatter you! You've been out with her, haven't you? With Donovan's daughter, Miss high and mighty bloody Donovan!'

Ceppi's fear diminished. She was well used to this. 'So what iffen I have?'

'Where is she? I'll bet the polis will want to speak to her.'

'What for? *She's* done nothing.'

'They'll want her to go to the hospital with him – if he lives – or to identify him, if he doesn't.'

As her brother stopped talking Ceppi heard the loud clanging of the ambulance bell. It turned the corner, passed them and went on down the street. It was followed by a police car, also clanging its bell.

Liam looked scornfully at his sister. 'You see, they *will* want to talk to her. Ask where she was.'

'We . . . she was in Beresford Square at a meeting. A big meeting.'

'You want *me* to believe that your one was at a political meeting?'

'She *was*. Anyway, why were you leaving? Won't the polis want to talk to you?'

He looked uneasy. 'I didn't see much of it at all. There was just a lot of . . . shouting.'

'Liar!' she flashed back at him. 'Ye said the lads were

15

belting him, ye couldn't just hear that. Ye must have seen it, I bet you got in a kick and a clatter yourself!'

'All right! I'll tell you what happened. Donovan caught Da as he was passing the shop. He was fierce angry and calling Da everything under the sun. Then he punched Da in the gut and when he fell down he started to kick him.' Liam's voice cracked with emotion but the look in Ceppi's eyes made him continue. 'That's when a couple of old shawlies started screaming and we all ran into the street. They told us what he'd done. Da was in a desperate state, there was blood coming from his mouth and he had some kind of a fit and then he . . . he stopped moving. The three Dolan lads laid into Donovan and then . . . everyone, he was on the floor and *he* wasn't moving either . . . Then the priest came and stopped it, but Donovan still wasn't moving. Does that suit you?' He scowled at her, then shuddered as if haunted by what he'd seen. 'I'm going for a smoke. I've a decent-size butt end I found in the road and one of that lot would have it off me before I'd a chance of a single drag.'

Ceppi watched him hurry off and then looked down the street. She couldn't see her mam but she could hear her ranting and raving and asking how was she going to manage now. Ceppi pressed her lips tightly together. Mammy seemed to have 'managed' for years. She shrank back into a doorway as the ambulance passed on its return journey to the hospital. Now the polis *would* be looking for Katherine; she'd have to get back to her quickly and without being noticed. She darted across the street into the open-doored Farrelly house, all the occupants of which were out in the street. She pounded down the lobby, through the kitchen, the scullery, the yard and finally reached the laneway and the corner house where she'd left her friend.

Katherine's teeth were chattering and there was nothing she could do to stop them. Her heart thumped against her ribs and her head ached. A wave of guilty relief passed through her when she recognised Ceppi's footsteps.

'Ceppi, come here to me, I've been so worried about you.'

The child took the outstretched hand and sat down on the cobbles, huddled against Katherine's side.

'It's true. Da's dead. I . . . I saw our Liam. He said your da started on mine, belted him hard and then . . .' Suddenly the full realisation hit the child and she began to sob. 'Oh, me da, me poor, lovely da. He wouldn't have hurt anyone. He never clattered me like Mammy did.'

Katherine gathered Ceppi in her arms and held her tightly. Her own predicament was bad enough but Ceppi didn't deserve this. Joe Healy shouldn't have died for the few pounds he owed. In that moment she *hated* her father: for Joe's death, for the way he'd treated the people who had depended on him just to keep a roof over their heads and have a bit of fire and food. At this very moment she didn't care if he were alive or dead.

At last the child's sobs diminished as Katherine soothed her. 'Hush now, we have to think of ourselves.'

'Liam said the polis would want to talk to you.'

'Well, I've nothing to say to them. If . . . if my da's dead, he's dead. If he's alive I'm never going to see him again.'

'Then what will we do? I'm not leaving you.'

'But I can't offer you anything. I *can't* go back there. I can't let you roam the streets . . .'

'I'm *not* going back. I don't care.'

'But I *do*. I care for you, you're only a child.'

Before Ceppi could reply they both heard loud, ominous footsteps and the beam of light from a lamp pierced the darkness. They clung tightly to each other until the footsteps stopped a few yards away from them. They both shrank backwards as the beam settled on them.

'Begod! Isn't it you two again?'

Katherine glimpsed the silver buttons on the dark green uniform and relief surged through her. It was the policeman from Kerry, she'd know that accent anywhere.

'Come on out of that, sitting on the cobbles, you'll catch cold.'

'What are you doing around here?' Katherine asked. 'You were at the meeting.'

'I was and isn't it well for you that you left early. There was fighting the whole length of Sackville Street the like I've never seen before. There'll be murder before the night's over. And that's why I'm here. Some eejit of an inspector told me to get down here as at least one man has been murdered, possibly two, and me that's never been this far north in my life. Sure, how did they expect me to find my way through this maze of streets? Two or three of the lads are already here and they came in style – in a car. It's last I am.'

Katherine got to her feet, pulling Ceppi with her. Oh, to hear a friendly, reassuring voice. 'We're glad you came. There . . . there *has* been a murder, maybe two.'

'How do you know?'

Katherine tried to keep her voice calm. 'I know because it was my father who . . . who murdered Mr Healy. This . . . this is Ceppi Healy and I'm Katherine Donovan.' She couldn't disguise the anguish in her voice. 'We'd just got back from the meeting; we didn't see anything. Ceppi's brother, Con, told us and . . . and we just ran.'

'Holy Mother of God! Well, there'll be nothing to fear now. You can both go home. I'll make sure you are not interfered with.'

'No, you don't understand. They all hate me as much as they hated Da. They've always despised me because I never went short of anything and he was so cruel to them all. I can't go back.'

'What about her? Who's going to look out for her?'

'Katherine will,' Ceppi retorted. 'I hate them – all of them! And Mammy doesn't give a tinker's curse about any of us.'

He looked perplexed. 'Well, I can't be leaving you here like this.'

Katherine's overwrought nerves snapped and she began to sob, her face buried in Ceppi's tangled mop of curls.

Ceppi looked at the tall, strong-looking policeman. He might make her go back home or put her in the Workhouse. Of the two, she'd sooner go to the Workhouse.

'Have you brothers or sisters?' he asked Katherine.

She shook her head.

'Look, if you go back home, I'll stay with you for as long as I can. If people think we're watching them no harm can come to you. Either of you. And the priest will look after you too. You *can't* stay out in the street all night.'

Katherine looked up. He was a big man and he was trying

19

his best to help. She was sure it would have been different if he'd been one of the Dublin City lot.

'Will you stay, really stay?'

'Didn't I say I would? Come on now, the both of you, you're in a desperate state altogether. I'm Sean, Sean McGovern, by the way.'

Katherine wiped away her tears with the back of one hand while Ceppi's cold little fingers were clutched tightly in the other.

In mute trepidation they walked down the street. Most of the neighbours were still out, though the gapers had gone away. About a dozen small children sat on their respective doorsteps, watching in silence, their eyes wide with amazement. There were other policemen there too, those that had arrived in the car, Ceppi surmised. They were questioning people but were clearly not getting much in the way of firm witness statements.

'Where have you been, McGovern, and who the hell are these two?'

The young policeman saluted the senior officer. 'Sir, didn't I tell Inspector Quinn I'd get lost altogether in finding my way here. I'm RIC. I'd have been wandering around all night but for these two. Can I have a word, sir, it's a bit delicate?'

The sergeant moved a few paces away. 'Now what?'

'They're daughters of the parties concerned. Are both men dead?'

'Healy is and the priest got word to us that Donovan died in the ambulance. This lot appear to be deaf, dumb and blind. There's little use in trying to get information from any of them. They all know what happened – I'd lay down my life that half the men here were responsible for Donovan's death and the rest stood around and watched.'

'True for you, sir. I wouldn't disagree at all.'

'So, which is which and do *they* know anything? Will *they* talk?'

'The older one is Katherine Donovan, an only child. The other one is . . . was Healy's daughter, the youngest I think. I found them in a dark laneway – I think it was a laneway. They were terrified and half frozen. They'd both been out together. It wasn't until they came back that . . . Ah, well, you know the rest, sir.'

The sergeant snorted in disgust. 'It's all a waste of time anyway. Himself that murdered Healy has gone to meet his Maker and by all accounts I wouldn't want to be in his shoes. So, no case to answer. A bloody waste of time and men. Go and tell the lads to pack it in and then get back to the station. We've enough on our plates as it is with Larkin's lunatics fighting and looting. In Sackville Street, there were kids with bare feet climbing over broken glass to get at the stuff inside the shops. I wish to God that man would go back to Liverpool where he belongs and stop inciting half the bloody city to riot.'

'What will I do with them? What can I tell them?'

'Tell the Donovan girl to go down to the mortuary at the hospital, she'll have to formally identify her da. The younger one can stay put. The widow will do the honours. That's if she's sober enough – she's had women running up and down to the pub for "a wee drop" for her nerves. Nerves, that one, she's got as many "nerves" as a bloody scald-crow!'

21

'Can I ask a bit of a favour, sir?'

'What?'

'Can I go with Katherine Donovan to the mortuary? It's not a pleasant class of a thing for a young girl to have to do alone and I said I'd stay with them – for a bit – if I could. Sure, I think they think they'll be killed too.'

The older man nodded slowly. He'd heard the comments that had been made on old man Donovan's character. He glanced over towards the two girls. They looked an incongruous, pathetic little pair: the slim, dark-haired girl with anguished blue eyes holding tightly on to the scrawny, none-too-clean and badly dressed little rossi with the mop of curls. Momentarily he wondered what class of a friendship it was, but then he dragged his mind to more important matters.

'Go on, get off with you. Your reinforcements are not much use at all, hardly knowing Sackville Street from College Green. But the fault doesn't lie with you.'

The neighbours were going back into their houses and Katherine looked anxiously as Constable McGovern came over to them.

'I've cleared it with the sergeant. I can stay but I'm afraid there's something you have to do first.'

'What?' Katherine was fearful.

'You've to formally identify your father.'

Katherine was appalled. 'No! No! I never want to see him again!'

'I . . . I'll come with ye, Katherine,' Ceppi offered, still clutching her hand.

'You're far too young. Your mammy will go and see your da, God rest him. You should get yourself back home.'

22

'I don't want to go home! I want to go with Katherine.'

Katherine shook her head in bewilderment.

'It'll only take a few minutes,' the policeman coaxed.

It would. The problem was getting them to the hospital and back across a city centre that resembled a battlefield. The hospitals were rushed off their feet, the police were hard pressed, there had even been talk of calling out the military.

With reluctance, Katherine agreed to accompany the policeman, who in turn agreed that Ceppi too could come. They went quickly through the maze of dark and dirty streets until they crossed Butt Bridge and a scene of pure carnage and chaos met their eyes.

'Holy Mother of God!' Sean McGovern breathed.

'What's been going on?'

'A bloody war by the look of it! It's glad I am that I was sent out to you.'

Ceppi's wide-eyed, fearful gaze swept over the Quay and beyond. 'Will we be murdered?'

'No, I think it's all over.' But he looked at Katherine with apprehension for they could both hear the faint noise of the battle that had moved to the side streets.

'Come on, let's get up to the hospital and back before they return here, though God alone knows there's nothing much left to loot or destroy!'

Sackville Street was dark – most of the streetlamps were out – but they picked their way cautiously over the debris of glass; cobbles that had been ripped up; sticks; police batons; an abandoned tram, its windows all shattered; and assorted merchandise that had been looted and then dropped before the police charge and the battles that had followed.

When they reached the hospital, they were all relieved.

'Wait now while I go and speak to someone about . . .' The policeman's voice trailed away as he set off through the crowd of injured people – police among them – who were obviously casualties of the riot.

Ceppi's thumb was in her mouth and her other hand gripped Katherine's tightly. In one short night the world had gone mad.

Sean McGovern made his way across the room, careful not to step on or push the casualties, until he reached a nurse. 'Could you direct us to the mortuary, please?'

She looked up from bandaging the head of a youth. 'And haven't you lot been busy the night? And aren't we left to deal with the consequences of your truncheons? Is it murder you're all intent on?'

'It is not, and I've no intention at all of getting into a fight with yourself over the day that's in it. The mortuary please?'

When he finally had his directions he beckoned to Katherine and Ceppi.

'Oh God! Isn't this a desperate place?' Katherine said as she and Ceppi joined him.

'Sure, I've never seen anything like it and I didn't join the police to be after half killing the population of Dublin. Follow me. Are you all right?'

Katherine nodded and they followed him.

The stairs were badly lit and he told her to hang onto his arm so as not to slip. 'Otherwise you'll both finish up back there with all those half-broken men and women.'

As he opened the door the smell of formaldehyde made

Ceppi's stomach turn over. 'I don't want to go in there. It smells . . . and there's all those dead people!'

'Then stay here, we'll only be a minute.'

Ceppi looked up gratefully at Constable McGovern as he ushered Katherine through the door. It took less than a minute for her to formally identify her father. His face was cut and dirty but even in death he looked hard and unrelenting.

'Yes, that's him. Can we go now, I feel . . .' She swayed and closed her eyes.

He caught her before she fell and carried her bodily out of the room, kicking the door shut behind him.

Ceppi began to cry, her bravura finally overwhelmed by the sight of Katherine.

'Give over with that now, she's only fainted. The smell down here would buckle the legs of a carthorse.'

McGovern carried her through a side door he'd noticed before they'd gone into the mortuary and as the fresh air hit her Katherine began to come round.

'Ah, Katherine, I thought you were dead and all,' Ceppi whispered.

Katherine shook her head as she was set down on her two legs.

'Right then, now let's get you back and pray to God we don't run into any riots or we'll be destroyed altogether,' McGovern said bracingly.

They reached home without seeing anyone, except a few drunks and shawlies.

'Have you got a key?'

'No. I . . . I didn't think I'd need one. He . . . he always got back from Dollymount early.'

'You're lucky the place isn't looted but I expect they were all too preoccupied with the fight. Well, here goes.' He put his shoulder to the door and it burst open, the sound of splintering wood loud in the now quiet street. Inside it was pitch dark and smelled musty. He let the beam of his flash lamp hover around the room.

'He has some stuff here.'

'Yes, but I've always hated it. It's full of people's misery. I don't want to be in here.' She led the way to the back living room.

'Will you be having a match so I can light the gas?'

Katherine reached for the box and passed it over. A small flame burst from the bracket and Katherine placed the frosted glass mantel over it.

The room was comfortable, he thought. There was even a damped-down fire still in the range.

'Will I be putting the kettle on or will you while I mend this fire?'

'I'll see to it,' Katherine said. 'Ceppi, put on this cardigan and sit on the fender.'

The child nodded, picked up the navy woollen cardigan, wrapped herself in it and sat on one of the raised seats of the brass fender.

Sean McGovern's gaze travelled around the room. There was everything a person would want in the way of comfort: heavy green chenille curtains; a good rug on the floor; a carved sideboard; two winged easy chairs covered in a faded green tapestry-type material. There were pictures on the walls, ornaments and brassware on the overmantel. A square table was covered with a red and white gingham oilcloth, with four chairs arranged around it. There was a food press and even a small sofa. Compared to the homes that surrounded it this was palatial. Compared to his parents' home he'd left in Kerry it was luxurious.

Katherine was feeling calmer, too calm. It was as if she were standing still and the world was moving around her.

'Will you take off the helmet? It's giving me the horrors.'

He did so, placing it on the sideboard, and she noticed he had very dark hair, like her own. On closer inspection and in better light, she could see that he was young, possibly only twenty-five or -six.

Her hands were still shaking as she got the cups and saucers from the sideboard and milk and sugar from the press.

'I wouldn't be getting into a state about staying here, hardly anyone saw you.'

'They'd have heard the noise of you breaking the door in.'

'I suppose you'd have to be deaf not to, but don't be fretting yourself about them. They'll get over it in time.'

As she passed him his cup of tea there was a loud knocking on the kitchen door and both Katherine and Ceppi cried out fearfully.

McGovern was instantly on his feet and, grim-faced, he flung open the door. He knew he had the element of surprise if there was to be trouble.

'Constable! I thought you'd all gone.' Father Flynn was surprised.

'I stayed with them, Father. They're both badly shaken.'

'And the blessings of God be upon you for it.' The small rotund figure sat down in the chair McGovern had just vacated.

'A cup of tea, Father?' Katherine asked automatically. Hospitality, no matter what deprivations it caused to the family, was always offered. She handed him a cup.

'Now, I've come to see about the arrangements.'

'Arrangements?' Katherine was confused.

'When will you bring him to the church and at what time will the Funeral Mass be?'

She shook her head, bewildered. Why was he worrying about all that? Hadn't she had enough to contend with? This day seemed to stretch on and on. It must be nearly midnight.

Sean McGovern was thinking along the same lines. 'Can't it all wait until the morning, Father?'

'Not at all, it's best to get it all prepared now. Mr Donovan was a man of some standing, importance even. He was always very generous to the Church.'

Sean's eyes narrowed and Katherine ignored them both. She had decided what she was going to do. She fumbled under the turf basket, pulled out the tea caddy and opened it. She counted out the gold sovereigns and then passed them to the priest.

'That's enough there to bury him decently, but . . . but I don't want to have anything to do with it. I won't come to the removal, or the Mass or the burial.'

Father Flynn was taken aback. 'You . . . you're saying you won't even show a little respect to your father?'

'That's right. He deserves no respect. He is . . . was a murderer.'

'Thou shalt not kill,' Sean McGovern said in a loud whisper.

'He confessed to me in the ambulance just before he died. He departed this life without a stain on his soul.'

'How convenient of you to be there at the exact moment,' Sean said drily.

'If I hear any more remarks like that from you, I'll go straight to your superiors. They won't take kindly to insolence to a priest.'

Sean pursed his lips. Father Flynn should hear some of the things that were said about the clergy at the station.

Father Flynn turned again to Katherine. 'It's your duty as his only child to mourn him publicly.'

'I *won't* do it, Father.' She was adamant.

'It wouldn't go down too well with the neighbours is what I think she means.'

'They all hate me because of the humiliation they suffered at his hands. All my life they've hated me.'

'Don't be so ridiculous, girl. No one "hates" you. I'll give it out at the Mass that no one should attempt to intimidate you.'

The man was a fool, Sean thought. Men in parishes like this ignored the likes of Father Flynn.

'I'm still having nothing to do with it,' Katherine insisted, 'and now can we get some sleep, please? It's been a desperate, desperate day.'

Sean went and stood in the open doorway and the priest, white-faced with anger, stormed past him and out into the shop.

'Do you really mean it?'

Katherine grimaced as Sean closed the door behind him. 'I won't be a hypocrite. I won't pray at my father's funeral.'

'Then you have my admiration.'

She smiled. 'And you have mine. There's not many who'd answer a priest back.'

'The man's an insensitive fool.'

'You've been very good to us.'

He grinned. 'Ah, think nothing of it, all part of the service.'

Despite her mood, Katherine smiled back.

'Did anyone ever tell you that when you smile you're a fine-looking girl, Katherine Donovan?'

She frowned. 'I'm no beauty and now isn't the time for discussing such things.'

'Sorry. Now it's me that's the insensitive fool.'

'You meant well.'

'When this is all over, will you open up the shop again?' he asked.

'No! Never! I won't make my living out of the misery of others. He . . . he turned a woman away last week because all she had was her shawl and her boots. She was crying with despair. I don't know what she did, things must have been really appalling for her. No, I'll find some other way of making a living.'

'You could sell up.'

'And who in their right senses would be buying a business at a time like this?'

'You've a point. But if I were you I'd go to bed now and try to get some sleep. Things always look better in the light of day.' Seeing the look of fear that came into their eyes, he hastily added, 'I'll wait down here for a while.'

Katherine breathed more easily, for a second panic had swooped down on her again.

'Thanks for everything and goodnight to you, Constable McGovern. I hope you'll be able to go back to Kerry soon. We . . . we'll be going away from here too.'

'I don't blame you. Maybe you'd come to Kerry? We're not all eejits, you know.'

Katherine smiled. 'I know. Maybe . . . one day I will.'

Chapter Three

KATHERINE TUCKED THE quilt around Ceppi and brushed the strands of unruly red hair from her face. She'd put one of her own nightdresses on the child. The little girl really needed a good wash but it was so late and they were both exhausted. The garment swamped Ceppi but she didn't care, she'd never had a proper one before and it smelled clean and fresh. Sometimes in winter when it was very cold, she slept in all her clothes, for there were no blankets. A pile of old coats, rags, were what they had to cover them. And here she was given a proper mattress, not a sack of straw. There were pillows too, a real novelty, with clean white pillowcases and soft blankets. Three of them no less *and* the quilt.

'I never had any of these things before.' Ceppi rubbed the edge of the blanket against her cheek as she let her gaze wander over the room. It was so very different to home. The light from the oil lamp made it look warm. There was a fireplace – something she'd never seen in a bedroom before

– a chest of drawers, a small wardrobe, a washstand with a marble top and a delicate bowl and jug with a pattern of roses on them. There was a mirror on one wall, a crucifix on the wall over the bed and above the fireplace was a picture of the Blessed Virgin.

As the child snuggled down in the bed Katherine knelt beside it as she always did and said her prayers, remembering Joe Healy especially. There was nothing decent she could think of to say about her father. She hoped desperately that God would understand.

Although exhausted she slept fitfully. Ceppi slept soundly beside her, her red curls just visible above the quilt. What was she going to do? She didn't want the shop but she'd be hard pressed to find someone who would take it off her hands even to rent, nor was she trained to do anything but keep house. The worry was still there when she drifted off into a light sleep again.

It was the breaking of glass that woke her. She sat up in the bed, instantly awake. Sean McGovern must have gone back to the station. They were on their own. She was filled with panic. The noise grew louder and she began to shake. Voices mingled with the cracking and splintering. Who was down there and what were they doing? Then she remembered Da's money. She fought down the panic and got out of bed. She hardly noticed the coldness of the lino under her feet when she stepped off the bedside rug. They could take whatever they wanted to, but not the money. Dear God, that was all she had!

The scene that greeted her in the shop made her cry out.

There was total bedlam. She couldn't distinguish faces, only forms, for the shop was dark at the best of times and the light from the streetlamp was feeble and half shrouded in mist that had spread over the city from the Liffey. There were shouts and cries and oaths as her father's old customers searched for their pledges and even things that didn't belong to them. Clothing, blankets, lamps, ornaments, boots and shoes, kettles, pans and dishes were being discarded or fought over. For there were women as well as men in the group. She backed away slowly. She could do nothing to stop them, she was one against God knows how many. She prayed they wouldn't come further in, into the kitchen and upstairs. She reached the door of the living room, but it was too late. Even in the dismal light one of the women had spotted her.

'There she is, the owld devil's daughter! *She's* never gone without boots or shoes in the winter snow and ice!'

'Look at the style of her,' someone sneered, 'a nightdress and dressing gown and with the gold chain around her neck. Whose neck did it hang around before, that's what I want to know?'

They surged towards her, grabbing at her clothes and the gold cross. Her fear diminished and anger took its place. She had rights too. She'd put up with her da, she'd suffered too and no one was going to take what was rightfully hers from her. The cross was the only piece of jewellery Mam had ever had, apart from her wedding ring. No, they weren't going to take that from her. Screaming and lashing out she tried to fight them off but there were too many of them and they were stronger than she was. With her last bit of strength, she shouted louder and louder and then gradually the noise subsided until at last she could make herself heard.

'Take what belongs to you, I don't care. Take the whole flaming lot! I hate the whole bloody place! He treated me and Mam the same way he treated you!'

'Your mam didn't have to listen to her kids crying with the hunger,' someone called out from the crowd of dark faces. 'Some of us are after having to root in the ashcans for food. Your mam never had to do that!'

They surged forward again and she felt the solid wood of the living-room door against her back. She was cornered. Her eyes, now accustomed to the semi-darkness, darted from face to face, hoping to recognise someone who would help but there didn't seem to be anyone. Then her resolve strengthened. They'd have to kill her before she'd let them take the money. It was tainted, but it was all she had in the world.

The shouting started again, as did the grasping hands that tore at her nightdress and dressing gown. Again she fought back as best she could but she was tiring. Did they intend to beat her to death as they had her father? That thought gave her strength and she began to kick out, but with bare feet it was hopeless. With her hands over her head she turned to face the door, trying to protect herself. Suddenly, everything stopped. The level of noise dropped and slowly she turned around.

In the doorway stood Father Flynn, his face puce with anger, a small vein over his left eye throbbing.

'What have we here?' he thundered in the voice of the pulpit. 'Wasn't I on my way back after a sick call and heard this commotion? Is this a good Catholic way to be carrying on, two men dead this day?' His voice rose an octave. 'Thou shalt love thy neighbour. Thou shalt not covet thy neighbour's goods. Have you forgotten the simple rules of life – the Ten Commandments? Get out of here and leave this girl alone. Get out, before I excommunicate all of you!'

Muttering curses they all left, but not empty-handed.

'Are you hurt, child?' Father Flynn's voice took on a quieter, concerned tone.

Katherine shook her head but her face was scratched and the collar of her dressing gown was hanging off. One sleeve hung loose, ripped away at the shoulder seam. Katherine broke down. She didn't know how much more her nerves would take.

'I . . . I . . . couldn't let them take the money, Father, it's all I have. I was going to give everything back today but I didn't get a chance.'

He guided her into the living room and she sank down on one of the chairs.

'It was very fortunate that I was passing. Sometimes I fail to understand their behaviour, I really do.'

She shook her head in despair. 'They're just so . . . desperate. It's all the strikes.'

'Indeed it is, and that man Larkin inciting them to defy their employers – this is the result. They are poorer than ever. That socialist has turned them into animals!'

She was too upset to argue. 'I'll make some tea, Father, but first I must see if Ceppi's all right.'

He nodded his agreement.

She found Ceppi crouched at the top of the stairs, shivering and with tear-streaked cheeks.

'It's OK now, they've all gone. Father Flynn's downstairs,

he threw them all out. You're cold, go back to bed. I'll bring you up a mug of tea. I'll be up myself soon.'

She made sure the child was in bed before she went downstairs, leaving an oil lamp in the bedroom to allay Ceppi's fears.

To her amazement the priest had put the kettle on the range. Usually they just sat and were waited on hand and foot.

She went through the ritual of making the tea and took a mug upstairs before sitting down herself.

'Thank you, Father, for the kettle. Oh, it's been a terrible day altogether. How can so many things go wrong at once – people dying and fighting . . . How can I stay here now, after this?'

'They've all taken the things they pledged and more, and I'll be saying a few words on Sunday about the deplorable behaviour here this night. They won't bother you again.'

How could she believe him? He didn't understand that her life was over.

'You have the money safe and sound?' he asked.

Katherine went to the basket of turf and thankfully drew out the tea caddy from beneath it.

A man like Albert Donovan could have, should have found a better place than that to keep his money, Father Flynn thought, but then the pawnbroker'd always been full of pride and arrogance. And look where those sins had led him. To murder and in turn to be killed himself. An eye for an eye. He drained his cup. There was nothing more to keep him here and, as she'd said, it had been a long day for everyone – himself included. The last thing he'd wanted was to get out of a warm bed, get dressed in a cold room and go out into the dark, mist-shrouded streets.

'Thank you, child. Get some rest now. I'll send someone around in the morning to board up the window and help clean up.'

Katherine showed him out, climbing carefully over the debris that had been discarded at the arrival of the priest. Slowly she went upstairs again, this time taking the money with her. Ceppi was still awake, sitting up in the bed, the quilt pulled up to her chin.

'Has anyone come back?' she asked in a whisper.

'No. Father Flynn's just gone.'

'*Will* they come back?'

'I don't know. I hope and pray they don't but . . .'

'That polis feller said he'd stay.'

'I know he did, but he couldn't have stayed all night, Ceppi, not with all the trouble in the city. But I know one thing for sure and for certain.'

'What?'

'This time I'm leaving for good.'

'You won't leave me here, will you, Katherine? Please don't leave me or take me back to Mammy.'

Katherine looked down at the pale little face, the eyes brimming with tears. It was a hard decision to make. Ceppi would be an extra responsibility, one that she really didn't need, but how could she leave her? She was her little shadow. And what was the alternative for Ceppi: a lonely struggle for the rest of her life? Memories of Katherine's own childhood were all too vivid in her mind. She couldn't just leave her here.

'I won't take you back but I'll have to see your mammy about it or she might think I've kidnapped you.'

'No! No, please don't go.'

'I'll *have* to. What if she goes to the police?'

The child started to cry and Katherine took her in her arms and tried to comfort her but it was nearly dawn before either of them slept.

Katherine was still half asleep as she slid out of the bed. She didn't want to wake Ceppi. She dressed quickly and went downstairs to make herself some breakfast. She glanced through the kitchen door at the shop: it looked as if a bomb had exploded in it. She closed the door quickly; she'd think about clearing up when she came back. She'd just put on her jacket, taken a deep breath and turned to leave the room when she saw Ceppi standing at the foot of the stairs.

'You promised you wouldn't leave me!'

'Come here to me. I wasn't leaving you, I'm going to see your mammy, I told you I had to go. I won't leave you – ever. Now go back to bed.'

Comforted, the child went back upstairs.

'Right, Lily Healy, here I come!' she said grimly to herself as she closed the door behind her.

It was still dark but here and there a light burned in the upper storey of the houses. Their dilapidated condition was masked by the darkness and the mist that hung over them. The air smelled damp and was infused with other odours: coal; soot; rotting garbage; unwashed, unhealthy, hungry humanity. Poverty had a smell, a distinct smell. A dim light burned in the Healys' window. They had a two-pair front.

She pushed open the door which was half ajar anyway and knocked loudly on the first door on the left. A scruffy lad eventually opened it and peered out, still half asleep.

'Is your mammy there?'

He looked hard at her. 'At this time in the mornin' and she wailing on half the night like a bloody banshee. And what will ye want her for?'

'To see her about Ceppi.'

He looked at her suspiciously. 'Ye killed me da.'

'*I* didn't and I've got to see her. It's important,' Katherine insisted, making her tone brusque and businesslike.

The boy shrugged and turned away, leaving the door wide open. Katherine wrinkled her nose at the odour that came from the room. The sound of raised voices carried through the door but eventually Mrs Healy came down the hallway.

She was a short, fat, slovenly woman, with greying hair hanging over her shoulders in a greasy tangle. An old overcoat covered the skirt and jumper which she'd obviously slept in. Her small, dark eyes took in everything Katherine was wearing.

'Where's your hat? Did ye forget it, Miss High and Bloody Mighty?'

Katherine ignored the jibe.

'Anyway, what the flaming hell do ye want? Yer owld feller killed my poor Joe and iffen ye've come to say sorry ye know where ye can stick it.'

'It wouldn't be any use saying it, would it? But for what it's worth I *am* sorry. He was a nice man and he'll be missed.'

Lily Healy crossed her arms over her ample bosom. 'Don't go expecting me to feel sorry over yer da.'

'I don't. Even I'm not sorry, and he was my da.'

The older woman glared suspiciously at her. 'So what is it you'll be wanting then at this time in the morning?'

'It's about Ceppi. I . . . I'm going away. I'm leaving Dublin altogether and I want to take her with me.'

'That bold little article, what would ye want to do that for?'

'Because she's asked to come with me – she doesn't want to stay here.' Katherine very nearly said 'with you', but stopped herself in time.

'So how come she's not here to ask herself?'

'She's too young and too frightened, especially after last night.'

'I heard about all that commotion.' Mrs Healy didn't say she'd been one of the instigators and had managed to get quite a lot of stuff out before the priest came. And now here was the opportunity to be rid of one mouth to feed and get some money too.

'How much would it be worth?'

Katherine was taken aback. 'How can you put a price on your child? It's . . . it's like selling her as a slave.'

'Well, I've just lost me man. Me daughter's worth a lot to me.'

Katherine was in control of herself again. 'I haven't seen much evidence of that up to now,' she answered coldly.

'Any more of that and ye can get off me bit of a doorstep.'

'Will five pounds be enough?'

Mrs Healy debated it for a minute. Five pounds was a lot of money, easy money too.

'Have ye the money with ye?'

41

Katherine nodded and took a white five-pound note from her pocket. She felt terrible. How could anyone be so selfish and hard-hearted to just sell a child? But at least now Ceppi would have someone who really cared for her.

'Where are ye going then?' Lily Healy asked in an almost friendly tone.

Katherine was wary. 'I haven't decided that yet, just to get away from here, that much I know. I've had enough of Dublin.' She turned the collar of her jacket up and walked away.

Ceppi was sitting on the step, shivering.

'You'll catch your death of cold, why are you sitting out here?'

'I . . . I was worried.'

Katherine helped her to her feet. 'There's no need to be, she says you can stay with me.'

'Always?'

'Always. Come inside, we'll have something to eat, tidy up a bit and then go shopping. I can't take you anywhere looking like that.'

The light of joy filled Ceppi's eyes and she flung her arms around Katherine's waist. She'd lost her da but she had Katherine now and she *knew* the older girl would take good care of her. For the first time in her life she felt safe.

Chapter Four

———◆◆◆———

KATHERINE BEGAN, OUT of habit, to tidy up the kitchen. She was tired – no, she was *exhausted* – but an idea was forming in her mind.

Ceppi automatically began to collect up the dishes and took them into the scullery, returning with a kettle full of water to be boiled on the range to wash them.

It was something she'd often done at home. Her thin little face bore a look of curiosity mixed with anxiety.

'Where are we going? Far away? America?'

'Good grief! Not *that* far away. Why did you think of America?'

'Because Mary Sweeney's got three sisters there and they have great jobs and they send money home every month to their mam. They had to leave in the end, so they did.'

'The sisters?'

'No, not them.' Ceppi thought that sometimes Katherine was a bit slow to grasp things.

'The Sweeney family?'

'All of them.'

'Why so?'

Ceppi looked up at Katherine and sighed. It was like explaining something to a baby. 'Because they had more than anyone else had. What with the strikes and everything. Everyone's desperate with the hunger, so the women in the houses wouldn't speak to them. Especially when they wouldn't spare a bit of bread or milk or sugar. Didn't they say they needed it for the little chisellers?'

'I can understand how Mrs Sweeney must have felt, going away, I mean, but not why she wouldn't share,' Katherine said in a voice full of sympathy.

'Well, you wouldn't, because you're different,' Ceppi said, as she equally automatically started to dry the dishes Katherine had washed.

'Why so?' Katherine asked.

'Because your da *always* had money. But me poor da used to say he was a bad man, trading in people's mis . . . mis . . .'

'Misery,' Katherine finished for her. Out of the mouths of babes, she thought bitterly. Ceppi's innocent remarks had made her vague idea a certainty now. 'We're going to Liverpool.'

'Liverpool? Is that far?'

'Far enough. Eight hours by ferry boat.'

'We're after going on a ferry boat? A long way?'

Katherine really had no idea at all why she had chosen Liverpool. Probably because so many Irish emigrants over hundreds of years had settled there. She knew it was a bigger city than Dublin, that it was a thriving port with huge ships sailing up and down the River Mersey day and night. She'd heard that there was work for the taking, so hopefully she'd get something even though she was trained for nothing. Ceppi would get a decent class of education whether she liked it or not. At least when she left school at fourteen years she'd be able to read, write, spell and have a grasp of arithmetic.

'Right then, we'd better get organised,' she said briskly as she led the child upstairs.

As she watched Ceppi eat her way through the menu in Bewley's Café, Katherine thought how different the child looked now. It had been a busy day but the time had seemed to fly. She'd concentrated so hard on the things they'd had to do that the traumas of last night seemed to be in the dim and distant past. Of course she'd had to take Ceppi to the Public Baths and that had caused a tantrum. Ceppi had looked in horror at the big cast-iron bath.

'I've never been in anything like that. Wouldn't I be drownded in it.'

'You will not drown in it, believe me. They're a bit on the "careful" side with the amount of hot water. It's only sixpence worth and that includes the soap and a towel.' Many's the time Katherine'd been here with her mam. Oh, they all had a good wash each day, but Mam had always insisted that for women and girls a bath was necessary for good hygienic purposes. Da had never complained, although she knew he hated them for what he always called 'making a holy show of him'.

Once Ceppi'd got over her fear the child had been pleased to be allowed to stay, splashing about in the now dirty water.

'God knows what I'm to do with your hair, there's so much

of it,' Katherine said in despair, looking at the mop of curls.

'Mam always used to just leave it to dry itself.'

'Well, that will do a lot of good, you'll get rheumatism in your head when you're older.' She'd rubbed the mop of unruly curls as much as she could with the damp towel, then she'd tried to hold it back with hairpins taken from her own hair. Then, with Ceppi at least clean, they'd set off for the shops in the city centre.

Their shopping trip had cost Katherine quite a lot of money but the expression on Ceppi's face as they'd looked through the coats, dresses, underwear and nightwear was worth it. Ceppi, who had often not even had any knickers, was stunned at all the things Katherine chose. She was to have not just knickers but vests, petticoats, nightdresses, skirts and some jumpers, a good dress and a coat, hat, stockings and boots.

'Won't I be as grand as the gentry?' Ceppi had said, peering at her newly clothed self in the mirror.

Katherine had smiled. 'You will so.'

She had bought herself some new underwear and stockings, and, laden down with the clothes Ceppi wasn't wearing and her own parcels and bag, they'd gone into Bewley's, a nice sort of a place that was renowned for its coffee and sticky buns.

'If you eat any more, it's sick you'll be,' Katherine said as she finished her tea. 'Drink up that milk, we're nearly ready to go.'

Ceppi pulled a face. 'I don't like milk, except in tea.'

'It's good for you. It's fresh, not the tinned stuff you water down. I wish now that I'd left all these parcels somewhere.

My arms are aching. But never mind, we'll soon be on our way.'

Ceppi looked at her questioningly as she finished her milk. 'Are we not going back at all?'

'What for? No one ever liked me and they can help themselves to everything in the shop and the house bit of it too. I don't want anything from that place.'

Ceppi felt relieved and yet disappointed at the same time. She certainly didn't want to see any of her family and yet she wanted to show off her new clothes. They would all be green with envy, and that thought pleased her until it was replaced with another one. What if they took it all off her? Mammy would have it down to the pawnshop like lightning and be drinking the proceeds in a flash too.

As they left they crossed O'Connell Bridge and walked along the Quays. They both noticed that the crowd was getting bigger as they approached the ferry berth.

There were people of all ages, shapes and sizes and they all carried something: battered suitcases, their lids secured with string; brown-paper parcels; bulging shopping bags. Some had bundles which probably contained everything they owned in the world.

Liverpool must be a huge busy place if all this lot want to go there, Ceppi thought, clinging tightly to Katherine's free hand. In her hand Katherine had the strong Gladstone-like canvas bag that now held all *they* possessed. Ceppi had been dressed in the navy skirt and the pale blue jumper. Over them she wore the navy coat and hat, both of which were trimmed with white to make the outfit look nautical. She wore stockings and a pair of button-up boots. She was so taken with them

47

that she kept looking down every few minutes to admire them.

'You'll be walking into a lamppost if you don't look where you're going,' Katherine admonished.

'I'm watching that they don't get walked on and spoiled.'

'They won't be the only things to get walked on. I never realised so many people wanted to leave Dublin. It's going to be a desperate crush.'

It was, but she patiently waited her turn. She bought their tickets and managed by a stroke of good luck to get somewhere to perch at the end of one of the long wooden plank-like seats set out in rows. Ceppi sat on Katherine's knee, commenting on all and everything.

'Yes, it is better than a circus,' Katherine said with a smile, after Ceppi had pointed out two men, obviously having had drink taken, trying to play Pitch and Toss – which was illegal anyway – in the narrow aisle between the benches that was already cluttered with bags and bundles. At last an official appeared and announced that the ferry was now ready to be boarded.

'In an orderly fashion, if you please! If anyone attempts to rush the gangway' – he nodded in the direction of the group of police officers standing at the bottom of the wooden slatted gangway – 'they'll be penalised or maybe arrested if things get out of hand.'

'What's "penalised" and will the polis be going with us?'

Katherine sighed at yet another question. 'Punished, sort of sent to the back of the queue, and no, the police are not coming too. Hang onto my skirt and *don't* let go or I'll never find you again in this crowd.'

Once they'd given in their tickets and climbed the gangway

they joined the rush to get a seat. There weren't enough of them for everyone so Katherine was grateful to get one for herself and Ceppi, even though it wasn't very comfortable. She ignored the comments of two women about the bad manners these days when a Dublin City child got a seat and a poor decent country woman didn't. The crossing was going to take eight hours and Katherine wasn't going to have Ceppi sleeping on the floor. She'd had enough of that in her short life. Nor would she have Ceppi sitting on her knee for so long. Again the seats were plank-type but at least they could lean their backs against the bulkhead. There was a small bar selling whiskey and port, but nothing else in the way of food or non-alcoholic drinks was available. Still, there were plenty of men who took advantage of what was on offer. She wished now she'd had the sense to buy something in Bewley's to eat on the journey. They'd both be starved and thirsty when they finally arrived.

She tried to get some rest, as did most of her fellow passengers – once the bar had run dry. They slept anywhere they could: on the deck; on the staircases; some even on the open deck above them. She could see now why these were called 'cattle boats'. She gave a sympathetic thought to the poor creatures if *this* was how they were treated. God help the passengers in the winter months in the storms, it would be really desperate and dangerous. She shivered and crossed herself at the thought.

It wasn't a bad crossing. To Katherine it seemed choppy but the woman sitting beside them told them firmly it was nothing compared to how it could have been. Katherine closed her eyes and pretended to be asleep. The last thing she wanted now was a litany of bad ferry crossings with all the horrors that went with them. She felt a bit queasy but Ceppi was fast asleep, her head against Katherine's shoulder.

'Kids!' her neighbour chirruped just as Katherine felt herself drift into unconsciousness. 'They're all the same. Sleep on a clothes line, most of them. Course they 'aven't gorrany worries like what we 'as.'

Katherine reluctantly opened her eyes and managed a weak smile. There would be no rest for her until they reached Liverpool unless the woman fell asleep herself.

Her travelling companion finally did so some time in the early hours, by which time Katherine knew her whole life story and those of every single one of her friends, relations and neighbours. Plus all their arguments and fallings out. She made the Liverpool slums sound worse than those in Dublin, and that was something Katherine didn't want to know about at all. She'd hoped they'd escaped from all that. At least she'd learned some useful things: the names of the better neighbourhoods; the price of food and coal; the location of the shops and markets. She'd learned that in Mount Pleasant there was bed-and-breakfast accommodation at reasonable prices. Of course that was well beyond her own means and always would be, the woman had said tartly. She'd never heard of anyone who had actually taken advantage of such luxury – having a decent bed under you, one you didn't have to make in the morning? Having a good breakfast put before you? And when you'd finished, the dishes washed by someone else? Oh, that was luxury indeed. Wearily, Katherine had agreed.

*

Katherine was relieved but still very apprehensive as they made their way up on deck in the half-light that passed for dawn. It was getting lighter by the minute and they could see the bulk of the buildings on the waterfront. She knew – from her travelling companion – that they were recognised by sailors the world over. They were certainly impressive, as was the whole waterfront. It was busy even at this time in the morning. The river too was desperately crowded and choppy with white bow waves covering its surface from the ferries, the luggage boats, the tugs and the huge ocean liners they were manoeuvring. There were cargo ships and dredgers and the increasingly old-fashioned sailing ships. It was almost like a busy street, there was so much coming and going.

Ceppi rubbed her eyes to get rid of the sleep. 'It's big and it's busy,' she said in wonderment.

'It is, but I know where to go and which tram to get, thanks to Mrs Green.'

'Herself that talked all night?'

'Hush, she might hear you and be offended. She was only trying to be friendly and helpful. Anyway, miss, she didn't keep you awake. You slept the whole way.'

'I'm hungry,' Ceppi stated flatly.

'So am I. I gather there's some sort of café a bit further down the Landing Stage. We should thank Herself for that information too. She said you can get rashers, eggs, fried bread, black pudding and a pot of tea for two shillings. There's no white pudding over here, apparently. Well, Herself said she'd never seen or heard of such.'

Ceppi tugged at Katherine's sleeve looking anxious. 'We'd better hurry to get off in case crowds go there.'

'We'll have to wait for the gangway to be lowered.' Katherine looked around her. In the grey light of a morning which held the promise of imminent rain, everyone looked drawn, pale and tired. They were not exactly in any state to allow themselves the luxury of being overjoyed at this first sight of what was for many a new home. Some were going on to America, Canada, South Africa and Australia and she wished them joy of their long journey, especially if conditions were similar to those of last night. She was very thankful now she hadn't chosen America. Eight hours were bad enough. Four days and four nights would have been a nightmare and that was on Cunard's huge, fast liners that carried the mail. Other ships took longer, much much longer.

Weary although she already was she knew there was a busy day ahead of them. They had to find somewhere to lay their heads, a school and a church and then tomorrow she'd have to start looking for work. One journey was over but another one was just beginning, she thought as she felt hope begin to surge through her.

Chapter Five

———————

'WHERE IS THE café?' Ceppi asked. She was wide awake now, looking around her at the milling crowd.

'Over there, I think. Mrs Green just said, "Push your way through to the floating roadway, go up it, turn right and walk across towards the Custom House and you can't miss it". She said we were to be careful and avoid all the construction that's going on between the Mersey Dock Board building and the Cunard Building. Apparently it's another grand edifice. It's to have two clock towers and they are going to put statues of huge birds on top. She did tell me what kind of birds they were, but I couldn't make it out at all.'

'Why not?'

'Because she said they weren't "real", that no one has ever seen a bird like it!'

'That's daft. Is she some class of an eejit?'

'Ceppi! Your tongue will be the death of you! Oh, now I remember. They're "Liver" birds.'

Ceppi gave her a sceptical glance before returning to her main quest – the café.

They found it and fortunately it wasn't packed out. They took a table in the window, and Katherine was thankful that the oilcloth that covered it was clean. The other customers were either people like themselves or men – obviously dock workers – in old jackets, hobnail boots, moleskin trousers and that badge of the working-class male, the grubby white muffler tied around the neck.

'We can see all that's going on from here while we have our breakfast.'

'Will I go and ask when someone will come?'

'No, look, that woman is coming over now.'

The waitress was a large, middle-aged woman dressed in a plain grey frock with a grubby white calico apron over it and a cap worn back to front, which made it look more like a helmet than a cap. She obviously suffered with her feet because she wore a pair of laceless men's boots with the toes cut out.

'Right, now what's it ter be?'

'What have you got?'

'Bacon, sausage, egg, fried bread an' black puddin'.'

'Can I have it all?' Ceppi asked eagerly.

'Yer can, an' yer look as though yer need feedin' up a bit.'

'Thank you, two of everything please and could you be wetting the tea, we haven't had anything to drink for hours.'

The woman looked perturbed. 'What's with this "wetting the tea" then?'

'I'm sorry, I mean we'd like a pot of tea.'

'Yer look wore out, the pair of yez. 'Ave yer just come off that ferry?'

Katherine nodded.

'God 'elp yer both. I went on one once, ter see me 'usband's mam, but never again! The crossing was worse than meeting that sour-faced owld bitch! I told me husband straight: "I don't care if she's got the bloody crown jewels, I'm not comin' over 'ere again! Yer sisters can 'ave the flamin' lot!"'

'They got stolen,' Ceppi said.

Both Katherine and the waitress looked mystified.

'What got pinched?' the waitress asked.

Katherine smiled at the child. 'She thinks you know what happened when the King and Queen were over last summer.'

'Over where?'

'They visited Dublin in July but the Irish crown jewels had been stolen and there's not been hide nor hair seen of them to this day.'

'Well, it just goes ter show, yer can't trust no one these days! Where are yer off to then? Scottie Road, that's where most of yer lot go.'

'No, first of all we're going to Mount Pleasant and later – when we've found our feet – I hope to get something permanent.'

'Aye. Well, I'd make it quick, the prices them lot charge.'

When the tea and breakfast arrived they both ate in silence they were so hungry. Then Katherine went to the counter to pay while Ceppi struggled with the bag.

When they were once more out in the cold damp daylight, Katherine looked down at Ceppi. 'How is it you know that the crown jewels were stolen?'

'Wasn't it all me mammy went on and on about – what she'd do with the reward money, if she found them? Our

Maureen said if she found them, she'd keep them and then sell them and buy a great place to live in. Me mammy said she'd have a grand place all right, in Kilmainham Jail!'

'Let's just forget about all that. Wait now while I try to remember the number tram your one on the boat told me to get. It was numbers ten, eleven and twelve. Give me the bag now, it's heavy.'

They walked across the busy cobbled street and waited at the tramstop. The rain had now become heavier and they had no umbrellas. Katherine turned up the collar of Ceppi's coat and then her own.

'Shouldn't be long now, luv, they always come in threes,' the woman standing next to her said. 'I swear ter God I don't know 'ow they do it, but they do, an' all the time! Are yer goin' far, like?'

'I don't really know. I've directions for a place called Mount Pleasant . . .'

'That's only a couple of stops. I'll see youse get off at the right one.'

'Thank you, I don't know Liverpool at all yet.'

'You just take care of yer valuables, the place is overrun with pickpockets. Kids mainly, but they do it because they're desperate hungry.'

'There's thousands like them in Dublin too.'

'Well, what did I tell yer, 'ere they come, three in a bloody line,' the woman said triumphantly.

They boarded the tram. It was already crowded and as she pushed her way up the centre aisle Katherine thought that maybe it would have been better to have got the one behind, in which there probably wasn't so much of a crush. Nearly every man had gone on the upper deck to have a smoke and she wasn't at all surprised to see a notice screwed to the front partition which said 'No Spitting'. So far there didn't seem to be much difference between Liverpool and her native city.

It wasn't far, the conductor shouted to her, having been briefed by the woman they'd stood waiting with.

''Ere yer are, girl! Mount Pleasant! Take yer time. Give us the bag then yer can see ter the little one!'

Katherine passed the bag over with just a second of hesitation. It didn't go unnoticed.

'I'm 'ardly goin' ter run off with the bloody bag, luv! What 'ave yer gorrin it? Bricks?'

'Everything we own,' Katherine answered. 'Come on, Ceppi, give me your hand, it's a big step down.' Then she took the bag from the conductor and thanked him for his help. 'Everyone has been so kind,' she said gratefully.

He shrugged and smiled. 'What did yer expect, luv? The folk in this city are known for their 'earts of gold. Rough and ignorant we may be, but we'll never see anyone in trouble go without 'elp, like.'

Mount Pleasant lived up to its name, she thought: a sloping hill with houses, quite big ones, on both sides. They all had names and signs in the windows, 'Vacancies' or 'No Vacancies'. Her spirits dropped when she saw two or three with 'No Irish' displayed.

She finally decided on Taylor's Commercial Hotel. It looked clean and had a 'Vacancies' sign up. The paintwork was good and the windows were clean, as were the white cotton lace curtains. The brass knocker and letter-box shone.

She knocked on the door apprehensively, a worrying thought creeping into her mind. What if this place wouldn't take them? What if they couldn't get *anywhere*?

A tall, angular woman, dressed entirely in black, opened the front door and surveyed them with suspicion.

'Ma'am, I would like to rent a room for myself and my niece. We have just arrived and it's my intention to find employment as soon as possible. I can pay for accommodation. I do have money. I would be very grateful,' she said quietly.

'Straight off the boat?'

'Yes, ma'am.'

'I don't normally take children, they're more trouble than they're worth.'

'Oh, she'll be no trouble. She'll be at school all day and in the evenings I intend to set her some homework and teach her to knit and sew.'

This was news to Ceppi and she looked up at Katherine with suspicion.

Gladys Taylor hesitated. They looked respectable. They wore decent clothes and the child didn't have that look of mischief in her eyes. In fact with her pale skin and all those red curls she reminded her of a picture of a cherub she'd once seen. Of course the cherub had had more flesh on its bones.

'Just how long were you thinking of?'

'A matter of weeks, that's all,' Katherine said, a note of hope in her voice.

The landlady debated. She had rooms to spare, her regular clientele were travelling salesmen or the better-class emigrants who were just awaiting Sailing Day.

'Very well. It will be two shillings a night for yourself and the child. Breakfast is at seven sharp. The other meals you'll have to sort out yourself. There are a list of rules on the back of the door, please read them carefully. The front door is locked at ten-thirty, after that you'll have to knock. And there are definitely *no* men allowed in at the door without inspection by myself, and *no* men upstairs.'

'I can assure you, ma'am, there will be nothing at all like that.'

'I'll have to have one week's lodgings in advance.'

Katherine counted out the coins, thinking it was a bit pricey. It was a respectable place, though, clean and comfortable. She handed the money over.

'Come inside then or I'll have people complaining you're lowering the tone of the neighbourhood,' the landlady ordered. With a quick glance to the right then the left, she hurried them into the hall.

Both Katherine and Ceppi looked around and then exchanged glances. Everything was so dark, painted brown and bottle green; even the pictures on the wall were depressing. There was a coat stand and a large brass tub for wet umbrellas.

'Is that all the luggage you have?' the landlady asked, eyeing the bag.

'I'm afraid it is. We left a bit . . . hurriedly.'

'You're not wanted by the police? If you are it's out that door you go this minute.'

'No! No, ma'am, it was nothing like that. It's all the strikes and lockouts, you see. People are going hungry and are never knowing from day to day if they'll be able to feed their families.'

Gladys Taylor's face looked as though something nasty

had entered the room. 'Well, I don't blame you for leaving all that. We've had enough unrest here, what with that man Larkin . . . No one wants the likes of him stirring up trouble.'

'What's that?' Ceppi suddenly broke into the conversation. She was pointing at an over-decorated jardinière topped by an equally over-decorated pot which held a large aspidistra.

'Is she always so rude?'

'No. No, she's . . . she's just curious. Questions, questions, questions, that's all I hear out of her.' Katherine frowned at Ceppi as the landlady turned and made for the stairs. They were covered in highly polished lino that wasn't scuffed or faded.

It wasn't a bad room, Katherine thought, glancing around. Not small but definitely not large either.

'I'll leave you to settle in then.'

'Thank you. Thank you, ma'am.'

'I'd be obliged if you'd stop calling me ma'am,' their landlady said. 'I'm not royalty.'

'What am I to call you then?'

'Mrs Taylor will do.'

'Well, thank you, Mrs Taylor.'

When the door had closed behind her Ceppi went to the window. It overlooked a side wall. 'It hasn't got a garden. I thought it would have.'

Katherine sighed. 'And I would have thought she'd be more . . . friendly and not charge the rate she does, but we'll have to make the best of it, I suppose.'

A large and very ugly double bed made of black cast iron took up most of the space. There was a quilt over it, clean and quite heavy, Katherine thought as she felt it. The floor was covered with lino and beside the bed were two rag rugs. There was a chest of drawers and a small wardrobe, and on the wall hung a picture, a rural scene which looked completely out of place with all the dark green paint.

'I don't like it,' Ceppi announced as she sprawled on to the bed.

'Ceppi Healy, if I hear one more complaint about anything I'll send you back on the next boat. It's clean and comfortable and certainly better than anywhere you've ever slept.'

Ceppi wasn't in the least contrite. 'It's desperate, all this green paint! Ugh!'

'That's to keep out the bugs. Mam told me that once. And that's another thing in its favour, there don't appear to be any bugs of any kind. Now help me unpack these things and then we'll go and see some more of this new city that's to be our home.'

'Will we find somewhere to eat?'

'Don't you ever think of anything else but food? You've just eaten a meal that would fill a man's stomach, never mind a child's.'

'No. When you've never had enough, you . . . Oh, it's hard to explain.'

Katherine sighed. 'I suppose it is. But we'll have to find somewhere cheap if we're to get our meals ourselves. She doesn't look as though she'd care if we ate or not.'

With their meagre wardrobes hung up or laid in the chest of drawers, they went in search of a café or somewhere they could get cheap food. They walked to the junction of Mount Pleasant, Ranelagh Street and Renshaw Street. They spent some time staring into the windows of Lewis's department store.

'Will we ever be able to buy things from there?' Ceppi asked.

'I don't think so. Well, not for a long, long time anyway.'

'But can't we just go in and look?'

'Well, I don't suppose it will hurt, but no touching things.'

The doorman held open a door for them and Katherine smiled. Had Ceppi been wearing her old clothes he'd never have allowed them in. But the smile left her face as soon as she stepped over the threshold. She'd been into Brown Thomas in Grafton Street once and it had stunned and overawed her. She was feeling like that now.

Ceppi was struck dumb, her eyes wide with amazement.

A floorwalker, in formal morning suit, approached them. 'May I be of assistance?'

Katherine's heart sank. 'Er . . . We . . . She wanted to see . . .' She looked at him pleadingly.

'Our zoo perhaps?'

'Zoo! You have a zoo here?'

'We do. A small one. I'll get someone to show you the way. It's around the back of the building.'

They both stood in silence until at last a girl of Katherine's age appeared.

'He says I'm to show you the way to the zoo. Is it for her?'

'Yes. Well, both of us. If the truth be told I've never been to one, even though we have one in Dublin. Well, in Phoenix Park.'

The girl shrugged. 'Come on then. I'm warning you, it stinks to high heaven! I think it's a daft idea anyway. At least they only have a parrot in Blacklers.'

It was smelly and Ceppi peered into the cages with trepidation.

'These are all monkeys, from all over the world, like. Then there's the birds, and snakes. Ugh, God! They make my flesh creep. That thing in there with the long legs and tail is a wallaby all the way from Australia! That furry looking bear-like thing is a koala bear. That came from Australia too.'

'You know an awful lot about them.'

'All the junior staff have got to, it's part of our job. We do it on a rota basis.'

After their tour both Katherine and Ceppi were relieved to get out into the fresh air again. Katherine thanked the girl and they began to walk down towards Church Street to look at the shops there.

'Fancy me being after seeing all those creatures,' Ceppi marvelled.

'They did smell and I didn't like those snakes.'

'Maybe they got them from Ireland?'

'How so?'

'Sure, didn't St Patrick chase all the snakes out of the country?'

Katherine laughed. 'Ceppi, that was hundreds of years ago. They couldn't possibly be *that* old. You have some desperate ideas sometimes.'

They couldn't find a café they could afford to eat in in Church Street, so in the end Katherine approached a police-man standing on the corner of Church Street and Lord Street.

Ceppi eyed him with suspicion. She'd never seen a policeman in a dark blue uniform before.

'Sir, do you know of a café that's cheap but clean?'

He noted the accent but also that they were decently turned out.

'Well, there's one at the junction of Berry Street and Great George's Street. Go back along Church Street, up to Lewis's, around the corner to the top and you'll see St Luke's Church. Go along Berry Street, it's only about two hundred yards long, and at the top is the junction with Great George's Street.'

'Thank you, sir.'

'Have you anywhere to stay?'

'I have, sir, thank you.'

'That's all right then. This is a rough city for girls alone. Stay away from the dock areas and you'll be fine.'

Katherine thanked him again.

'Are all the polis like him over here? Sure at home they haven't a tinker's curse to throw after you.'

'I don't know, but we'll take his advice.' She knew it was only because they were decently dressed and she'd spoken respectfully to him that he'd taken any interest in them at all.

They followed his instructions and found the café. Katherine peered through the window but she couldn't see much because it was dark inside. 'Come on, in we go. If we don't like it we can try somewhere else.'

It wasn't very much lighter inside but it looked clean and at the smell of food cooking they wrinkled their noses appreciatively.

A girl, not much older than Katherine, came out of a door at the back of the room. 'Is it a breakfast or a lunch you want?'

'What's the difference?'

'Breakfast is bacon, egg, sausage an' fried bread. Dinner is cottage pie an' gravy. It's really only just dinnertime but I think there's some breakfast stuff left.'

'We'll have the dinner, please, we had breakfast earlier on.'

'Anythin' ter drink?'

'Tea please and a glass of fresh milk for herself there.'

Ceppi pulled a face and the girl laughed.

'I can't say I like that stuff much meself either.'

'Where we come from there's no fresh milk at all, it's all tinned. No one drinks just milk.'

'Ye're Irish, aren't yer?'

'We came over on the ferry last night,' Katherine said. 'We've got a room in a sort of hotel but she doesn't do any meals except breakfast so we're looking for somewhere clean and cheap to eat.'

'Well, I think yer just found it. Dinner is from twelve to two an' is a set price, an' tea is from 'alf past five to 'alf past seven and that's a set price too.'

'That'll be grand. I've got to find a job and a school for this one here. Mind you, she doesn't want to go to school at all.'

'You've no choice. Iffen yer don't go, the School Board feller comes around an' yer 'ave ter pay a fine an' it's a big one, an' iffen yer carry on not goin' then they'll cart yer sister 'ere ter jail.'

For Ceppi that was a very sobering thought.

'Can they really do that?' Katherine was equally impressed.

'Oh, yeah. I know one lad who gets regular 'idings, like, because his da's more often in clink than 'e is at work. Doesn't stop 'im skivin' off though. Mind you, meself I think 'e'll end up at the end of a rope.'

Katherine looked at her in horror. They had some very strict rules here.

'Yer could send 'er to the one in Maryland Street, that's not far and run by the nuns from the convent.'

Ceppi scowled at the girl. When she *had* gone to school, she'd been taught by the nuns in Dublin, and she hadn't thought much of them. This lot would probably be the same.

'Thanks, I'll go and see the Reverend Mother this afternoon. The sooner she goes, the sooner I can find work and then somewhere decent to live.'

'Well, yer won't find much of either around 'ere, luv.'

'But . . . but I thought there was plenty of work?'

'Casual labour, navvyin', factory work. Can yer do anythin'?'

'No, except for housework.'

'Try the factories. The wages is shockin' and so are the conditions, but it's a job of work.'

'Oh,' Katherine replied, disappointedly.

'The match factory pays the best. The more boxes yer do, the more yer earn, but it's a stinkin' place and it's dangerous.'

'Dangerous?'

'Yeah. The stuff they put on the sticks – yer know, that red stuff – well, it can give yer somethin' called "phossy jaw" an' that's real bad, but—'

'Thanks, I'll try there.' Katherine ended the conversation quickly. She didn't want any more doom and gloom.

'Let me know 'ow yer get on.'

'I will. What's your name?'

'Joan. Joan Robinson.'

'I'm Katherine Donovan and this is Concepta . . . Ceppi Healy.'

'I thought she was yer sister, like.'

'No, we're not even related,' Ceppi blurted out. 'But none of the real brothers and sisters wanted me at home, and neither does Mammy.'

Joan looked questioningly at Katherine.

'It's true,' Katherine confirmed, smiling sadly.

Ceppi turned to Katherine. 'I don't give a tinker's curse about them any more. I've got Katherine, *she's* my mammy now.'

Chapter Six

— • ❖ • —

THE INTERVIEW WITH Reverend Mother had been far from successful for the nun made it plain that she had no wish to have Concepta Healy in her school.

'You say she was . . . er . . . educated by nuns in Dublin?'

'She was, Mother,' Katherine replied.

'Which order?'

'The Sisters of Charity.'

'Indeed.' The word was uttered in such a tone as to leave Katherine in no doubt whatsoever what her opinion of them was. It held precious little charity.

'Can she read and write her own name?'

'She can write, she likes writing, but I help her as much as I can with the reading.'

The nun leaned her elbows on her desk and pressed the tips of her fingers together in a gesture that Ceppi thought looked like a roof. Ceppi hadn't uttered a single word yet. This nun with a face like a half-starved cat terrified her.

'Well, I suppose we *can* take her.' There was heavy emphasis on the word 'can'. 'Bring her tomorrow morning at eight-thirty sharp, and make sure she wears something . . . *sensible*.'

Again the emphasis on 'sensible'. Katherine didn't like the woman. If only she knew of another suitable school, she'd have turned down the grudging offer.

'Thank you, Mother.'

Still seated, the nun moved her head slightly in acknowledgement. 'And we shall see you in the morning, Concepta.'

Ceppi could only nod. It was clear that she was not going to be called Ceppi here. She'd have to be careful to answer to her full name while she was at school.

Katherine sighed when they were out in the street. 'Well, that's you sorted out.'

'Do I *really* have to go? She was desperate altogether!'

'Yes, you do. I didn't like her much either, full of her own importance, but it's a good school from what I saw of it and you'll do well. I'm not having you grow up wild and ignorant. I want you to get a good job at the end of it so you'll never be cold and hungry again.'

Ceppi debated this for a while. She'd always trusted Katherine; maybe she was right. She didn't want to let her down. Maybe this school wouldn't be that bad. As they made their way back to Mrs Taylor's establishment, she turned her attention to wondering what her classmates would be like. Would she find a friend?

They both slept well for the first time in months and were washed and dressed – in 'sensible' clothes – by seven o'clock ready for breakfast.

'Have you found a school for her yet?' Mrs Taylor asked as she carefully placed the teapot – covered with a blue-striped cosy – on the cork mat in the middle of the table.

'I have so, I'm taking her to Maryland Street and then I'm going to look for work.'

The woman nodded her approval. In the navy blue skirt and a navy blue jumper, black stockings and boots, her hair held tidily off her face with a blue-and-white ribbon, the child looked very neat and tidy.

But when Katherine left her at the Convent gates, there were tears in Ceppi's eyes and a lump in her throat. She wouldn't cry, though. She wouldn't let anyone see she was acting like a baby. She clutched her dinner money tightly in her hand and walked towards the stone doorway, her head held high.

The iron gates of Bryant and May's match factory were closed but there was a small hut-like building to one side of them and a man sat inside. Katherine knocked on the window and he got up.

'What do you want, luv?'

'Are there any jobs going, please?'

'It depends. Wait now and I'll find out for you from Ted Morris – he's the foreman. There may have been some absentees this morning.'

She watched him walk across the yard and disappear inside the building, a little more hopeful now, since he'd been cheerful. The place looked a bit like a jail, but if they had a job she didn't care.

Katherine sniffed. There was a strange smell in the air and

she remembered what Joan Robinson from the café had told her about phossy jaw.

The man was grinning when he came back. 'You're on. Two didn't turn up this morning and it's the sack for one of them; she's been absent for two days with not a word from her. You can start now.'

'Oh, I didn't expect to get anything so soon! Oh, thank you! Thank you!'

'It's not me you should thank, luv, it's divine providence and luck. Being at the right place at the right time.'

After thanking him again Katherine walked across the yard to the first real job she had ever had. Her stomach felt as though it was full of ice water and her legs as though they were made of jelly.

She gave her name to some sort of clerk and was handed a brown overall. Then she hesitantly went through the door. There seemed to be a series of small rooms, all full of women and girls assembling boxes. The pungent smell of phosphorus was almost overpowering. A man in an overall coat but with a shirt and tie and dark trousers underneath came towards her.

'Have you done this kind of work before?'

'I have not, sir, but I'm very willing to learn.'

'Right then, this way.'

She followed him down the long corridor aware that at each room they passed silence descended and work speeded up. He at last ushered her into a much larger room. 'Collect your materials over there, find somewhere to sit and' – he looked around – 'Dot will show you the ropes. You do know it's piece-work?'

'Yes, sir.'

71

A place was made for her at the workbench after she had collected the foul-smelling glue and cardboard. She was relieved to see they were making boxes. Maybe the matches were made elsewhere and she'd no need to worry about phossy jaw.

'I 'ope ye're not goin' ter slow us down. We work as a group. We all have to work as fast as we can so we all get a decent wage. Me mam went mad last week because I was short in me wages an' all because of bloody 'ilda and 'er bloody hands.'

'That's not fair, Dotty, she's got arthritis.'

'Well, all I know is I was short. What's yer name?'

'Katherine Donovan.'

'An' which part of the Emerald Isle do yer come from? Yer've an accent yer could cut with a bread knife.'

'Dublin and not the nice part. The slums. Will you teach me what bits go where and I promise I'll soon be able to keep up. I want to earn as much as I can.'

'Be thankful too that yer've not been put in the phossy shop.'

'Oh, I am. I heard about it and what can happen.'

'Only last week a girl who used to work 'ere was buried. Dotty an' me went ter the funeral. It was terrible, she was only twenty-four. It eats away at yer mouth and then gets inter yer blood.'

'God 'elp 'er, she was a good worker too.'

Katherine was watching Dotty assemble a matchbox at what seemed to be lightning speed and didn't really hear the rest of the story of the former worker's gruesome end.

She struggled for an hour. It wasn't as easy as it looked: the tiny pieces of cardboard stuck together or ended up in all the wrong places and the glue covered her fingers making it even harder to carry out the fiddly process.

'Oh, would you look at the mess I'm in. I'm sorry, Dotty, but I don't think your mam will be very pleased with your wages this week either.'

'Go and wash yer hands. Use that little scrubbin' brush to get the glue off and we'll start again,' Mavis instructed, darting a warning glance at Dotty.

Dotty remained silent and got on with her work while Mavis patiently went through each stage with Katherine. 'Don't try an' rush, take yer time an' learn properly, then yer can worry about 'ow many yer can make in a day.'

'This is desperate. We'll all have no wages by the end of the week,' Katherine said apologetically.

'No, we won't. By the end of the week yer'll be just as fast as us,' Mavis said firmly, once again looking at Dotty with gimlet eyes.

'Well, I 'ope that'll keep me mam 'appy,' Dotty interrupted regardless. 'Just because I'm not out scrubbin' floors she thinks this is an "easy" job. She changed her tune though when that poor girl died. She said I wasn't ter go anywhere I could catch somethin'.' Dotty screamed with laughter. 'As if we gets a bloody say in it. Beggars can't be choosers!'

When the hooter sounded everyone downed tools.

'We always go an' eat our butties sittin' on the wall outside, providin' it's not rainin' or blowin' a gale. Just a bit of fresh air helps to get rid of the stink in 'ere.'

'Fresh! That's a bloody joke. There's more soot in the air than there is in the bloody chimney.'

'For God's sake, Dotty, will yer stop puttin' the mockers on every bloody thing,' Mavis retorted. 'Come on out with us, Katherine.'

'I will so, but . . .'

'But what?' Mavis asked.

'Well, I didn't think I'd get a job so soon, so I didn't bring anything . . .' She felt embarrassed.

''Aven't yer gorrany butties, like?' Dotty asked.

'I have not.'

'Well, that doesn't matter, girl, we'll give yer some of ours. Share an' share alike.'

'Oh, I *couldn't!*'

'Of course yer can. I've got meat paste on mine.'

'I've only got drippin', Mam's a bit short this week. Me da only got three days' work and what with 'ilda stopping off . . .' Dotty shrugged.

Katherine's protests were silenced and she was grateful for their generosity. It would be hours before she had a meal at the café.

It had turned out to be an interesting afternoon, Katherine thought. She had not yet reached the designated speed nor could she work and talk at the same time. But although the rest of her co-workers were rough diamonds they'd been friendly and included her in the general chit chat and gossip. Haltingly, her mind half on her job and half on what she was saying, she told her story. Not the bit about her father murdering Ceppi's father or his subsequent death at the hands and feet of the men in the street, though. She told them that she'd had enough of being at his beck and call and waiting on him hand and foot and getting nothing back in return, so she'd left him. Ceppi's story was edited in the same way. Of course they all said she was stark raving mad to cart someone else's child to Liverpool with her. Life here was bloody tough on kids, especially hard-up ones. Katherine said nothing about her father's money.

At four o'clock the clanging of the bell marked the end of the school day and Ceppi was more than glad. She'd never been so quiet or put as much thought and concentration into her lessons before, and Sister Imelda terrified her. The nun walked up and down between the rows of desks holding a small, thin piece of wood that had been secreted somewhere beneath the long, voluminous skirt of her habit.

At break time she'd stood in a corner and watched the others playing. She'd eaten her dinner in silence and it hadn't been until the afternoon playtime that anyone had spoken to her. And that was only a thin, plain girl in glasses who was obviously the class brainbox.

She'd never felt so intimidated in her life. She didn't belong here. She wasn't like them. They were all cleverer than she was. The tears pricked her eyes as she walked back to Mount Pleasant. On top of everything, she'd been given homework for the first time in her life.

'You are so far behind everyone, Concepta, you will have to work in the evenings. What kind of a school you attended in Dublin I dread to think!' had been Sister Imelda's parting words.

Now she was going back to a silent house. She wondered how Katherine had got on. She hoped she'd got some class of a job, then they could leave Mrs Taylor and maybe even change her school. The thought made her cheer up a bit and quicken her steps.

Mrs Taylor answered the door. 'Well, how did you get on?'

'Oh, grand, ma'am. Sorry, Mrs Taylor. I've a bit of work to do at home.'

'Then I suggest you go straight up and do it. I presume you can light a gas jet?'

'Yes, Mrs Taylor.'

Her legs felt tired as she climbed the stairs and her heart sank as she opened the door to the dark, chilly room. She dragged the quilt off the bed, wrapped herself in it and began to cry.

She had cried herself to sleep by the time Katherine got in. Katherine shook her awake.

'Ceppi, Ceppi, what's the matter?'

'It was desperate, really desperate. No one spoke to me, they didn't ask me to join their games and I'm as thick as the wall. I've even got to do homework to catch up.'

Katherine held her in her arms, memories of her own unhappy, isolated childhood flooding back. What had she done, coming here and dragging Ceppi with her? The last thing she wanted was for the poor child to be unhappy, the way she'd been. Her own miserable experiences had begun long before she was Ceppi's age. Oh, how often had she come home in tears like Ceppi? How often had she been lonely, hurt and humiliated but – in the years after Mam's death – received no sympathy? No arms to hold her, no one to dry her tears, no one to soothe her and sympathise with her. She didn't want anything like that for Ceppi. She prayed she'd made the right decision coming to Liverpool.

'Hush now,' Katherine murmured as the storm of Ceppi's weeping died down. 'I'll help you with your homework after we've been to eat. I'll ask Herself downstairs if we can use the parlour or the dining-room table. Come on now and wash your face.'

'Did you get a job?' Ceppi asked, brightening up.

'Yes I did, and I started right away. It won't be long before we can find somewhere else to stay.'

'Can I go to another school, please, please?'

'We'll see, Ceppi. But I want you to have a good education.'

The child began to cry again.

'Well, we'll see, Ceppi. Get your coat on, I'm starving hungry, even though the girls I work with gave me a couple of their sandwiches. They called them "butties".'

They both felt much better after a meal that consisted of potatoes, carrots and brisket, followed by a sponge pudding with custard.

'Joan, can I ask a favour?' Katherine said hesitantly.

'What do yer want?'

'Well, I got a job at the match factory, making boxes, and I didn't have anything with me for my dinner. Could you make me some butties please, for tomorrow? I'll pay of course.'

'Course I will, an' I won't charge a penny. She'll never miss a few slices of bread and there's always food left over. What the eye doesn't see, if yer get my meanin'.'

'Oh, I wouldn't be wanting to get you into trouble.'

'It's no trouble. I'll slip the packet to yer on yer way out.'

'Thanks.'

'There's no need. What are friends for?'

Katherine smiled back, warmed by the girl's words. She had found a friend.

'She's nice, isn't she?' Ceppi stated as they walked home.

'She is so, and she's generous and I . . . I've never had a friend before.'

'Never?'

'No. Nobody would let me join their games, or play with me because . . . because of my da.'

'I had lots.'

'And you'll have lots here soon too. It's just a matter of breaking the ice. You talk to someone, instead of waiting for them to talk to you. I bet you'll soon have them hanging on your every word when you tell them about your life in Dublin. I bet none of them has ever been on a ferry boat, apart from the ones that go across the Mersey.'

Ceppi brightened a little further. She still hated the place but maybe tomorrow she *would* talk to someone.

When they'd arrived back and Mrs Taylor had let them in, Katherine touched the woman's arm.

'Mrs Taylor, could I ask a favour of you?'

'That depends on what it is.'

'Ceppi has to do some homework to catch up at school. Could she do it on the dining-room table? I promise faithfully that not a mark will be made on it. I'll be with her all the time and I'm sure it won't be for long.'

The landlady thought for a few minutes and then nodded. 'On the condition that not the tiniest scratch will be made.'

'Thank you so much. Could you not leave the felt overlay on it?'

'I intend to.'

'I've had a good day, Mrs Taylor.'

'I'm glad to hear it.'

'I got a day's work and start full time in the morning.'

'Indeed. What kind of work?'

'Making matchboxes. I've never done anything like that before but I picked it up fairly well and the girls I work with are very nice.'

The landlady was staring at her, her eyes full of disapproval.

'Is there something the matter, Mrs Taylor?'

'Oh, indeed there is. The child attending school is one thing, you working in that . . . that . . . stinking factory is quite another. I can smell that stuff on you now.'

'It's work, Mrs Taylor. I have to earn money to keep Ceppi and myself and pay you.'

'I thought you had money?'

'I do but it won't last for ever.'

'Indeed it won't.'

She turned leaving Katherine looking blankly at the door as it closed behind the landlady.

'I hate her! She's desperate! Really desperate!' Ceppi cried.

Katherine could do little else but agree.

Katherine was actually looking forward to work the following morning. She'd have someone to talk to all day and in the evening she would have Joan. She smiled to herself: she liked Liverpool, she really did, and the people were so kind and humorous. Mrs Taylor was the exception, she told herself, determined to be positive.

She watched Ceppi go through the school gates and gave her a wave.

Ceppi waved back nervously. She had promised she would try to talk to the other girls in her class but she wasn't looking forward to it. At least all her homework had been done. Katherine had helped her so much and she'd said that by no means was she as 'thick as the wall'; she was, in fact, quite clever. But Ceppi hadn't believed her.

When the four o'clock bell sounded along the narrow corridors with their polished floors and statues and holy pictures, Ceppi was once again feeling very miserable. She'd done her best, she really had, but no one had been very friendly to her. They all seemed to have their own little groups.

She was waiting with her coat and hat on when Katherine came in.

'I tried! I tried!'

'Oh, Ceppi! Ceppi, I want you to be happy. I want you to have a better life, that's why I brought you with me.'

'I hate it!'

'Come on, let's go and see Joan, she'll cheer us up.' She was still in her working clothes but she wouldn't stop to change; she had to distract Ceppi.

They went straight to the welcoming little café to be greeted by Joan's cheerful smile.

'And 'ow did things go terday then?'

'For me, it was grand, but not for Ceppi.'

'I hate it! I hate them all, even that Sister Imelda!'

'Oh, cross yerself an' say ye're sorry! Quick! It's terrible bad luck ter speak like that of a nun!' Joan almost shrieked but Katherine caught the gleam of mischief in her eyes.

Ceppi did what she'd been told to do and looked pale.

'Right, ternight it's 'otpot with red cabbage, and sponge puddin' with custard.'

'Oh, Joan, that sounds like—'

'You 'aven't seen the state of the cook. She's 'alf cut most of the time an' I swear she's gettin' worse. They'll come ter cart 'er off ter the loony-bin one day!'

'I don't care if she's as drunk as ten lords, I'm starving!'

'Oh, I didn't mean the food is bad, it's good considering the state of '*er*.'

'I'd watch yourself just the same or you could end up working in the match factory like me.'

'God, I'd 'ate that. I suppose Mrs T. is 'appy now?'

'No, I couldn't believe it. You'd have thought I'd told her I was starting up a house of ill repute, the carry on out of her! It's honest work, and it will pay the rent, but she's far from happy.'

Ceppi was pushing her knife and fork around the table and kicking her heels against the legs of the chair. She felt that her position was worth being voiced again.

'At least you *like* your job and people talk to you. Nobody likes me and I hate them!'

Katherine and Joan exchanged glances and Katherine sighed. Joan became very businesslike. 'I'll go an' get yer tea.'

As Ceppi watched Joan disappear into the kitchen, her expression was still one of deep misery. Katherine leaned over the table to give her a hug. 'Give it some time. It's only been two days. Maybe tomorrow everything will be different.'

Chapter Seven

———◆———

LIFE WAS BEGINNING to fall into a pattern, to have some normality at last, Katherine thought as she pulled a sleepy-eyed Ceppi from her warm and comfortable bed. Katherine was already washed and dressed.

'Ceppi, come on, wake yourself up. The sooner we get downstairs, the sooner we get our breakfast.'

'Don't want to go to school.'

'You *have* to. Don't you remember what Joan said? If you don't go to school I'll be fined. I'll lose all our money and I might even go to jail. Now, put on those clothes and then I'll try to do something with your hair.'

Ceppi sat on the end of the bed while Katherine carefully plaited her hair.

'Can we go for breakfast now? What time is it?'

'Time to go!'

Breakfast was served as usual by their landlady, whose look of disdain had not diminished. But today there was one other diner: a middle-aged man in a well-worn grey suit.

'I see we have some new arrivals.' He addressed Mrs Taylor, but smiled over at Katherine and Ceppi as he spoke. They both smiled back.

Mrs Taylor nodded curtly.

'Well, aren't you going to introduce us?'

'This is Katherine Donovan and the child's name is Concepta Healy. They're Irish, from Dublin. This is Mr Fortesque, a commercial traveller who always stays here when he has to come to Liverpool.'

'Well, Miss Donovan and Miss Concepta Healy, it's very nice to meet you. Are you staying long?'

'No, a couple of weeks, that's all.'

'Well, you'll have to work day and night in *that* place to be able to afford to rent somewhere decent,' Mrs Taylor remarked scathingly.

Katherine felt her cheeks getting red but she was determined not to let the woman get the better of her so she ignored her. 'Ceppi, eat up now, it's time to leave for school. I'll see you there before I catch the tram for work myself.'

Mrs Taylor left the room, closing the door firmly behind her.

'Do I detect a slight "coldness" in our landlady's manner? What have you done to upset her – not that it's hard to do that?'

'I've got a job in a match factory.'

'She doesn't approve, I gather?'

'You gather right.'

'Take no notice. Don't let Mrs Taylor put you off, the people in this city are a friendly lot. Better than some other places I go to.'

'I won't. I meant what I said about moving out. Well, I suppose we'll see you tomorrow morning?'

'You will but I'm off later in the day.'

'I hope you have a successful day.'

'You too, both of you.'

The whole morning Ceppi struggled to keep up with the other girls and as the bell rang for lunch her teacher called her to the front.

'Concepta, your homework was satisfactory but did they not teach you your tables back home in Dublin?'

Ceppi looked down at her boots and nodded.

'Well then, why don't you know them? You couldn't answer a single question.'

Ceppi didn't raise her eyes. 'I . . . I . . . well, Mammy never really . . . made . . . me.'

'Ah, I see. You were left to run the streets instead of going to school. Are there no education inspectors in Dublin?'

'I . . . I . . . don't think so, Sister.'

'You *do* know the laws here?'

'I do so.'

'Then I expect to see you every day and with your tables learned. You will recite the six, seven, eight and nine times tables for me tomorrow morning. Now go and get your lunch.'

'Yes, Sister.'

She dragged her feet as she went towards the refectory as it was called, a word she had never heard before, let alone known what it meant. The smell coming from it was good and despite everything she was hungry. Katherine had already paid for her lunches for the week. So she gave her ticket to a nun standing by the door. There were long scrubbed tables with benches to sit on. On each table was a big glass jug of water and several glasses. You had to stand in line to get served, it was all very orderly, and if anyone spoke at all it was in a whisper. Talking and eating at the same time was extremely bad manners, she'd been told by Katherine, as was cramming the food into your mouth, no matter how hungry you were. Grace was said and then they were allowed to sit. It was minced beef with carrots and mashed potatoes and as she ate, in silence and with the right knife and fork, she thought with something akin to wonder that these days all she seemed to do was eat, and for that fact alone she was glad that Katherine had brought her to Liverpool.

Plates were collected up by the monitor, an older girl who sat at the head of the table, and when they'd finished the knives and forks were laid neatly side by side. Then Grace After Meals was said and they filed out into the cloakroom to put on their coats to go into the playground: a rectangular yard covered with fine gravel. The wind tore at her hair and it was in danger of falling out of its plait so she stood in a corner to try to shield it from the gusts. Despite the good meal she felt miserable again.

'What's the matter with you?'

Ceppi looked up. Maddy Coyne, the class bully, was staring at her.

'Nothing,' Ceppi answered.

'Then why aren't you playing like everyone else?'

Ceppi shrugged. She'd quickly come to hate the other girl.

'I'll tell you why: you've got no friends. You don't belong

here with us. You're Irish and me mam says all the Irish are thick as the wall.'

At this insult Ceppi glared at her. 'We're not! I'm a bit behind but it's nothing desperate. You wait and see, I'm cleverer than you. *You're* the thick one! You can't read as good as me and look at you!' Her body was tense and her eyes blazed. 'A great thick lump of a bold article, that's what you are!'

Maddy's face turned bright red. A small crowd had gathered around them, listening and watching, wondering if Ceppi thought she was a match for Maddy. Suddenly Maddy lunged forward and caught Ceppi by her hair which had now escaped from its plait.

'I'll show you how "thick" I am! I'll pull all the hair out of your head!'

Ceppi screamed in agony but kicked out, catching the other girl on the shin. Maddy gave a yell of pain and her grasp on Ceppi's hair loosened.

As quick and as slippery as an eel Ceppi twisted herself from Maddy's grip and, with all the strength she could muster, launched herself at her tormentor and they both fell, screaming, yelling, scratching and tearing at each other's hair and clothes. Fury drove Ceppi on. She'd had many a fight like this in Dublin, but not for the same reason. But as they rolled around Ceppi realised she was no match for Maddy who was a big strong girl. Ceppi was tiring. Maddy now had the advantage; she was pinning her to the ground with strong arms when suddenly she bellowed in pain and the pressure on Ceppi's shoulders was released.

'Pick on someone your own size, Maddy Coyne, you big coward! You're just what she called you, "a thick lump of an article",' Mary Boland yelled, dragging Maddy away by her hair.

Maddy was screaming with hurt. Ceppi sat up, her face and hands dirty and scratched.

The group of girls that surrounded them drew back and they all faced a furious Sister Imelda.

'What is going on here? Get up off the ground, all three of you!' she demanded.

They did as they were told, Ceppi trying to tidy her hair, Maddy brushing down her skirt and Mary Boland trying to look innocent.

'Perhaps you can tell me why you were rolling around and fighting like dogs in the gutter?' Sister Imelda's tone was like ice breaking.

They all remained silent.

'I see. Then you'll all go and tell Mother Superior what you were doing.' The nun's face was a mask of barely concealed fury. 'You are supposed to be decorous Catholic young ladies, following the example of Our Blessed Lady!'

'She . . . Maddy Coyne was picking on Concepta. Calling her names. It was all *her* fault!' Mary said, glaring at Maddy.

'Behaving like wild animals is never justified by the provocation! This is not the end of the matter. Your parents will be informed and if this carries on you will all be expelled!'

There was a collective gasp amongst the other girls and Ceppi, Maddy and Mary Boland were despatched to the cloakroom to tidy themselves up.

All afternoon Ceppi was worried; she couldn't concentrate on her work. She'd only just started here and now . . .

At afternoon break Mary Boland came up to her. 'My mam will kill me, but I couldn't let her get away with it. She's much bigger than you and you were giving as good as you got until . . .' She shrugged.

'I'm sorry that you'll get into trouble, but thanks. At least you weren't like the others, just standing around gaping.'

'I *hate* her! Everyone does, even that lot who hang around her. I hope she does get expelled; she's done this before but she usually waits until school's over.'

'Katherine will kill me too.'

'Who's she?'

'She's sort of an older sister, but she's not. She's my friend. And she says I'm to have a good education.'

'Where did you go to school before?'

'Before what?'

'Before you came here.'

'In Dublin.'

'Was it a convent?'

'No, but we had nuns to teach us and the boys had priests. Christian Brothers.'

'And you came all the way over here in a boat? I've been down to the Pier Head and watched the ships but I've never been on one, not even the Mersey ferries. What was it like?'

'Desperate.'

'What?'

'Desperate . . . like . . . awful, horrible.'

'Oh, I see. You say things different. You were "brought" to school, not "taken".'

'I know, but there's lots of words you say that I don't understand.'

'Well, just ask me. I won't bite your head off.'

'I've got homework to do as well as all this . . . trouble. I have my six, seven, eight and nine times tables to learn tonight.'

Mary looked appalled. '*All* of them? That's terrible!'

'Well, I never went to school much in Dublin. I only went if I felt like it. The mammy didn't care if I went or stayed at home, so I am behind everyone.'

Mary was amazed. 'Imagine, being able to please yourself when you went to school. Is that really true? What about the fellers from the School Board?'

Ceppi shrugged. 'Like I told Sister Imelda, I never saw any of them and neither did the mammy.'

'Where do you live?'

'In a house called "Englefield" in Mount Pleasant but I hope we'll be leaving it soon. Herself . . . Mrs Taylor who runs it is really desperate.'

'I live in one of the streets that run off it so I'll walk home with you tonight. I don't much feel like walking on my own.'

'Thanks, neither do I. What will . . . happen to us?'

'God knows, but it's bound to be bad,' Mary answered gloomily. Then she returned to the interesting facts of Ceppi's life before she'd come to Liverpool. 'When you came here with Katherine, didn't your mam say anything about it?'

'No. Sure, she couldn't care less. There's a crowd of us and every one of us had to take care of themselves. I'm the youngest. I . . . I didn't have anything, sometimes no boots even, until Katherine brought me with her.'

Mary looked at her with pity. 'Why did Katherine come? Didn't anyone want her either?'

'Her mammy died years ago and her da . . . her da died not long ago.'

'Oh, that's awfully sad.'

'It is so.'

'Well, when all this is over and things have settled down again, do you think Katherine will let you come and play on Saturday afternoons and maybe Sunday afternoons too?'

Ceppi looked taken aback. Considering the dire position they were in, Mary Boland was looking a long way into the future.

'You mean that you'll be my friend? Even after today?'

'Why shouldn't I? I like you and we've got to get through this together.'

'You mean I can *really* come to play in your house?'

'Yes, but it's mainly in the street we play, all kinds of games. Did you play street games before you came here?'

'Not really. We were always too tired and cold and hungry.'

'Oh.' Mary didn't think she should press on with this subject.

'I think I like Liverpool better than Dublin. Have you got brothers and sisters?'

'Two brothers and one sister. Our Alfie's fifteen, he works as a messenger boy for the Tramways, but our Eddie is younger than me, he's two. In fact he's really only a baby. Mam calls him her "bloody little accident".'

'Why?'

'Because she didn't want to have any more kids after me. She was always saying having a lot of kids made you poor and drove you round the bend with the antics out of them.'

'What about your sister?'

'Our Tilly's fourteen, she left school and she was dead lucky to get a job in service, though I wouldn't want to have anything to do with them rich people, no matter how grand a house and a life they have. I don't call scrubbing floors, fetching coal and peeling tons of potatoes much of a job, and they pay her almost half of nothing! She comes home sometimes to see us, but not often and I don't blame her. She's hardly got the coat off her when Mam starts on about money and our Eddie. She knows Mam'll have half her wages off her before she goes back to that posh house.'

'What do you want to do, when you're grown up I mean?'

Mary shrugged. 'Oh, I dunno. Shop work, I suppose. What about you?'

'I don't really know either, but I do know one thing.'

'What's that?'

'I'm never going back to Dublin.' The bell told them that time was up.

'I'll walk home with you. I daresn't speak again in class.'

They made their way together to the stone archway that led into the schoolrooms.

'Do you think your Katherine would let me come round one night to help you with your times tables? I've never been in one of those bed and breakfast places and neither has Mam and we're both dying to see the inside.'

Ceppi looked at her. 'I thought you said your mam will kill you?'

'She'll get over it. When we were younger we were always fighting in the street.'

'But the street's not school. I think . . . we should wait and see what happens, but, Mary, thanks. I really mean it.'

All three of them were given an envelope with instructions to hand it to their parents right away and under no circumstances to let it 'go missing' or open it.

Ceppi's mood deepened. She'd spent the last hour thinking what Katherine would say. She'd even toyed with the idea of not telling her, letting her find out in time, but that option wasn't open to her now.

Neither she nor Mary spoke much on the way home. They parted company at the top of St Andrew's Street and Ceppi slowly walked the remainder of the way.

She went straight upstairs and sat on the edge of the bed, turning the envelope over and over in her hands. It *hadn't* been her fault. Surely Katherine would understand?

It seemed an age before she heard Katherine's voice in the hallway below. She bit her lip as Katherine came into the room.

Katherine took one look at the solemn little face and sighed. 'Ceppi, now what's wrong? Did you still not make any friends?'

Ceppi handed over the envelope and steeled herself.

Katherine was at first a little confused then as she read the note her temper began to rise. 'Ceppi Healy! I despair of you! Fighting! FIGHTING in school!'

'I didn't start it! Maddy Coyne called me names and said everyone Irish is thick, and I lost my temper—'

'Oh, you did that all right if all this is true!' Katherine interrupted. The note was very graphic, saying it had been the very type of behaviour Mother Superior wanted to eradicate in 'this uneducated child of the Dublin slums'.

'I despair of you, Ceppi! I'm working to give you a good

education and what do you do? Not a week in there and you're carrying on like a little cat and an alley cat at that! Now I'll have to go up there and apologise and hope they'll keep you on. Isn't that a grand way of spending an evening after a hard day's work, and there'll be no supper until I come back! You, you bold little rossi, will stay here!'

Ceppi dissolved into tears as Katherine slammed the door behind her and almost collided with Mrs Taylor, her arms full of clean towels, who had obviously heard every word.

'Trouble, is it, Miss Donovan?'

'Not at all, Mrs Taylor! Nothing that I can't sort out or for you to worry your head about!' Katherine answered acidly. Oh, she could kill Ceppi, Mrs Taylor was bound to hear of it somehow.

Katherine's interview with Mother Superior was not an easy one, but at least she wasn't alone in her predicament. Mary Boland's mother was there, as was Mrs Coyne, and both of them were as angry as Katherine.

'I'll swing for our Maddy yet! I've belted her, her da's belted her for picking fights. Well, it's the buckle end of his belt she'll be getting if they throw her out!'

'God knows why our Mary got involved. She can't mind her own flaming business!'

'I'm sorry Ceppi involved you in all this, Mrs Boland. I know she was provoked' – she glanced with some hostility towards Mrs Coyne – 'but to go fighting "like dogs in the gutter"' – she quoted from the note – 'after all the trouble I've gone to . . .!'

'Well, girl, let's hope this will teach the flaming little

hooligans. I swear to God I never had this trouble with our Alfie.'

'I never had any trouble with my lads either, but the girls . . .' Mrs Coyne shook her head.

'All we can do is apologise and swear it will never happen again,' Katherine said through gritted teeth.

Chapter Eight

CEPPI AND MARY Boland became firm friends, which on occasion brought them into contact with Sister Imelda's stinging little cane. They had to go to school on Saturday mornings but in the afternoons they played together, either with the other kids in the street or in Mary's house if it was too wet or cold. Ceppi was only allowed to play quietly on Sunday afternoons as Katherine said it was 'God's day' and they should show some respect.

After some persuasion on Katherine's part Mrs Taylor allowed Mary to come and help Ceppi with her homework, provided they were supervised by Katherine herself. The arrangement worked well for both girls, for as Mary said she didn't get much peace and quiet in her house with Eddie crying and Alfie and her da always arguing.

Sometimes she couldn't come, when her mam went on a night out with her friends and she had to mind Eddie.

'You should see all the performance and palaver out of her!

You'd think they were all dead young an' good-looking, instead of being old and wrinkled. They only go and sit in the snug at the Red House. Our Alfie said once that she was "mutton dressed as lamb" and she gave him such a clout across his ears that he said he saw stars. Mam said if he ever said it again it would be more than just stars he'd be seeing. It would be the sun and moon and all those other things up there in the sky.'

Ceppi laughed with her new friend, but shuddered inside as she remembered the 'clouts' her mammy used to deal out to her brothers and sisters. But that was behind her now. She wouldn't think about it again.

As Katherine walked home from the tram stop she smiled to herself. She almost had enough money. In another couple of weeks she could realise her dream, a dream that had started very simply. After Mr Fortesque had left, two other commercial travellers, very similar to Mr Fortesque, had arrived. It hadn't been a very pleasant atmosphere in Mrs Taylor's dining room or parlour where the gentlemen were allowed to sit – without a fire – and write up their order books. The poor men were always tired after their day's work of talking to the buyers of their respective trades, trying to persuade them to purchase more and more items. Consequently there was little conversation in the evenings. No wonder they looked so miserable, she'd thought, far away from their homes and family and friends, travelling all the time and probably getting no sense of 'home' or comfort in the places they stayed. They certainly got none here. So she'd thought, why couldn't she rent a house and make it welcoming for people like the salesmen? Or perhaps she might take a permanent lodger or two? Make a 'home from home' for them. A cup of tea when they first came in and with a good fire to warm them and cheer them up in the winter, and maybe a bottle of beer instead of the tea in summer. She would even wash and iron their shirts if they wished so. She'd have a room specially set up for them to write up orders, a card table each, a comfortable chair, pictures on the walls and a couple of big ashtrays. She'd do evening meals too so they wouldn't have to go out again, and the parlour would be as homely as she could make it.

With what she had earned, less all the expenses, she had nearly fifty pounds which she kept in an old brown wallet under the mattress. A small fortune, though most of it was her father's money. Things would be tight at first, especially if she was to furnish it the way she wanted. Maybe she would have to work for a bit longer, but how could she do that *and* look after her 'guests' as Mrs Taylor called them? Still, she was determined to find a way – somehow she'd make her plan work.

She turned the corner, and smiled to herself. After a shaky start, thanks to the encouragement of Dotty and Mavis she'd become one of the fastest workers. The other two made jokes about it but they didn't mind because it increased their wages as well. They worked as a team and were the envy of other teams, which often led to some back-biting. For Katherine it was much easier than housework and she enjoyed the company of the girls she worked with. She'd even been out with a few of them for a drink in one of the fairly decent pubs in the area. Once they all went to a dance hall called the Rialto which she hadn't liked much, but when they went to the cinemagraph, she'd really enjoyed it.

Mrs Taylor had nothing to complain about at all. She paid their bed and board regularly, she didn't bring friends home and she made sure Ceppi and quite often Mary did their homework quietly at the big table, while she herself read. She had joined the public library and discovered a wealth of knowledge. In the evenings, when she would sit reading, she was oblivious to almost everything, except for Ceppi's interruptions. She'd even registered Ceppi at the library, something Mary had refused to do with stubborn horror.

'Don't we have enough reading at school? Don't we even do our homework? We need a rest,' she'd complained.

'You might find you like it. There's lots of books to choose from and they are very different from those you have at school,' Katherine had urged, to no avail. Mary wouldn't budge.

Children had to be able to prove they could actually read before they were allowed anywhere near a book, and they were only allowed to take out one book a week. It was enough for Ceppi, who held similar views to Mary, but her reading was slowly improving.

Tonight, as Katherine walked into the house, she could sense there was something wrong. Mrs Taylor was standing in the doorway of the dining room with a face like thunder. Of Ceppi there was no sign.

'Where's Ceppi?'

'In the bedroom and in disgrace!'

'In disgrace? What is it she's done?'

'This is what she's done.' The woman held up a small

tablecloth which was a patchy pale blue in colour.

'It's ruined! Completely ruined. She knocked a whole pot of ink over it. That stuff is almost impossible to get out.'

Katherine sighed. 'I'll speak to her.'

'It's more than "speaking" to she needs!'

Katherine walked up the stairs to their room to find Ceppi lying on the bed in the dark. Katherine quickly lit the gas.

'Oh, Ceppi, you've been crying. She told me about knocking over the inkpot. She's annoyed but I'll pay for the damned thing and you'll have to be more careful in future.'

'Oh, Katherine, it was an accident! I wanted to get my story finished for tomorrow and the pot sort of wobbled and spilt. She came in and she said . . . I was a nasty little pest and then she slapped me!' The child dissolved in tears.

'She did WHAT!'

'She slapped me across the face and sent me up here. I don't want to live here any more, Katherine.'

Katherine was furious. 'Hush now, acushla, we won't be staying here after the weekend. Leave *her* to me!' She cradled Ceppi in her arms until at last the sobs diminished. 'Go and wash your face – there's water in the jug – then wait for me here. We'll go to Joan for our tea after I've sorted this out.'

Katherine's tone of voice when she'd spoken to Ceppi had been soft and reassuring but inside her the anger was growing. She ran lightly down the stairs and to the kitchen door. This was no time for niceties like knocking and opening the kitchen door quietly, as she usually did when she needed to speak to the landlady. She almost took it off its hinges and Mrs Taylor looked up in alarm from the range.

'How dare you! How dare you slap her!'

Caught off her guard, the woman began to stutter. 'She . . . she deserved it. She's an insolent little vandal! Everything . . . everything she touches she breaks or ruins!'

Katherine's face was white with suppressed fury. 'She does not! She's quiet and polite all the time she's here, which is practically never. She doesn't finish school until four o'clock and by the time she gets back it's nearly half past. She usually reads or if Mary is with her they work quietly until I come in. Spilling that ink was an accident, pure and simple, and you have no right at all to smack her. A few stern words about carelessness, fine, but I'll not have anyone raise a hand to her. She's been through enough in her short life. I'll pay for the cloth, and you won't have to trouble yourself about either of us for much longer. We'll be leaving at the end of the week.'

The cups and saucers rattled as she slammed the door behind her, but as she stormed upstairs some of her anger died. She'd acted too quickly. They had nowhere else to go to and she was sure that the old hag would tell everyone in the houses on the hill that Ceppi Healy was not a child to entertain under their roofs. She had three days to find somewhere else to live.

'Katherine, you won't let her hit me again, will you?' Ceppi asked as they walked up Berry Street.

'Of course not. Now turn the collar of your coat up. It's so cold here it'd perish the crows.'

Joan was highly indignant after Katherine had told her what had happened.

'The 'atchet-faced old cow! Yer know, a lot of these jumped-up snobby old bitches won't even 'ave kids over the door step. Yer should 'ear what me mam calls them. It's not fit for 'er ears!'

'I can imagine and she's heard worse, believe me.'

'Well, I'll give yer two 'elpings of puddin', it's yer favourite – baked apples an' custard.'

Ceppi cheered up a little. Joan left and then reappeared with their meals.

'What will yer do, like? Where will yer go? I know me mam would take yer in in a flash, but 'onest to God, Katherine, our 'ouse is like a lunatic asylum! Two up, two down and there's ten of us. Like bloody sardines we are and there's always a row goin' on between one or other of me sisters and brothers.'

'Thanks, Joan, it's really kind of you, but that was the sort of house she lived in before and I want better for her now. I don't want to sound ungrateful.'

'Ye're not. I understand. God, iffen it was one of our lot she belted, they'd belt 'er back!'

Ceppi had finished her meal and looked up. 'Will we go and live in another house like that one or with a proper family?'

'It won't be somewhere like that, but I don't know just where we'll go yet.'

'Mary says she's fed up listening to her mam moaning about not enough money and no one to help with the housework.'

'And 'ow many of them are there in that house?' Joan asked.

'Mary, her mam and dad, Alfie and Eddie, he's the baby.' Sensing she had caught Katherine's attention she carried on,

'Will I be asking Mary can we stay in their house? I'm sure her mam would be grateful for the money and it'd be cheaper than back there.'

'What are yer sayin', Ceppi?'

'I can ask Mary Boland's mam if we can live with them.'

'Well, it's an idea. I don't really know 'er, like, but me mam does. Isn't she the one with the "birrof an accident"?'

Katherine smiled. 'Yes. Mary always complains about the little one. Does the whole parish call him "an accident"?'

'Oh, yeah. Maggie Boland 'as a mouth like a parish oven! If yer want everyone ter know yer business, tell 'er. She's good-hearted though, I'll give you that.'

Katherine made up her mind. 'Ask Mary to ask her mam if I can go and see her. She might not be serious about not having enough money or anyone to help, just moaning and hoping for some sympathy. A lot of women do that, but they don't necessarily mean it.'

'Will I still ask though?' Ceppi was eager, the prospect of living with her friend had banished all the miseries from her mind.

'Yes.'

'It's not all overcrowded, like ours was, always a mess. Everything is tidy and clean; Mary says she never stops scrubbing and polishing. Monday is wash day, Tuesday is ironing day, Wednesday shopping and baking and the rest of the time she cleans. Bedrooms one day, downstairs another, the stairs a third.'

'Good God, the woman must be in a desperate state of tiredness,' Katherine remarked. Joan cast her eyes to the ceiling.

'Well, she is always sayin' things like "the Devil finds work for idle hands" and "there's no excuse for dirt, soap and water don't cost much".'

'I'm beginning to like her more and more,' Katherine said.

Mrs Boland might be a bit of a fusspot, Ceppi thought, but surely it would be better than having to live in another house like Mrs Taylor's? And a hundred times better than living with the family in Ireland?

'I'll ask Mary tomorrow,' Ceppi said.

The next day Ceppi explained everything to Mary.

'I'm sure Mam will say yes. I mean she *knows* you and she's seen Katherine lots of times.'

'I do hope we can come and live with you. I won't even mind Eddie.'

'No one could get to like *him*!' Mary said darkly.

'Oh, Mary, sure he's not *that* desperate, he's only a baby.'

'He's two and he *is* that desperate, as you say. Wait until you have to listen to him day and night and have him putting his sticky, dirty fingers on everything.'

'Your mam doesn't let him.'

'Well, he would if she did.'

'I wouldn't mind, honestly. Oh, I hope she says yes!'

After school they ran all the way to Mary's house.

'Mam, Ceppi's got something to ask you.'

'If it involves money you're out of luck. The rent feller's been today and I won't get your da and our Alfie's wages until tomorrow.'

'It's sort of . . . can be . . . might be about money,' Ceppi blurted out. 'Katherine wants to come and see you.'

103

Maggie Boland carried on wiping the patterned oilcloth on the table, prior to setting it. 'Katherine? What for?'

'She'd rather let Katherine say what for,' Mary interrupted hastily.

'We don't like it at Mrs Taylor's. She belted me last night.'

'What in God's name for?'

'I spilled the inkpot on the tablecloth. It was an accident, really it was. I didn't do it on purpose but you'd think I had. So she belted me across the face, called me names and told me to get out of her sight.'

Maggie Boland's expression became grim. The coldness in her dark eyes added to the air of outrage. 'She's no right to go belting you over something like that. She could have soaked the cloth in bleach. It'd come out.'

'So when Katherine got home she said we were going to leave.'

Understanding was beginning to dawn on Mary's mam. 'Have you got somewhere else to go, like?'

Ceppi shook her head.

'Well then, tell Katherine to come down tonight after she gets in from work.'

'Thanks, Mrs Boland.'

'Oh, *thanks*, Mam,' Mary added with feeling.

Chapter Nine

———❦———

IN THE END it wasn't until the following day that Katherine went to see Maggie Boland.

'Oh, please, please can we live there?' Ceppi begged as she danced along beside Katherine.

'Will you walk properly or it's after falling over you'll be doing. I told you that we'd have to wait and see,' she answered as they walked towards St Andrew's Street where the Bolands lived.

It was Mary herself who answered the door, her eyes shining, her cheeks pink with excited anticipation. 'Mam's in the kitchen, come in.'

As Katherine walked down the lobby she looked around. She'd been here before a couple of times, but hadn't really given more than a passing thought to the state of the place except that it was clean and smelled of carbolic soap. Now she noted the polished lino, the tough, hard-wearing, but far from elegant jute matting on the stairs, held in place on each stair with metal rods to keep it from slipping. There was a small table covered with a clean white cloth on which stood a statue with a nightlight in a small bowl set before it. The paintwork was the uniform dark bottle green, widely believed to keep the bugs at bay.

Maggie Boland was a big woman with dark brown hair arranged in the 'cottage loaf' style. Katherine noticed that there was not a strand of grey in it. She wore a paisley-patterned blouse tucked into a grey skirt with a calico apron tied over it. She was engaged in tidying away the dirty dishes but she stopped and smiled at Katherine.

'I'll just put this lot in the sink in the scullery, they can soak. Sit down and take the weight off your legs, Katherine.'

Katherine sat down in a rocking chair, much used but well polished and with a clean, if faded cushion on the seat. On the opposite side of the obviously well-black-leaded range was a small chair covered with faded blue-and-yellow tapestry-type material. The furniture wasn't good, by any means, but it wasn't falling apart. The dishes on the dresser were cheap imitations of blue delftware but the flagstoned floor was clean and before the range was a green-and-yellow rug, a bit thread-bare and with the occasional small hole where hot coal or ash had fallen on it, but not in need of half an hour's beating over the line in the yard. The other furniture in the room was polished, but it too had the look of being well used. Two brass candlesticks, two black-and-white spotted pot dogs and a small clock held pride of place on the overmantel which was covered with a runner of green baize. Of Alfie there was no sign but Eddie was sitting on a small stool with his thumb in his mouth.

'At least he's not kicking up a row,' Mary whispered to Ceppi.

Maggie returned and took off her pinafore and sat opposite Katherine.

'Our Mary tells me you had a row with that one up there and now you've nowhere to go?'

'No, we haven't. I told her we'd be gone by the weekend and it's Friday tomorrow.'

'Well, if you don't mind sharing with our Mary we can manage. Myself and Frank and Eddie have the downstairs front room, and our Alfie has the other bedroom, but that's no bigger than a cupboard anyway. You can't swing a cat in it and it's got no window.'

'But there's only a single bed in my room,' Mary protested.

'Don't worry, I'll buy a double bed,' her mother reassured her.

'I can't be letting you do that,' Katherine objected.

'Won't I get one for half of nothing in a second-hand shop?'

'Thank you! We won't mind sharing. So how much rent will you need?'

'Oh, let's not bring money into it now. We'll have a cup of tea first. Mary, fill that kettle and put it on to boil.'

Katherine knew this was part of the ritual before any major decisions or changes were made.

It was Ceppi who went to fill the kettle while Mary set out clean cups from the dresser and brought the tea caddy to the table.

'Make sure that teapot is empty, Mary.'

'I don't want you to be after thinking I'd not pull my weight as well. I'll help out with the cleaning and the ironing, I know with little ones all you seem to do is wash and iron. In Dublin, in the houses around where I lived, that's all the women seemed to do.'

'Don't I know it and there's that much soot in the air that when the wind is in a certain direction you'd think the clothes had been dragged in the gutter and you have to do them all again. Then there's times when I have to dry them in here. It drives Frank mad, he says it looks like a second-hand clothes shop. But what else can I do with them, for God's sake?' Maggie sniffed. 'I'm not one to be going to the public wash-house and having everyone gawping at what you've got and what sort of state it's in.'

'I could do some shopping on my way home too,' Katherine volunteered.

'Thanks, luv, but I like to choose my own stuff. No offence.'

'Oh, no. I just thought it might be a help. I'll see that Ceppi keeps her things tidily.'

'Well, that will be a help. I have to nag at Alfie and Mary to be a bit more tidy. In these small houses the place looks like a midden after a few days. But you work hard enough all day.'

'Yes, but it's not bad, it's sitting down at least.'

'I heard from Mavis Holland's mam that your little group gets paid almost double what the others do because you're all so fast.'

'We do. It's a bit fiddly but not hard. That's why I want to help in the house. You're on your feet all day.'

Ceppi carefully handed a cup of tea to Maggie and then Katherine.

'Why don't you two put on your coats and go to Sullivan's? I'll give you a threepenny bit to buy some sweets.' Katherine opened her purse and handed Ceppi a silver coin.

'That was good of you.'

'Well, I thought it would be better to have them out of the way while we talk about the rent.'

Maggie thought for a few seconds. 'Well, let's say five and sixpence and that's to include everything.'

'Ah, sure that's not nearly enough.'

'I don't want any more, not if you're going to do other things.'

'Make it seven and I'll do my fair share. From what Ceppi and Mary have told me you seem to be working yourself into the ground.'

'To keep anywhere decent around here, luv, you have to. I know they all think I'm nagging them, but when I've been on my knees scrubbing the step outside or swilling down the back yard, it makes my blood boil when they come in traipsing muck on their boots.'

'That's a feeling I know only too well. Da never gave it a thought either and poor Mam worked herself to death. She really did. She was never strong and she caught the influenza. She tried to carry on but she . . . she collapsed and died.'

'Ah, God rest her, the poor soul. I've heard that the Dublin slums are as bad as ours.'

'They are, maybe a bit worse. That's why I want to give Ceppi a chance in life. She didn't have much of a start. That's why I make her do her homework and get books from the library.'

'Well, our Mary's reading and writing have come on in

leaps and bounds since she started to be friends with Ceppi and that's something I never thought I'd see.'

'Life is hard enough for the likes of us, I want better for her.' Katherine smiled. 'For them both.'

Eddie had decided he wasn't getting enough attention and began to wail.

'God in heaven, that child will be the death of me! I thought I'd got it all over and done with and then he comes along.'

Katherine picked him up. 'He's a grand boy, aren't you, Eddie? Maybe we can find something for you to do, so you won't be after driving your mammy up the wall.'

He'd stopped crying and was regarding Katherine with large solemn blue eyes.

'Well, if you've any ideas, tell me them. I'd pay you just to amuse him and give me a bit of peace and quiet.'

'We'll have him sorted out, won't we, my bonny boy?'

The two girls arrived back, flushed and each clutching a paper cone full of a variety of sweets.

'Wipe your feet, Mary Boland,' Maggie instructed. 'God, I feel just like a flaming parrot sometimes.'

Mary dutifully took off her boots and Ceppi, taking her lead from her friend, did the same.

'God, you've managed to shut him up!' Mary said with satisfaction that the bane of her life had obviously taken to Katherine. Eddie was fascinated by the small gold hooped earings Katherine always wore, patting them in wonder.

'Don't you go taking the Lord's name in vain in this house, Mary Boland! You'll tell that to Father Scanlan in Confession tomorrow.'

Mary looked suitably chastened.

'When will you want to move all your stuff in, then?' Maggie asked of Katherine who had sat down and was bouncing Eddie up and down on her lap.

'On Sunday, if that's all right. We haven't really got much to bring.'

'I'll send our Alfie around to help just the same. It'll keep him out of mischief. That lad will be the death of me! I'll tell you all about *him* when we've got you settled. I'll go and see about a bed and bedding and get them to deliver it all here tomorrow night. Frank and Alfie will get it upstairs and I'll have it made up and aired for you.'

Katherine thanked her again, wondering what Alfie did that was so bad that his mother thought she'd be dead with the worry of him. He was only fifteen after all, and surely his da would keep him on the straight and narrow?

She passed Eddie back to his mother and rose. 'Come on then, Ceppi, let's go and see Joan for tea, then we can go back and start to pack up.'

'Haven't either of you had anything to eat yet?'

'No. As soon as I set foot over the door she almost dragged me around here!'

'You should have said, luv. You could have had something with us. Will I make you something now? I can do a bit of a fry-up?'

'That's very kind, Mrs Boland, but Joan will be expecting us.'

'If you're sure then, and will you stop calling me Mrs Boland? It's Maggie from now on.'

Katherine smiled back. It would be nice to live with a

family. Even when her mam was alive she'd never felt they were a *real* family. There was seldom any laughter or noise, only muttered complaints and questions from her da. In so many ways her life had got better.

Between them Maggie and Mary had everyone in a state of high excitement. Neither could wait to have Katherine living with them. Alfie Boland was the exception. He was not pleased at all about the arrangements. As if he didn't have enough to put up with already. His da was always on and on at him, telling him he had to work hard and make himself useful to the right people – whoever they were – to get on. His mam only left him five shillings out of his weekly wage and out of that he had to take his expenses. He usually walked to work to save money but got the tram home as he was tired and hungry at the end of the day. When he mentioned having a bit of fun, a night out, that usually started the arguments off. He was too young to go out to pubs or dance halls, too old to be hanging around street corners. All there was left were the moving pictures or the music halls and you really needed a partner for the music hall. He was trying to save up for a new suit, one like the one he'd seen in the window of Hepworth's. Like everyone else in the neighbourhood, he had navy serge for Sundays, but it wasn't what he wanted and he seemed to have had it for years and years too. What he wanted was something better, something a bit more 'classy'.

With a sullen look on his face he knocked on the door of the bed and breakfast in Mount Pleasant while his sister jumped up and down beside him.

Ceppi opened it. She had on her coat and hat and was

clutching a canvas bag in which she kept her clothes and things she needed for school.

'We're ready. I've had my bag packed since last night, and Katherine is just finishing!'

'We'll none of us get any peace if she doesn't come soon. Is that all you've got?'

'Yes,' Ceppi replied, stung. 'Sure, what did you expect, great big suitcases?'

'It wasn't worth me flaming well coming,' Alfie complained.

'Katherine's got more stuff, she's coming down now.'

Alfie peered down the lobby but there was no sign of Mrs Taylor or Katherine. He shoved his hands into his trouser pockets and looked pained. After a few minutes he heard footsteps on the stairs and peeped inside again. He'd seen Katherine Donovan before, but only fleetingly when she'd come round to collect Ceppi; now as he saw her come down the stairs he was struck by just how beautiful she looked with that black hair, pale skin and blue eyes. She wasn't that much older than he was, he thought, at least she didn't look to be.

'Here, I'll carry that,' he said gruffly, holding out his hand for one of the bags.

'Thank you, Alfie. It was good of you to come and help. I know you don't have much spare time.'

'That's all right. I . . . I don't mind.'

'Alfie Boland, you liar! You've done nothing but moan about helping since Mam told you Katherine and Ceppi were coming to live with us!' Mary cried.

Alfie glared at her. 'You can never keep your bloody mouth shut, can you?'

'I'll tell me da you swore and then you'll be in for it.'

113

'Oh, for heaven's sake you two, is this what it's going to be like? The pair of you fighting and your mam giving out to you all the time?' Katherine's words and frown were tempered by the sparkle in her eyes. 'Come on, let's shake the dust of this place off our feet and go . . . home.'

It sounded strange to say the word, but she had the feeling that life with the Bolands was going to be her first experience of a real home.

Chapter Ten

———◆———

LIFE HAD CERTAINLY changed and for the good, Katherine thought as she gazed out of the tram window at the decorated shops on Church Street. Christmas Day was only two days away. The weather was cold but there was no wind. Liverpool – like Dublin – was often windy. It seemed to drive in from the estuary. But unlike Dublin where it hurtled down the Quays and under the bridges of the Liffey, here it swirled and twisted its way across the whole city. By day the skies seemed immense and were a shade of cornflower blue. The weak sunlight made the frost that covered everything sparkle and glisten. By night the sky was filled with stars and the light of a silver-coloured moon tried to add its feeble rays to that of the streetlamps.

Henderson's, Marks and Spencer, Bon Marché and George Henry Lee all had their windows decorated with festive colours and scenes. Outside the butchers' shops geese, capons, turkey and legs of pork were hung in rows, with the prices marked on pieces of cardboard, which often displayed sales captions too, such as 'Fresh From the Farm' or 'Best Price in Town'. At the junction of Church Street and Ranelagh Street there was a huge Christmas tree and the band of the Salvation Army played Christmas carols. Oh, of course she'd seen the decorations in Grafton Street and Sackville Street in Dublin, but this year it was so very very different. For one thing she'd promised to take both Ceppi and Mary to Lewis's grotto, which by all accounts was the best in the city. Tableaux of fairy grottos, caves with elves, a living fairy story and a chance to sit on Santi's knee and get a small present were what had been described to her by Dotty and Mavis.

Most of the workers found it was too cold now to sit outside on the factory wall to eat their butties, but Katherine and her friends wrapped up well and took advantage of the crisp dry weather, seeing as it had rained for most of November.

'Thank God the bloody rain 'as stopped. I used ter be wet when I got ter work and bloody soaked to the skin by the time I got 'ome an' then me mam 'ad the cheek ter tell me not ter go trailin' water everywhere! God, there's times when I could cheerfully strangle 'er!'

'What are yer goin' ter do, Dotty? Anythin' special for Christmas, like?' Mavis asked as she brushed the crumbs from her sandwiches off her coat.

'Special! In our 'ouse? All me mam's sisters an' their families come round an' yer can't move. All the fellers go ter the pub and most years the bloody dinner's stuck ter the roof of the oven by the time they get back and then there's always the mother an' father of a row. Me Aunty Vera's got the right idea. If yer can't beat them, join them. She always brings a

116

bottle of dead cheap sherry an' usually drinks the lot. What with all that, an' the kids all moanin' about being hungry an' then startin' to fight! Is that what yer'd call "special"?'

'I know 'ow yer mam feels, it's pretty much the same in our 'ouse,' Mavis said, shaking her head.

Katherine thought of last Christmas and the ones before that. She and Da had gone to Mass but afterwards only Father Flynn wished them 'Christmas greetings'. Sullen looks were all they got from the rest of the congregation. Nearly all of them were Da's customers. Then it was home to a miserable, undecorated house. Da had said there was no need to dress the place up after Mam had died. They ate the meal in silence and then exchanged the customary but begrudged presents. Da usually had a couple of glasses of Powers and then dozed off, leaving her to wash the dishes.

This Christmas would be so different. She was part of a family – almost – and she could afford little treats.

She'd bought small gifts for everyone, and Ceppi and Mary were going to hang out their stockings, Ceppi for the first time in her life.

'Are you sure Santi will come?' the child had asked, doubt struggling with eagerness in her grey-green eyes.

'I'm absolutely certain he will this year.'

'Sure, he never came to our house. Me sisters and the lads bought themselves stuff but I didn't have the money for that. Then Con was after telling me there's no such a person as Santi.'

Katherine's heart went out to the child. 'Wasn't he the eejit then. If you don't believe there is a Santi then he won't come, will he?'

117

Ceppi considered this and it seemed to make sense. After that there had been no holding either girl. Katherine and Maggie had decided what they would buy to put in the stockings that were to be hung up on the overmantel.

'But it's not fair for you to buy for our Mary,' Maggie had said.

'It's not fair for you to buy for Ceppi,' Katherine'd answered so they had agreed to split the cost. Eddie was still little more than a baby and couldn't even understand what all the fuss was about, but they'd got him a rattle and a small fluffy ball with a bell inside anyway.

'I know we can't leave him out, but I've the feeling that with bells and rattles he'll drive us all to drink,' Maggie said.

'Ah, but they won't last for ever.'

'They won't if I've anything to do with it. They'll be taken away and hidden and only brought out to shut him up when the yelling gets too much,' Maggie had answered.

Katherine tucked her knitted scarf more closely around her neck as she got off the tram and began to walk home. It was freezing hard already. There was a thin coating of frost on the pavement and she walked slowly, afraid of slipping.

The level of noise coming from the Bolands' kitchen surprised her. There was always some but now there appeared to be a very loud fight going on.

'You wait until your da gets in, Alfie Boland! By God, he'll take his belt to you!' Maggie yelled at her eldest son as Katherine walked in.

'What's going on? Sure you can hear the row from the street!'

Alfie was looking very pale and downcast.

'Would you look at the state of him?' Maggie asked, still on top note.

'Why so? He looks great to me, if a bit pale.'

'Pale! Pale, is it? Drunk more likely! Can hardly stand up, and at his age!'

Both Mary and Ceppi were watching, Mary with concern and Ceppi with only mild interest; she'd seen too many drunken men and women in her life to worry about Alfie. Eddie was howling with fright so Katherine went and picked him up.

'How did he get like this?' she asked Maggie. She could see now that the lad was indeed drunk.

'Them other lads at the parcel depot thought it a huge joke to go pouring bottles of ale down him and he let them. And most of them should know better, they're all older than him. And him letting us all down. What will Mr Lawson and the other foreman think of us?'

'I'm sure they'll understand, especially when Alfie explains. I bet Mr Lawson has been in this state too at some time in his life.'

'Well, I'll be having a few words with Mr Lawson and I don't care how bad meladdo feels in the morning, he's going to work!'

Alfie's knees began to buckle and his eyes were closing.

Katherine thrust a still crying Eddie into Mary's arms. 'Quick! Catch him, Maggie! Won't he hurt himself if he falls awkward?'

They both supported Alfie's dead weight.

'What's the matter with him now, Mam?' Mary asked, trying to quieten her little brother.

'Ah, 'tis nothing. I've seen men like that before. And haven't I seen many fall down and lie on the ground! He's as drunk as a tinker at a horse fair. He'll just sleep but he'll have a desperate headache in the morning,' Ceppi answered off-handedly and turned back to the making of a chain of red and green paper to decorate the kitchen.

'Katherine, we'll never get him upstairs, he's too bloody heavy.'

Katherine was struggling. 'I know. Ceppi, go and fill up that big enamel jug with water and bring it into the lobby.'

Ceppi pulled a face but did as she was told.

'What are you going to do with it?' Maggie demanded.

'Tip it all over his head – that should bring him round enough for us to get him upstairs. Drag him into the lobby first. We can mop up later.'

With some difficulty they heaved Alfie into the lobby and Ceppi handed Katherine the heavy jug. She'd spilt some of the water in the kitchen and told Mary to mop it up 'before your mam sees it'. Eddie was abandoned on the rocking chair.

Katherine was just in the act of pouring the icy cold water on the lad's head when Mary yelled from the kitchen that her da was home.

Frank strode into the lobby.

'Oh, thank God you've arrived! We can't manage him! Would you look at the state those lads have got him in?'

'Right,' Frank Boland said grimly. 'Get out of the way Katherine, we won't be needing the water.'

They both loosened their grip on Alfie and his father picked him up, slung him over his shoulder and went upstairs.

120

The two women looked at each other as they heard the bedroom door slam.

'I'll get your tea, luv,' Maggie said as her husband reappeared. 'You must all be starving. Mary, Ceppi, get those things off the table and then set it. You can finish them off after we've eaten. We're all behind with ourselves, thanks to *him*.'

'Ah, Mam, it's Christmas Eve tomorrow, we'll never finish them. We're going to the grotto with Katherine, don't forget,' Mary complained.

'Don't you start, milady! I've enough to put up with. I said move those things and I meant it. *Now!*'

The meal was eaten almost in silence. Maggie and Frank sat with faces like thunder. Mary, taking her cue from Ceppi, concentrated on her food and Katherine looked around with trepidation tinged with concern. The poor lad would feel like death in the morning when, no doubt, there would be another row.

Maggie washed the dishes and Katherine dried and put them away. Frank settled down to read the *Echo* and the two girls resumed making their paper chains.

'I'll just go and check on him, Maggie, to see if he's all right. He might be sick and—'

'If he's sick he can bloody well clean it up himself in the morning!' Maggie interrupted. 'We'll be the talk of the neighbourhood.'

Katherine took the big old-fashioned oil lamp which was used instead of the gas jet in the hall and went up the stairs. She opened the door to the tiny bedroom quietly and placed the lamp on the small chest of drawers beside the bed. Alfie looked ridiculously childish, she thought. His father had just flung him on top of the bed, so she took off his boots, then his jacket. He'd have to sleep in his trousers, she wasn't going to take *them* off. Maggie would be scandalised. It was with some difficulty that she managed to drag the bedclothes from under him and replace them on top of him. It was so cold in the room that up here he'd be frozen to death if left uncovered like that. She went and removed the quilt from her and the girls' own bed; they could wear old cardigans or jumpers over their nightdresses and keep their stockings on to stay warm.

He was still sound asleep, or so she thought as she tucked the quilt around him. He reeked of beer and she turned her head away.

'I love you, Katherine. I . . . I'm drunk but I know I love you.'

She looked down at him with amazement and then collected her wits. 'Yes, you are drunk, Alfie, and you'll suffer for it, so you will, but I'll pretend I never heard that or you'll be having embarrassment to add to everything else. I'll shut the door and go down.'

He was asleep again and she sighed deeply. He didn't mean it. It was the drink talking. She knew of men who became pathetically romantic towards their wives, in fact to any woman, when they'd drink taken. He'd have forgotten he'd ever said it in the morning. But would he after he'd got over his hangover? She stopped herself. You eejit, Katherine Donovan! He's fifteen. You're filling yourself with vanity.

'Well?' Maggie asked as she came back into the kitchen.

'He's fine. I took his boots and jacket off and I've wrapped him in the quilt from our bed. It's so cold up there it would perish the crows.'

'Won't we be frozen too?' Ceppi interrupted.

'Just for once we can sleep in old jumpers and our stockings. We can put our coats over the bed. We'll be grand, it's only for one night.'

'We'll be frozen stiff, so we will,' Ceppi murmured to Mary.

'If I hear another word out of you, Concepta Healy, there'll be no outing to the grotto.'

'Ah, Katherine, you're too good to them, all of them.'

'Sure, it wasn't all his fault, Maggie. You know what young lads are like, all boasting and bragging. He'll be so sorry in the morning.'

'Oh, he *will* that!'

'But don't let it spoil our Christmas, not after all the hard work we've done for the day that's in it.'

'I suppose you're right, luv, but I could murder him!'

'Will you go and see this Mr Lawson?' Katherine asked.

'No, it'll only make things look worse.' Maggie turned away. 'Come along, you two, it's time you were in bed anyway. You've a big day tomorrow,' she instructed.

'You *will* take us to the grotto and Santi *will* still come, won't he?' Ceppi asked before she left the room. There was anxiety in her eyes. That eejit Alfie might have ruined everything.

'Yes, you'll both go to the grotto and yes, Santi *will* come. Now, off to bed.'

When the girls had gone up, Katherine went on, 'I'll put the kettle on. I think we all need a bit of calming down. We've all got work of one sort or another in the morning. At least we finish at dinnertime.'

'Thanks, luv, you're a treasure. When you've got them at the grotto I can go to St John's market for the veg and the last bits of things.'

Katherine smiled. Rows notwithstanding, this was going to be the best Christmas ever.

Despite a spectacular hangover which made him look like death warmed up, Alfie was bullied into going to work.

'Oh, Mam, do I *have* to go? Every time I move my head I think it's going to burst open.'

'Well, you should have thought of that, meladdo, before you let that lot fill you with ale! Get out of my sight!'

'Try to drink lots of water, Alfie, it helps, it really does. I used to hear the women in the street back in Dublin saying that after a night on the batter, all the men drank pints and pints of water to clear the drink out of their systems,' Katherine said sympathetically.

Alfie'd nodded and then groaned at the pain of the action.

'I'll have the girls all washed and ready for when you get in, Katherine, luv.'

'The quicker we get there the better, or so Mavis says. She said you can queue for hours. I don't feel much like that, not in this weather, but I've promised, so, even if it's past teatime before we get back, I'll have to wait. Sure I'd never be forgiven if I didn't, and, to be honest, I'm looking forward to seeing it all myself!'

'I'll get the pair of them to put up the decorations and

sort out the Christmas tree, that should keep them quiet. I'm worried about those little candles though.'

'Tell them that on no account are they to be playing about with candles and matches or Santi will see them.'

'That should do the trick. Now off you go while I clean up and write down what I still need.'

Everyone seemed to be in high spirits. Even the tram driver had been cracking jokes about holly and mistletoe and 'if yer can't be good, be careful'. Katherine arrived at work feeling very cheerful.

'What's the matter with you, Dotty?' she asked of her workmate, who was looking pale.

'God, I feel awful. Me mam and da were rowin' so much that I took me Aunty Vera's advice.'

'Sure to God, you didn't drink a whole bottle of sherry?'

'Not quite a whole bottle, but I've spent 'alf the night in the freezing privy down the yard bein' sick!'

'Oh, Jesus, Mary and Joseph, not another one.' Katherine told them all about Alfie.

'It's a good job we're only 'ere fer a few 'ours or we'd be down in our wages. At least we've all bought our Christmas pressies. Let it be a lesson to yer,' Mavis said with some annoyance.

'I'll never touch another flamin' drop again.'

'Oh, yer will. Yer'll forget, either that or yer'll learn how ter 'old yer drink. Go and see old Perkins – he might 'ave a few aspirins.'

The morning passed quickly and after wishing her workmates a 'Happy Christmas' Katherine caught the tram home. Ceppi was standing on the step looking neat, tidy and cold.

'What are you doing out here?'

'I was waiting for you.'

'Ceppi, didn't I promise last night that we *will* go?'

'I know, but . . . well, the mammy was always promising things and then . . . forgot.'

'Oh, aren't you the little eejit! Come inside while I get washed and changed.'

The child's eyes lit up and Katherine wondered how many times in the past she'd been cruelly disappointed.

'Sure, someone's been busy this morning,' Katherine commented as she entered the room. The paper chains looked well and the small tree stood in a corner of the room and was decorated with home-made bits and pieces and tiny red candles, which were not lit. Maggie had promised they could light them after tea.

'I'll have to put a chair in front of it or meladdo here will have it ruined,' Maggie said, scooping Eddie up and away from the tree for the umpteenth time. 'As soon as Frank comes in I'll go into town. I can't take Eddie with me, he'd have me demented and get knocked and pushed. Frank's going for a quick drink with his mates but he's promised to be in for half past two and I've never known him to break a promise yet, especially this time of year and after the performance out of our Alfie. Go on, hurry up, I've made you a couple of butties to eat while you wait and make sure you wrap up well!'

At first Katherine's heart sank as she saw the line of people waiting. It stretched halfway up Ranelagh Street.

'How long do you think we'll be?' she asked the woman in

front of her who was trying to placate two little girls with a bag of sweeties.

'God knows, it depends on how quickly the people in charge can get everyone through. It's the best, you see, that's why it's one and sixpence each. Blacklers is cheaper but not as good. Here.' She offered the paper bag to Katherine.

'No, we couldn't. I didn't think to bring sweets. I've got a few sandwiches as I came almost straight from work.'

'Oh, give the kids a sweet or two. Mine have eaten so many I'll not be surprised if they're sick on the tram going home – whatever time that will be and if we can even *get* on a tram. They'll be packed later on.'

Katherine sighed deeply. She hoped it would be worth it. The wait seemed interminable and they were all getting colder by the minute. Both girls complained they couldn't feel their feet. But gradually the queue moved forward until at last they were in the shop and it was warm. Only two flights of stairs to go, the information was passed down the line and the children became excited again.

Katherine could hardly believe her eyes when at long last they reached the grotto. She'd never seen anything so beautiful, not even in Grafton Street. It was magnificent, even breathtaking. It was the story of Sleeping Beauty. Each scene was in a small glass-fronted room, the walls painted in silver or gold or pink and blue. Special electric lights had been used to heighten the effect. The real people were dressed to look like the servants and courtiers, the good fairies and the wicked one who cast the spell in each scene, the king and queen and the prince. Both children were overawed, eyes wide with wonderment, and when they caught sight of the old man dressed in red with his long white beard who was sitting on a chair shaped like a sledge she had to push them both forward when it was their turn. Neither of them could answer when asked what they would like him to bring them but were sat on his knee and given a small present by a girl dressed as a fairy. The gifts were wrapped in red-and-gold paper and came from the sack at his side.

'Well now, wasn't that grand? Wasn't it worth all that time standing waiting?'

Ceppi had recovered her wits. 'Can we open these now?'

'No, you can't, Ceppi, you can give them to me and I'll leave them for Santi to put in your stockings.'

'He asked me my name and what I wanted. I sat on *his* knee!' Mary was enraptured.

Katherine smiled down at the two excited little faces. It was worth the three shillings and the wait. Yes indeed, this Christmas would be the best she and Ceppi could wish for.

Chapter Eleven

———◆———

THE WIND, THAT had come screaming down the Mersey from the estuary and had bullied its way between the buildings on the waterfront, had almost torn the hat from Katherine's head twice. With one hand she struggled along, hanging on to it while in the other she clasped the bag that contained some groceries Maggie had asked her to get.

This wind was so unseasonal for the end of April. It was a gale and a bad one too. She'd heard on the tram that it had affected the tide on the river, whipping up huge waves that crashed over both Landing Stages and surged up the floating roadway. The spray could be felt as far as Mann Island.

'God 'elp them at sea, even out in the bay the waves are twenty feet 'igh. Most of the ships are lying to in the docks or the Sloyne,' a man had informed the tram passengers.

''Ave Cunard stopped their ships?' another asked.

'No, you know them, sail in all weathers because of the mail.'

'I know they're big but God 'elp them just the same.'

All the passengers fell silent, their thoughts on the biggest shipwreck ever, the loss, earlier that month, of the *Titanic*.

The conductor broke the silence. 'Look what happened to the *Titanic*. "Unsinkable" they called her! No bloody ships are unsinkable and anyone who thinks they are is a bloody fool. You could build ships two and three times her size and they'd still not be unsinkable.'

'Well, what do you expect from them bosses down there? Probably half of them have never been to sea while most of the fellers in this city are seafarers and always will be,' another man said derisively.

The conversation ended abruptly as they all reflected on the terrible tragedy. The loss of a ship – any ship – had a profound effect on the people of Liverpool. Although *Titanic* had carried the name of Liverpool on her stern it had been simply her port of registry. She'd never been near the Mersey, but it hadn't stopped the sense of loss everyone had felt, for there had been men from Liverpool working in her stokehold.

As Katherine turned into St Andrew's Street there seemed to be some sort of commotion going on and a small crowd had gathered. Now what? she thought as she hastened her steps.

'What is it? What's wrong?' she asked.

'It's the bloody wind and these ramshackle houses,' Ida Irving informed her.

'So, what's happened?'

'Maggie Boland's chimney has come down.'

Katherine caught her breath. 'Oh, Holy Mother of God! Is anyone hurt?'

'The two kids, they were just about to go in when down it came with no warning, bringing half the tiles with it!'

'No! Ceppi! Ceppi!' she cried, pushing her way to the front of the crowd. The pavement and road were littered with the debris and Maggie and Mary Bradley were on their knees beside the two children who lay on the ground.

'Katherine! Oh, thank God you're here,' Maggie cried, catching sight of her.

'Are they badly hurt?' There was fear in Katherine's eyes.

Maggie dabbed at her eyes with the tea towel she'd had in her hand when she'd run from the house. 'I don't know, really I don't. Our Mary hasn't opened her eyes and Ceppi's head is covered with blood. Someone has gone for the ambulance, the police and the fire bobbies. I hope to God the whole flaming lot doesn't come down.'

Katherine knelt down amongst the slates, bricks and chunks of mortar and cradled Ceppi's head in her lap. Ceppi was at least conscious but her red curls were matted with blood.

She looked up at Katherine with tears in her eyes, her face white with shock. 'Katherine, it hurts, it hurts bad.'

'Where does it hurt most, Ceppi?'

'My head and my foot.'

Katherine looked down to see that the child's feet were trapped beneath a pile of bricks. 'For the love of God, will some of you stop just standing there gaping and start moving these bricks?' she pleaded.

'We're afraid to, Katherine, girl, there's no knowing what'll happen,' Mr Bradley said with concern.

'The fire bobbies will be here soon, they're much better

131

than the likes of us at dealing with things like this,' Mrs Irving said with a confidence she didn't feel.

Katherine was very worried about Mary. 'Maggie, is Mary still breathing?'

Maggie could only nod.

'Where's Eddie?' Katherine suddenly remembered to ask.

'I've left him with Edna. He doesn't understand what's happened, thank God, but he was screaming just the same.'

It was with great relief that they all heard the furious clanging of the bells of both ambulance and fire service vehicles.

They both came to a halt and the crowd parted to let the ambulancemen through.

'It's all right now, luv, we'll take over.'

'She's bleeding badly, it's her head. Her feet are trapped too, but Mary . . .' Katherine felt near to tears with shock and worry.

'Let's take a look at these bricks,' one of the firemen instructed while the ambulanceman gently lifted Mary in his arms. Maggie got up, still holding the child's hand.

'Can I come with you?'

'Of course, luv, get in.'

Katherine watched as the firemen carefully moved the bricks that were covering Ceppi's feet. She bit her lip and dashed away the tears with one hand. They seemed to be taking for ever.

She held on to the child tightly as, with a cry from Ceppi, her feet were freed.

'Do they hurt bad, Ceppi?' she asked.

'Only this one.' Ceppi tried to move her right foot but cried out in pain.

The ambulanceman, who had been watching, now came

forward and took Ceppi's foot gently in his hands. The movement caused Ceppi to cry out again.

'Looks like it's broken, but let's get you all to hospital.'

'Move back! Move back!' a fireman shouted as he urged the crowd backwards.

'Oh, what's going to happen to us now? We've not even a roof over our heads,' Maggie cried. She was very worried about Mary. At least you could see Ceppi's injuries and, with the help of God, they'd not be serious, but with Mary it was a different story altogether. She was pale as a ghost and apart from her shallow breathing she looked as if she were dead. 'Oh, don't let her die. O Blessed Mother, don't let her die,' she prayed as, with the bell ringing loudly in their ears, the ambulance was driven through the cobbled streets to the Royal Infirmary.

They weren't allowed in the room into which the two girls, on stretchers, had been taken, in, followed by a doctor, a sister and two nurses.

'You can see them when the doctor has found out what's wrong,' Sister told them firmly. She was a short, thin woman with iron-grey hair confined by a stiff pleated cap. Her apron crackled with starch when she moved. Her manner was very officious and authoritative.

'But Ceppi's awake,' Katherine begged. 'She's in pain and she's frightened. Please, please, just let me have a few minutes to reassure her.'

Sister was adamant in her refusal and left them to wait alone with their fears.

'Oh, Katherine, what am I going to do? She . . . she's . . .' Maggie broke down.

'Stop that now. They'll do everything they can. She'll be grand.'

'And we've nowhere to lay our heads.'

Katherine put her arms around her. 'Don't worry, we'll manage somehow.'

'But the roof's almost gone and what'll Frank and Alfie think when they come home and poor Edna will have a terrible time with our Eddie! Oh, God have pity on us!' Her shoulders shook as she gave way to the panic.

'When Frank comes home the neighbours will tell him, that is if he doesn't read about it in the late edition of the *Echo*. He'll know what to do.'

'But there's no one in the street we can live with and I don't want to live with anyone else. I want my own home and our Mary awake and out of here and . . .' She couldn't speak, her throat felt as though it had closed over and Katherine couldn't console her.

A young nurse brought them a cup of tea with plenty of sugar in it. 'You're to drink this. It's good for shock, Sister says.'

Katherine thanked her and turned to Maggie. 'See, she does think about us. Is there any more news yet?' she asked the nurse.

'No, but I'm sure there will be soon.'

They both drank their tea in silence but Maggie's hand was shaking so much that she had to clasp the mug in both hands to stop the tea from spilling over. Ten minutes later Sister appeared and beckoned them to follow her, their footsteps echoing along the white tiled corridors.

'Mrs Boland, will you come in here please? Miss . . .?'

'Donovan,' Katherine supplied.

'Will you wait here for just a minute? Doctor will see you shortly.'

The minute seemed to be endless as she fretted about Ceppi and Mary. At last Sister appeared and she was led into a small curtained cubicle where Ceppi lay on a narrow black iron-framed bed.

Ceppi tried to get up. 'Katherine! Katherine, I was frightened.'

'Lie down,' Sister ordered and Katherine pushed the bewildered child back down gently.

'Oh, Ceppi, you'll be just grand, I *know* you will. They will do everything to help make you better.'

'They were after saying my ankle is broken.'

'She's a nasty gash on her head, just above her left ear, but we've cleaned it up and Doctor will be back to put a few stitches in it. Then we'll see to her ankle. Of course she won't be allowed to leave until we're sure that there are no complications.'

Ceppi began to cry. 'I don't want to stay here, Katherine. Take me home, please? Please? I don't care how much my ankle and head hurt.'

'Hush now, Ceppi, you have to stay and I'm sure it won't be for long. I'll come and see you, I promise. I'll come as often as I can. Did I ever break a promise to you?'

Ceppi tried to shake her head but the movement hurt too much.

She stood holding the child's hand until the Sister and doctor appeared and she was asked firmly to go back to the Casualty waiting room. She found Maggie there and a grim-looking Frank who had just arrived. He had an arm around his wife's shoulder.

'I read it in the paper and came straight here. I sent our Alfie to see what state the house is in and to ask Edna if she'll keep Eddie overnight. Alfie's useless at anything like that.'

'Ceppi's got a broken ankle and a gash on her head, but she'll be all right. What about Mary?' Katherine asked.

Maggie burst into renewed tears, her shoulders shaking. Frank patted her arm. Maggie was unable to utter a word.

'They say she's in a coma, whatever that means. That doctor tried to explain it to me; she's sort of asleep but they don't know when or . . . if she'll wake up. There's hardly a mark on her, just a little cut on her forehead. I don't under-stand it at all. They say all we can do is wait and trust them,' Frank answered.

'And God,' Katherine added.

'Those bloody houses should be condemned, the state they're in, but they won't be.'

'Will . . . will we send for the . . . priest?' Maggie managed to ask.

'I don't think we should, not yet.'

'It might help,' Katherine said quietly but Frank shook his head emphatically. Mary wasn't at death's door – yet.

They were all physically and emotionally exhausted when they left the hospital. They had been told they could not possibly stay in there overnight.

'It's against all the rules. We can't have people roaming at will through the wards, there would be chaos and my staff just couldn't cope. It's not good for the patients either, they need rest and they won't get it if the place resembles Lime Street Station.'

'She's a child and we would sit with her quietly. What if something happens or if she wakes up? She'll be terrified,' Frank had asked determinedly, but Sister wouldn't budge. She told them that if anything did happen during the night, then word would be got to them and with that they had to be content.

No one spoke on the tram going home. As they walked down the street they could see that all the rubble had been cleared and a tarpaulin sheet had been fastened over the roof. It flapped in the wind which, fortunately, had died down somewhat.

At their approach Edna appeared from her doorway. 'I've been watching out for you, Maggie, luv. Come on in here, I've a fresh pot of tea just made and both Alfie and Eddie are here.'

Katherine thanked her and pushed Maggie gently up the lobby.

'Will you send our Alfie out here, Edna, please? I'm going to see just what kind of a shape the house is in.'

'Take care, Frank. If it's not fit to live in you know you can all stay here. We'll have to double up but that's no problem.'

'Thanks, Edna.'

A pale-faced Alfie was told to go out to his father. Eddie was asleep on the sofa, his thumb in his mouth.

Edna put a shawl over him. 'He's wore himself out with crying, poor little mite. Now sit down both of you and if you feel faint I've got some smelling salts here.'

'I don't think we'll be needing them, but thank you,' Katherine replied.

'Now tell me what happened to cause it and what they said at the hospital about Mary and Ceppi,' Edna asked as she handed out the tea.

'I don't think Maggie can talk about it. I saw nothing, the chimney was all over the street when I saw it first. Ceppi has a broken ankle and a cut on her head and they won't let her out.'

'Well, it's for the best, Katherine,' Edna said.

'I know. But they said that Mary is in a coma. A sort of very deep sleep.'

Edna's expression became even more concerned. She'd once heard of someone who'd been in a coma. You could be like that for ages until you died or woke up. She said nothing about what she knew, however. 'Drink that tea up now.'

'They gave us a cup in the hospital but it was so full of sugar—'

Katherine broke off as Frank, Alfie and Bernard O'Brian came into the room.

'It's not too bad. It's better than I thought it would be. I've been upstairs and had a good look. It's very cold but there don't seem to be any big cracks.'

'I looked downstairs: no real damage done there,' Bernard reported.

'Oh, when can we go home?' Maggie pleaded. She wanted the familiar comfort of her own kitchen.

Frank looked at Bernard for support. 'It didn't look too bad at all, did it, Bernard?'

'No.'

'I'll go and see the authorities in the morning to see if they think it's safe to go back. Apart from a hole in the roof where the chimney broke away, it's just dust and soot and that can be cleaned up. That sheet thing they've put over the hole will keep out any rain. We were damned lucky the chimney didn't come crashing down through the roof. It seems to have just toppled over and slid down the slates.'

'It could have been so much more serious,' Alfie added.

'Well, let's start to get things sorted out for the night. Maybe you'll be able to go home tomorrow, Maggie,' Edna said with a note of cheer in her voice.

Katherine sincerely hoped so. She knew there wouldn't be much sleep for either herself or Maggie, Frank and Alfie tonight. They were all too worried.

Chapter Twelve

ALL OF THEM were heavy-eyed next morning, but they were thankful that no one had come knocking on the door with bad news in the hours of darkness when worries are magnified often all out of proportion. Frank and Alfie were going to work, for there was no use in them just hanging around, losing a day's pay. Maggie was going up to the hospital and Katherine insisted she go with her.

'But what about your job?' Maggie asked.

'Ah, to hell with the job! Aren't Ceppi and Mary more important?'

'Will I send word down? It might help.'

'Thanks, Frank. It will help today but not if I don't turn up tomorrow, and I'm not going in if they aren't any better.'

Her lodging-house dream had been pushed to the back of her mind. It wasn't worth it compared with Ceppi's health.

A different Sister, but built in the same mould and wearing the same type of uniform, sat at the desk.

'Excuse me, I'm Miss Donovan and this is Mrs Boland. We've come to see how Mary and Concepta are?'

Sister stood up. 'Ah, I see. Will you wait here and I'll go and ask if the doctor will see you.'

'But . . . but can't we go in and see them?' Katherine asked anxiously.

'I'm sorry but no. If there is any danger of course you will be called, but the visiting times are very strict, they have to be.'

'But our Mary's in a co . . . coma.' Maggie struggled with the unfamiliar word and the fact that she couldn't see her own daughter, her own flesh and blood. 'When can we see them?' she begged.

'Visiting is from half past six to half past seven weekdays, and from half past two to half past three on Sundays.'

Katherine was outraged. 'You're after telling us we can't see them until tonight?'

'Yes. I don't make the rules, Matron does. We all have to abide by them.'

'What kind of a place is this that a mother can't see her own poor sick child?' Maggie was near to tears and Katherine was furious herself, but she reined in her temper in order to soothe her friend.

'It's for the best,' she urged. 'Don't get upset again, Maggie, we'll wait until we see the doctor.'

Sister looked relieved; she had begun to wonder if she should send for help to remove them from the hospital. It was something she frequently had to do. 'That's very sensible. Take a seat over there, away from the door; the draught is terrible, you'd catch cold.'

141

'Thank you.' Katherine's anger died and she led Maggie to the bench the Sister had indicated.

'She isn't *that* bad. Isn't she only obeying orders?' Katherine tried to calm Maggie, but she thought that Matron must be the most hard-hearted of women to be making rules like that.

It seemed an age before the doctor saw them. Sister ushered them into a small, austerely furnished room, painted green, with a big sash window that looked out over the yard. A middle-aged man wearing spectacles and a white coat was sitting at the desk reading the notes he had set out before him.

'Mrs Boland and Miss Donovan, Doctor,' Sister announced deferentially.

He looked up. 'I believe you are Concepta's guardian?'

'I am so, sir.'

'Apart from a broken ankle and a small wound to her head, both of which will heal, there doesn't seem to be any reason for us to keep her here.'

'Is it telling me she can come home you are, sir?'

At his terse reply, 'I am,' Katherine was filled with relief.

He turned his attention to Maggie. 'Mrs Boland?'

'Yes, sir.'

'I'm afraid your daughter's state of health is not the same as Concepta's. She is still in the coma – unconscious – and we have no idea when she will come out of it.' He paused, moved some papers around and looked very grave. 'I am a man who believes in telling the parents or spouse the truth. I also know many of my colleagues don't agree with my methods, but I find it helps people to adjust and cope. If Mary doesn't regain consciousness then she can't eat or drink and I'm afraid that

– in time – she will, unfortunately, die. We'll all do our best but it's in the hands of a greater authority now.'

Maggie couldn't take it in. No! He *must* be wrong. Mary wasn't going to die.

'Doctor, please, is there anything . . . anything at all you can do?' Katherine was as stunned as Maggie but someone had to ask.

'Just make her as comfortable as possible and pray to God.'

'Can . . . can I see her . . . now, please?' Maggie pleaded pitifully.

'It's not usually allowed but I think the rules can be broken this once. Sister will show you the way.'

Katherine put her arm around Maggie's shoulder. 'Thank you, sir.'

He nodded grimly. What was there to thank him for? At times like this he felt so angry and frustrated.

In a daze they followed the Sister. Her shoes squeaked and her apron crackled, everyday sounds in a world turned upside down.

Mary was in a side ward. It felt so cold, Maggie thought, glancing around. Mary's face was almost the same colour as the walls and she just looked as if she were peacefully asleep.

Maggie bent over the bed and stroked her forehead. 'Oh, Mary, Mary, luv . . .'

'Can she have a few moments with her while I see Ceppi?'

The Sister, who was a charitable woman, nodded and opened the door quietly.

Ceppi was sitting up in bed, a bandage around her head and her foot, heavily bandaged, in a splint. Her pale little face lit up as she saw Katherine.

'I've come to take you home,' Katherine said, gathering her in her arms and pressing her cheek against the child's soft curly hair.

'Now? This very minute?'

'Well, I'll have to go back and get you some clean clothes and one boot, but I won't be long, I promise.'

Much cheered, Ceppi smiled. 'I knew you'd come today. I *knew*! I told the night nurse you would. Can Mary go home too? They wouldn't let me see her at all.'

Katherine was gentle. 'No, Mary can't come home today, in fact we don't know when she will be home . . . She banged her head, you see, and she's . . . she's asleep.'

'Why can't someone wake her up?' Ceppi demanded.

'It's not the kind of sleep someone can wake you up from; she has to do it herself, naturally.'

'But she hasn't got a broken ankle or a cut on her head, has she?'

'Not at all. She's got a tiny little cut on her forehead, that's all.'

'Then she'll be coming home soon. She'll wake up and she'll want her mam to bring her clothes.'

Katherine exchanged glances with the Sister. How did you tell a child of Ceppi's age that her best and only friend was going to die if she didn't wake up?

'We'll not think about that yet. Now be good while I go back for your things. Don't move off that bed. Promise me?'

'I will so.'

All the way home Katherine tried to bolster Maggie's spirits, but it was hard when she was so terribly upset herself.

'She looks like a little angel in that white gown thing they've dressed her in. They've combed her hair and she . . . she just looks . . .' Katherine fought down a sob. 'All we can do is pray. I'll go to see Father Scanlan and ask him to say a Mass for her and ask from the pulpit that everyone prays for her. I'll ask *everyone* we know – surely God will hear us?'

'It's . . . it's those damned rules. They won't let me sit with her. I can only see her for an hour a day.'

'I know. Maybe if I see Matron and ask her . . .' Katherine shuddered at the thought of meeting the woman but she would do it if it helped Maggie.

'Would you? Would you really, Katherine? I . . . I couldn't face her. I'd either be crying so much I couldn't speak or I'd lose my temper and call her all the names under the sun and that wouldn't do any good at all.'

'I'll ask when I go back with Ceppi's clothes if I can see her.'

'God bless you, Katherine.'

God help me, Katherine thought to herself.

As promised, before she went to collect Ceppi, she plucked up courage to ask the Sister if she could possibly make an appointment to see Matron.

'It's very unusual, Miss Donovan. In fact it's almost unheard of.'

'I know, but I promised Mrs Boland I'd try.'

'What do you want? Can I help?' Sister didn't relish the thought of having to go and see Matron and make such an outlandish request. Matron was a holy terror. Even some of the doctors were wary of her, particularly the younger ones.

It was only the likes of the consultants and surgeons who would argue with her.

'She wants to know if it will be possible for her to come and sit with Mary for longer than an hour a day.'

'Ah, I see.' Sister also saw very clearly what Matron would say but she felt sorry for the poor woman. So many children died in this city, of disease usually. But what had happened to Mary was a different tragedy. 'I think it might be better if we saw a doctor first.'

Now it was Katherine's turn to say, 'I see,' and she nodded to let Sister know that she knew what the nurse meant. Matron would hardly refuse a doctor.

'If you come at visiting time tonight, I might have some news for you.' It was still against all hospital protocol. She should go to Miss Travis the Deputy Matron, but she was almost as bad as Matron herself.

'Oh, thank you. Thank you. It's so hard on Maggie, she cares and worries about them all. She mightn't have much but she's a good wife and mother.'

'I don't doubt it. Well, come along and let's get this little madam ready to leave. Have you organised transport? She can't walk far without help.'

'I . . . I haven't. I was too concerned about Mrs Boland and Mary. I'll get a cab, she's too heavy for me to carry on and off the tram and down the street.'

'I'll send a porter to find you one.'

'You really are very kind.'

'Oh, we're not all dragons, Miss Donovan.' When Sister smiled she looked like a totally different person, Katherine thought, smiling back at her.

*

She told Maggie of her conversation.

'Oh, thank God. You're so good and so brave, Katherine.'

'We should have some news by tonight.'

'I'll be first in line when they let the visitors in,' Maggie said firmly.

They were and Sister called Katherine to one side.

'Tell Mrs Boland that Matron has ruled that she can come in for an hour in the afternoon. Two till three. But *only* Mrs Boland.'

'Oh, that's a blessed relief. How can we thank you?'

'You can't. It was Dr Spencer, who saw you both earlier. He went to see Matron.' Her voice dropped to a whisper. 'And I believe that swords were crossed but of course he had the final say.' She wasn't sorry she'd approached him but she knew she would soon face Matron's wrath.

'Then God bless him. Will it be all right for me to send him something . . . a thank-you note?'

'I think I'd let things lie for now,' Sister advised.

'Is it good news?' Maggie begged when Katherine got back.

'It is. You can come in for an hour in the afternoon as well. Two to three, but just you. Not Frank or Alfie or me.'

Maggie smiled with relief. 'I bless the day you first set foot over my doorstep, Katherine Donovan. What would I have done without you and all the help you give me, to say nothing of the extra money? I feel . . . better now.'

'I'm glad. Now all we have to do is pray.'

Maggie went every afternoon and in the evenings Frank went with her. Once Alfie was allowed to see his sister and once

Katherine was allowed to join Maggie. It was only two visitors to a bed and they were very strict.

Each night they all prayed. In fact the whole neighbourhood prayed. 'Storming heaven's gates' was how Edna described it, but each day Maggie could see her daughter slipping further and further away from her.

A fortnight later, almost to the day and hour of the accident, Death kept its appointment with little Mary Boland. Dr Spencer spoke to them after, a note of anger in his voice. 'Death is a thing we all have to face. You can't shut it out or lock it away. It's the biggest thief of all,' he said bleakly. He'd seen it all too often.

Ceppi was unconsolable. She just couldn't understand even though Katherine explained it all to her, time and time again.

'But she was *asleep*. She was going to wake up one day. She was my friend. She was my best friend and I loved her.'

'I know all that, acushla, and she's awake now but up in heaven, not down here. God sent His holy angels to take her to heaven to live with Him and all the angels and saints.'

'But I didn't *want* Him to take her up there! I've got no one now! I don't like that God! He's nasty and cruel. He took Mary and she didn't belong to Him. She was *my* friend.'

'Ceppi, please don't think like that about God. We all *do* belong to Him. One day, when you're an old lady I hope, God will take you too. He takes all of us and everyone is happy to go. He's not nasty or cruel. I know that Mary is very happy in heaven and she's looking down on you and always will do. And you'll have more friends. I know how it hurts you, but the hurt will go away in time.'

'Is she *really* happy? Is she *really* looking down on me?'

Katherine nodded. 'She *is* happy and she *is* looking down on you, I promise.'

Ceppi's sobs at last diminished for Katherine never broke a promise.

Chapter Thirteen

———◆———

T HE WHOLE OF St Andrew's Street was plunged into mourning. They'd seen dozens of funerals over the years, including those of children, and there were decades-old traditions to observe. Curtains remained closed; the kids were not allowed to play their noisy street games; everyone called to extend their sympathies to Maggie and Frank and Alfie and collected pennies, sixpences and shillings for flowers. At times like this the whole neighbourhood put aside all the bickering and arguments and pulled together. There had been occasions when there was no burial fund to draw upon and money had been collected to give the deceased a decent funeral. To have a member go to a pauper's grave was one of the worst things that could happen to a family.

The women closest to Maggie came to hang white sheets around the walls of Alfie's small bedroom. Alfie had to sleep on the sofa but he didn't mind for a few nights. They draped black crêpe around the door and at each corner of the narrow bed, which almost filled the room, were four white candles in brass candlesticks lent by Mrs Neale from the corner shop.

When they brought Mary home in her small coffin she looked like a wax doll. She was dressed in a plain white cotton shroud. Her hands were crossed over her chest and a set of rosary beads was threaded between her fingers. Although she knew that the neighbours had made a collection for wreaths, Katherine bought flowers, expensive white Madonna-lilies, which she arranged at the top and bottom of the bed in vases also borrowed from Mrs Neale. She could have bought daffodils for half the price but they seemed wrong somehow. They were looked upon as a herald of spring and of new life. Lilies were considered by many people to be the flowers of the dead but they were also symbols of purity and innocence and who could have been more pure and innocent than Mary, a little child of eight?

Katherine was worried about Ceppi, who was very subdued. Once she found her nursing Mary's old rag doll, tears running unheeded down her cheeks. So she had had a discussion with Maggie about Ceppi, when both Alfie and Ceppi had gone to bed and before Frank came in from his nightly drink.

'I know it's customary for everyone to see . . . Mary . . . but I don't think it will do Ceppi any good. I told her that the angels came down and took Mary to heaven, but it was a long time before she believed me. Of course I had to promise that that is where Mary is. If she sees Mary she's going to start to question and doubt me.'

'I know, Katherine, I'm so mithered that I can't think straight. There seems to be a constant procession of people coming and going through the house. I know they mean well and I know it's customary, but . . .'

Katherine took her hand. 'Maggie, don't I know how upset you are? You haven't slept properly for weeks. But . . . but when everything is over perhaps you will be glad of people calling. When my mam died no one came, not a single one except Father Flynn, and I would have given my right arm for someone, anyone to talk to.'

Maggie squeezed her hand. 'You've not had much of a life up to now, luv, have you?'

'Not really.'

'Then you do whatever you think best for Ceppi.'

'I'll just tell her that we've made Alfie's room into a sort of chapel where the neighbours come to say special prayers, and as for the funeral . . . well, I think it best if she goes to school. Everything will be over by the time she comes home. I'm trying to keep things normal for her, she's very confused. She really doesn't understand. How can she?'

'Aren't we all confused, luv? God knows I'll never be able to forget seeing her in that hospital bed, slipping away, day by day, and me not being able to do a single thing.' Maggie broke down again, and Katherine cried with her. How would Maggie get over this? Katherine too knew she would never ever forget Mary Boland, and she was not her mother.

The day of the funeral was as windy and cold as the day of the accident. How Katherine'd wished over the weeks that she'd never stopped off to get those groceries Maggie had asked for. If she'd gone straight home she might have been able to do something . . . anything to get them out of the path of the bricks and mortar hurtling down the roof. She'd confided her guilt to Father Scanlan who had comforted her by saying there was absolutely nothing to be done. It was Divine Will.

Katherine looked around at the people who were crammed into Maggie's kitchen. The women all wore black but most of the men wore their Sunday suits with a black armband over the sleeve. The mood was heavy. Katherine wished it was all over.

As they stepped out of the front door the wind almost plucked their hats away. The sky was full of grey clouds that threatened rain. The assembled neighbours stood waiting to follow the hearse to the church. The black plumes on the horses' bridles were being almost flattened and the animals tossed their heads and stamped their hooves, uneasy in the gusts of wind that lifted the rubbish in the gutter. To stop them from bolting the driver stood at their heads.

Frank helped Maggie and Katherine into the carriage. It was a good turnout, one Katherine had generously contributed to. Everyone saved for a decent funeral for their family, but it was very expensive. Even Tilly had taken a day off from work to attend.

The small coffin, covered with flowers, was borne on the shoulders of Frank, Alfie, Bernard O'Brian and Mick Irving. Katherine supported Maggie as they followed it down the aisle of the church.

Father Scanlan said the Mass and his touching speech about little Mary Boland left half of the congregation in tears; many of the women present had buried children too. Liverpool could be a harsh, comfortless city at times.

The burial was even harder to bear. A scattering of

raindrops, borne on the wind, were like icy pinpricks on their faces and the senior altar boy struggled to keep the large black umbrella over the priest. She was glad she'd sent Ceppi to school. The child still cried often for Mary, mostly in the night. Katherine wondered how she'd got on that day.

Maggie was sobbing uncontrollably and Frank held her tightly, his face pale with suffering and the determination not to break down. Men didn't cry, although he felt like it as he watched the coffin containing his youngest, precious daughter being lowered into the open grave. Both he and Maggie refused to take the handful of damp soil one of the undertakers had offered them. Maggie simply couldn't have thrown it into the grave; she could barely stand without Frank's help.

Katherine refused too. Instead she threw one of the lilies and it lay, a white splash, against the background of dark soil.

Ida Irving and Eliza Neale, who had shut her shop for a few hours, had stayed behind and had hot soup and tea ready for the mourners. There were plates of ham sandwiches and meat pies cut into squares and beer and whiskey for the men. Katherine had bought a bottle of sherry and a bottle of Madeira wine for the women. She didn't want anyone to speak disparagingly about the funeral and the tea that followed it and she knew there were some, like Martha Mulrooney, the neighbourhood's most vindictive gossip, who would, even though they'd eaten Maggie's food and drunk her wine.

People stood around in groups, talking quietly. Maggie was sitting on the old sofa, a glass of Madeira in one hand, a sodden handkerchief in the other. She didn't know what she was saying, she was in such a state.

It was all dreadful, Katherine thought, utterly dreadful.

*

Ceppi was still lost in an unreal world. She didn't want to go to school but Katherine said it would be for the best. She'd given her a note to give to Sister Imelda.

The nun had heard all the details of the accident, and prayers had been said in the Convent too. 'Come here to me, child,' she instructed as the girls trooped into the classroom, Ceppi clutching the note. Ceppi did as she was bid and gave Sister Imelda the note. The nun opened it and read the few lines, then she folded it and put it in one of the many pockets in the skirt of her habit.

'It's a sad day for you, child, we'll all help you get through it.'

'But . . . but Katherine said we are only sad for ourselves. She said Mary's happy now.'

'And so she is, don't ever forget that, or that you'll see her again some day if you are good. Sit down now and get out your exercise books,' she commanded and the whispering stopped.

As Ceppi went to her desk the nun thought that Ceppi's guardian had a lot of common sense for someone so young.

Everyone in her class was very nice to Ceppi that day and she wondered why.

'We're all your friends now, Ceppi,' Mary Jane O'Hanlan said at playtime.

'Yes, we are,' Maddy Coyne added.

Ceppi didn't believe her for Maddy Coyne had tormented and tried to bully her every day, though she'd never succeeded for Ceppi knew very well how to look after herself. Quite often it had been she who had defended Mary against her.

'She doesn't really mean it, Ceppi, it's just because Sister Imelda has told her to be nice to you,' Celia Murphy whispered. 'But some of us do mean it.'

'Who?' Ceppi asked suspiciously.

'Well, me and Bridget and Tessa. You can play with us now.'

'I'd sooner have Mary,' Ceppi replied and started to cry.

Sister Imelda was sent for and she took Ceppi into the private chapel to talk to her and to calm her and say some prayers.

Katherine was trying to make Maggie go to bed. Frank was going for a pint with Bernard and Mick, and Edna O'Brian was keeping Eddie. He had become used to being with her now and didn't make a fuss.

'Maggie, you're exhausted. You've got to get some sleep.'

'I can't. I keep thinking of her. All alone, under all that soil.'

'Maggie, you *know* she's not there. It's . . . it's just an empty shell of a . . . body. We all keep thinking of her and will continue to do so, but you've had the heaviest burden to shoulder. Please, please go to bed?'

After Maggie had gone up Katherine sat down wearily in the old rocking chair. Alfie was sitting opposite with his head in his hands. Katherine felt so sorry for him. He seemed to have been left out. She got up and went and put her arm around his shoulder.

'I know you're unhappy, It's been a terrible day and you shouldn't be afraid to cry.'

'Nobody thought of me. I felt I didn't even belong there.'

'Of course you belonged and I know that your mam and dad *did* think of you.'

'Hardly anyone spoke to me when we all came back. It was as if I wasn't here, I wasn't a "real" person at all and she was my sister.' He burst into tears and Katherine sat on the arm of the chair and put her other arm around him. The poor lad, he'd been so neglected and he was hurting as much as the rest of them but had somehow managed to 'act like a man' as Frank called it – until now. Surely it was good to cry? To let all the misery out?

'Oh, Alfie, I know it's been hard and it's going to be hard for quite a while, but we *do* think of you. We really do.'

He looked up at her, his face pinched and white with grief. 'I know *you* do and . . . and that's the most important thing.'

She was so taken aback by the intensity of his words that for a couple of seconds she let her guard slip. Before she knew it Alfie was on his feet, had clasped her in his arms and was kissing her. She pushed him away.

'Alfie! Alfie, stop it!' she cried.

'No! I love you, Katherine. I love you so much. Don't you remember? I told you so at Christmas.'

She stepped away from him, wanting to be out of reach. 'You don't love me, Alfie, you only think you do.'

'I don't think, I *know*!'

'You're only a boy, Alfie. You're only fifteen!' She tried to keep her voice calm, but she was shaken and she didn't want to hurt him.

'I'm *not* a boy! You're only nineteen, that's just four years older than me,' he pleaded. Since he'd first seen her that day at Mrs Taylor's house he'd never stopped thinking about her.

Sometimes the desire to touch her, hold her, kiss her had almost overwhelmed him. His life now centred on her.

'Alfie, listen to me,' she commanded. 'Yes, I am only four years older than you but those years matter so much because of the way I lived in Dublin. I've had to cope with things my mam would have dealt with. It wasn't an easy life. My da was a very hard man to get on with.' She paused. If only he knew just what she had had to cope with. 'And my mam died when I was twelve and I had no brothers or sisters I could turn to for help. I *had* to grow up quickly, too quickly. In four years' time you'll look back and think, I was only a kid. I *am* fond of you, Alfie, you must believe that, but I don't love you. I don't love anyone.'

'I'll wait, Katherine.'

'For what?'

'For me to grow up and then I can marry you.'

He was serious. Obviously he was obsessed. She didn't want to hurt him, but this had to stop now.

'Alfie, you're distraught, you don't know what you're saying. I can't marry you – ever. I don't love you and for a marriage to work it's not enough for only one partner to be in love. The last thing I want to do is hurt you, so go to bed before your da comes home. We don't want any more upsets.'

There was naked longing in his eyes. 'Is that all I am, Katherine, an "upset"? I love you, I *really* love you! There will never be anyone else, I know that.'

He reached out to her again but she backed away.

'You're far more than an "upset" and you know that. But, Alfie, it's just not meant to be.'

'Katherine, you're my whole life,' he whispered. 'I never

stop thinking about you. What kind of a life will I have without you? There's nothing worth living for.'

Now she was really worried. 'Alfie, stop talking like that! Promise me you'll do nothing . . . stupid or I'll have to tell your da about . . . everything.'

'I don't care!'

'Well, I *do*! I'm not going to inflict more pain and grief on your mam, she's had more than most women can stand. I mean it, I'll *have* to tell them both. Is that what you want? To see your mam bowed down with worry and your da too? Is it?'

Slowly he shook his head and she sighed with relief.

'Go on up to bed now before your da gets in.'

With reluctance he did so but the look in his eyes as he turned at the door made her feel deeply anxious.

She was sitting in the rocking chair beside the range, engrossed in thought, when Frank came in.

'I thought you'd have gone to bed by now, Katherine, it's been a long day.'

'It has so, but . . .'

Frank looked at her closely. 'Katherine, is there anything wrong, apart from it being a terrible day?'

She thought quickly. Should she tell him about Alfie's delusions of love or would he get annoyed and start shouting at the boy? Poor Alfie was in a bad enough state as it was. No, she couldn't tell Frank, it would cause so much unnecessary suffering. She might have to one day, but not now.

'No, I'm just tired and I feel so helpless. I suppose it's because of the day that's in it: I'll go up now. At least it's all over.'

Frank nodded wearily. 'Yes, perhaps things can get back to some kind of order.'

The following morning Alfie appeared subdued as if he'd had hardly any sleep. He was pale and there were dark circles under his eyes.

'Are you all right, lad?' Frank asked him. Maggie had noticed nothing, she seemed to be in a daze as she moved around the kitchen like an automated doll.

'I didn't get much sleep last night, Da, that's all,' he answered in heavy tones, casting a glance at Katherine.

'None of us did, Alfie,' Katherine said quietly, but was sorry she'd spoken when she saw that intense look come into his eyes. Oh, this was terrible but what could she do about it? Certainly nothing at this precise moment. She just prayed that he would keep quiet.

After half-heartedly eating their breakfasts, Frank, Alfie and Katherine went to work and Ceppi, reluctantly, went to school. Life, however hard it was, had to go on.

Chapter Fourteen

—◆◆◆—

K ATHERINE LOOKED UP at the cloudless blue sky as she
sat with the others on the factory wall. She found it
hard to believe that such a short time had elapsed since Mary's
death and funeral. To herself, and indeed everyone in the
house in St Andrew's Street, it seemed so long ago.

Ceppi was getting over it and she often spoke about the
girls she now looked on as her friends, although Katherine
knew she would never really forget Mary. Children are very
resilient, Father Scanlan had told her, and she had to agree.

With Maggie and Frank it was different. Frank always put
on a brave face but she often heard Maggie crying in the night
and Frank's voice as he tried to console her. Alfie had put on
a brave face too. She knew it was hard on him. Maggie had
Frank's shoulder to cry on, Alfie had no one: Tilly had of
course gone back to work and Eddie was far too young to
understand. At times Alfie had no patience with his baby
brother.

She sighed heavily as she thought of poor Alfie.

'God, that was cheerful, what's up with yer?' Dotty asked as she rolled up the sleeves of her overall to let the sunlight warm her arms.

'Take no notice of 'er, Katherine, she's got no tact. She probably doesn't even know the meanin' of the word.'

'I do!' Dotty shot back, incensed.

'Then don't go sayin' daft things. She can sigh if she wants to.'

'All I said was—'

'For heaven's sake will you give it a rest, the pair of you!' Katherine pleaded.

'There is somethin' wrong, isn't there, luv?' Mavis asked.

'Yer know yer can tell us. I know I've a big mouth but if people ask me ter keep it shut I can.'

Katherine looked at them and wondered if she could trust Dotty. She made her decision: she had nobody at home to confide in without upsetting the whole family – again.

'There is so. It's Alfie—'

'That's Maggie's lad?' Dotty interrupted and received a look of venom from Mavis.

'Yes. He . . . he's got a crush on me. He thinks he loves me and is going to marry me some day. The poor lad, I've tried to talk to him, tried to keep out of his way but he's still gazing at me like a lovestruck calf and I'm afraid he'll say something and there will be more heartache. And it's affecting Ceppi, she's all mixed up. She keeps looking at me sort of question-ingly, but she won't ask me why I hardly ever talk to Alfie.'

'What did yer say to 'im, exactly, like?' Mavis asked.

'It was on the day of the funeral. I told him he was too

young, that he didn't love me and he'd get over it in time and that I couldn't ever think of marrying him because I don't love him. He's only four years younger than me, but he hasn't had to grow up so fast.'

'Fellers are like that, they still act like kids even when they do grow up,' Dotty said.

'An' some never grow up properly,' Mavis said tartly, thinking of her own fiancé.

When Katherine arrived home that evening she was surprised to find no one in the house. Obviously Frank and Alfie were working late; Maggie must have taken Eddie to Edna's and stayed to chat. She was still struggling to get over Mary's death and needed all the support her friends could give. As for Ceppi – no doubt she would have some excuse for being late.

Katherine had laid the table and started to peel potatoes when she heard the scullery door open.

'Ceppi, is that you? Where have you been?' she called.

'It's not Ceppi, Katherine, it's me.'

Katherine turned to see Alfie standing in the doorway.

'Where's your da?'

'Working. He got the chance of a bit of overtime, I didn't.'

Katherine returned to her task but felt uneasy.

'Where's Mam?' he asked.

'Probably with Edna. I expect she'll be in in a few minutes, she'll have forgotten the time.'

'Is Ceppi in?'

Oh, Lord, this was getting worse. Katherine was becoming more agitated by the minute. She'd kill Ceppi for being late. She kept her eyes firmly fixed on the potato she was peeling.

'So, there's just you and me. At last I've got you alone for a few minutes.' There was a note of triumph in his voice.

She looked up. 'Oh, Alfie, please, please don't start again. I've told you I don't love you. I've been fair and open with you. Forget me!'

'Katherine, you know I can't!' He reached for her hand but she pulled away.

'You *can*! You've got to make an effort, Alfie. Go out more with your mates, please? You'll meet a nice girl who can love you.'

'No! No! I could never love anyone else. I don't want anyone else!' He reached for her again and she realised she would have to be cruel to be kind.

'Alfie, I'll never, never love you. How can I when you're just like a young brother to me? That's how I think of you. Like a ten- or twelve-year-old brother. Never as a grown man.'

She pressed her lips together as she saw the hurt in his eyes turn to shock, but she had to put an end to this.

He struggled to speak; there was a huge lump in his throat and his eyes were over-bright with tears. 'Then . . . then . . . there's nothing . . . nothing left for me. I've nothing to look forward to so I might as well be . . .'

'NO! Alfie, don't even *say* it! It's a sin and would you add to your mam's sorrows? It would kill her, I know it would!' She reached out and held his hands tightly in her own. 'Promise me that you won't do anything like that. Alfie, if you love me then promise me, please? If anything . . . happened to you, I'd never forgive myself, I'd be in bits for the rest of my life. Is that what you want? Do you want me to be so miserable and guilty that my life would be ruined?'

Slowly he shook his head.

'Then promise me?'

'I . . . I promise, Katherine, but I'll always love you.'

She sighed with relief and gently touched his cheek. 'Thank you, Alfie. I know you won't break your promise.'

'Whose life would be ruined and why does he have to promise you?'

Katherine's relief turned to apprehension as she saw Ceppi standing in the doorway. She'd obviously heard some of the conversation.

'It doesn't concern you, Ceppi, and just where have you been?'

'I went home with Cecilia and some of the others. Where is everyone?' she demanded to distract Katherine from the fact that she'd dawdled home.

'Frank's working late and Maggie is—'

'God in heaven! Didn't I forget the time and there's no start made on the tea!'

Katherine smiled with relief as Maggie bustled in with a tired and hungry Eddie on her hip.

The following day Katherine's friends noticed that she still wasn't her usual cheerful self.

'What's up?' Mavis asked.

'Oh, Alfie started again last night. He even threatened to . . . to kill himself.'

'Jesus, Mary an' Joseph! What did yer do?' Dotty asked.

'I had to make him promise he wouldn't but I feel so helpless . . .'

Mavis looked serious and even Dotty was frowning with concentration.

'The only thing yer can do, Katherine, is ter leave. That way no one will get 'urt.'

Mavis had voiced her own thoughts.

'I know, but I feel as though I'd be letting Maggie down. It's not that long since Mary died. I'd feel as if I was deserting her in some way and I know she would miss what I pay her for our board and lodgings.'

'Well, she wouldn't 'ave ter feed either of yer, would she? That should save 'er money.'

'For once in yer life, Dotty, yer've actually said something sensible.'

'I suppose I should say "Thanks", but I won't. You always think I'm a thicko.'

'That's because most of the time you are,' Mavis answered, but for once there was no note of sarcasm in her voice.

Katherine was deep in thought. She had enough money now to open her lodging house, but she really did feel that it was too soon to leave Maggie. She'd be so hurt and upset.

'Well, where would she go?' Dotty asked.

Mavis shrugged. 'We'll have to think about it.'

Katherine decided to take the plunge. 'No, no you won't. I've already got plans. I've had them for ages, ever since I came to Liverpool. It was living with your one in Mount Pleasant that gave me the idea.'

Dotty looked pained. 'Well, tell us! Fer God's sake, don't leave us guessin'!'

'I . . . I want to open my own lodging house, mainly for travelling salesmen.'

They both gaped at her.

'I know you both think I'm the biggest eejit in the world, but I mean it.'

Mavis was the first to recover. 'That takes money, girl, a lot of money. 'Ow will yer furnish it? There'll be all those beds an' sheets an' blankets. A whole 'ouse?'

'Yer must 'ave a fortune!' Dotty was equally incredulous.

'I had most of it when I came over from Dublin. My . . . my da sort of left it to me.'

'Yer said 'e was a skinflint an' yer were sick of him.'

'I know. He . . . he's dead. He had a pawnshop, the Harp and Shamrock, and he was a moneylender and he was worse than a skinflint. But he was . . . killed.' The word was sticking in her throat but she was glad the truth would come out at last. 'He was . . . murdered.'

Mavis crossed herself. 'Jesus, Mary an' Holy St Joseph! Who done fer 'im then?'

Katherine could see she was going to have to tell them everything. 'The men in the houses. He'd killed . . . murdered Ceppi's da and poor Joe was a cripple who couldn't fight back at all. That's why I brought Ceppi with me. Her mam didn't care a fig for her, she'd had to bring herself up. I . . . I just left the shop, I didn't want anything from either it or the house. There was rioting at the time.'

'I remember me da sayin' somethin' about all that,' Dotty remarked. ''E said 'e didn't blame them, 'alf starved they were or so me da said.'

'What did the police do then?'

'Nothing. What could they do? Nobody would give them a shred of evidence and I'm glad they didn't. Both Da and Joe Healy were dead, so I took the money and Ceppi and came here.'

'And now yer've got enough money?' Mavis asked.

'Yes, I suppose I have, but I didn't want to leave Maggie's just yet. I've got enough to pay about two months' rent and furnish the place but managing until I get people in to stay is going to be hard.'

'But fer yer own peace of mind an' ter save poor Maggie any more 'eartache, yer'll have ter go soon, luv.'

'We won't 'alf miss yer, Katherine.'

'I'll miss you too and I'm sorry that your wages will drop.'

'Aye, they will. Unless we get another one like you.'

'Fat bloody chance of that! They're always useless or they don't stop long,' Dotty retorted.

'When will yer tell Maggie?'

'I don't know. Will it be better to tell her when I've found something or tell her now?'

'Do what yer common sense tells yer, Katherine. Yer won't judge it wrong,' Mavis advised.

She decided to tell Maggie at the first opportunity. She waited until their evening meal was over and Frank was reading his newspaper, Ceppi was doing her homework and Alfie had gone out.

'It's a lovely evening, let's go and sit on the front step,' she suggested. During the hot summer months both front and back door were opened and the women sat on their steps and talked. Although it was only May the evening was warm.

'Go on, luv, a bit of fresh air will do you both good,' Frank urged. It would leave him with some peace and quiet to read his newspaper.

The step was still warm and they both tucked their long skirts around their legs and sat down.

'Maggie, there's something I want to tell you, that's why I asked you to come out here.'

Maggie looked at her with apprehension.

'It's . . . it's nothing bad. It's just that . . . I . . .'

'You're telling me you're going to leave, get somewhere of your own.'

Katherine gasped in astonishment. 'You *know*! How did you know? I never even said a word . . .'

'Katherine, luv, I might be three sheets to the wind at times but I've noticed the way our Alfie looks at you – and so has Frank.'

Katherine nodded her head. 'I just don't want to cause more upset. I really don't, you've had enough to last a lifetime. But there's nothing more I can do. I . . . I have spoken to him about it.'

Maggie looked very concerned. 'What did you say? More to the point, what did *he* say?'

Katherine gave her an edited version.

'Oh, the stupid fool!' Maggie said, shaking her head.

'Don't blame him, he's upset still over Mary. It'll pass. He's only fifteen, he'll find a girl he can love and then all this will be water under the bridge. Don't say anything to him, Maggie, please?'

'I won't. I'll have to tell Frank though.'

'Of course you will.'

'It's . . . it's for the best, luv.'

'I won't go far, I promise. I'll see you at every opportunity.'

Now that it was out in the open Maggie was relieved. At first she'd taken no notice of Frank's comments about his son's behaviour, she'd been too upset, but gradually she'd started to watch him and had to agree that Frank was right. Frank had said he'd give him another good talking to but she had wondered if that was the answer. Probably not. Katherine's solution was drastic but was probably the only way out. Somehow she didn't mind.

'What will you look for? A couple of rooms?'

'No, I want more than that.' Briefly she told Maggie the same story she'd told Mavis and Dotty. At each revelation, Maggie's expression changed, reflecting her shock, amazement and finally determination. When Katherine fell silent they both sat like statues for a moment before Maggie broke the silence. She got to her feet purposefully. 'Well, let's start straight away then.'

Katherine had also risen. 'Why so?'

'Before our Alfie finds out. Will you tell milady in there?'

'No, not until I . . . we've found somewhere.'

'Let's get Frank's paper. The *Echo* always has notices of houses to sell or rent.'

When Maggie asked Frank for the *Echo* he looked surprised. 'What for?'

'The housing pages,' she mouthed, jerking her head in Ceppi's direction.

He looked mystified until realisation began to dawn on him. He breathed a sigh of relief. Katherine had taken the matter into her own hands.

*

They found two possibilities, only a few streets away, and decided they would go and see them on Saturday. Ceppi would be playing with her friends from school and wouldn't want to go on a shopping trip, which was what Katherine would tell her they were doing.

It was a very warm day. The sunlight was bright and strong. There was no breeze and the wisps of cloud across the blue sky hardly moved at all.

They walked along the main road looking at the details Katherine had cut from the paper before it was used to light the fire. Even in summer they had to keep a fire going in the range for heat to cook on and hot water.

The first house looked decidedly run down.

'We didn't expect it to be a little palace but even to my eyes it looks as if it's going to fall down any minute. I've experience of that.'

'It is pretty desperate, isn't it? Is it worth a closer look, would you say?'

'No,' Maggie answered firmly.

They turned away and began to walk up the street.

They finally found the second house on her list and they stood on the opposite side of the street to get a better view. It was a big ugly-looking, awkwardly shaped old house.

'Well, what about this one?'

'It's big, I'll give you that. Let's go and have a proper look.'

The windows were dirty; some were missing panes of glass. The paintwork was peeling and the front steps were worn. It had a terrible air of neglect but for some reason Katherine was drawn to it. They crossed over and opened the gate whose

171

hinges screeched. Nothing a bit of oil wouldn't cure, Katherine thought, looking upwards. The roof looked to be sound, it was of grey slates but the rest of the house had been red brick originally. Now, like every other building in the neighbourhood, the bricks were black with soot. There were two large windows on the upper level and one big bay window on the ground floor.

'It's shaped a bit like the bow of a ship,' Maggie said as they walked along the narrow overgrown path that led to the other side of it.

Again there were two bedroom windows and one ground-floor window, but this one wasn't a bay, it was flat. They both went and tried to look inside but that side of the house was out of the sunlight and the window panes were so dirty that they could see nothing. They walked back again to the sunny side and, with both hands pressed against their faces and the window to keep out the glare, they peered in. It was a big room and completely bare. The sunlight filtering in through the grime showed a fireplace, an old one. She'd seen many of them in the once grand houses in Dublin and it didn't look to be in much need of repair. There were remnants of wallpaper clinging to the walls and the ceiling was decorated with plaster motifs, with some bits missing. It was just old and neglected, but with some repairs and furniture and rugs it could be made into a home. She couldn't afford to restore it to its former glory, nor did she want to.

They went and sat down on the worn sunwarmed steps and Katherine touched the iron boot scraper with her hand.

'Well, what do you think, Katherine? Myself I think it's not too bad. If the feller that owns it will do some repairs, and we can scrub it from top to bottom, it wouldn't be too bad at all.'

Katherine nodded. She'd found it. She knew she'd found just what she wanted.

'Eh, youse, what are yer doin' there?'

They looked up to see a young man of about twenty-three standing at the gate.

They got up. 'Don't you be so hardfaced, meladdo,' Maggie answered him.

'We were just having a look round,' Katherine added.

'Are yer thinkin' of rentin' it then? It's been empty fer a long time.'

'How long?' Maggie asked.

'Oh, about two years.'

'What's up with it then?'

'It's too big. Yer could fit six families in it.'

'Then why is it still empty?'

''is nibs, the landlord, like, wants too much rent.'

'How much?' Maggie demanded.

'Me mam said she'd heard 'e wanted eighteen shillings a week. No one round 'ere has that kind of money fer rent. Me mam moans at payin' seven shillings, let alone eighteen.'

'It's nearly three times what I pay too. It's scandalous, that's what it is.'

'What's his name, the landlord?' Katherine asked, trying to work out in her head how much a month it would cost her.

'Dunno. It's rented out by some fancy agency.'

Katherine looked down at the piece of paper. 'Marsden, Carpenter and Yeates, Dale Street,' she read aloud.

'I'd beat him down, Katherine,' Maggie advised. 'If it's

173

been empty for that long he might come down a bit. Don't tell him what you want to do with it though. And there is the problem with the street.'

'What's the matter with the street? It looks like all the others.'

'Everyone calls it Lonely Street.'

'Why?'

'Because nearly all the fellers who lived in it went down with the *Titanic*. They all worked in the stokehold and never stood a chance. Widows and orphans are all you'll find in this street.'

Katherine looked up at the house again. The House on Lonely Street, she thought. Well, she'd do as much as she could to make it a happy place. There was little she could do for the widows and orphans but there was a lot she could do to the house. She wasn't put off by its unofficial title. It was a challenge.

Chapter Fifteen

———◆———

AS THEY WALKED BACK, Katherine's head was full of ideas. Maggie was concentrating on the practical side of things, although, as they'd sat together on the doorstep, she'd glanced at Katherine and wondered how she had survived such a bleak and lonely childhood to become the young woman she was now: strong, thoughtful, generous and loyal.

'When will you go and see those agent people?'

'Now. Why not?' Katherine was decisive.

'Why not indeed. Strike while the iron's hot, I always say.'

'We'll get a tram at the next stop.' Katherine was eager now.

The office of Marsden, Carpenter and Yeates was on the first floor of the dimly lit, austere building on the left side of Dale Street. As they climbed the narrow stairs, Maggie wheezed a bit.

'I'm not as young as I used to be. Thank God we've not got two more flights to go.'

Katherine knocked hard on the glass window in the upper part of the door that bore the name of the business in black letters.

A young man appeared.

'I'm interested in renting a house.'

He looked over his shoulder. 'You'd better come in and I'll see if Mr Carpenter will see you.'

They stood in the small square hall that served as a waiting room but lacked even a bench to sit on until he reappeared. He beckoned them to follow him into a room that was just as gloomy as the corridor had been. A bald-headed man in a dark suit with a stiff white-collared shirt and grey tie indicated that they should sit down.

'Your name, ladies, please?'

'Miss Katherine Donovan and Mrs Margaret Boland,' Katherine answered. 'We . . . I have come to enquire about the house on the corner of Kildare Street.'

Mr Carpenter took a brown folder from one of the drawers in his desk and opened it.

He looked over the top of his spectacles at Katherine. 'It's a large property.'

'I know. We've just been to look at it. Not inside, of course, it's all locked.'

'Someone told us it has been empty for two years,' Maggie added.

'It has.'

'I believe the rent is eighteen shillings a week?'

'It is.' Privately he thought the landlord was mad to ask for such an amount, considering the size of the house and its shabby neighbourhood.

'Do you think the landlord would drop it?' Katherine asked tentatively.

He looked over his spectacles at her again, a habit that had begun to irritate Maggie.

'He might well do. What kind of a sum were you thinking of?'

'Well, considering it's so run down and where it is, I would think about fourteen shillings. I would see to decorating if he has the major repairs done – if there are any.'

He looked at the papers again. She obviously wasn't the naïve young Irish girl he'd taken her for and it was a fair enough amount. 'Structurally it seems to be sound. Leave it with me. I'll contact him and tell him about your offer.'

'When . . . how . . .?'

'If you leave me the address you are living at now, I'll write as soon as I have any news.'

They both stood up.

'Thank you, sir. Do you think it will be long?'

'Possibly by Wednesday you should have heard from me.'

Katherine gave him the address and, after thanking him again, they left.

They were both on tenterhooks and it was hard to keep silent about it in front of Ceppi and Alfie until Wednesday. Frank knew and many was the time he had to shake his head at both his wife and Katherine to stop them giving it away.

She'd told Mavis and Dotty all about it on Monday morning but the post didn't come until Katherine had left for work and by Wednesday they were all in a state of excitement.

'Ye're like a cat on 'ot bricks. Go back 'ome in yer dinner-time. I don't think I can purrup with an afternoon of yer not knowin',' Mavis said.

'Go on, we'll cover fer yer if ye're a bit late, as long as it's not too long,' Dotty offered.

When the hooter sounded at half past twelve, Katherine took off her overall, handed it to Mavis, smiled at them both and walked quickly towards the gate.

She walked as fast as she could and when she reached the top of St Andrew's Street her heart began to pound and she ran the few remaining yards. She burst into the kitchen, startling both Eddie and Maggie.

'Has it come? Has the letter arrived?'

Maggie was just as excited and had found it so hard to wait that she'd even deliberated on steaming it open. She was glad now she hadn't as she handed it to Katherine.

The girl tore it open. 'Oh! oh!'

'What? What is it? For God's sake tell me before I have a heart attack.'

Katherine's eyes were sparkling and her cheeks were flushed. 'I've got it! I've got it! Fourteen shillings a week. He's agreed, look – it says so here.'

Maggie scrutinised the lines of neat copperplate writing.

'I can have the key any time, I've just got to go to that office and pay a month's rent in advance and then they'll give me the key.'

'When will you go?'

Katherine thought hard. By the time she finished work and got to Dale Street they would have closed the place for the day. 'I'll have to see if I can get a few hours off tomorrow but

I'll have to get back now. I can't ask for time if I'm late back today.'

'Can't I go for you?'

Katherine read the letter again. 'No, it says "in person".'

'What will you tell the factory? They won't let you off to go and look at a house.'

'I'll think of something. Mavis and Dotty will help. The pair of them are always full of ideas.'

'Have a cup of tea to celebrate,' Maggie offered.

'Sorry, I've not got the time!' Katherine replied.

She ran the whole way back so as not to be a second late and arrived with five minutes to spare.

She couldn't speak at first as her breath was coming in short gasps.

'She's got it! I know she's got it just by the look on 'er face!'

'Did 'e agree to the rent?' Dotty asked.

Katherine nodded and having recovered her breath she sat down on the wall. 'He did. As soon as I take the money they'll give me the key, but . . .'

'But what?'

'How am I going to get there while they're still open?'

'Yeah, that's a bit of a problem,' Dotty agreed.

'What can I say?'

Mavis looked thoughtful. 'Yer only want ter go 'alf an hour early, we could say yer fainted.'

'It's so bloody 'ot in there yer *could* faint,' Dotty said.

'I don't like tempting fate.'

'Well, that's the best I can do.'

'All right. When will I do it?'

'Ternight, 'alf an hour before knocking-off time. 'Ave yer got the cash?'

'I never thought of that, I'll have to go home first.'

'Ye're going ter need a bit more time then.'

'Can't yer ask Fred on the gate ter watch fer anyone passin' an' ask them ter go ter Maggie an' tell 'er to bring the money down ter the gate?'

'God, Dotty, sometimes yer amaze me. Yer go an' ask him, quick, like.'

Dotty ran quickly to the gate and then back.

''E says 'e'll do that. 'E said 'e likes yer—'

'We're not interested in that!' Mavis cut her short.

'Oh, ta very much, after I've 'ad ter speak nice to him, like. I can't stand 'im either.'

'We'll still do it a bit earlier in case there's a delay and yer 'ave ter go home first.'

'Right, we'll both insist ye're not well and then 'e'll 'ave ter let yer go. Yer can catch the tram around the corner. Thank God the tram stop is out of sight.'

'When will yer be leavin' then? I mean fer good?'

'In about a week, I think. It's in a state and needs scrubbing and painting and things like that.'

'Well, we'll come an' 'elp yer, after work an' on Saturday afternoon, won't we, Dotty?'

'Speak fer yerself, Mavis. I've got me da's tea ter get when I go 'ome on Saturdays. Me mam has a bit of a rest.'

'I wouldn't be wanting you to go putting yourself out, Mavis. Maggie will help.'

'We'll come on two nights an' Saturday afternoon. Yer da can 'ave somethin' cold – I know yer mam, she wouldn't mind

– an' iffen 'e doesn't like it 'e can bloody well lump it!'

'I'm so grateful to both of you. You've been good friends.'

'An' we'll go on bein' friends. We'll come an' visit, like.'

'You'll be welcome at any time, I mean that.'

'What do you want me to do?' Katherine whispered as the afternoon shift drew to a close.

'Yer just lie down on the floor an' sort of spread yer arms out an' close yer eyes.'

'I'll go yellin' ter the office an' tell 'im. I'll run.'

'When we 'ear 'er comin' back I'll kneel down beside yer and yer can be sort of strugglin' to sit up,' Mavis said determinedly. 'Right, 'ere we go.'

Dotty's screeching filled the whole place.

'God Almighty, she's overdoin' it a bit. Quick, get on the floor. She'll 'ave the bloody place up.'

Katherine lay down with her eyes closed and her arms outstretched. Mavis knelt on the floor beside her.

Footsteps came down the corridor. ''Ere they come. Gerra grip of yerself, luv.'

Dotty and Bert Madigan, the foreman, burst into the room.

'I told yer! I told yer, she's out fer the count. Just sort of groaned an' then fell on the floor, didn't she, Mavis?'

Mavis was trying to sit Katherine up. 'She did. Dropped like a stone. I wouldn't wonder if she 'asn't broke somethin'.'

'It's the 'eat in 'ere. It's like a bloody furnace.'

'Well, there's nothing I can do about that. The windows are sealed. Are you hurt anywhere, Katherine?' Mr Madigan asked as Katherine slowly opened her eyes. Mavis was still supporting her.

'No, I don't think so. I just . . . I was just so hot . . . and then . . .'

'If she goes out again yer'll 'ave ter send for the ambulance,' Mavis said flatly.

'Oh, yer will. She could be really sick, maybe she's caught somethin',' Dotty added.

'I don't need you to stick your oar in too, Dotty.'

'Well, yer never know. People get all kinds of things in the summer, what with the rubbish in the streets and the flies and the stinking privies.'

Bert Madigan hesitated as Mavis and Dotty helped Katherine to her feet.

'Sway a bit,' Mavis hissed into her ear under the guise of feeling Katherine's forehead.

Katherine obliged and the foreman's mind was made up.

'If she can walk, Mavis, take her to the gate, but don't be hanging around there. Can you find your own way, Katherine?'

'I . . . I . . . think so.'

'Right then, off you go.'

'I'm sorry, Mr Madigan. I'll be in in the morning.'

'See that you are,' he said tersely as he swung on his heel and left. He hoped she wasn't very sick. She was one of the best workers he had.

Katherine stripped off her overall and gave it to Mavis. 'Thanks, I would never have got out but for both of you.'

'Never mind all that, gerra move on!'

It was with huge relief that she saw Maggie standing on the corner.

'Some feller called an' gave me the message. I've got it all counted out. Two pounds and sixteen shillings. There's plenty of fellers who don't earn as much as that in a week.'

'I know, but—'

'Forget all that, here comes a tram!'

Katherine put the notes and coins in her pocket and jumped aboard with Maggie. As they sat on the tram heading into town the full realisation hit Katherine and she wanted to leap up and hug the conductor and tell all the passengers that she, Katherine Donovan from the slums of Dublin, was to be in business in her own right. She'd done it. She'd made her dream come true, with the help of all her friends – and they were good friends, each and every one of them. Never had she been so thankful that she'd made the decision to come to Liverpool. Soon the key to the House on Lonely Street would be in her hand. Suddenly a sobering thought struck her: how would Ceppi and Alfie take the news?

Ceppi had been sent to fetch Eddie from Edna O'Brian and both Frank and Alfie looked curiously at Katherine while Maggie bustled around the kitchen, making a start on the tea.

'Where've you been, Mam? You always have the tea ready for when we come in,' Alfie asked.

'Out with Katherine,' his mother answered sharply.

'Right, Ceppi, sit down, I've got something to tell you.'

'Is it a surprise?'

'It is so. A big one too.'

Ceppi stared at Katherine. She was clearly excited about something so it couldn't be going back to Dublin or even about changing schools. Now that Ceppi'd made her new friends she really didn't want to go to another school.

'We're moving. I'm renting a big house on the corner of Kildare Street, or Lonely Street as they call it down there.'

Ceppi stared at her. This was a surprise and she really didn't know if she wanted to move.

'Well?' Katherine asked. She could see that Ceppi was perturbed.

'Is it far from here?' Ceppi asked, still unsure.

'No. About a ten-minute walk. Not even a tram stop away.'

'You're . . . you're leaving us?' Alfie interrupted. His voice was hoarse with pain.

Katherine sighed. 'Yes, it's for the best, Alfie,' she said quietly. 'But, as I've just told Ceppi, it's not *that* far away.'

All Alfie could do was stare at her, stunned.

'So, when do we get to see this house?' Frank asked.

'Tonight, if you like. It doesn't get dark until late. Ceppi, you'll love it and I'm sure there will be a bedroom you can have all to yourself.'

Ceppi was already changing her mind about the move. 'I won't have to share with anyone at all?'

'Not a one.'

Ceppi had never known anyone to have a bedroom all to themselves except Alfie and you couldn't call that attic room much of a bedroom, it was more like a press. A room – all of her own! She couldn't quite take it in.

'Right then, Maggie, you'd better get on with the tea if we're all going down there after,' Frank said cheerfully.

Alfie didn't want to see the house, the house that was taking Katherine from him. He wouldn't see her every morning and night, as he did now. He lived for these few hours.

'I don't want to go,' he said, his voice full of emotion.

The three adults exchanged glances.

Frank broke the silence. 'Well, you don't have to, lad. It's not really the thing fellers of your age want to do. You won't be upset, will you, Katherine?'

'No, of course not. As you said, what possible interest could a lad of Alfie's age have in a house?'

Maggie cast a grateful look at Katherine.

'Has it got a garden?' Ceppi asked.

'I think there's a bit at the back, we didn't see it but would you like it if it did?'

Ceppi deliberated. Very few of the girls she went to school with had gardens. 'I would so.'

'Then we can grow all kinds of flowers, daffodils in spring, roses in summer and a few shrubs for the autumn and winter.'

Frank raised his eyes to the ceiling. 'I can see us getting no sense out of these three, Alfie lad, they'll be too busy with flowers and the like.'

'You can come and help us,' Ceppi said seriously. She didn't want Frank and Alfie to feel left out.

'Ceppi, after a day's work the last thing we'll feel like is planting flowers.'

Heartened by his father's treatment of him as an equal, a man who wouldn't want to have anything to do with such feminine things as flowers, Alfie nodded in agreement.

'Right, Ceppi, you set the table while I help Maggie or we'll never get up there tonight,' Katherine instructed, thankful that her breaking of the news had gone so smoothly.

Chapter Sixteen

———◆———

KATHERINE'S HANDS WERE shaking a little as she tried to get the key in the lock of the front door.

'Oh, give it here,' Frank said. He turned the key with no difficulty but the door remained closed. 'It's warped, the wood's swollen. I'll put my shoulder to it. Stand back.'

'You be careful, Frank, it might give easily and you'll end up on the floor,' Maggie warned.

It only took one push and the door opened on its creaking hinges.

'A bit of oil on those hinges and a bit shaved off the door and it'll be fine.'

Suddenly Maggie shivered. 'I hope to God that door isn't a bad omen.'

'Don't be such a fool, woman! What nonsense. It's a door that's stuck and that's *all* it is,' Frank told her.

They all trooped into the dismal hall.

'It needs a damned good clean,' Maggie said as her

gaze went rapidly over the walls and stairs.

'Isn't it *huge!*' Ceppi said in almost a whisper.

'You've taken a lot on, Katherine, I hope you know what you're doing,' Frank said doubtfully.

'I do so. It's going to take all the money I have and it will be hard work. I'll have to go on working for a bit. I thought I would be able to give my notice in in about a week, but after furnishing it, I'll need money to tide us over until I get some guests.'

They had all progressed down the hall and into the room where most families lived, the kitchen.

'Well, it's nice and bright but . . .'

'It needs painting and the windows need cleaning, to say nothing about that range. That hasn't seen blacklead for years by the look of it. You'll need to take a wire brush to it, Katherine, to get rid of the rust.'

Ceppi had disappeared and when Katherine called her, the answer came back into the room like an echo.

'Ceppi, where are you?'

'In here. What class of a place is this?' the child asked, emerging from the pantry.

Maggie looked inside at the shelves that ran around the walls and the marble slab where you put things to keep them cool in summer. 'It's a pantry! I've never seen a house with a pantry before. You won't need a food press, there's plenty of room in there. A good scrub and it'll do.'

'We can line the shelves with oilcloth, then they'll only need a wipe over,' Katherine said, poking her head around the door.

They moved on to the front room with the bay window.

'It's *huge*!' Maggie said in awe.

Frank was making a mental note of the state of the window frames and the plaster cornices.

'You'll have to get someone who knows what they're doing to get that back to rights.' He pointed to the ceiling.

'You're never going to have a fire in that, are you?' Maggie asked, pointing at the fireplace.

'Why not? It's the main feature of the room.' Already Katherine was mentally visualising how the room would look after she'd finished it.

'It'll cost you a fortune in coal and what with all the gaslights, you're going to have to go on working for ever to pay the bills!'

'There's another grand room in here,' Ceppi shouted from the hall and they all moved on.

'I'll have this as a dining room. It's nice and bright,' Katherine decided.

Maggie raised her eyes to the ceiling. 'Katherine, I just hope you've not bitten off more than you can chew. Although it's big it's not in the right kind of neighbourhood and when they see it being done up, people might get envious, especially if they're half starved and living on the Parish.'

'I never thought of that. I don't want to upset them.'

'Well, I know I'd get a bit "upset" if it were me.'

Katherine looked pensive. 'I wonder if there's anything I can do to help them, but I wouldn't want them to be thinking it was all a "Lady Bountiful" act. I want them to know me, to understand how I came to be able to do all this. To know what kind of a background I come from. I want them to accept me, Maggie. I was never accepted back in Dublin and I never would have been, not even if I'd given my neighbours every penny I had. Can you understand that, Maggie?'

Maggie nodded. It was important to Katherine, and she *had* been accepted in St Andrew's Street. But even if Alfie hadn't carried on like he had Katherine would have left in the end. This was her dream.

'Of course I understand, luv. Just try to get to know them better first.'

'There's another room here.' Ceppi was darting in and out of doorways.

It was a small room with a window looking out into the street, but it had a black cast-iron fireplace with what looked like ceramic tiles as decoration. Katherine wet her handkerchief and dabbed at one, revealing a cream and russet pattern.

'I could use this as the room where the commercial traveller guests can write up their orders. Cotton lace curtains for privacy and some heavy drapes for winter.'

As they left the room Maggie was shaking her head. It was a very big house and it was going to take some decorating and furnishing.

Their steps sounded loudly on the bare boards of the stairs. Ceppi's footsteps were pattering on the landing above them.

The landing was wide but very dark, only a small window in the side wall giving any light at all.

'God, this is miserable, Katherine.'

'It is so. I wonder what I can do to lighten it up?'

'Can I have this room, Katherine? Can I? Can I, please?'

They all walked into the room Ceppi had chosen for herself. It looked out over a yard and a pocket handkerchief of a garden that was full of weeds.

Katherine and Ceppi peered through the dirty window pane.

'Can I?' Ceppi persisted.

Katherine smiled at her. 'Of course you can, now let's see what else there is.' There were five bedrooms in total, all in the same dilapidated condition – and to their utter amazement, a bathroom with a flush toilet!

Maggie was the first to speak as they gazed around. 'An *inside* toilet! A *bath* and *wash* basin. It said nothing about that in the paper and that Carpenter feller didn't tell us. I'd give my right arm for an inside toilet. No running down the yard in winter, no more flies in their hundreds or the smell in summer.'

'When was it built?' Frank asked curiously, looking at length down the toilet pan and then pulling the handle on the chain. They all gazed at the flow of water.

'I don't know exactly,' Katherine replied. 'I'd say about twenty years ago. The feller who owned it must have been mad to build something like it in this neighbourhood. No wonder no one wanted it, they couldn't afford it, nor could they keep it in a decent state. You'd get four families living quite comfortably in it.

'I told him I was opening a boarding house and I had to sign something when I went to pick up the key: "Single Tenancy". I think that means I *can't* have four families living here, not permanently. No one I can charge rent for. But my guests will only be here for a day or two so I don't think it counts.'

'Well, you've certainly got your hands full, girl,' Frank said.

'We'll manage. A good scrub and you'll begin to see a difference. We'll start tomorrow night, but if you don't mind, Katherine, I'll come tomorrow afternoon and give all those windows a damned good clean,' Maggie offered.

'I could give you a hand, luv, with the heavy work and bits and pieces that need mending,' Frank offered.

'Thank you both. You've been so good to me.'

'We haven't done much, Katherine.'

'You gave me a home and took me into your family – and hearts. You'll never know how much that means to me.'

She couldn't get to sleep that night, planning which rooms she would do first. Then she went onto furniture and colour schemes. She'd have that parlour done in green, different shades of it mixed with cream. She'd have the dining room in varying blues and the 'work room' in warm colours of rust and brown and cream. There were so many rooms to think about that it was just before dawn by the time she had fallen asleep.

When she arrived at work she was pale and there were dark circles under her eyes.

'God, yer look terrible! What's up with yer?' Mavis asked.

'I couldn't sleep. All night furniture and colours kept going round and round in my head. I think I'm going to have to work for longer than I first thought.'

'What's it like then?' Dotty demanded.

'It's very big. Much bigger than I thought it would be.'

'Me da was sayin' that it was built by some rich owld feller years ago who 'ad daft ideas about "livin' with the poor". Me da said 'e didn't live there long; 'e'd soon 'ad enough of living with the likes of us.'

'It can't 'ave been empty fer that long,' Mavis said sceptically.

'No, it's been lived in on and off since then but 'e 'ad it built so well that it 'asn't got inter the state of the other 'ouses in that street.'

'It's badly in need of a good clean. Some of the panes of glass in the back windows are broken and the front and back doors stick. But it's got an inside flush toilet in a proper bathroom.'

They both stared at her in disbelief.

'It 'asn't,' Dotty said at last.

'It *has*!'

'Do yer think Dotty and me could come as payin' guests? A *bathroom*, a *toilet*!'

'I know how you feel, I've never lived in a house that had one.'

Dotty was first to recover her wits. 'Are yer goin' ter paint it or will yer 'ave wallpaper?'

'I'll only have wallpaper in a couple of rooms to start with, I can't afford to do them all. The ceilings are so high too: Maggie said it will cost a fortune in coal. I've been thinking that when I haven't got anyone in, Ceppi and I could just use the kitchen. It's big and light and it's got a pantry.'

'God, what next? Would yer listen to 'er, a pantry! Our kitchen is probably as big as that.'

'It probably is, Dotty. It's much bigger than Maggie's kitchen anyway.'

'Right then, when do yer want us ter come an' clean?' Mavis asked, she being more practical than Dotty.

'Maggie is going down today to clean all the windows, but

192

I hope she doesn't wear herself out. There's so many of them and they are so dirty.'

'We'll make a start termorrow night, won't we, Dotty?'

Now that the idea of helping was a reality Dotty wasn't as enthusiastic.

'*Won't we?*' Mavis laid heavy emphasis on the question.

'Oh, aye, we will.'

'I'll have to leave Maggie some money for cleaning stuff. We'll need scrubbing brushes, buckets, a yard brush and shovel and cloths, scrubbing soap, Jeyes fluid, bleach, washing soda, a wire brush and blacklead for the range.'

'An' a new pair of 'ands if we're using all that. Me nails will be down ter me knuckles,' Dotty said gloomily.

'I've told yer, Katherine, yer'll not get much work out of this one 'ere. She needs a gun let off behind 'er.'

'Oh, shurrup, Mavis! I'm not *that* bad,' Dotty retorted.

'Well, we'll soon see, won't we?'

Dotty glared at Mavis but for once said nothing.

Katherine decided to buy all the things they needed from Lockwood's Hardware shop.

'Are you going to clean the *Mauretania*? You've enough here to do it.'

Katherine laughed. 'No, just a house, thank you. Could you possibly deliver it all?'

'Seeing as you've bought so much I'll get one of my lads to load it into the handcart and push it up. Will later tonight do?'

'That would be grand, thank you, Mr Lockwood. I'd best be getting home. Maggie will start to worry.' Katherine couldn't keep the smile off her face, despite all the hard work awaiting her; she was on her way!

Maggie was stirring a big pan of scouse and Ceppi was setting the table when Katherine got in.

'You're late, luv.'

'I know. I stopped off at Lockwood's for some things; one of his lads will be bringing them up later.'

'And we won't half need them. You should have seen the colour of the water after I'd finished those windows. It was like mud. How long it's been since they were cleaned, God alone knows. It's a good job I'd saved some of those old newspapers of Frank's.'

'Why so?'

'They give the windows a good shine, it's something to do with the black print on them.'

'Mavis and Dotty will come around tomorrow night. Even though they've got boyfriends, they're going to help. Mavis told Dotty to tell her feller that she was going to give their usual night out a miss this week.'

Maggie wondered if Katherine ever noticed that both her friends were courting and she wasn't, but now wasn't the time to mention it. Instead she said, 'That's good of them. I know Dotty's mam and she says a lazier kid than their Dotty would be hard to find.'

'I think she'll be all right. Mavis has the knack of getting her moving.'

'I'll tell that to her mam next time I see her. Perhaps she could get some tips from Mavis! Now, could you cut some bread for me, luv? Frank and Alfie will be in any minute.' She lowered her voice so Ceppi, who was avidly curious about everything, couldn't hear. 'Our Alfie's taking it hard. He tries to put on a brave face, but I know what he's thinking and feeling.'

'Oh, I hate to see him so miserable, I really do.'

'So do I but it's for the best. Here they come, pass those bowls over to me. Frank, take those boots off in the scullery and you too, Alfie. I've not long mopped it.'

Mutterings came from the tiny scullery.

'I suppose you'll be asking to see the state of our hands, like kids,' Frank replied.

Maggie cast her eyes to the ceiling. 'I might just do that!' As they sat down to eat Ceppi started up again with her endless questioning. When could they move? As always Katherine gave the same answer. 'When it's clean and we've got some furniture.' It was an answer that Ceppi wasn't satisfied with.

'When will that be?' she asked doggedly.

'I don't know! For heaven's sake, Ceppi, will you have a bit of patience because I'm losing mine with you.'

'Well, can I come and help with the cleaning?' Although she'd been promised a bedroom, actually having and sleeping in it seemed to be a long way off.

'You can come on Saturday afternoon, but you'll have to work as hard as everyone else.' Katherine glanced at Maggie, who nodded. If they managed to wear Ceppi out then she wouldn't want to come again.

'We're going to have to light a fire in that range for hot water, but God knows what state the chimney's in; it probably hasn't been swept for years and years.'

Lyn Andrews

'Maybe we'll do that first, before we start to try to put water on to boil.'

'I'll go down tomorrow morning and call in to see the sweep on my way. If he's not booked up I'll get it done. There's no sense in having smoke get into every room.'

'I didn't know Maggie Boland knew me mam,' Dotty said suspiciously next day.

'Neither did I until last night,' Katherine replied.

'Yer see, Dotty, yer reputation's known fer being a lazy little madam.'

'I'm bloody not! I can work with the best when I feel like it.'

'Then yer'd better "feel like it" ternight. We might as well leave our overalls on ter go down there.'

Mavis had brought sandwiches and as soon as Dotty noticed them her face fell.

'What's up with yer now?' Mavis demanded.

'I never thought ter ask me mam ter do me some butties.'

'Ah, don't worry about that, Dotty. I told Maggie you were both coming to help so there'll be something to eat to give us the energy. Then she'll see that Frank and Alfie are fed before we all leave.'

Dotty looked pleased. All she would have got on her mam's butties was dripping.

'What is it then, fer tea, I mean?'

'Blind scouse iffen ye're lucky,' Mavis answered tartly.

'It's not. Maggie always manages to have meat in the stews. I think it's liver and onions and mashed potatoes.'

'That should give yer energy, Dotty – it'll do it fer me,

196

we only 'ave meat four times a week. Sunday roast, Monday cold meat an' potatoes, Tuesday scouse. Wednesday and Friday we 'as fish, Saturday it's a bit of a fry-up and Thursday it's cold meat.' Mavis's menu for the week was the same as most, but it differed in one thing. There was no salt fish for the traditional Liverpool Sunday breakfast.

'Yer weren't joking when yer said it was big an' it was dirty. I've never seen the like in me life. This muck will take some shiftin',' Mavis said grimly as she looked around.

'It will,' Maggie agreed. 'At least we can start now, but I had to get the sweep. At first he said he was busy, but I told him where the house was and he said he'd always wanted to see inside the place so he fitted us in.'

'Was it bad?'

'Bad! I've never seen so much soot and there were two dead starlings and their nest stuck up there. Imagine if I'd have lit a fire, the place would have been full of smoke. We'd all be gasping for breath and the place would be worse than it is.'

'It was good that you did call him. And those windows! You couldn't see through them they were so dirty, now they're just grand,' Katherine praised Maggie's efforts.

'Right then, what do you want to do? A room each or all of us working on one room at a time?'

Mavis glanced across at Dotty. 'I think all of us in one room.' That way she could keep her eye on Dotty to avoid any shirking.

'Then let's get going with the hall and if we've got time we'll make a start on that big room with the bay window. It doesn't get dark until it's nearly eleven o'clock,' Maggie said.

'Just 'ow many rooms are there?' Dotty demanded.

'Twelve, counting the hall and landing and the bathroom,' Katherine replied.

''oly Mother of God! We'll all be fit fer nothin'.' Seeing the expression on Maggie's face Dotty carried on, 'Not that I'm complainin' or anythin', like.'

'Once we've got it clean, then she's going to have a couple of rooms wallpapered. Our Frank and Mick Irving will whitewash the rest.'

'Ye're goin ter 'ave ter spend a fortune on furniture, Katherine.'

'I know. That's why I'll have to go on working. I'll just get the kitchen and a bedroom for me and one for Ceppi sorted out first, then we'll move in.' She glanced at Maggie, who nodded. She was doing the right thing for Alfie. She'd hated the whole sorry episode. He was only a boy; he had his whole life ahead of him. If he didn't see her for a while, a long while, she was sure he'd get over it all.

Chapter Seventeen

FOR A WEEK they all scrubbed and polished and cleaned, and all the activity had not gone unnoticed. On Friday evening when she'd at last finished Katherine closed the front door behind her and, turning, saw a group of women standing watching her. She decided that now was a good time to introduce herself to her neighbours.

'I'm Katherine Donovan, I'm renting this house. It's been empty for quite a while, so I believe.'

She was met with a stony silence.

'I . . . I'm going to make it into a sort of boarding house, for travelling salesmen.'

'On yer own?' one of the women asked.

'No, I have one of my neighbours' children living with me. Ceppi, she's nine.'

She took a deep breath. She had to keep trying, she didn't want her life here to be as solitary as it had been in Dublin. She stared at the grim expressions and suddenly the memory

199

of that terrible night in her father's house came back. No, that would *never* happen again. If she had to plead and beg and grovel she'd do it. She wanted these women to like and accept her and any help or relief from the terrible blow fate had dealt them that she could provide.

'I come from the slums of Dublin and conditions are as bad there as they are here. I'm only renting the house. I could never buy it. I could never buy anything.'

'Then 'ow did yer get the money ter rent it?'

'I worked. I've worked all my life and I've saved every half penny. Having a boarding house was just a dream, but a dream I held on to every step of the way.'

'An' where do yer live now?' another woman asked.

'St Andrew's Street.'

'Are yer sure yer 'aven't come inter a fortune?'

'No. As I've said I work and I'll still go on working at Bryant and May's until I get the place fixed up. I . . . I heard what happened to your husbands and sons and I'm very, very sorry. I know what it's like to live with poverty and grief and I hope that there is something I can do to help you, all of you—'

'We don't take charity,' the oldest of the women said tartly.

'I know that, but I'm sure there's some way we can help each other.'

None of them answered so with a short farewell Katherine turned away. It wasn't going to be easy but she would never stop trying.

'You're going to have a time of it with that lot!' Maggie said after Katherine had relayed the events to her.

'I think they'll come round.'

'I wouldn't count on it. They're bitter, very bitter and with good reason too. No one cares about them. Their men were only stokers, the lowest of the low, but the first to go, God rest them. Down there in the stokehold they didn't stand a chance. These poor souls haven't even got a grave to visit and that makes it all the worse. They're making ends meet as best they can but on the Parish that's no joke,' Maggie said sadly.

'Well, you've got ter agree it looks a damned sight better now,' Mavis said the following weekend as she stood back to admire the scrubbed boards and clean windows in the hall. Frank and Mick Irving and Bernard O'Brian had given the windows, gutters, downspouts and front door of the house a fresh coat of paint and had whitewashed the hall, the bathroom and two bedrooms.

'It does,' Katherine agreed. It seemed lighter and she wasn't going to give in to everyone's advice about green paint and bugs. 'Now I can start to buy things.'

'What about curtains?' Maggie asked.

'There's a woman at the top of our street, Mrs Savage, she's a widow, she does sewing. Will I ask Mam to see her?'

'Thanks, Dotty, that would be a help. I'm getting no peace with Ceppi wanting her own room. She's driving us all mad.'

'Where will yer go fer the stuff, like?' Dotty asked.

'I'll go with her to London Road, they have the best second-hand furniture shops there,' Maggie answered. 'And if I go with her I can beat them down on the price.'

'I don't know where to start. I need so much, even just for a couple of rooms.'

'I'd get a big table an' chairs an' a couple of easy chairs fer that kitchen, as well as pots and pans an' the like,' Mavis advised. 'Yer can make it inter a living room.'

'And yer'll need beds an' bedding an' rugs an' wardrobes,' Dotty added.

Maggie sighed. 'She'll be having to go to a moneylender herself if she—'

'I'd *never* do that. *Never!*' Katherine interrupted heatedly. 'I know what they charge. Da was one and I saw the misery he caused and I'm not getting involved with the likes of them!'

'That's all very well, but we 'as ter pawn things, it's sort of a way of life. The Sunday clothes go in on Monday mornin' and come out on Saturday. Even me mam who's got a fairly steady wage comin' in 'as ter go,' Dotty informed them.

Maggie had commandeered the help of half the men in the street to bring home everything she and Katherine had bought. Things were reasonably priced for second-hand stuff but she'd managed to beat the dealers down, seeing that they'd bought so much. The men were told that they were to bring it all home.

'Bloody hell, Frank, it would have been easier to have hired old Dobson's horse and cart for that lot. How the hell are we going to get it all back? We'll be backwards and forwards all bloody day.'

Bernard looked at the list Maggie had given Frank. It started with items they'd bought and each shop they'd been purchased in.

'I know. Our Maggie argued and argued, she said, but

none of them will deliver because they bought stuff from other shops! Christ! Would yer believe it? And them rolling in money. Scared to death of one another's business.'

'Well, Bernard's got a point, why don't we ask old Dobson? He doesn't work Saturdays, he stops off at the Unicorn and is paralytic by dinnertime. It's a good job the horse knows its own way home.'

Maggie and Katherine and Ceppi waited in the empty house until Frank appeared.

'Where's the stuff?' Maggie demanded.

'Still up there in the shops, and before you get all airyated, Mick's going to see about borrowing old Dobson's horse and cart. There's too much stuff for us to move; even with a fleet of handcarts we wouldn't get it all here before they close and you know as well as I do that we haven't *got* a dozen handcarts. We'll have to make a couple of trips even with a horse and cart.'

'And just what do you think we're going to be doing here waiting for you? That's if you don't join Percy Dobson propping up the bar, his favourite occupation on Saturdays – the busiest day of the week for most people!'

Katherine thought it wisest to intervene. 'When you get back we can sort out the things you've brought and put them in the rooms where they're needed, and we can arrange them the way we want. Can you bring the kitchen things first, please?'

Katherine was right to ask for the kitchen stuff, Maggie thought. At least they could make themselves a cup of tea. She had a fire in the range even though it was a hot summer's day and they were all perspiring with their efforts.

'And no going and asking for "a smell of the barmaid's apron"!' Maggie warned.

'I'll have one pint with Mick, Bernie and old Dobson and that's it, I promise. It's hot out there,' Frank answered.

'It's flaming well hot in here too, but are we complaining?' Frank looked at Mick and they both left.

By eight o'clock they were all exhausted, hungry and thirsty, but the beds were up and made. The lino had been laid in the rooms Katherine was going to use first. The rugs in the kitchen and bedrooms were down. A big square table and six chairs dominated the kitchen but looked well. All the pots and pans hung beside the range and the blue-and-white delftware dishes (enough to cater for a small army as Maggie had described the dinner service) were in the pantry – for the time being. She'd get a dresser soon and hopefully some curtains. She had cotton lace ones in the bedrooms, on loan from Maggie until she could get her own, and she'd borrowed a pair of draw curtains for the side window that overlooked the street from Dotty's mam, who had come to admire her daughter's handiwork and was heard to comment under her breath something about getting their Dotty to do as good a job at home. Dotty had glared at her back and muttered that this was what became of people not minding their own business.

Katherine and Ceppi were to move in the following weekend when she had more of the necessities of life, for there was still a lot to buy.

Exhausted after working so hard in sweltering heat, they all sat outside in the yard on upturned empty paint cans, orange boxes and a rusty old bucket. Katherine had brought some bottles of beer and Maggie had tea and sandwiches for them all.

'I suppose this is where you'll grow your roses then, Katherine?' Frank said, taking a swig of the bottle of beer.

Katherine laughed. 'Not for a while yet.'

Frank was looking round the yard and the piece of scrubby land beyond, which was full of weeds and old bricks and rubbish.

'You know, if you shifted all that rubbish, whitewashed the walls of the yard, dug that lot up and got rid of the weeds, it might well be able to grow some veg. I could have a go at it for you.'

Maggie looked at him in disbelief. 'Since when have you wanted to take up gardening? What the hell do you know about things like that? It's hard enough for me to get you to swill the yard down in summer and then I'm accused of nagging!'

'Bert Brinkley I work with has an allotment.'

'What in God's name is that?' his wife asked.

'A bit of land you can rent from the council and grow things . . .' Frank replied a bit sheepishly as Mick was looking at him in an odd way too.

'Would you listen to him! Bloody allotments it is now when I can't get a hand's turn out of him most of the time!'

Frank, who was now warming to the idea, was sticking to his guns. 'You're always saying I should take an interest in things.'

'Yes, but things around the house and yard.'

'Don't start an argument over it, please?' Katherine laughed but she could see that Frank wasn't going to give up his idea. She wouldn't mind, of course, as long as it was all right with Maggie. They could all have fresh home-grown vegetables. She wasn't concerned about roses, food was far more important.

'Do you think we could dig up some of the yard?' she asked Frank.

'For God's sake, Katherine, don't encourage him!'

'I mean when he has the time. I don't want you falling out over it, but it would save on potatoes and vegetables.'

Maggie nodded slowly. Perhaps it wasn't such a ridiculous idea after all.

Ceppi, who had gone out to play with the other kids in the street, to get to know them better, now appeared with a young girl of her own age. She was dressed in a faded print dress that was too short for her and had a pair of broken-down old shoes on her feet.

'This is Nancy Maynard. Can I bring her in to play?'

'Of course you can,' Katherine answered.

'Her da was drownded when that big ship sank. Nearly all of the kids had brothers and das drownded.'

'Drowned,' Katherine corrected her before smiling at the other child. 'I know. I'm very sorry, Nancy.'

She exchanged glances with Maggie. It was good that Ceppi had found a playmate. They knew she still missed Mary and they suspected the friendship wouldn't last. When Nancy saw how much more Ceppi had of everything then the child's mother would put a stop to it.

'Give Nancy those last butties and that drop of tea,' Katherine instructed. The child's face brightened and Katherine's eyes misted. Nancy reminded her forcefully of

Ceppi before she'd brought her to Liverpool, but poor Nancy's future wasn't at all rosy, not unless she could find some way to help without it being seen as charity. The wives and mothers of Lonely Street had their pride and she respected that.

Everyone came to give a hand on moving day. Frank, Ida and Mick Irving, Edna and Bernard O'Brian, Mavis, Dotty and again, surprisingly, Dotty's mam.

'I don't know what your one has come for this time,' Katherine said to Maggie.

'I do. Apart from seeing the miracle worked on her Dotty, she's the neighbourhood gossip.'

'Well, is that so bad? I'm glad of every pair of hands,' Katherine replied, wiping the perspiration from her forehead. It was so hot and it was only just after noon. They had the whole scorching afternoon to get through.

She'd managed to get to London Road after work one day, when some of the shops stayed open late. She'd bought a kitchen dresser, a sofa, and two armchairs covered in tan-coloured leather. The leather had cracked in places, but nothing a good polishing with beeswax wouldn't cure, Maggie had remarked. Mrs Savage had been down and measured for curtains in all the rooms although Katherine had explained she couldn't afford to have them all made yet. But she had bought a lot of material and more rolls of lino for the hall, landing, parlour and dining room. She would have the stairs carpeted and buy a matching runner for the hall. There was a hallstand with a mirror and a drawer, and a shallow brass tray at the bottom for wet umbrellas. She'd also bought a large brass mantel clock, wondering as she did so if she was mad when she needed so many other things. She'd ordered almost a ton of coal which was very cheap during the summer months. It would, she hoped, last her quite a long time in winter.

The kitchen was where everyone congregated for tea and fish and chips. Ceppi and Nancy had been sent with the money and a huge bowl to Black's Chip Shop while Katherine cut slices of fresh bread and butter. As Maggie was making the tea Katherine realised that she would have to buy a much bigger kettle and teapot. She also noticed how Nancy crammed the food into her mouth.

'Well, it looks like a home now, Katherine,' Edna remarked.

'It's a start.'

'How soon will yer be takin' in payin' guests?' Dotty's mam asked.

'I don't honestly know. I've nearly used up my savings and the place is still far from ready.'

'Yer'll 'ave ter charge enough ter keep the place goin',' Dotty's mam said, hoping Katherine would tell her how much she intended to charge. But one look at Maggie's face silenced her.

'It's got more than we 'ave,' Mavis said, a little enviously.

Katherine sighed. 'I know and if it was just for Ceppi and me I wouldn't need a quarter of it, but . . .'

'What about the neighbours?' Dotty's mam asked.

'What about them?' Maggie demanded.

'I know what you mean,' Katherine intervened. 'It will take them a long time to accept me. A young, single girl being able to afford a place like this and furnish it when they've lost everything. I wish to God there was something I could do.'

Surprising everyone, Mavis made a suggestion. 'Yer could start a tontine or a Christmas club.'

'A what?' Katherine asked.

'Yer start collectin' a couple of pence every week, more if they can afford it, then when the time comes, they've gorra few bob to spend. Did yer never 'ear of that before?'

'No, I didn't. It's a good idea but we've not all that long to Christmas.'

'Six months – half a year is long enough, and iffen . . .'

'If what?'

'Iffen yer started it off with a couple of bob of yer money they might just agree.'

Katherine stared at Mavis, then nodded decisively. 'Nancy, tomorrow after Mass will you ask your mam if I can go and speak to her? The sooner we get this tontine thing going the better.'

'God Almighty, Katherine, don't you think you've enough on your plate as it is?' Maggie asked.

Katherine shook her head. 'No, we'll manage,' she said stubbornly.

'But this place on its own will keep yer occupied,' Maggie insisted, taking off the pinafore and rolling down her sleeves.

'I know that, but I'm young and stronger than I look and besides, it's important for both Ceppi and me to sort of "fit in".'

'Katherine, just look at yourself. Even in that old dress and apron you're better dressed than most of them. You've got stockings and shoes, they're lucky to have an old pair of boots. When you're dressed up to go out anywhere you'll only make them feel worse about themselves.'

'Isn't that all the more reason to want to help?'

'Oh, I can see it's no use trying to change your mind. Work yourself into the ground if you want to.'

'If it means I can help then I will. Mind you, I can't see them trusting me with their money. I *am* a stranger and their few pennies are hard come by.'

'They are. Try to get one of *them* to keep the money, that's your best chance,' Maggie advised.

'I think you're right, Maggie.'

'At least you'll take *some* advice!'

Katherine smiled. 'Sure, I'm not an eejit!'

After Mass Katherine changed into one of her shabbier dresses and went down to see Mrs Maynard. The front door was wide open but she knocked hard on it just the same. She knew that everyone's doors were always open but she was a stranger in this street and viewed with suspicion.

Nancy herself came to the door.

'Me mam says will yer wait a minute an' she'll be out ter see yer. I told her it was you.'

'Thanks. Now why don't you go and play with Ceppi?'

The child flashed a smile and then ran up the street thinking that perhaps there would be something to eat.

Katherine waited. It wasn't too hot as this side of the street didn't get the sun until late afternoon. She sniffed and then sighed: what she smelled was the too familiar odour of poverty and need. Her mind went back to Dublin. There had been nothing, absolutely nothing she could have done to help her neighbours there and she'd often fumed at her impotence. Now she was determined to help.

When she heard footsteps in the dark lobby she smoothed back her hair and straightened her skirt, although neither needed attention.

'Mrs Maynard?'

'Yes. What do yer want from me? Our Nancy 'as told me how ye're fillin' that 'ouse with lino an' furniture.'

'I *did* tell you why I need all that stuff.'

Nancy's mother crossed her arms over her chest. 'Oh, aye, yer did.'

Katherine plunged on. 'I've come to see if I can start a tontine for Christmas. I'll join it too. It's not going to be all money, money in my house.'

Lizzie Maynard looked at her suspiciously. 'Don't try an' pull the wool over my eyes. Yer'll 'ave plenty of money comin' in. Do yer know 'ow much us widows get? I'll tell yer. Nothing. Bloody nothing.'

'I know, it's a living disgrace. Your men risked death or injury every time they went away, that's bad enough to live with, but when it actually happens and you don't get a penny, it's criminal. Have you tried to get anything?'

'What fer? The likes of us will get nothin'.'

'You should try. I could write to the White Star Line myself, and try to find someone with authority to speak for you.'

'It'll be a waste of time. They won't care iffen we starve or freeze in winter and the kids 'ave no boots or 'ardly a rag to their backs.'

Faced with such pessimism, Katherine decided to leave that issue and pursue the original reason for her visit. 'About the tontine? I don't expect that you'll all trust me with your money, I wouldn't blame you in the least, so would *you* collect and keep it, please? I don't want to appear pushy or hardfaced, because I'm neither, but it would help us all to have a few extra shillings saved for Christmas.'

Lizzie Maynard looked at her hard. She was a strange girl, with some strange ideas, but she acted and sounded as if she were genuinely concerned, and they all needed extra money, God alone knew how much. She nodded slowly. 'I'll talk ter them all an' then iffen they agree I'll collect the money, yours as well.' She paused, and suddenly became uneasy.

'Yes, collect mine too,' Katherine said, hoping to learn what was bothering the woman.

'Yer'll 'ave ter keep the book, like.'

Katherine understood. Nancy's mam couldn't read or write the names and addresses of her neighbours but was too proud to say so.

'Of course I'll keep the book. We can sort it out together, say once a fortnight. You can deal with the actual money side of things and I'll do the boring bit, entering it all in the book.' She smiled. 'We'll call it "Doing the Accounts". Doesn't that sound grand?'

For the first time Katherine saw a glint of a smile in the older woman's eyes and inwardly she felt relieved. She hoped she had taken the first step to lessen the distance between them.

Chapter Eighteen

⁂

FOR THE REST of June and part of July Katherine continued to work and save and gradually get the house sorted, but what she really loved was the peace of her new home. In the long, warm evenings she would sit on the stairs and watch the last rays of sunlight coming in through the glass panels of the front door. The prisms of light were multi-coloured and the specks of dust they carried looked like tiny coloured beads. She liked the light paintwork, no matter what Maggie said; she would keep to light colours in all the rooms in the house. She almost had enough to start up her business and she'd paid a proper painter and decorator to come in and finish the rooms she'd need. Frank had advised her on that.

'The likes of me or any feller in the street hasn't got a clue about hanging wallpaper—'

'Don't we all know that,' Maggie had interrupted.

Frank had ignored her. 'Although we're great at slapping a coat of whitewash around the house.'

'And didn't yourself and the others make a grand job of the bathroom and the other rooms you did for me,' Katherine had added.

'But you'll need someone whose trade it is. I'll ask around.'

She and Ceppi used the kitchen as a living room. She had had the walls in the parlour wallpapered in cream with a tiny diamond pattern in light green. There was lino, the pattern of which made it look like highly polished wood. There was a decent rug on the floor. Cotton lace curtains and the heavy dark green draw curtains, made by Mrs Savage, now covered the bay window. The curtains had been lined to give them more body and would help to keep out the draughts in winter. Besides the leather three-piece suite there were two winged armchairs both covered in dark green tweed and all had comfortable and colourful cushions. There was a small table and fancy glass mantles over the gas jets. She'd even acquired some small ornaments for the mantelpiece to complement the clock. Their reflection in the mirror above the fireplace pleased her. There were two pictures on the wall, both of rural scenes, and a small footstool was placed beside the brass fender.

'You know, you've got a sense of, oh, I don't know . . . you just seem to know what goes with what,' Maggie had commented as Katherine had shown her her handiwork.

'Do you not think the jardinière and aspidistra are a bit too much? Do they make the place look cluttered? Men don't like rooms to be too fancy.'

'Don't talk daft, it's just right and that jard . . . jar . . . the thing with the plant on top of it looks very . . .' Maggie paused while she searched for the right word. 'Very tasteful,' she finished. 'Where did you get it?'

'In Great Homer Street market and the job I had in getting it home in one piece! It was cheap because it's got a few chips in it but I added to them getting it home and the plant took a bit of a battering too.'

As yet the dining room had only a second-hand table that was scratched and which she'd covered with a white tablecloth. There were six chairs to go with it. They weren't new but they polished up well. She did have curtains at the window but the room was more functional than decorative, for the time being.

The small room that overlooked the street had a rug in front of the empty fireplace and three card tables with green baize tops. There was a chair for each one. Each table had a large ashtray, a cheap pen and a sheet of blotting paper on it. The curtains she'd borrowed were now a fixture as Dotty's mam said she might as well keep them. She hadn't bought them, they'd been a gift, and were a bit impractical.

'You've got every comfort. Are you sure you're not going to make them too comfortable?' Maggie asked.

Katherine laughed as she led the way to show Maggie the three bedrooms she had done up. They were all identical. The off-white wallpaper had a blue stripe which matched the curtains and the rug beside the bed. The beds were all single ones and had sheets and blankets as well as a quilt. There was a small bedside table, a combined wardrobe and chest and a frosted glass mantle over the gas jet.

'I think I'll come and rent a room myself. You must have spent a fortune.'

'Not really, I shopped around and bargained. The most expensive things were the beds themselves and the bedding and extra towels for the bathroom.'

'That's what I mean, too comfortable. A bathroom they can go to in the warmth of the house in winter and no smells or flies in summer. If we all had one, even if it was still outside, I'm sure there wouldn't be so much disease.'

Katherine sighed. 'Will that day ever come? I certainly have spent a fortune on cleaning things. I seem to use gallons of bleach and Aunt Sally,' she said, using the brand name of the liquid soap that came in bottles.

'What will you call it? The House on Lonely Street?'

'God, no! That would put them off. I was after thinking of something like "Donovan's Commercial Boarding House".'

Maggie looked thoughtful. 'Say it again?'

Katherine repeated it.

'Yes . . . yes, that sounds good. I like the "Commercial" bit. How will you find the people, these commercial travellers?'

'I'll advertise. I'll put a postcard in one of the shops in Mount Pleasant.'

'What'll you say?'

'Oh, something like "Donovan's Commercial Boarding House. A Home from Home. Five shillings a night, breakfast and evening meal included". That's a bit less than Mrs Taylor charged and she wouldn't put herself out for you.'

'Serves her right if you take business from her and the rest of that lot up there. How's the tontine going?'

'Very well. I started it off with a pound and Lizzie Maynard collects in the pennies, whatever they can afford, which isn't much. She keeps the book with the money and at the end of the month she comes here and I fill it in, and we work out roughly how much everyone will have by Christmas. At least this year they'll have a bit more than they did last year, so Lizzie says.'

'You've done better than I thought you would with them in this street.'

. 'They were in a desperate state. Lizzie is slowly beginning to accept me. Of course she's envious of all the comforts we have here – but I would be myself – she wouldn't admit it and I told her I'd been more than fortunate having a bit of money left to me. Do you know, she won't even have a cup of tea off me?'

'That's carrying pride a bit too far.'

'I know but what can I do? I'm hoping one or two of the others will help out with the cleaning and the washing and ironing when I get this place up and running properly.'

'There was nothing from the shipping people then?'

'Not a single word but I'm not giving up. Do you remember Mr Carpenter?'

Maggie nodded.

'Well, I'm going to go and ask him if he'll help or if he can recommend someone. No one's going to take any notice of me, I've not even lost a man.'

'Katherine, they'll charge.'

'I don't care. When I see the likes of little Nancy and the rest of the children my heart goes out to them. Their das and brothers all dead and their mammies worried sick about trying to feed them and keep a roof over their heads.'

'Well, if you want I'll come with you when you decide to go to see that feller.'

'Thanks, Maggie.'

'I still think you're doing too much.'

'How can I not help?'

'You must be the only one who will try.'

'That's as may be.' She changed the subject, not wanting to dwell on what she was doing for Lonely Street. 'Now I'd better write out my little advertisement.'

'I'll be off then. Here's hoping they all come knocking on your door . . .' Maggie hesitated.

'What's the matter?'

'I . . . I just want to say this quickly because I don't want to keep on about it.'

Katherine looked at her curiously. 'What?'

'Is it "proper" for a young unmarried girl to go taking men in, however respectable they are?'

Katherine sighed. 'Probably not, but I don't care and anyway I've got Ceppi with me and there'll be all kinds of people popping in and out once I give up work.'

'I just thought I should mention it, luv, that's all. You'll have to be very strict about who you take in.'

'I know.'

'Why don't you send for Frank to give them the "once over"? That way they'll know you're not entirely alone without a man to call on in times of necessity?'

Katherine nodded. 'It's a good idea. Will you ask him?'

'I won't have to, he brought the subject up.'

She placed her neatly written advertisement in the window of Sullivan's, knowing that most men went there for their cigarettes or pipe tobacco, but she still didn't give up her work. She told herself she'd give her notice in any day now. There was still a doubt in her mind as to whether these men would be happy about the area the house was in.

''Ow soon will yer know, like? Iffen any of them fellers are interested?' Dotty asked.

'I'll not get anyone at the weekend, but maybe Monday or Tuesday morning.'

'I wish it were me, Katherine, yer own place and done up all fancy like that,' Mavis said wistfully.

'But we won't lose touch, you'll both have to come down once a week to keep me up to date with all the gossip.'

'That won't be much,' Dotty said gloomily. She was going to miss Katherine.

'Well, come just the same.'

'We won't be dumpin' ourselves on yer every week; every couple of weeks will do.' Mavis was just as gloomy.

'I'm going to meet Maggie in Dale Street on Monday afternoon.'

'Are yer *still* goin' on with writin' about the women in yer street?'

'I am. They deserve someone to help them.'

'Sometimes I think ye're clean around the bend, Katherine. Boarding 'ouses, letters to shippin' companies . . .'

'I'm hoping to succeed with both of them.'

'We 'ope yer do, but don't be disappointed iffen yer don't.'

'I won't fail. When I was growing up I learned to hold my own. I'm not a silly, empty-headed bit of a girl, you know.'

'Ye're definitely not that. Yer've more sense an' guts than a lot of fellers 'ave, mine included,' Mavis stated.

*

On Monday as arranged she met Maggie at the tram stop in Dale Street and again climbed the dark narrow stairs to the offices of Marsden, Carpenter and Yeates.

Mr Carpenter was surprised to see them again but pleased too. He'd liked Katherine.

'I'm very pleased to see you both again, ladies.' He looked from one concerned face to the other and raised his eyebrows questioningly.

'Thank you, but it's not over a house this time,' Katherine said.

'Oh, I rather thought it was. Perhaps hoped it was.' He smiled.

She smiled back at him. He was a very nice man really once you got past the stiff, formal appearance. 'Maybe one day, but not for a long time yet. I've got the place done out and I'm just waiting to see if I get any replies to my advertisement.'

'It's like a little palace now, sir, it really is. They'll be standing in line at her front door,' Maggie informed him with pride.

'I'm sure it's grand. So what can I help you with this time?'

'Kildare Street is known locally as "Lonely Street" because nearly every man who lived there went down with the *Titanic* and their widows and mothers haven't had a single penny from anyone to help out.'

He shook his head sadly. He knew that the King had some ideas about setting up a fund for women such as those Katherine was talking about, but it was only talk and he wouldn't raise her hopes. 'Tragic. Utterly tragic, the whole affair.'

'I've written to the company but I've not heard anything and I was wondering if . . . well . . . if . . .?'

He was surprised. He knew what she was trying to say. 'You would like me to write?'

'Or someone else, sir, if you feel you can't.'

'It's a very worthy cause, Miss Donovan. It was all in the papers at the time, the deaths of the Black Gang, the stokers and trimmers. But it isn't "news" any longer, and so they're forgotten. But I think you should have someone more qualified than I am to take up their cause. It's a solicitor you need and they cost money. A good deal of it, I'm afraid.'

'About how much money, sir?'

'I would estimate twenty or thirty pounds if there was no initial settlement.'

She was stunned. She didn't have money like that. 'I don't have nearly enough money. I used all my savings on the house.'

He was thoughtful, turning the pencil he was holding around and around in his hand. 'Leave it with me and I'll see what I can do to get someone interested. It's a deserving cause and I'm sure the owners wouldn't wish for more bad publicity at this time.'

'I'd be very grateful for any help. Just a letter would do, at least it would be *something*,' Katherine pleaded.

'Can you call back and see me, say, Wednesday?'

'I can so, sir, it's very good of you to offer.'

He smiled, wondering if she realised what a fine-looking girl she was . . .

'Do you really think that feller can do something?' Maggie asked when they were once more in the street.

'I hope he can. At least, I can tell Lizzie that I've talked to him about it.'

As soon as she got home she changed, had a quick cup of tea and then went down the street to see Lizzie. She always knocked; it had become a sort of ritual of respect for the older woman.

'It's me, Katherine,' she called down the lobby.

'Well, don't stand there clutterin' up me bit of a doorstep, come in,' Lizzie called back.

She had been in the house before and on every occasion she tried not to notice the lack of furniture and home comforts. Lizzie did her best and had her pride. She was stirring a big pan on the range.

'It's blind scouse. I couldn't afford ter put meat in it, not even scraps, and the veg is mostly fades, but it's somethin'.'

Katherine sighed. It was a home like this that Ceppi had come from. 'I don't want to get your hopes up, but I've been into town to see the estate agent who helped me with the house and I asked him would he or someone else take up your case. I couldn't afford the thirty pounds a solicitor would charge, but he's going to try to help. I've got to go back and see him on Wednesday.'

Lizzie stared at her. 'THIRTY POUNDS!' She was scandalised.

Katherine nodded.

'Yer'd get a letter from the Pope fer less than that!'

'I probably would but let's hope this person Mr Carpenter knows can help. We'll just wait and see. Will you tell the others, please?'

'I will.'

222

Katherine rose. 'I'll let you know as soon as I hear anything, good or bad.'

'Thanks. Oh, by the way, thanks for them things yer gave our Nancy. She was made up with them.'

Katherine smiled. They were clothes she'd bought at Paddy's Market in Great Homer Street but she'd told Nancy they were things Ceppi either couldn't or wouldn't wear. The child had been delighted and she'd sworn Ceppi to secrecy.

Lizzie was now looking at Katherine closely. She'd never met anyone like her before. She was a stranger – although no one was a stranger in this city for very long – she had money enough to furnish that big old house, and though she couldn't afford to pay that outrageous sum of thirty pounds she was willing to fight their corner anyway.

'Have you always been like this?'

Katherine was puzzled. 'Like what?'

''Elping people, strangers. Our Nancy told me that Ceppi was terrible poor and that her mam was always 'alf drunk.'

'She was. I paid her mother five pounds to bring Ceppi here with me.'

Lizzie was scandalised. ''Oly Mother of God! She *sold* the child?'

'She did so. Now you can see why Ceppi is spoilt – she deserves some fun after the awful time she had in Dublin. I had no brothers or sisters. No friends even, except Ceppi, so please let me do what I can for Nancy and the rest. I know you've all got your pride, but I can't stand by and see your children with no boots or coats in the cold days of winter if I can find the money to help.'

223

Slowly Lizzie nodded. She was an unusual person but you couldn't be offended by her offers of help. Lizzie still didn't know much about Katherine, but she was clearly sincere and respectable.

On Tuesday morning there was a knock on her front door and her heart quickened. Was this her first guest? She automatically patted her hair as she went down the lobby.

A young man was standing on the doorstep. He was tall, slim, fair-haired and was dressed in what had once been an expensive suit, but was now a little shabby. He looked down at her with eyes that were a piercing shade of blue.

'Er . . . Mrs Donovan?'

'Yes, but it's Miss. Have you come about the room?'

He smiled. 'I have. I saw your card in the newsagent's, it's very reasonable for what you are offering: bed, breakfast and evening meal.'

'Come in then and I'll show you around. If you decide to stay we'll have a cup of tea.'

'Are you alone?'

Katherine stiffened, remembering Maggie's words.

'No, I have my niece living with me, she's nine, and there's a sort of "interview" you have to go through before I finally accept you. Mr Frank Boland, the husband of my closest friend, will give you the "once over", so to speak.'

He grinned and gave a mock bow. 'Oh, I'm happy to undergo "fire and sword" for you, Miss Donovan. My name is Edwin Sackville and I sell medical supplies.'

'That's a coincidence! The main street in Dublin is called

Sackville Street. Would you be related to the one they named it after?'

His smile had a hint of amusement in it. 'Not that I know of. It would have been named after someone very illustrious and there's certainly no one like that in my family.'

'Isn't selling medical supplies rather important?'

He laughed. 'No, it's a job like any other. I was a medical student but unfortunately my family fell on hard times and couldn't support me.'

Katherine looked more closely at him. He must have been looking forward to a great future. What a disappointment for him to be reduced to this.

'I'm sorry to hear that.'

He shrugged. 'Ah, well, I really wasn't cut out for all that studying anyway.'

'And are you quite happy with what you do now?'

'Yes, strangely I am. I have more freedom, meet more people but of course I don't earn a great deal. I've stayed in some terrible houses in the past, Miss Donovan.'

'I can believe that. Well, leave your bags in the hall and I'll show you around.'

She took him around the house and he was amazed.

'I've never been anywhere like this before. It *is* a real "Home from Home". Usually it's just a bedroom and a dining room that's provided for you, but a lounge and a writing room, I've never come across either.'

'I saw the commercial travellers when I lived in Mount Pleasant. I stayed there for a few weeks, in a bed and breakfast place. It was a cheerless experience for my fellow boarders so I decided to open my "Home from Home". There will be either a cup of tea or a bottle of beer awaiting you when you come back tonight.'

'Oh, beer, please. You really *are* a treasure.'

She laughed. She didn't think she'd have much trouble with him but Frank would have to see him first.

'You can leave the bags you don't need in your room. They'll be safe. When you come in this evening Mr Boland will be here.'

'That's fine by me. You can't be too careful, a young, and might I venture to say, lovely young lady living in a house full of men.'

Katherine felt the flush creeping up her neck to her cheeks. She'd never been called a 'lady' before.

'There are a couple of other men I know, decent sorts, in the same line of work – although not medical supplies. I'll certainly tell them about this little jewel of a place. You'll have people fighting to get a room here.'

Frank came down after his tea to interview the first of Katherine's guests. He found her with Ceppi and Edwin Sackville in the parlour. Katherine had called earlier in the day to tell Maggie the good news.

'Ceppi, go and play with Nancy and all the others. Take those biscuits with you, they're always starving hungry,' Katherine instructed.

'Right,' Frank started. 'I know you were a medical student and your family lost all their money. How?'

'My father, God rest him, was addicted to gambling. It was like a disease with him, he couldn't stop. He'd gone through a small fortune, as much of Mother's jewellery as he could sell, plus all the silver, and he mortgaged the house. But at last he had to tell my mother and sisters and myself about the huge amount he'd wasted gambling.'

Frank looked grave. 'You said, "God rest him". Why?'

'The truth of the matter is that he shot himself.'

Katherine crossed herself. 'God forgive him.' Suicide was a mortal sin.

'He might, my mother and sisters never will.'

'Where are the rest of your family?'

'Living in genteel poverty in Shropshire.'

'Why did you come to Liverpool?'

'Because I was at the university and I liked Liverpool. People accept you for what you are, there's no side with them.'

'You must have friends here. What would they think?'

'I was only in my first year so fortunately there are no "friends" who could look down their noses at me and criticise.'

'And this job, does it pay well? Enough for you to manage on?'

'Oh, I can pay Miss Donovan, if that's what you mean. It's not a bad job.'

'How often do you come to Liverpool?'

'About once a month for a few days, sometimes more frequently.'

Frank stood up. 'Well, I think you're a safe bet. But I'm warning you, anything, anything at all that upsets Katherine and you'll have me to deal with.'

Edwin Sackville looked at the older man. Frank was strong and wore a thick leather belt around his waist and Edwin was certain that he would have no qualms about using it as a weapon.

'I can assure you, sir, I won't put a foot wrong.'

'Right then, I'm off home.' Frank was flattered; he had never been called 'sir' in his life before. And the lad seemed to be genuine, he was happy about him staying with Katherine.

Katherine showed Frank out and thanked him.

'Then I'm acceptable?' Edwin Sackville asked as she came in from the hall.

She smiled at him. 'You are so. Now, take up your sample case and there'll be a bottle of beer and a glass waiting for you in here and I'll make a start on your meal.'

'Might I have a wash first?'

'Of course you can.'

'I can't get over it, Miss Donovan, it's truly remarkable. I'm being treated better than I was in my own home. I wonder why someone hasn't come up with the idea before? We travellers do miss home comforts.'

'I've only myself and Ceppi to worry about keeping, so I can afford to offer a bit more. And I enjoy making everyone comfortable. It makes *me* happy.'

'What a gift, Miss Donovan, what a gift!'

She just smiled as he went up the stairs.

They were getting on very well, she thought as she watched Ceppi reading aloud from one of her books while Edwin sat and listened. He was still praising Katherine and marvelling at her house.

'You've thought of everything, even down to a sheet of blotting paper.'

'Not quite, the yard and garden are a bit of a mess.'

'Well, we don't want to sit in a garden now, do we? It's

much more comfortable here in the sitting room.' That was the name they'd all decided on. Katherine thought 'lounge' was too grand and he'd said a 'parlour' sounded even more formal. In the end it was Ceppi who came up with 'sitting room'. 'No, you can put up your feet, relax, read the newspaper or swap stories with other guests.' He paused. 'Are you worried about something, Miss Donovan? You seem a bit distracted tonight. If there's anything I can do you only have to say the word.'

Katherine sighed. 'You must have noticed how this house stands out from all the others in the street. There's real poverty in those homes, as bad as any I've lived with in Dublin.'

He didn't seem very interested, Katherine thought, so she went on, 'Do you know why this is called "Lonely Street"?'

'It's a very odd name to give a street. I thought it said Kildare Street in the advertisement.'

'It is officially, but its other name is because there wasn't a husband, brother or son that didn't go down with *Titanic*.'

'Surely not? All of them? It was a dreadful, dreadful tragedy but I understood that there were only first-class and steerage passengers, officers, stewards . . .'

'And the men from this street, this city, who stoked the boilers. The "Black Gang" from Kildare Street.'

'Ah, I understand. A shocking business all round.'

'Tomorrow I've got to go and see someone who may be able to help the widows.'

'A very worthy cause, Miss Donovan,' he answered off-handedly. Katherine thought maybe it was his upbringing. He seemed totally uninterested in the plight of her neighbours.

All the way to Dale Street on the tram she prayed Mr Carpenter would have some good news and when she finally arrived at his office she could tell from his face that her journey hadn't been in vain.

'Is it good news, sir?'

'It is and it isn't.'

She looked bewildered.

'Mr Greenwood, who is a friend of mine and has a little influence with the City Council, has agreed to write, putting the case of the widows and orphans of the men lost to the proper department.'

'Thank you! Thank you so much!'

'Don't get your hopes up, Miss Donovan, it may take a very long time before you get a reply.'

He didn't add that a reply might never come.

Chapter Nineteen

────◆────

I T DID SEEM A long time before she heard from Mr Carpenter, but now she had two other guests she had little time to brood on it. She'd had, as Edwin Sackville had predicted, to turn away four men, explaining that she already had guests for that week, but not without a kindly word and a cup of tea.

She wrote down the address for them and said to keep calling or write in advance as there would be times when she did have vacancies. Not everyone had the same schedule of work. The two she had had room for, Mr Forrester and Mr Dunne, were middle-aged men, quiet, respectful and delighted to come back after a day's work tramping the sweltering streets of the city to a decent bathroom, change of clothes and a drink while Katherine cooked a simple but filling meal for them. Ceppi always laid the table in the dining room which now was a pleasant place, owing to more pictures on the wall and a large sideboard on which the condiments were set out on a small tray. Every single one of them praised her foresight in providing a writing room.

'Many's the time I have had to write up my orders in a dismal, cold room, Miss Donovan,' Mr Forrester had said appreciatively.

Both Mr Forrester and Mr Dunne were only staying two nights this time, but Edwin still seemed in no hurry to move on and she didn't ask why.

At the beginning of the following week Maggie arrived with Eddie.

'I had to bring him with me, he's at that age when he drives you mad, so I can't get anyone to mind him. I can't take my eyes off him for more than two minutes or he's at something he shouldn't be. I can't remember the other three ever being as bad.'

'That's probably because you've forgotten. Come on in and I'll put the kettle on.'

Maggie sat Eddie on one of the kitchen chairs from which he instantly wriggled down and was away across the kitchen to the gleaming copper pans that were hung on hooks by the range.

'Holy Mother! Would you look at him! As slippery as an eel.'

'He's after going for the shiny things.' Katherine laughed and took down a little brass bell from the dresser. 'Come here to me, Eddie, and have this to play with. You'll burn yourself there by the fire.'

Eddie's chubby little fingers closed firmly around the ornament and a look of surprise and wonder came over his face as he heard the tinkling sound.

'Katherine, luv, couldn't you have found something that doesn't make a noise? We'll be tormented with him and probably end up with a headache.'

'Ah, he's no trouble. Will I give him a biscuit?'

'Give him what you like as long as it doesn't make a noise,' Maggie replied a little wearily.

The biscuit had the desired effect and Katherine made the tea.

'Frank said you've three nice gentlemen staying.'

'I have, I've been lucky, and Frank's been very good, Maggie, giving up his evenings.'

'A few hours isn't an evening and we both care and worry about you and milady.'

'Oh, she's taken a liking to Edwin, he sits with her and helps her with her homework. In fact he said to me that she's clever enough to be a doctor one day. As if, I said. No, he said, there are lady doctors. But I said they came from better backgrounds than this and anyway I couldn't afford to pay fees and all the other things. Becoming a nurse would be more practical.'

Maggie looked at Katherine sceptically. 'Can you see that one in a starched apron and cuffs? And she'd have a terrible time keeping all that hair under one of those daft caps they wear.'

Katherine laughed. That was certainly true!

'Have you heard anything yet from Mr Carpenter?'

'No, and time is getting on. I need some money now. Those women need money *now*.'

'Why don't you go and see him again?'

Katherine pondered on this. 'Will you come with me? It's

school holidays and Ceppi needs clothes but I couldn't trust her to sit quietly while I see him. Sure, she'd have the whole place in uproar. You know what she's like, questions, questions. Fortunately Edwin seems to know all the answers.'

It hadn't escaped Maggie's notice that Katherine now referred to her first guest only by his Christian name. 'Is that feller going to become a permanent fixture or what?'

'I was wondering about that myself. The hospitals and doctors can't keep ordering that many supplies. I'm sure he'll need to move on soon. I think I'll ask him tonight when he comes in.'

'I'd do that, luv,' Maggie agreed.

It was hot in the city centre: the buildings seemed to trap and hold the heat and the flowers and shrubs in St John's Gardens were wilting for lack of water.

'I'll be glad of some rain, this weather gives me shocking headaches,' Maggie remarked as they reached Mr Carpenter's building.

The estate agent looked solemn as he asked them both to sit down. Katherine's heart dropped like a stone.

'Mr Greenwood wrote and retrieved a very terse and quick reply, but I'm afraid the reply he received is not the one you wished for. There will be no money forthcoming for the widows of the Black Gang.'

'Not even a shilling or two?' Maggie was outraged.

He shook his head. 'I agree with you both, they should have been compensated, for decency alone, but . . .' He shook his head again.

'Thank you, sir, we're very grateful just the same,'

Katherine said, but she couldn't hide her disappointment.

'Oh, let's go for a cup of tea. My head is pounding,' Maggie suggested as they emerged from the gloomy building.

'There's a Lyon's Corner Café over there; I could do with something myself.'

It was only marginally cooler than the street but Katherine ordered a pot of tea for two and two toasted teacakes.

'Maggie, what am I going to tell them? No matter how many times I've told Lizzie not to get their hopes up, they have and I don't blame them. How can anyone just ignore their plight?'

'Easily, Katherine. Quite easily. What do they care about a couple of dozen stokers and trimmers? Have you an aspirin by any chance?'

Katherine delved into her bag and produced a long strip of paper containing tablets.

'Here, take what you need and I'll have one myself.'

All the way home on the tram Katherine thought about the situation. In the end she decided it would be better to tell them all together. She'd invite them in for a cup of tea and then break the news.

When she arrived home she asked Lizzie to go around and collect some of the women. Not all were in, for some had managed to get a few hours' work cleaning everything from offices in India Building to the public toilets.

She and Maggie moved all the chairs she had into the back yard where it was cooler – as Maggie remarked, the kitchen was as hot as the hobs of hell.

Lizzie had got everyone together but they all looked anxious, hoping against hope that she had some good news.

Katherine passed the mugs and cups of tea around.

'It's not good news, I'm afraid. Mr Greenwood, the friend of Mr Carpenter, wrote on your behalf, putting forward your case for some kind of compensation, but the answer he got back was "No". I'm sorry, so very sorry.'

There was a brief silence and then Lizzie spoke. 'At least yer tried, girl. At least yer care enough about us ter go an' see that feller.'

'I'm sorry I haven't got thirty pounds which is what it would cost for a solicitor. I would have paid it if I had.'

'Jesus! Is that what they charge?' Astounded, Vi Watson rolled her eyes dramatically. 'I've never even seen that much money,' she said. 'I can only remember 'avin' a five-pound note once in my life when Mam died and I got the Burial Club money, but the Co-op are very good.'

'Isn't there *something* we can do?' Lizzie asked.

Katherine looked solemn. 'I'll need someone to help me clean and do the washing and ironing, but I can't afford to pay much.' She paused. 'Did you say the Co-op, Vi?'

'Yes.'

Katherine seemed sunk in thought, a frown of concentration on her face. Then she spoke. 'It might work. Yes, it just might. Why don't we have our own Co-op? We pool everything and then divide everything equally – that way we'll all be sure of the rent and food.'

'Can yer see Cissy Cassidy turnin' up her wages?' Lizzie muttered to one of her neighbours.

'No, I bloody can't,' came the reply.

'It'll only work if we all pull together, if the ones who can afford to put more in do so. I will for a start. I know it doesn't *look* to be very fair but it will be. We've all got to do it.'

Lizzie considered her words. 'I think that if anyone isn't 'appy with it then they just don't join. Let them get on with it an' starve if they 'ave ter. I'd sooner turn it up and know that I'd at least 'ave a roof over me 'ead and food on the table.'

'If there is ever anything over the weekly sum it can be saved and used to buy the kids boots and a coat for the winter,' Katherine suggested.

'Could we sort of borrow fer big things, like quilts an' blankets?' Vi asked.

'God, Vi, let's not go down that road just yet. It's goin' ter be 'ard enough to get everyone ter agree,' Lizzie answered.

'Well, does everyone here want to do it? There're enough of us to start with and maybe when those who don't join see how it's working they can come in on it later.'

Everyone nodded, a few albeit reluctantly.

'I'll put in the same as everyone here,' Katherine promised.

This was the cause of some fidgeting.

'What's the matter now?'

'We don't want charity, Katherine. You don't *need* ter pay. Ye're in a different position altergether,' Vi said at last.

Katherine lost her patience. 'It's not flaming charity! I don't earn a fortune, I have to buy food, cook it, strip the beds and wash the sheets and pay the rent and all the other bills. I've got Ceppi to clothe too and you all know how quickly kids grow out of things.'

'Oh, don't get all airyated about it, Katherine!' Lizzie exclaimed. 'Yer know what Vi means. But iffen ye're sure?'

'I am,' said Katherine firmly.

It was with some reluctance that they all finally agreed.

Katherine worked it out and what each family would get wasn't much but it would pay for the rent, food and coal, but not for extras like clothes.

'What about the Parish? As soon as they 'ear about this we'll get nothin'.'

'We don't bloody tell them and if yer'll keep yer big gob shut, Vi, they'll not find out!' Lizzie said vehemently.

'The Lord 'elps those who 'elp themselves,' someone muttered.

'You're a very strange girl, Katherine,' Lizzie said as they all trooped out.

'Strange? How so?'

'You seem to have good ideas and then you make them work.'

'Maggie said something like that only the other day.'

'Well, it's true. No one thought about turning that 'ouse inter a bit of a decent place fer people to stay in. None of us ever thought about tryin' ter get some money after losing our fellers, and no one thought of this . . . this scheme.'

'Lizzie, I've known poverty, despair and destitution. My da had a pawnshop and he lent money and when he . . . died, I swore I would never ignore other people's misery. With the help of God and a bit of luck, in time we can change the name of this street to "Happiness Street".'

'There'll always be a sadness 'ere, Katherine,' Lizzie said quietly and with that she left.

September brought blessed relief from the sultry heat of August. Katherine's house was always full, except at weekends, and now she had her regulars. She'd heard from them that her venture had caused some anger amongst the landladies of Mount Pleasant.

Edwin had finally paid his bill and left, saying he'd be out of a job if he lingered much longer. She'd miss him and so would Ceppi for he'd always taken time to help her with her school work. He'd told her that studying hard would open lots of doors to her when she was older and she should think about her future. He'd told Katherine that she should think about sending the child to learn typewriting and office skills when she left school at fourteen. Katherine was considering this carefully. It wasn't such a flight of fancy as being a doctor had been.

September also brought the monthly visit of Mavis and Dotty. They had been going to come every fortnight, but they didn't want to be always troubling her when she had her hands full, Mavis had said when the two of them made their first visit, so they came regularly but only every four weeks.

Now they sat in the kitchen and looked around with pleasure at the welcoming, cosy place.

'Do those fellers appreciate all yer do fer them?' Mavis asked.

'Fellers don't appreciate *anything* yer do fer them, except of course iffen yer do what ye're not supposed ter do,' Dotty said tartly.

'That's all she ever thinks about these days, fellers. I keep tellin' her they're useless, even the best of them.'

'Yer sound just like me mam, Mavis.'

'Well, why don't yer take some bloody notice, Dotty? We all *know*.'

'Katherine doesn't,' Dotty shot back. 'Do you?' she added, turning to Katherine.

Katherine paused for a minute before she answered. There were a few seconds of regret that she'd never had someone special in her life. Then she laughed. 'You two never change, always bickering. And I don't have time for "fellers" as you call them.'

'And talking of things "ye're not supposed ter do",' added Mavis, 'do yer remember Maureen Grey? A mousy-lookin' girl, wore 'er 'air parted in the middle, always po-faced.'

'I do so.'

'Well, she's gone an' got 'erself inter trouble. 'Er mam told me mam that 'er da gave 'er a good 'idin' and she still won't say who the father is.'

'Yer wouldn't believe it, would yer? A plain, mousy bit like that. Myself I've 'eard that Ted Morris 'as somethin' ter do with it.'

'Dotty, wash yer mouth out with soap! That's only a rumour and we shouldn't repeat it. God 'elp us all if we had mouths on us like this one 'ere.'

Ceppi appeared and Dotty gave a cry of surprise which diverted Mavis's attention from her.

''Asn't she grown? What 'ave yer been feedin' her, Katherine?'

'Food, food and more food. I don't know where she puts it and she certainly isn't what you'd call bonny.'

'This letter was lying on the hall table,' Ceppi said.

Katherine opened it and scrutinised the few lines. 'It's from Edwin, he says he'll be back next Monday.'

'What's 'e like, this Edwin feller?' Dotty asked.

'He's nice. He speaks very correctly and has perfect manners.'

'What's 'e doin' travellin' around the country?' Dotty demanded.

Katherine told them briefly.

'Is 'e sort of . . . special, then?' Dotty asked.

'Not really. But I do like him.'

'And so do I,' Ceppi chipped in.

Dotty raised her eyes to the ceiling. They'd get no more information about this feller with Ceppi standing there with her ears flapping. 'Do yer think we could just 'ave a birrof a look at them?' she asked cautiously.

'God, Dotty, they're not animals in a flamin' zoo!'

Katherine smiled. 'I'll introduce you but they're all middle-aged men. At this time they're usually writing up their orders.'

Dotty was disappointed, she'd thought one of them might be interesting. 'Oh, don't disturb them then.'

Mavis grinned. 'Yer can read 'er like a book. She was after flirtin' with the younger lodgers.'

'I haven't got any "younger" gentlemen.'

'Except that Edwin feller. Will yer introduce me when 'e's 'ere next?'

'Of course.'

'Dotty, get yer jacket an' put yer 'at on.'

'I'll walk up with you, it's a nice evening. Ceppi, make another pot of tea and take it in. I won't be long.'

''Ow are the neighbours doin' with this Co-op idea?' asked Dotty.

'Who told you that? Jesus, Mary and Joseph, if it's all around the neighbourhood we'll have the authorities down on us.'

'I 'eard Maggie sayin' something about it to Vi,' Dotty replied hastily. 'I didn't mean to listen in. I didn't mean no harm. I only told me mam.'

'So, who's got the biggest mouth around 'ere, next ter Dotty's mam?'

'Dotty's Aunty Vera,' Katherine answered.

'Right first time. This one 'ere can't keep 'er flamin' trap shut and yer know what 'er Aunty Vera's like.'

'I told Mam not ter tell anyone else but she always blabs ter me Aunty Vera. I'm sorry.' Dotty was remorseful.

'Yer shouldn't 'ave said "a few words". Yer shouldn't 'ave said anythin' at all!' Mavis snapped.

'Well, it's starting to work, if you want to know. Lizzie does all the washing and ironing for me and Vi comes in to help clean. There weren't many to start with and there were some fierce arguments too, but lately some of the other women have joined in. There's only three of them who won't and never will join but, as Lizzie says, it's tough if they lose their jobs, they needn't come to us for handouts. We've even managed to save a bit, which is a miracle for every single penny has been worked and sweated for. It's made me really grateful for all the things I have and have always had. We've sorted out Ceppi and the older kids into a sort of "minding" group for the younger ones while their mams go to work. Nearly everyone has a job now, only a couple of hours at a time usually and mainly cleaning, but it all helps. When one of those Cunard ships come in they have such a quick turn-round that everyone gets work, sometimes as much as eight or nine hours, and Cunard pay well. That's when we need the help of the older kids. A lot of them have found bits of jobs, delivering for shops, running errands, collecting glass bottles and jars, anything that will pay a penny or two.

'There's the tontine money too, that's separate from everything else, but we'll have some extra for Christmas.'

'Well, I'd be 'aving a few words with Vera or they'll lose what bit they get from the Parish and with winter comin' on they'll need every 'alfpenny they can get.'

Katherine watched the tram that Dotty and Mavis had boarded disappear slowly in the distance. She was undecided. Should she go now to see Dotty's aunt or should she go back home first? Ceppi would worry a bit but she wouldn't be that long. She walked quickly along the main road and turned into one of the side streets and almost collided with a man dressed in the uniform of the Liverpool City Police.

'Begod, it can't be you! It *is*!'

Katherine was also astounded. 'It . . . it's . . . you!'

'Katherine Donovan, as I live and breathe!'

'Sean McGovern! What on earth are you doing here and wearing that uniform too?'

'Ah, now there's a bit of a tale that goes with the uniform.'

'Look, I only live around the corner, come back with me?'

'Well, I don't know. I'm on duty, you see, and the sergeant is very fond of fining us if we step out of line.'

'Sure, he wouldn't fine you if you said I'd called you as I was sure there was someone prowling around the house, now would he?'

He grinned. 'That's a fine answer but we'll both have to confess to it on Saturday or there'll be no taking Communion on Sunday!'

He walked beside her swinging his truncheon idly,

something his superiors disliked, and the few women who were on their doorsteps called their kids inside and shut the door hurriedly.

'They're all terrified of you,' she explained.

'Ah, the police here are more respected than they are in Dublin.'

'That's true,' Katherine answered, praying he hadn't heard about their defrauding the Parish.

'I often wondered what had happened to you. I stayed for a couple of hours but . . .'

'It wasn't long enough.'

'Why so?'

'The mob must have waited for you to leave, then they came for their belongings. It turned desperate and only Father Flynn saved me from being beaten and having Da's money stolen. After that—'

'It's sorry I am to hear that. Is this place yours?'

'It is so. Donovan's Commercial Boarding House. I rent the house and give the commercial travellers a decent place to stay.'

'How did you do it? What made you decide on Liverpool?'

'I'll answer all that if you tell me why *you* came to Liverpool and why you're wearing that uniform.'

'Well, the fighting and rioting got worse, far worse. Meself I blame the employers – there's going to be a full lock-out before long. They'll bring the city to a standstill and I'd had enough. As I told you once before, I didn't join the police to be after half killing the population of Dublin. So I came over. God, but they're fierce strict with the rules and regulations here!'

'Where do you live?'

'At the Station House in Warren Street. Not being married or having a home to live in with an old father and mother, I live there. It's not bad. It's a damned sight better than the barracks back in Dublin.'

'Is this part of your beat?'

'It is so. I work shifts but I could always drop in for anything that was on the go.'

'Like a mug of tea and a sandwich?'

He grinned at her and she thought how nice he was. There was a bond between them after that desperate night they'd shared. It was good to have someone from home to talk to.

'Ceppi,' she called down the lobby, 'put the kettle on, we have company!'

Ceppi appeared in the kitchen doorway.

'Look who I found wandering up and down the street.'

'It's *you*!' Ceppi cried. 'You tried to help us and now you're *here*!' She ran down the hallway and hugged him around his waist.

Both Katherine and Sean McGovern laughed. Who could have asked for a warmer welcome?

Chapter Twenty

———◆———

SEAN MCGOVERN CALLED frequently and at various times of the day and evening. Maggie told Katherine it was a good thing to let all her guests see that the Arm of the Law was in constant attendance.

'You've got a soft spot for him, haven't you, Katherine?' Maggie asked one afternoon while she was helping the girl to fold all the extra blankets she'd just bought.

'I have. He once helped us and I'll not forget his kindness.'

'And he must be a reminder for you of home.'

'My home is here, Maggie,' Katherine said firmly. 'You should know that by now.'

'You'd be better off with Sean McGovern than that Edwin Sackville. A good, steady job with a decent pension at the end of it. The other one's job isn't safe by any means and he'd always be away, leaving you on your own and perhaps getting up to no good as well.'

Katherine laughed. 'Maggie, I'm not thinking of either of them as a husband.'

'Well, you should be. You're getting older. Eddie, give that to your mam now before you hurt yourself,' she finished, taking the poker from her small son who then had to be pacified with a biscuit.

'I'm only twenty, for heaven's sake! I know I act older but—'

'Time is ticking by, Katherine.'

'Maybe I'm cut out to be a spinster.'

'God forbid! You're better looking and have more sense and personality than any other girl of your age around here. You need a man of your own.'

'Please don't go on about it, Maggie?'

'I won't say another word but you just think about it.'

'I will so,' Katherine promised.

She did think about it when she was alone in the kitchen at night and everyone was in bed. She often sat staring into the fire. What was it like to be 'in love'? She was sure she would feel very differently than she did now. She just didn't know. She was fond of both men but she inclined more to Sean than to Edwin, perhaps because of the horrors of that night. She'd tried to banish them from her mind, but there were times when they wouldn't go away. She was aware though that she was young and successful and if she married, then the business would automatically belong to her husband and she certainly wasn't prepared to hand it over just yet.

As the days grew shorter with the approach of winter, Katherine saw that all the fires were lit and burning cheerfully when her guests arrived back. It was so gratifying to see the look on their faces when they hung up their coats and hats in the hall and went into the sitting room where a pot of hot tea was waiting for them. They greeted each other as friends now, for many came to stay at the same time each fortnight or month, swapping stories and information on how their respective businesses were doing. Mr Forrester had once said it was just like a gentlemen's club, they were treated so well. They hadn't minded when Katherine had said she was desperately sorry but she would have to put her rate up by a shilling, owing to the fact that things had become so dear, particularly coal. The success of her Commercial Boarding House was gaining momentum and other people were catching on to the same idea.

'But they'll never be quite like this because they won't have you, Katherine,' Mr Dunne remarked.

She liked him very much for he often told her about his wife and children. He missed them but he had to earn a crust and at least his company treated him very well. He'd been working for them for years. His wife, he said, was very thankful that he'd at last found somewhere nice to stay; it helped her to worry less about him.

Katherine noticed Edwin's visits grew shorter after Sean started to call.

'He's jealous,' Maggie remarked.

'He isn't! He hardly ever sees Sean, who always sits in the kitchen with us. And anyway, he's a cut above me, coming from a family like that.'

'Oh, aye, a family like that is a good recommendation, I'm sure. His father gambling away the roof over their heads. Very nice, that is.'

'He shot himself, Maggie, I told you.'

'If it had been our Frank I'd have been the one doing the shooting and it wouldn't be myself I'd shoot,' Maggie answered tartly.

But Katherine was particularly grateful to Edwin for the fact that Ceppi was doing very well at school – even Sister Imelda admitted as much. Katherine had praised the child when she'd come back from seeing the nuns and had taken Ceppi and Nancy for a meal in Reece's as a reward, Nancy in clothes borrowed from Ceppi. She watched them both eat. Ceppi was a different child altogether now and Nancy was her shadow. She followed Ceppi everywhere. She always reminded Katherine of the kind of life she'd rescued Ceppi from. The co-operative scheme was working well now and for that she thanked God. The poor always dreaded the approach of winter for the freezing weather took its toll of the old and the very young.

There was enough money in the tontine to bring a bit of festive cheer at the Christmas that was drawing ever closer. Katherine had also heard of a charitable fund with a peculiar name, the Goodfellows Society. They gave out parcels of food to poor and needy families recommended to them at Christmas.

She'd gone to their office in Tithebarn Street and left the names of all her neighbours. The clerk had been surprised.

'We don't often give so many to one street. The poor often share.'

'In this case, sir, they have all "shared" the loss of husbands and sons and are "poor" because of it. Am I now to go back and tell them that yet again they have been refused help?'

He'd looked over his spectacles at her. She was young but she had an air of confidence and authority about her and she was well dressed, in a neat way.

'Could you explain that please, miss?'

'I can so and in three words: "*Titanic*'s Black Gang".'

His expression changed. 'Oh, I see. Then there are special circumstances. I'll see to it that everyone's name is put forward and the reason.'

She had thanked him and left. Why was it so hard to get people to understand that the poor were not poor from choice? They lacked education and therefore were only offered the lowest of jobs. They were forced to live in squalor because the houses they could afford to rent were in need of demolition and there was a terrible shortage of basic things like running water and proper sanitation.

'I'm a bit worried about Christmas,' she confided to Sean one evening.

'Why so?'

'Well, last year Mary, Ceppi's best friend, was alive. I took them to the grotto and Ceppi said it was the best Christmas she'd ever had. Will the memory spoil this Christmas for her?'

He was off duty and, as he often did, was spending his free time with her. His superiors didn't like it but he'd explained to them she was a friend from Dublin. He viewed her as a sister (he'd lied) who needed the presence of authority in the person of himself, a constable of the Liverpool City Police, to deter any form of trouble arising. And besides, he'd explained, there were always other people in the house as well as a young girl of nine. Now he looked perturbed.

'Will I ask her, in a roundabout sort of way?'

'Would you? I'd be so grateful. I don't think she's even thought much about Christmas yet but she will soon. Are you coming to us for your Christmas dinner?'

'If I can. I've nowhere else to go, but I don't know yet whether or not I'll be off duty.'

'We can wait for you if you're late. I've invited Edwin too. He doesn't want to go to Shropshire and have a cheerless Christmas with his mother and sisters. I know he does send money to them from time to time because I've posted letters for him, but I don't think they appreciate it. He never gets a reply.'

'Lovely manners they have over here, the middle classes at least,' he said with heavy sarcasm.

'You won't mind him joining us?'

'Why would I mind at all?' he replied with a show of indifference. But deep down he didn't like Edwin Sackville one bit. There was something in his manner, especially towards Katherine, that didn't sit right.

'We'll have all the trimmings. I thought last Christmas was wonderful, being with a family and all, but this year I have my own bit of a family, isn't that great?'

'It is so and thanks, Katherine, for including me. It's a long way back to Kerry and I don't relish the thought of Christmas in the Station House.'

Ceppi brought the subject of Christmas up herself the following day.

'Katherine, can I have Nancy in for Christmas like I had Mary last year?'

'You had Mary because we lived with them.'

'I know but she's gone to heaven, she's happy, but poor Nancy . . .'

Katherine was baking but she stopped rolling out the pastry. 'Ceppi, poor Nancy would only be upset by the things Santi will have brought you. Don't you remember how you felt when Santi didn't come to you?'

The child nodded, although those memories were now fading.

'I've asked Sean and Edwin to have their dinner with us, then we can go and see Maggie and Frank. Besides, I think Nancy and the rest of the children in the street will get a surprise.'

'How so?'

'Well, all their mams have been saving up for half a year so as to be able to get them things and I'm going to buy a Christmas tree.'

'For in here?'

'No.' Then, seeing the expression on the child's face she hurried on, 'Of course we'll have one but this will be the biggest I can find and I'll get Frank and Sean and some of the others to put it right in the middle of the street, there's hardly any traffic down here anyway. Then we'll decorate it and everyone can enjoy it.'

Ceppi's eyes lit up. 'And we'll have Sean and Edwin and I like them both and I know Mary would too. I know she's always watching me, that's why I work so hard at school. I don't want to let her down.'

Katherine breathed a sigh of relief. So that's settled, she thought thankfully.

*

From then on the weeks seemed to fly past. The tontine money had been given out and everyone was amazed at just how much they'd managed to save. Only Lizzie knew that Katherine had added extra. All kinds of plans were made and shopping trips organised. Katherine had given out packets of red and green crêpe paper and Ceppi had shown all the older kids how to make plaited chains to decorate the kitchens. Katherine's present to her neighbours was the subject of a great deal of talk and envy in the neighbourhood.

'Well, she can afford ter buy a bloody big tree like that with all the money she's got,' a woman from the next street was heard to say. Unfortunately for her, Vi Watson was standing in the queue behind her and made verbal mincemeat out of her, to the satisfaction of the rest of Mrs Neale's customers who all liked a little bit of gossip and argument to liven up the day.

Vi had the last word. 'She works damned hard for what she gets.'

All the kids in the street were in a state of high excitement and couldn't believe they had a Christmas tree of their own to stand and wonder at. One they could touch without fear of parental disapproval. One they fought many battles over with kids from the surrounding streets who were green with envy. And then on the day before Christmas Eve the parcels arrived. They contained tea, sugar, flour, oranges, Christmas pudding, a slab of fruit cake and a good-sized piece of ham. There was also jam and butter, and even a few sweets.

Ceppi and Nancy came bursting into the kitchen.

'Oh, Katherine, yer should see what some feller has brung us!' Nancy cried.

'There's oranges and sweets and cake and tea and all kinds of things!' Ceppi was as excited as Nancy.

'Now isn't that great. Did everyone get one?'

'Yes, they did. Every single 'ouse, Katherine.'

At the change of voice Katherine looked up and her eyes met those of Lizzie who was standing in the doorway with tears falling down her cheeks.

'When yer first came 'ere, girl, everyone was suspicious of yer. Not one of us 'ad a kind word fer yer, not even ter pass the time of day, an' now . . . yer've done so much fer us, all of us. Because of yer there'll be a good fire an' a table full of food. Some of us were facin' the Workhouse before yer arrived. We were so poor an' bowed down with grief an' no one seemed ter care; we were the forgotten ones. You gave us back our pride an' determination an' the means to carry on, fer the kids' sakes. You were even thinkin' of payin' someone ter take up our case. There's not many who'd do all that. Now we've all got enough ter be able ter give them some little—'

She was stopped from saying 'toys' by Katherine placing her finger on her lips and shaking her head.

'Well, fer anythin' Santi might bring.'

'Oh, Lizzie, come here to me,' Katherine cried and the older woman threw her arms around Katherine and began to cry all over again.

'I wish I could bring him back to you, and all the other men too,' Katherine said with a sob in her own voice.

Ceppi and Nancy looked at them in amazement.

'Why is me mam cryin' like that?' Nancy asked.

'I don't know. Grown-ups are eejits some of the time,

there's no understanding them. Take no notice. Sure, don't they go acting the fool over daft things,' Ceppi answered.

Edwin arrived later that day, loaded down with presents for both of them.

'Oh, you shouldn't have spent so much money on us!' Katherine said, but she was smiling.

'I've no one else to buy for. Well, that I want to buy for.'

'Not even your poor mother and she having to live with all the sorrow your father left behind?'

'I sent her a card.'

'Could you not even have sent her a small gift? Chocolates? She could have shared them with your sisters.'

'I sent her money.'

'Why do you speak so coldly of her?'

'She was – is a very selfish woman. She had no time for me. For my sisters, yes, but never me. She didn't want any more children, I'm seven years younger—'

'You were her "little accident", as Maggie calls Eddie,' Katherine interrupted, but not unkindly.

'No. I was her "big disaster". Father had always wanted a son, or so he said. He really didn't show me much affection when I was little and then he was "involved" with gambling and there were terrible rows, until—'

'Stop it! Don't say any more, don't think of it any more. I want you to have a good Christmas.'

He smiled. 'You are the exact opposite to any woman I've ever known.'

'Right, well, your room is ready, the bed is aired and if you go and warm yourself by the sitting-room fire, I'll bring you some tea.'

'Will you join me?'

'Of course, if you want me to.'

'I want you to. You're always too busy to just sit and talk.'

'First, will you give me the things you've bought for Ceppi? I'll have to hide them.'

'What on earth for? They're presents from me.'

'She thinks, expects, that all presents come from Santi.'

'I don't want to ruin her belief in that, but I'll just keep one to give her when I give you yours.'

'Oh, Edwin, you really shouldn't have spent so much. It's so good of you.'

'No, Katherine, it's so good of *you*, even though I'll have to share you with our friend in blue.'

'You don't like Sean, do you?'

'It's hard to explain, Katherine. You have so much more in common with him than I have. You're easy in his presence.'

'Am I not with you?'

'Yes, but . . .'

'But what?'

'It's different somehow.'

'Edwin Sackville, all this is in your mind. Put it away from you, it's Christmas. Will you be going to church on Christmas morning?'

'Probably not. I'm not of your faith.'

'I already know that and I don't hold it against you as many in this city would,' she said cheerfully. 'We'll be going to Midnight Mass and when we get back we can all have a drink because by then it will be Christmas Day!'

*

The kitchen was decorated, the food all prepared and the table laid when Katherine, Ceppi and Sean went out to Midnight Mass. Ceppi had never been up so late, not even when she lived with her mammy. It was a cold, clear night. There was no moon but there seemed to be thousands of stars and the sky was like a huge, black piece of velvet. She danced along beside Katherine and Sean.

'You'll slip and fall if you don't walk properly, it's freezing hard,' Katherine chided, taking one of Ceppi's hands while Sean took the other one. He laughed. 'Right, you bold little rossi, will we play "Jumping the Cracks"?'

'Jumping the Cracks?'

'Sure to God, didn't you used to play that in Dublin?'

'No. How do you play it?'

'You keep tight hold of my and Katherine's hands and we'll move a bit faster and then swing you right off your feet and you'll be jumping the cracks in the paving stones.'

'Have you gone mad?' Katherine laughed too. 'Is this what they pay you to do above in the station? We'll all end up in hospital.'

'We will not. Come on, don't be a sour puss!'

All three of them were laughing by the time they reached the church, as Ceppi had demanded they play this new game all the rest of the way.

'The Lord save us! I've a stitch in my side so bad I can't stand up,' Katherine panted.

'Well, we'd all better wipe the smiles off our faces or Father Scanlan won't be amused by all this bold hilarity.'

'What does "hilarity" mean?' Ceppi asked.

'She doesn't change, does she?' Sean said and Katherine smiled back.

'We'll tell you after Mass. Now dip your fingers in the Holy Water and cross yourself or Himself will have a few words about "respect" too.'

As Katherine gazed around the packed church she felt both happy and sad. Sad because she remembered Mary and Maggie but happy because she was so fortunate and she'd been able, in a small way, to help her neighbours. It was their first Christmas without their menfolk and it would be hard for them, all of them. For Maggie and Frank too, as they missed their Mary.

She rose with the whole congregation as the parish priest, in gold and white vestments, preceded by altar boys of various ages, the oldest carrying the silver cross and another the silver thurible that contained the burning incense, processed up to the altar and the organ burst into life with the first bars of *Adeste Fideles*.

Everything looked so beautiful, Katherine thought. The holly, the Christmas roses, the red poinsettias that decorated the altar and the Stations of the Cross. The hundreds of candles that lit the side altars with their statues and flowers. She glanced at Sean and Ceppi and thought they looked like a family. A proper family. Then she turned her mind to the ceremony that was about to start.

When they arrived home it was to find a note from Edwin on the kitchen table.

'He never said he was going anywhere. I can't understand it. Here.' Katherine passed the note to Sean.

'"Gone out for a while just to absorb the Festive Spirit.

Don't wait up for me. Happy Christmas."' Sean looked grave. If that bloody toff spoiled this Christmas he'd feel the back of Sean's hand across his stupid, selfish head.

'I presume "Festive Spirit" means having drink taken,' Katherine stated flatly.

'I think you presume right. You and Ceppi go to bed. I'll wait down here to see what sort of a state he's in.'

'Sean, I can look after myself. I've seen men in a desperate state, destroyed entirely by drink. There's no need to stay, you'll have to be up early.'

He was working the early shift from six in the morning to four in the afternoon, so she was going to delay dinner for him.

'There won't be much going on, except the usual fights when families get together and the men have drink taken. Just a few "domestics", that's all.'

'No. I'll be just fine. I won't have you losing sleep over Edwin's night out. He was probably lonely sitting down here on his own. Now go and I'll see you at about half past four, by which time her ladyship here will have us demented – and that won't be confined to this house either. The whole street will be running mad with the antics of the kids.'

Reluctantly he left and she followed Ceppi upstairs. She was tired; it had been a long day. She'd been up early to go for the vegetables and fruit. On her way home she'd collected the goose from the butcher and a ham shank and – as a special treat for Sean – pigs' trotters, or cruibins as they were called.

She got an equally tired Ceppi to bed and was sitting brushing out her long dark hair. It was cold tonight, she thought, shivering as she pulled on her nightdress. Still, she thanked God for everything she had now.

She'd just risen from her knees when she heard the back-yard door slam and she sighed. Edwin, and very probably drunk. She'd have to go down and keep him quiet or Ceppi would think it was Santi – Katherine had already filled the girl's stocking. She slid her feet into her slippers and wrapped a heavy flannel dressing gown around her. She hoped he wasn't one of those men who were prone to singing loud and vulgar songs.

The light was burning in the kitchen as she opened the door. He turned around and she breathed a sigh of relief. He wasn't drunk.

'I somehow thought you'd gone out drinking when I saw your note. You must have been lonely sitting here by yourself.'

'I was, that's why I went out.' He turned away back to the sink.

'What are you doing?'

'Just swilling my face and hands. It's so dark in that entry I had to feel my way along and that wall is filthy.'

'Well, go on up now or we'll have Ceppi down on us thinking Santi's been and we'll get no sleep then.'

'It's Christmas Day. Don't I get a kiss, Katherine?'

She was startled.

'I'll bring in some mistletoe if you like,' he joked and she smiled.

'Aren't you an eejit sometimes. Come here to me.'

He did so and she stood on tip-toe and kissed him on the cheek. 'Happy Christmas, Edwin.'

'Can't you do better than that, Katherine?' he said softly

and leaned towards her. To her own amazement she was in his arms and was kissing him back until she pulled herself together and out of the circle of his embrace.

'No! No, I . . . it's . . . it's just Christmas, that's all.'

'I don't think it was that, Katherine, but I promise you I won't pursue you until you reconcile yourself to your feelings for me.'

Always the gentleman, she thought as she went upstairs. She locked her bedroom door, but not because she was afraid of him. She was afraid of herself and the feelings that kiss had awoken in her.

Chapter Twenty-One

———◆———

B Y EIGHT O'CLOCK THE whole street was awake and every child was full of excitement. Their little faces shone with happiness as they ran in and out of the houses of their friends. Katherine's home was no exception.

'Look! Look! Ceppi, look what I've got!' Nancy's eyes were sparkling as she showed Ceppi the first doll she'd ever had in her life. It was only a cheap rag doll with a papier-mâché face, but it could have been made of gold for the affection and pride that Nancy showered it with.

'Look what Santi brought me.' Ceppi was just as excited. 'It's a doll's house, isn't it just perfect?' She and Nancy were fascinated with it for it was a replica of a real house with furniture and carpets and curtains and even a family of small dolls.

Katherine smiled at them both. Ceppi had had a porcelain doll from Edwin that was so fragile and beautifully dressed that she knew she was going to have to lay down some rules about the length of time it could be played with. Sweets, an orange, an apple and a new penny had also been in Ceppi's stocking. From Sean there was a skipping rope with fancy wooden handles and a wooden top and whip.

'Aren't you the fortunate one? Santi must have noticed how good you've been.'

'I've been good, too, but I didn't expect 'im to leave anything for me, 'e doesn't usually,' Nancy said, clutching the doll tightly as if fearing it would be taken from her.

Katherine laughed. 'Well, all the children in this street must have been very very good this year.'

'And there's all the food. Me mam's been cookin' an' makin' pies but she said we can't 'ave the cake or the oranges or the sweets just yet. We've got ter make them all last. We've *never* 'ad food like that, not even when me da was . . . alive.' Her bottom lip began to tremble.

'Now, Nancy, stop that. We don't want to spoil the day. Your da wouldn't want that, would he?'

'Do yer think we got so much because 'e—'

'Nancy, your da would want you to be happy. Like Mary he'll be up in heaven—'

'And everyone is happy up there all the time,' Ceppi interrupted and the atmosphere lightened again.

'Here, I can't wait for dinner to be over, I want to give you this now.' Edwin passed a beautifully wrapped parcel to Katherine.

'The wrapping must have cost a pretty penny on its own,' she remarked as she carefully undid it. It was a beautiful pale blue silk blouse.

'Oh, Edwin! It's gorgeous, it really is, but I can't accept it. It's too much. It's far too good for me. When would I wear it?'

'Today, if you like.'

'You shouldn't have spent so much, really you shouldn't.'

'Why not? You deserve it.'

'It must have cost a small fortune.'

'Never mind about that, Katherine. Will you wear it for dinner, just to please me?'

'Of course, and it will be a pleasure for me. Mind you, I'll have to wear an apron over it until everything is ready.' She reached up and kissed him on the cheek. 'Thank you! It's very special.'

'And so are you.'

She laughed, but she felt a little awkward.

'What I have for you isn't nearly as expensive. Now haven't you made me embarrassed because it's so little.'

'That doesn't matter. It doesn't have to be expensive. Coming from you it will be better than gold or jewels.'

'Ah, I think you are the worst flatterer I've ever met. Pour yourself a drink and go into the sitting room, away from all this, for I've work to do.' She indicated the pans on the range and the goose, plucked, stuffed and trussed up with string, waiting to go into the oven.

'I'd sooner stay in here, our friend in blue does.'

'Are you jealous? There's nothing to be jealous about. And why do you never call him by his proper name?'

'Oh, it's just a bit of a joke but you're right, Katherine, I am jealous.'

'Get away with you into the sitting room,' she said, shooing him playfully out of the kitchen. 'At least you'll have a bit of peace until the food is ready and Sean has arrived – that's if I can keep Ceppi from being sick with all the excitement and sweets she's eaten.'

Oh, it really was such a beautiful blouse, she thought as she stroked it almost with reverence. It must have cost pounds. She held it against her cheek to feel its delicacy and she sniffed. It had a smell to it, a lovely smell. Lavender, that's what it was. He must have asked for it to be packed in sweet-smelling tissue paper. She'd heard from Maggie that on one of her very rare visits, Tilly had brought her a nice lace collar that her mistress had discarded, and that had been wrapped in perfumed paper. Well, it would have to be taken upstairs and hung up before it was destroyed entirely with splashes and stains.

By midday Ceppi had so many of her friends in the kitchen that Katherine almost lost her temper.

'Will you all go away and give me a bit of peace and quiet?'

'Where can we go? Everyone's mam is cooking,' Ceppi asked.

Katherine thought. Not the sitting room, Edwin was in there reading, and certainly not the dining room where the table was set – she'd taken great care in laying it.

'Right, into the writing room with the lot of you! Ceppi, fold up the tables in there, push the chairs against the wall and don't make too much of a mess.'

'It's freezing in there, there's no fire at all,' Ceppi complained.

'Then I'll bring one. Now go on.' Katherine wiped her hands and fetched the coal bucket. With a shovel she transferred some of the hot coals in the range to the bucket.

'Mind out of my way,' she called as she went into the writing room and deposited the fire into the grate. 'Wait now while I mend it for you.' She took the small brass shovel and heaped coal from the scuttle onto the burning coals.

'Now, can I trust you not to be burning the house around us?'

A chorus of agreement sent her back to the kitchen and then the dining room. It looked grand, she thought. She had set out her best dishes on a snowy-white tablecloth. She'd laid stripes of coloured paper in a diagonal pattern over the cloth, and she had glasses too. Nice ones, not the thick ones which were more serviceable but ugly with it. She had made a centrepiece with two red candles and some holly. Mrs Sullivan from the tobacconist had shown her one she'd made and the candles and other bits hadn't been expensive. She knew it was far above anything the women in the street would have but at least all their tables would have food and there'd be a fire in the room. She'd made a deal with Mr Perks the coal merchant. She'd paid for a half-hundredweight of coal to be left at each house. Just laid on the front step, late on Christmas Eve.

'It'll do my lads good to get a bit more exercise, running up and down with the bags. Lads today don't know the meaning of the word "work",' he'd grumbled. 'Anyway, I can't get the cart down the street because of your flaming Christmas tree,' he'd added as she'd counted out the coins onto the palm of a hand that had coal dust ingrained in the pores of the skin.

*

By five minutes past four everything was ready and they were all starving.

'Everyone's had their dinner, why are we having ours late?' Ceppi demanded. 'I'm hungry.'

'We are all hungry and you know why we're late. We're waiting for Sean.'

'Well, why isn't he here?'

'Because he doesn't finish until four, then he's got to get changed and come down here,' she answered.

By a quarter to five she had given in to the demands of both Ceppi and Edwin that she serve. Edwin was secretly pleased at the non-appearance of his rival for Katherine's time and attention. She'd be furious that he was so late: the meal would be ruined.

Katherine, looking at the overcooked vegetables and potatoes, was indeed thinking along those lines. It wasn't like him. Had he gone for a drink? She knew he drank very little but his colleagues might have persuaded him.

'Edwin, will you carve while I bring in the potatoes and vegetables? We can't wait any longer.' She felt angry and yet disappointed. He knew of the effort she'd put into this meal and he'd been looking forward to it so much last night.

They had cleared their plates and Ceppi had been allowed to pull one cracker with Edwin, getting a paper hat and cheap little toy from inside it, when she heard the kitchen door slam. She went quickly across the hall and into the kitchen.

'Katherine. Katherine, I'm so sorry! Believe me, if I could have got away earlier I would have! Did you get my message?'

'What message?'

267

'I gave a note to one of the kids, one of the Watsons I think, and told him to bring it to you.'

'I got no such a note.'

'He said he gave it to a feller. I wanted to tell you to start without me and not to let the dinner spoil.'

'In the name of God, what's going on? Notes, boys, fellers, are you sure he went to the right house?'

'I am so. Everyone around here knows the House on Lonely Street. He swore he gave it in.'

'He must have gone to the wrong house, sure, half of Vi's lot can't read.' She dismissed it. 'We have started, everything was getting overcooked and it's nearly teatime. So, why are you so late?' She took his plate from the small oven with canvas mitts.

'There was a murder last night.'

She nearly dropped the plate. 'Holy Mother! A murder! I've heard nothing.'

'You will soon.'

'Who was it?'

'A woman. A well-off young woman.'

'Oh, the Lord save us! How . . .'

'Strangled. The word is that she entertained the type of man she should have had nothing to do with!'

'You can't mean . . .?'

'She lived in one of those big houses in Abercromby Square.'

'But . . . they have servants . . .'

'They do – apparently they were all in the kitchen having their usual Christmas Eve drink. It seems they all get a bit more money at Christmas. But her maid says she caught a glimpse of someone just in the act of closing the French windows. She was too terrified to go after him, too terrified to scream apparently or he might have been caught. She'd only gone up to see if there was anything her mistress wanted. She says she'd finished her meal so Mr Hardcastle, the butler, told her to go and see. The dead woman must have known him. She must have let him in because everyone else was either out or cavorting in the kitchen. Because of where she lived and the type of family she came from, all leave has been cancelled. There's a manhunt on. I'll be having me dinner standing up. I've got to get back or I'll be the one who'll be murdered. My inspector is fierce mad to catch him.'

'Sit down here in the kitchen. You can't eat standing up. Will I fetch Ceppi to thank you for the toys?'

'No, you know what she's like, asking all kinds of questions. Just tell her I was very very busy and I'll see her soon. God knows when I'll be able to call next.'

Katherine watched him eat. It was a terrible thing. Maybe the woman had loose morals but that was no excuse for murder.

He finished his meal at a speed that Katherine said would cause him severe indigestion for most of the evening.

She reached up and kissed him on the cheek. 'Happy Christmas, Sean. Take this with you. It's not much.'

'God, I must be the biggest eejit in the whole city! Didn't I forget your present altogether? Thank God I gave you Ceppi's.'

'It doesn't matter, Sean, really. You keep it for a surprise.'

'I'll see you as soon as I can get away,' he promised. God knows when, he thought. Half of the entire police force were out and about in the part of the city where the rich lived, so it could be seen that they were actually doing *something*. If the victim had been a girl from the slums he was certain there would have been nothing like this turnout.

'Who was that?' Edwin demanded. Both he and Ceppi had waited for what seemed like an age but he had stopped Ceppi from going to look for Katherine. 'Maybe someone's in trouble or wants to borrow something,' he'd replied to the child's demands.

Katherine sat down with the pudding. 'Sean.'

'So, where is he?'

'Gone. He couldn't wait. He was in uniform.'

'I thought he was off duty at four?' Edwin said peevishly.

'All leave has been cancelled. There's been a bit of trouble.'

'What kind of trouble?' Ceppi asked.

Katherine sighed and realised that she would have to tell her; she'd hear it soon enough anyway from the neighbours' kids.

'A woman was murdered last night, up in the posh part of the city.'

'Good God! Who was she? Did Sean tell you her name?'

'He didn't. But she must have been quite wealthy to be living there. Her maid found her and the girl actually caught a glimpse of the killer. The poor creature, it must have given her a terrible shock.'

'It's dreadful, truly a dreadful experience for the poor girl. I hope they gave her leave to go to her family, but I doubt they will. They never consider other people or their feelings,' he said bitterly.

'They have half the police force knocking on doors up there.'

'Well, you can't have them thinking that the police are doing nothing to find this . . . monster,' he replied, and Katherine was surprised at the note of sarcasm in his voice.

They had spent a quietly pleasant evening playing word games. Then, just before Ceppi went to bed, Katherine had a visitor. She opened the back door to a pale and wild-eyed Alfie.

'What's wrong?'

'It's . . . it's . . . me mam . . .' he panted.

'But I only saw her when she called on her way home from Mass this morning – we arranged for me to come up tomorrow. Alfie, what's wrong with her? Is she ill?'

'No. She's in a state though and so is our Tilly. You've got to come, Katherine! Please!'

'Tilly? I thought your mam said she had no time off at Christmas?'

'She . . . she's been at the police station all day.'

'Tilly? What in the name of God for?'

'She's the one who worked for that murdered woman. She found her!'

'Holy Mother of God!' Katherine cried. 'Wait until I get my coat.'

'What's wrong?' Edwin asked in concern as he came into the kitchen.

'I've got to go to Maggie's. I'm so sorry to have to leave you on your own, it being Christmas.'

'Is she ill?'

'No, but her daughter, the one who is in service, actually found the poor woman who's been murdered. She's been with the police all day. Oh, Maggie will be in a terrible state and so will the poor girl.'

'You go then, Katherine. They're sort of like a family, aren't they?'

She nodded and then left with Alfie.

As they walked, Katherine's thoughts went back to the last time she'd spoken to the lad. After all the nonsense, Alfie had started courting Brenda Keegan from the bottom end of their street. Maggie had told her and she'd been so relieved.

He had calmed down a little now and was feeling embarrassed. 'Katherine, I . . . I want to say how stupid and—'

'There's no need, Alfie, it was just a crush. You see I'm twenty, an old maid, and Brenda is a really nice girl. What time did they let Tilly come home?' she asked to change the subject.

'Teatime; about half past six, I think. She says she's never going back there. She'd rather die than go back into that house and I don't blame her!'

When they arrived Frank was looking very serious and Maggie looked worn out. Of Eddie and Tilly there was no sign.

'Oh, Katherine, I'm so glad you've come.'

'Where is she?'

'In bed. I gave her a drop of whiskey with hot water to warm her up, she couldn't stop shivering. Thank God she's asleep.'

'It must have been a terrible ordeal for her. Finding the woman and then having the police swarming over the place and herself down at the station.'

'She says that was the worst part. They made her feel guilty that she didn't get a proper look at the feller but she swore up hill and down dale to her da and me that she couldn't remember what he looked like, even if her life depended on it. Just a quick flash of a glance at him and when she turned around she . . . well . . . she saw *her*.'

'Stay there, luv, I'll put the kettle on. She's exhausted,' Frank confided to Katherine.

'Did Tilly say anything about your one who was killed?'

'Not to the police she didn't, but when I was helping her to bed she told me that there had been a bit of trouble a month or so ago. Miss Madeleine Power was in a terrible state and wouldn't tell anyone what was the matter with her. She entertained . . . people . . . when her mam and da were away. They have another house by the sea somewhere in Wales, I think. So, she was no better than she ought to be, according to our Tilly.'

'Did Tilly say what the "bit of trouble" was?'

'No, but she said that when she got back from her afternoon off – and it wasn't visiting me! – Miss Madeleine was in bed, poorly, like. There was blood on the sheets.' Maggie lowered her voice. 'Tilly thought it was "the curse", and she was up and about the next day and as happy as ever, singing too.'

Katherine looked puzzled.

'It puzzles me too, luv, but she's not going back there. Her da and me would put a stop to that, but luckily she doesn't want to. Frank will go for what wages she's due, if they don't send them. I know it's a bad time for them, but she worked damned hard for that money and I bet they'll give her nothing extra for her ordeal.'

Chapter Twenty-Two

A S THE NEW YEAR passed so the police search for the murderer was wound down. No one had been caught and the official verdict was that it had been done by someone who had either left the city the same night or was being harboured by friends or relatives.

Sean at last got the two days off that were owing.

'I'd like to take you somewhere – and Ceppi of course,' he added. 'We'd need a sort of chaperone or your reputation would be ruined. I knows she's only a child, but . . .'

'Oh, I'm not really too worried about my reputation but where would we go at this time of the year?'

'Anywhere.'

'What would I do with my gentlemen?'

'They're not here at the weekend. Perhaps we could go to the Isle of Man? It's not far by ferry.'

'We'd have a terrible crossing, the weather's shocking.' Katherine was remembering her trip from Dublin and the stories Mrs Green had told her that night.

'We could stay in a boarding house overnight.'

'Are you mad? Holiday boarding houses won't be open at this time of year.'

'One of the lads is a Manxman, I'll ask him. If he can find us somewhere, will we go?'

'Oh, all right, but don't say anything to Ceppi or she'll have me demented altogether.'

'I want you to think of it as the real Christmas we should have had.'

She smiled and fingered the little silver cross and chain he'd bought her for Christmas.

She had been to see Maggie and Tilly who was still in a state about the murder but who was going to start next weekend as a shop assistant in Pegram's, the grocer's. On her return home she found Edwin standing on the doorstep.

She was surprised. 'You didn't say you were coming. Are you wet through?'

'Almost, and I'm sorry to descend on you like this, Katherine, but two of the places wouldn't see me.'

'Oh, that's so disappointing.'

It's more than that, he thought. He now had very little money left.

She put the kettle on while he went to take off his wet clothes.

She called upstairs that the tea was wet and would he bring down his overcoat and she'd dry it in front of the range.

He watched her as she draped the sleeves of his coat over a wooden clothes horse which she placed in front of the fire. 'We'll have to watch it doesn't scorch. Here, get this down you and you'll feel warm again. There's a drop of whiskey in it.'

'Thanks, Katherine.'

'I've been up to see Maggie. Tilly's got a new job.'

'Really? In service?'

'No. A shop assistant in Pegram's, the grocer's a few streets away. She was really lucky to get it and the pay is far better than she's been used to.'

'I'm glad of that. You don't mind me coming back?'

'Of course not, but I think I'm going to have to leave you to fend for yourself for two days at the weekend.'

'You're deserting the ship?'

'Sean's got this mad idea that Ceppi and me should have a little bit of a break, a sort of holiday.'

'Where?'

'The Isle of Man, would you believe? At this time of year too. He has a friend who originally comes from there; he's asking him to find a bed and breakfast place.'

'Do you want to go, Katherine?'

'I don't know and that's the truth of it. I'd like a break, it would be nice to have my breakfast cooked and served for me for once, but it's the weather.'

'Surely the ferry service will be suspended if the weather's *that* bad.'

'I don't think so. The ferry carries the mail and even if every other ship stays in port, they have to sail, like the Cunard ships. The mail has to get through even though they lost the *Ellan Vannin* in a storm four years ago.'

'Does he know that?'

She shrugged.

'Surely he won't risk your life and Ceppi's?'

'No, he wouldn't do a thing like that.'

'Did they catch anyone for that poor girl's murder?'

'No. The police have been twice to see Tilly to see if she can remember the slightest thing. Maggie told them to clear off the last time, Tilly was getting all upset again. She has nightmares, screaming and shouting, things like that.'

'The poor girl, they are insensitive fools at times.'

'Once or twice Maggie said she was rambling, saying what the man looked like, but she puts it down to all the pressure they keep piling on her.'

'If it had been a poor girl from the slums they'd not be carrying on a search for this length of time.'

Two days later Sean arrived with three tickets and an address.

'Now you've got to come, it's all arranged. Fred Quirk's mam will put us up. She's closed for the winter but she doesn't mind just for one night and I've booked the ferry. There's only one a day in winter but they go back and forth all summer.'

Katherine laughed. 'Then I suppose we'll have to go. Now you can tell Ceppi, she's at Nancy's, and leave me to get this bread in the oven.'

Ceppi was delighted, skipping for joy as she left Nancy's house with Sean.

'Oh, Katherine, it's to be a *holiday*. I've never been on a holiday before.'

'Neither have I and probably neither has Sean. It's all his crazy idea. We sail early on Saturday morning and come back on the Sunday afternoon ferry.'

'Is it like Mrs Taylor's house?' Ceppi was suddenly a little concerned.

'I don't think so. At least Sean's got the sense not to pay for a place like that.'

She'd made meat pies and there was cold ham and pork that Edwin could eat while she was away.

'Does he think you'll be going for a week with all that?' Maggie commented. Katherine had gone to say goodbye to her and Sean was picking her up from there.

'No, but I felt I had to give him some choice.'

'You're too good to him, Katherine, and he doesn't appreciate it. Anyway, what's he doing back again so soon?'

'He couldn't get an appointment with two of his places.'

'He's just a glorified brush salesman. Oh, they all give themselves fancy titles but he's a door-to-door salesman all the same.'

'You don't like him, do you?'

'I don't, Katherine. Now, if it were Sean . . .'

'Oh, get off with you, all this blathering about Sean.'

'Well, you know my feelings about him too. Maybe this "holiday" will make you see what a fine lad he is.'

'He's twenty-seven, he's not a lad.'

'They're all lads to me. Still, our Alfie and Brenda seem to be getting serious.'

'Do you approve of her then?'

'Oh, aye, I know all her family and have done for years. She's a good girl. Hard-working, clean and thrifty, which can't be said for a lot of girls around here.'

'I'm so glad. I *did* worry about him, you know.'

'Didn't we all, luv?'

The back-yard door slammed and both women rose.

'That'll be Sean,' Katherine said.

'It might be Tilly, she said she'd be back for her tea.'

They both arrived together and Katherine smiled; she was glad the girl was looking better, she had some colour in her cheeks now.

'Well, are we all ready for the off then?' Sean asked.

'Indeed we are. I just hope this doesn't turn out to be a disaster.'

'It won't. I promise.'

It wasn't a bad crossing. It got a little choppy once they were out in the bay but the sun was shining, tipping the waves with pale gold. They were all wrapped up so they went up on deck.

'At least it's an improvement on the Dublin ferry. There's enough seats and comfortable ones too. I heard they actually have cabins.'

'They do, but they cost.'

'Well, we won't be using one anyway. What's he like?'

'Who?'

'Fred Quirk.'

'A decent bloke and he says his mam is very friendly. She doesn't have a list of rules and regulations as long as your arm like most do.'

Katherine looked up at him. She really did like him a lot. He was so affectionate and dependable and thoughtful.

'Sean, I'm glad I came. I really mean that.' She felt the blush creeping upwards from her neck to her cheeks.

He put his arm around her. 'Katherine, I never forgot you. I was always searching the crowds for you and Ceppi. I didn't think I'd ever see you again and when I did, I knew it was meant to happen.'

She bowed her head. 'What?'

'Katherine, look at me.'

She raised her head and their eyes met. 'I love you, Katherine. I have done since that meeting in Beresford Place. Is there any hope for me?'

She didn't know what to say. She had never expected this.

'Sean, I . . . I . . . don't know what to say.'

'Then say nothing. Just think about it. And enjoy this bit of a holiday.'

She nodded. She felt a little of what she'd felt for Edwin rise up. She was confused. Who did she love? Was it love? Could you love two people? She saw more of Sean, and he was from a background similar to hers. He was the same religion; Edwin wasn't and that could be a major problem. If she was ever in trouble of any sort she knew whom she would turn to and it wouldn't be Edwin.

The weather had turned squally as the ferry tied up in Ramsey in the north of the island and they all held onto their hats as they walked towards the boarding house.

'Doesn't it look sort of . . . empty?' Ceppi said.

'All the beaches on the whole island are packed in summer, so Fred says.'

'It's a bit too cold and blustery to be on a beach.'

'It's invigorating.'

Katherine looked at him. 'Where did you learn words like that?'

'In the books I have to read.'

'Do you still have to read books for the job?'

'Yes and no.'

'And what's that supposed to mean?'

'Well, I wasn't going to tell anyone, but you're different. I'm studying for my sergeant's exam. I don't want to be a constable all my life. But that's as high as I'll get. No one with my background ever gets to be an inspector.'

'Sergeant McGovern. It has a nice ring to it.'

'And talking of rings, we've arrived, so ring on the bell.'

'Can I do it?' Ceppi asked, her eyes bright and her cheeks pink.

'Go on then.'

Mrs Quirk made them very welcome. They had a cup of tea first before she showed them their rooms.

'I've given you these at the back, it's more sheltered. In summer everyone wants a sea view, but in winter it's the other way around. Now I'll leave you all to unpack. I've put the little one in with you, Katherine, is that all right?'

'It is. She has her own room at home but with me being in a similar sort of business, I know what it's like with all the bedding, especially in this weather.'

'There's lots of things to see and do. You can go on the steam railway, see the Laxey Wheel, go over to Peel and see the castle and the fishing fleet – if it's in – and there's Douglas with all the shops.'

'I can see we're going to have a busy time,' Sean said.

'Well, you might as well take the opportunity, you might never come again. There're horse-drawn trams still and you mustn't go over the bridge without saying hello to the fairies.'

'There's fairies?' Ceppi was incredulous. 'What do they look like?'

'No one's ever seen them, they're very shy.'

Katherine smiled at the older woman. 'We have the "little people" and no one's ever seen them either.'

'It's all part of our history. We have our own Gaelic language and our own parliament and laws.'

'Then you've got more than we have in Ireland,' Sean said.

'If you want to go out tonight I'll keep my eye on Ceppi.'

'Where is there to go?'

'Some of the hotels have public bars and they'll be glad of the custom too.'

After a ride on the small railway to Douglas and back, they all had tea and at seven o'clock Ceppi was dispatched to bed. She was tired out and so for once there wasn't an argument.

'Will we go out?' Sean asked.

'Why not? After all, we *are* on holiday.'

They found a nice smallish hotel that had a roaring fire in the lounge bar although there was no one else in the room. The barman had a bit of a chat to Sean and he eventually returned with the drinks, a pint of beer for himself and a port and lemon for Katherine.

'Isn't this the life of luxury?' he said, holding his hands out to the blaze.

'It is so. It must be wonderful to spend a whole week here. That meal was grand and afterwards I could get up from the table and walk away from all the dirty dishes!'

'But you offered to help.'

'It was only manners. Sure, we both know how hard it is. She's very nice.'

'Didn't I tell you you'd enjoy it?'

She laughed. 'I am enjoying it, thanks. Thank you so much, Sean.'

He took her hand in his. 'It's my pleasure. I want you to enjoy it, to make up for a miserable Christmas.'

'It wasn't *that* miserable.'

'Well, it wasn't the way we'd planned it.'

'I know, but it couldn't be helped. That poor girl.'

'Did I tell you the bit of gossip that's going around? It *is* only a rumour so don't go telling Maggie. After the post-mortem they found she'd had an abortion. It was all hushed up, of course.'

Katherine looked at him with horror. 'An abortion! That's . . . that's . . . *murder*.'

'I know. I also know that many desperate girls have died after seeking one. They go to some backstreet place that's dirty and often the women who operate haven't a clue about just what they're doing. Not that it would have been the likes of them that Miss Madeleine Power went to.'

Katherine shivered. 'Oh, Sean, let's change the subject.'

'I'm sorry I mentioned it. I don't suppose it was the type of thing you'd want to hear.'

'I don't, but it goes on in Dublin too. Not very often because of the clergy.'

'Do you ever want children? Children of your own, I don't mean Ceppi?'

'Of course I do. What girl wouldn't? But I'd have to be married first.'

'I like kids too,' he replied before downing the last of his beer. 'Will you take another one?'

'I will. I've never tasted a drink like that before. I've only had sherry.' The thought prompted memories of poor Mary's funeral wake.

She watched Sean as he went to the bar counter. He'd make a good father, he'd be strict but fair and most of all he'd have the patience. The feeling of confusion returned but she shook it off. They only had one night here and she wasn't going to spoil it for herself or him.

Chapter Twenty-Three

———◆———

'IT'S ALL OVER,' Ceppi complained as they waited to board the ferry home. They'd only been to see the Laxey Wheel, there hadn't been time to go to Peel.

'I know, but one day we'll come again in summer. And you've bought all those sticks of rock for your friends.'

Ceppi cheered up. 'Nancy will love it, there's "Isle of Man" running right through it.'

Katherine was looking fearfully at the huge grey clouds that were moving across the sky and she prayed that the wind wouldn't get up.

It did as they left the lee of the land and Ceppi was dreadfully sick. Fortunately neither Sean nor herself were.

'I want to get off! Oh, Katherine, I want to get off,' she moaned.

'I'm sorry, Ceppi, but we can't get off, not until we reach Liverpool. It's not like a bus or a train.'

'She'll be grand when her feet are on firm ground again.

Poor kid, and she'd enjoyed it all so much.'

'We both did but I just hope this weather doesn't get worse.'

'So do I. It's going to take us extra time as it is. We'll definitely get a cab home. We can't drag her on and off trams after this.'

The journey seemed endless as the little mail boat ploughed through the heavy seas with waves twenty feet high breaking over her. Katherine began to feel afraid.

'Oh, Sean, would you just listen to it?' she whispered. She'd managed to get Ceppi asleep. The sound of the sea pitting its might against the frail craft was terrifyingly loud. 'It'll take us under if it goes on like this.'

He put his arm around her. 'Katherine, I'm a firm believer that when the Lord decides to call you, you go; it doesn't matter how or when, you just have to believe that. But if . . . if anything happens I want you to know that I love you and wanted to marry you and spend the rest of my life with you.'

She rested her head on his shoulder. It was comforting and despite his words she felt that he would never let anything bad happen to her or Ceppi if he could possibly help it. During those dark, terrifying hours she came to realise that he was the man she loved. She felt safe with him and he was fond of Ceppi. Then she remembered something her mam had once said: 'Better the divil you know, than the one you don't.' She *knew* Sean; she really didn't know Edwin.

They got a cab after the storm-battered ferry finally came alongside the Princes Landing Stage three hours late. Katherine felt exhausted by the experience and Sean felt relieved; there had been times when he thought the ship would be breached by the heavy seas and share the *Ellan Vannin*'s fate.

When they reached the house it was in darkness and Katherine's hands were so cold that she had to give Sean the keys. He found the matches and lit the gas in the hall and they went into the kitchen. The fire was out and the room cold.

'He might have had the foresight to build up the fire before he went to bed. I'll put the kettle on, a cup of tea will warm us all, then I'll take your bags up for you.'

'No, Sean, I'll have to try to get this fire started again before we can make tea.'

He took the bags up while she raked out the embers and coaxed the glowing coals into life. It would take ages to get going again, she thought. It was typical of Edwin. He just wouldn't think about things like this. He'd probably never had to do anything so menial in his life.

She'd wrapped Ceppi in her own coat and sat her on the chair nearest the range. The child was still very pale and tired looking. The sooner she got her to bed the better, she thought.

'This is going to take ages before I can even boil a kettle. I could kill him, he's so thoughtless!' she complained as Sean came back.

'He's not here,' Sean announced.

'What?'

'His room is empty, the bed not disturbed.'

'Then where is he? He can't have been gone all that long, there were still hot embers in the range.'

'If you bank those things up they can last for hours on end. What's that on the mantelshelf?' He reached up and took a folded piece of paper down. 'It's for you.' He handed it over.

'No, you read it.'

He scanned the lines. 'He had word that his mother is very ill and he's gone to Shropshire. He doesn't know when he'll be back, he'll try to let you know.'

'He hasn't usually got much time for his mother or his sisters, but I suppose she still *is* his mother.'

'He must have got the news by telegram but he'll be lucky to get a train. He'll have to change a few times too. Look, the fire's caught.'

'Oh, at last! Bring that kettle over to me,' Katherine instructed as the pieces of dry wood known as 'chips' started to burn.

'Will you stay and help me with Ceppi? She's still not well and she's too heavy for me to carry upstairs.'

'Of course I will.'

'I'll come up and turn back the bed. I'll only take her shoes and coat off. She can sleep in her clothes just for tonight: the bed will be so cold.'

Katherine awoke with a start and, glancing at the clock on the chest of drawers, saw it was nearly eight o'clock. She threw off the bedclothes. Ceppi was going to be late for school and she had Mr Dunne and Mr Forrester arriving any time now. She got dressed quickly, brushed her hair and pinned it up into a loose chignon, so at least it looked tidy. As she went downstairs she changed her mind about waking Ceppi. She wouldn't send her in to school until this afternoon; she'd give her a note to take in.

She had the fire going in the range and sitting room when there was a knock on the front door.

'Oh, Mr Dunne, it's yourself. Come on in. I'm afraid I'm a bit behind. We went to the Isle of Man for the weekend and were delayed getting back by the storm. I'll soon have the kettle on.'

'It was a terribly wild night. Mrs Dunne was afraid we'd lose some tiles from the roof but they held. I'll take my bags up, Katherine, if you don't mind. Has Mr Forrester arrived yet?'

'No, but I don't think he'll be long.'

'Apart from the storm, did you enjoy your break?'

'I did so. The weather wasn't too bad, the place we stayed at was clean and warm and the food was good too.'

He took his bag upstairs while she got the cups and saucers from the dresser. She'd just brought the tea caddy to the table when there was another knock on the front door.

Ah, Mr Forrester, she thought. Well, they could all have tea together; she hadn't had anything herself yet.

She gave a cry of surprise as she opened the door and found Sean, in uniform, standing on the step.

'If you've come for a cup of tea you're lucky, I was just making a pot.' Then she noticed how pale he looked; his lips were set in a thin line of anger.

'What's wrong?'

'Get your coat, Katherine, Maggie needs you.'

'Maggie? At this hour? What is it? For God's sake, Sean, what's the matter?'

'It's . . . it's . . . Tilly. She didn't come home last night. They . . . they found her this morning. She's dead, Katherine, she's been murdered.'

She stared at him, utter horror spreading over her face. 'No! No!'

'I'm afraid so. Get your coat. Have you anyone here?'

'Mr Dunne and Ceppi; I've left her in bed. I thought you were Mr Forrester.'

'I'll go and have a word with Mr Dunne, explain and ask him to see to Ceppi. Then we'll go.'

As she walked beside him she was shivering. It couldn't be true. It just *couldn't*. Not Tilly. The girl was so quiet, so inoffensive. Who would want to kill her?

Frank met them at the door. He looked haggard and stunned. His eyes were full of tears.

'Oh, Frank, is it true? Is it really true?'

He could only nod and Sean put an arm around his shoulder and guided him back into a kitchen that was crowded with policemen and neighbours. Maggie was sitting in the old rocking chair, sobbing wildly into Alfie's jacket sleeve. The lad looked confused and frightened.

'For God's sake, McGovern, get some of these people out of here, it's like bloody Lime Street Station!' his sergeant said.

Sean knew most of the neighbours and managed to persuade them to leave. They were followed by a couple of constables, colleagues of Sean's from Warren Street Station. Katherine nodded at Alfie who moved away from his mother and Katherine took Maggie into her arms.

'Oh, Maggie! Maggie! How . . . how did it happen?'

Maggie raised her head, her eyes half closed with crying. 'She . . . she said she was going to meet a girl from the place she was in service with but she . . . she didn't come back.' Maggie couldn't carry on, she was sobbing uncontrollably again.

Frank turned to Katherine. 'I went out looking for her

290

with Bernard and Mick and then the rest of the fellers joined in, but we had no luck and then . . . they . . . they came to tell us.'

'Oh, why her? Why poor Tilly?'

'We don't know. She wasn't robbed or . . . er . . . assaulted. Just left . . . in the entry. She'd been strangled,' Sean told her as gently as he could.

'Oh, Sean, it's terrible! It's desperate! Who'd do anything to Tilly? She wouldn't hurt anyone!'

'We don't know, but we'll make bloody sure we find out,' he answered grimly.

Katherine sat with Maggie while Frank went with the police to deal with all the formalities. Alfie had been sent to work.

'Oh, God, what have I done, Katherine? First Mary and now my poor Tilly!'

'Hush, hush now. It's nothing you've done, Maggie. They'll find whoever did this and he'll hang.'

Maggie couldn't reply. In the end Katherine prevailed upon the police sergeant to allow her to take Maggie to her own house for a few hours. A change of scenery might help calm her.

Mr Dunne was standing at the window and as soon as he saw Katherine and Maggie he went to open the door.

'Mr Dunne, I thought you'd have had to go out by now.' Katherine was concerned; what else had happened?

'No, I cancelled my appointment to stay with Ceppi. Is this . . .?'

Katherine nodded and took Maggie into the parlour and settled her into an easy chair. 'You'll be more comfortable in here. I'll be back in a minute.'

'I'm making some tea with plenty of sugar in it.'

'Mr Dunne, you are so kind. It's . . . it's terrible, unbelievable.'

'The poor woman and the poor girl. Have they caught anyone yet?'

'Not that I know of. But why? Why some quiet, respectable young girl like Tilly? She hadn't been robbed or anything.'

'Perhaps she knew whoever it was.'

'They didn't say there had been a struggle. But what chance would Tilly have had if she had struggled? Where's Ceppi?'

'At school. Mr Forrester arrived soon after you left and walked there with her and went in to explain.'

'You are both so thoughtful, thank you, thank you so much.'

'How could we stand by and do nothing?' He handed a cup to Maggie who shook her head.

'I . . . I . . . couldn't drink it, but thank you.'

Mr Dunne understood. 'Best to let her cry, it will help. Grief shouldn't be stifled, that's what I always say.'

Katherine nodded. 'This is the second child she's lost. I don't know if she'll be able to bear all this. Her younger daughter died in a freak accident.'

'The poor soul.'

Katherine nodded. Death was no stranger to Maggie Boland.

Everyone in St Andrew's Street was very good. Katherine had gone to see all the women to ask for their help.

'It was bad enough for her when poor Mary died, but this is . . . different. She'll have the police there by the minute asking questions,' Edna O'Brian said sadly. Little Eddie had spent so much time with Edna that he'd begun to look on her as a surrogate mother.

'Oh, surely not?'

'They will. I just hope they catch the bastard. I'll be one of the crowd outside Walton Jail the day they hang him!' Ida put in.

'Well, she's not in any state to do anything.'

'Don't you worry, Katherine, we'll all pitch in with the washing and ironing and cleaning and shopping.'

'And I'll cook the meals,' Eliza Neale from the corner shop added.

'Then there's the funeral. I don't know about the Burial Club money,' said Ida.

'Don't worry about that, I'll see to it.'

'You did last time, girl.'

'I know but she gave me a home. I'll never forget that, Ida.'

'Is she going to bring Tilly home? Will the authorities let her?' Eliza asked.

'Of course they will.'

Ida got down to business. 'Then we'd all better sit down and work out a plan. It's no good two of us doing the same thing, is it?'

Katherine thought how good everyone was. They all helped each other out; it was one of the few saving graces in all the slums she'd known.

Katherine felt as if she were living a dream as the day of the funeral arrived. It was cold and windy, just as it had been for Mary's, but somehow because of the circumstances of Tilly

Boland's death the funeral seemed to be a far worse ordeal. She felt numb as she stood and watched the coffin being lowered into the grave. Well, Mary would have company now. Poor Maggie could hardly stand. She was supported by her husband and son who both looked emotionally drained and physically exhausted.

She wondered hopelessly how they would all cope in the days ahead.

At the weekend Edwin came back. He looked so miserable too, Katherine thought as she opened the door for him.

'I'm sorry to just take off, leaving only a note and then descend on you again, but I've nowhere else to go.'

'That's all right. How is your mother?'

'She died. I was too late. By the time I got there she was dead, but I had to stay on for the funeral.'

'Oh, I'm so sorry, really I am. I know you didn't have much time for her, but it still must have come as a shock.'

'It did, and there was no money for a decent funeral. I had to borrow it.'

She made no comment. Having paid for Tilly's funeral she had nothing much left herself.

'How did your trip go?' he asked.

'It was grand even though the journey back was horrifying. We . . . we've had a terrible time here too.'

'Why?'

She told him about Tilly Boland.

'Dear God, who would want to do anything like that? A poor innocent little shop girl. How is Mrs Boland taking it?'

'As you would expect, badly, very badly. I try to get up for an hour a day and she has good neighbours.'

'Isn't life unfair to some people.'

'It is so. Poor Maggie, both her daughters . . . gone.'

'Have the police caught anyone?'

'No. They could find no clue and no motive. Sean said they think it must be someone who left Liverpool straight away or that someone was hiding him.'

'I know that parts of this city are dangerous – down by the docks they'd slit your throat for two shillings – but these are respectable, hard-working people.'

'I know that only too well.'

'I imagine our friend in blue is working overtime on it?'

She nodded. 'I suppose if they don't catch anyone soon they'll stop looking, like they did after that poor Miss Power's murder.'

'There's no similarity between them, nothing to link them. Miss Power was a wealthy young woman and was killed in her own home. Tilly was—'

'Only a shop girl from a working-class family and was killed in the alleyway.'

'Quite. I'll only be able to stay tomorrow, the rest of the week I'm really going to have to get down to work, to pay off the loan to start with.'

'Well, I'll make sure you go off with a decent breakfast. Have you eaten at all today?'

'No.'

Katherine smiled at him. 'At least that's something I can remedy.'

Chapter Twenty-Four

———•※•———

EVERYONE WAS GLAD when winter was over, Katherine thought as she drew back the curtains in the sitting room. Early spring sunlight flooded into the room making the light green and tan decor seem fresh. She'd get some flowers, daffodils, when she was out shopping. She folded the dirty sheets she'd stripped from the beds and made a bundle of them; Lizzie would collect them later. She had a busy week ahead of her, a house full but with gentlemen only staying two nights at most, hence a huge amount of washing and ironing. She felt for Lizzie for the many long afternoons she stood ironing; the constant swapping over of the flat irons made it backbreaking work. It had been one of the burdens she'd taken off Maggie when she'd lived in her house.

Her thoughts turned to her friend. Maggie in particular needed cheering up. There had been so much sadness in her life over the last couple of years that she was looking old and careworn. Well, she'd take her some daffodils too. It might give her a moment's cheer. A sign that the long, dark and tragic winter was over.

She hadn't seen much of Edwin, he'd been away working. She'd missed him, he always lightened her spirits and made her laugh. She often wondered why his mother had rejected him. Oh, she knew the reason, the reason he'd told her, but was the woman as bad as she'd been painted? Maggie often complained about Eddie's escapades, although since Tilly's death she had more patience with the little boy who was still not much more than a baby. The whole neighbourhood still referred to him as 'Maggie's little accident' but it was not said with any malice. Edwin's mother had had a different view, she supposed. The middle classes did things differently; they always sent their children away to a boarding school as soon as they were seven or eight. They were emulating the upper classes, of course, but Katherine thought it was a cruel thing to do to a young child. Why did they have children in the first place if all they were going to do was employ someone else to look after them: nannies, governesses and boarding schools? Edwin had been starved of affection, she thought sadly as she put on her short wool jacket and a small brown-and-cream hat which she adjusted in the mirror in the hallway.

She stared at herself for a moment. Did she look older? There were tiny lines appearing at the corners of her eyes but they were only laughter lines, so Lizzie Maynard had said.

'Wait until yer 'ave an 'usband an' kids of yer own, *then* you'll 'ave wrinkles. It's worry what causes them. I'm only thirty-three but I look about fifty-three. When I think back ter the day I got married, well, I never thought it would be like this.'

Katherine had been taken aback; she'd never realised that Lizzie was so young. Closing the door behind her, she walked down the street deep in thought. All the women she knew were probably much younger than they looked. They must all have been young, clear-skinned, bright-eyed girls when they married and look at them now. The exception was her mam. She could never remember her mam looking lined and wrinkled but then she'd only been twelve years old when Mam had died.

'Are you deliberately trying to walk into a lamppost?'

She looked up and her sober thoughts were banished as she laughed. 'I am not, Sean McGovern!'

'Strange, I thought you were.'

She laughed again. 'Sometimes you really are a desperate eejit!'

'What was it that had you so engrossed?' he asked, falling into step beside her and swinging his truncheon idly, a habit his superiors had still not managed to eradicate.

'Spring at last and age.'

'Age? Jaysus! What for?'

'I suddenly thought about how old Lizzie Maynard said she was and wondered if we'd all end up looking like her.'

'Ah, now that's a bit too profound and delicate for the likes of me. Wouldn't I go putting my foot in it if I started to speculate on things like that? Anyway, I know how old you are.'

'Do you?'

'Of course. Didn't you tell me yourself? You'll be twenty-one in June. Twenty-one and still "a Spinster of this Parish".'

'Will you stop that! I have enough of that from Maggie and Lizzie and Vi Watson.'

'Well, you know how to remedy it.'

She looked down at her feet, embarrassed. 'I know but . . .' She faltered. She was almost sure she loved him but was 'almost' enough to spend her life with him? To have children and the responsibility that went with them?

He was serious. 'I know you'll have to give up your business, my superiors don't approve even now, and I'll have to be the only wage-earner. Is that it, by any chance?'

'Oh, Sean, you know it's not,' she replied, but a moment of hesitation betrayed the fact she wasn't sure.

He sighed. They'd reached the bottom of the road and the shops. 'I'd better be off. If Sergeant Davies sees me "loitering" then it'll be the last straw. I'll be after paying a five-shilling fine, or more if he's in a bad mood.'

'Aren't they desperate.'

'Oh, I don't know. They have to keep us on our toes so the public will respect us and the villains amongst them will have a healthy fear of us. Trouble is, some of the biggest villains are in the police force, but for the love of God don't tell anyone I said that or I'll be out on my ear and probably in jail too.'

'I won't. Will you be round tonight? It'll be fairly quiet. The three I have in now write up their orders, have their meal and then usually read the newspaper or fall asleep.'

'You know, it's a job I would *hate*.'

'They don't have it easy but some of the older ones are well thought of. They're looking forward to retirement, though. Of course, they don't get a pension, unlike you.'

'Ah, so now it's my money you're after, Katherine Donovan?'

She gave him a playful swipe with her shopping bag. 'Get off with you!'

'Get off yourself. What must it look like, a slip of a girl like you clattering the feared Arm of the Law!'

'I'll deal with you tonight.' She laughed as she turned away and went into the greengrocer's.

By the time she got to Maggie's it was almost lunchtime and she was laden down with shopping.

'Maggie, could you wet the tea? I'm worn out with all that lot.' She placed her bags on the floor and sat down in the rocking chair.

'You should get them to deliver it all, the amount you spend on meat and groceries.'

'Ah, that's a bit too grand for me – and what would the neighbours say, having delivery boys calling at the house all day long?'

'I'd say to hell with the lot of them, Katherine, you've done so much for those women—'

'Could I have done less? It was only a couple of ideas. Where's Eddie?' she asked to change the subject.

'With Edna. That woman's a saint to take him off my hands for a couple of hours a day. He drives you demented, you never know what he's going to do next.'

'Here, I bought you these.' Katherine placed the bunch of daffodils on the table.

'You shouldn't go wasting your money, Katherine, but they're lovely.'

'I know. I got some to brighten up the sitting room.'

Maggie stood for a while with the flowers in her hand. 'If you don't mind, Katherine, I . . . I'll take them up to the cemetery on Sunday, for Mary and Tilly.'

Katherine sighed deeply. Maggie would grieve for her two girls as long as she lived. 'Of course I don't mind. Here, take this lot too. A bunch for each of them.'

'No, you take those home, luv. I'd like you to do that.'

'I will. They'll remind me . . . of them both.'

Maggie, with an effort, pushed her thoughts of her daughters to the back of her mind. 'Right, then, let's have a cuppa before meladdo comes back for we'll get no peace then.'

Katherine was surprised to see Ceppi's coat and hat on the hallstand.

'Ceppi! Ceppi! Where are you?' she called as she entered the kitchen. She fervently hoped she hadn't been sent home in disgrace for some escapade. She was teaching the child better manners, just as at the convent they were improving her academically, despite Maggie's gloomy claim that Katherine would never make 'that one' into a lady. Sister Imelda had told her that if Concepta worked hard then in four years' time when she left school she would probably be considered for a reputable Commercial College. One where they wouldn't accept you without the right qualifications, no matter how much money you were prepared to pay.

She found Ceppi hunched up in an armchair, still with her hat and coat on.

'What's the matter?'

'I wasn't well so they sent me home.'

This was something unheard of. Only if you collapsed with

some dire disease did they send you home. She laid a hand on the child's forehead.

'You're burning up. You've a fever.'

'I've got a cough and I feel desperate.'

'Right, stay where you are for now, I'm going for Dr Walsh.'

'Don't leave me for too long, Katherine, please?'

'I won't, I promise.'

As she reached the hall door she stopped dead in her tracks. Ceppi had begun to cough. Oh, merciful God! she thought. There was no need for her to go to the doctor now to find out what was wrong with Ceppi. That racking cough that left the girl gasping for breath told its own story. Ceppi had whooping cough and it could kill.

In a panic she ran back and with an effort lifted the child up and out of the chair. The spasm had passed.

'Ceppi, I've got to get you to bed. Can you walk?'

Ceppi nodded and Katherine helped her to get up the stairs and into her room. She took off her clothes, pulled her nightdress over her head and got her into bed. Katherine tucked the covers tightly around Ceppi.

'I'm going for the doctor and Maggie. I *have* to,' she forestalled Ceppi's pleadings that she stay. 'I'll be back soon.'

She went straight to Maggie.

'It's Ceppi. She . . . they . . .' Katherine was gasping, having run the whole way. 'They sent her home. Maggie, you've got to help me, please, she's got whooping cough!'

'Merciful Mother of God! I'll get my coat and take Eddie back to Edna. I'll write a note for Frank and Alfie.'

'I'll run on ahead, Maggie. I'll get Dr Walsh to come out.

Here, take my key, you'll be back before me,' Katherine urged.

Maggie nodded. Katherine was still a young slip of a thing able to run like the wind when necessity arose; she was middle-aged and too heavy to be running anywhere.

She was sitting beside Ceppi's bed when Katherine arrived with the doctor.

'This is Mrs Boland, a very dear friend.'

Dr Walsh nodded to Maggie who stood up.

He felt Ceppi's forehead, then sounded her chest. Almost as if on cue Ceppi started to cough.

He nodded slowly. Whooping cough claimed many young lives, especially babies, toddlers and under-nourished children. At least this one would have some of the advantages denied to the others. She was well fed, well clothed and her guardian was able to afford his fee and medicines. Yet even with all that she could still die.

'I'll leave you something, Miss Donovan, and I'd recommend camphor.'

'Sir, I've heard that it helps to keep a kettle or a pan boiling all the time,' Maggie interrupted deferentially.

'It does. The steam helps the breathing. If she gets any worse, Miss Donovan, call me.' He got up to leave.

'How much do I owe you?' Katherine asked in the hall.

'Just the money for the medicine, you made the diagnosis yourself. I have to tell you that even a child of Concepta's age doesn't always . . . survive.'

'Oh, God, no!'

'I'm sorry, Miss Donovan, but it's my duty not to give out false hopes. It's serious and it's contagious. Are there any other children in the house?'

'No, but Mrs Boland has a four-year-old son.'

'Keep him well away from here. I seem to remember that the poor woman has already lost two daughters, both tragically. Doctors hear these things.'

'She has and I'd never forgive myself if . . . if . . . Eddie were to get this.'

'Then send her home, Miss Donovan, as soon as possible, and don't let her come here again until it's safe.'

As Katherine closed the front door behind him she felt a weight descend on her shoulders. What had she done, exposing Maggie and her family to such a risk. And, selfishly, she was terrified at having to send away the only person she could rely on. Slowly, she went back upstairs.

'I've given her a dose of the stuff he left,' Maggie told her, 'but I'd get camphor and start boiling water. You've got that gas ring, you could bring it up here and use the biggest pan you've got.'

'Oh, Maggie!'

'I know it's worrying, luv, but—'

'Maggie, you don't understand. He said I have to send you home immediately and not let you come back until—'

'I'm not leaving you to cope alone, Katherine, I don't care what he says.'

'Maggie, it's for Eddie. If there's a single chance that Eddie might catch it then I'd never, ever forgive myself!'

Some of the colour drained from Maggie's face. She could see that the doctor had a point and she knew Katherine would understand only too well what the possible loss of Eddie would do to her.

'You see, I *can't* let you stay. I can't take that chance, it's not fair, Maggie.'

Slowly Maggie nodded. 'Oh, Katherine, after all you've done for me and now, when you need me most, I can't help you.'

'You can do something for me.'

'What, luv?'

'Ask Lizzie and Vi will they run the place for me? I'm fully booked and I can't turn them all away.'

'I will, luv, and I'm certain they'd both be delighted but—'

Suddenly Katherine remembered. They both had young children who were not as well nourished or as strong as Ceppi. Oh, she must be utterly distracted ever to have suggested it.

'No! I'll manage.'

'How can you?'

'I will. They'll have to cook their own breakfast and possibly find somewhere to have their evening meal, but I won't charge.'

'Katherine, you're going to have to close, they'll understand. Most of them are family men. I'll get the gas ring and the pan of water, then I'll go and buy some camphor, then I'll get off home. Oh, Katherine, luv, I feel terrible . . .'

'Maggie, don't think like that, please.'

The woman nodded sadly and left.

Katherine covered her face with her hands. Just when she was doing so well – but she'd not move from Ceppi's bedside until . . . No, she wouldn't let herself think like that! Ceppi *wasn't* going to die.

*

The room was full of steam and the smell of camphor. Katherine's hair had escaped from its pins and damp strands clung to her cheeks and forehead. After each terrifying bout of coughing that left the child weak and gasping, Katherine held her hand tightly. When she was in the throes of an attack, Katherine sat her up and held her. She didn't know what time it was, only that darkness had descended and the wind had got up.

She jumped as the bedroom door opened. 'Sean! Sean, thank God it's you!'

'I came as soon as I'd finished my shift. Lizzie told me, I saw her coming out of Mrs Neale's. How is she?'

'I don't know, really I don't. The medicine the doctor left doesn't seem to help and I've never experienced this . . . this cough before. Oh, Sean, it's terrible to watch and hear her. I *had* to send Maggie home because of little Eddie. I said I'll manage, but . . .'

He put his arm around her shoulder and she leaned her head against him.

'We'll manage, Katherine. I'll stay and I'll take leave if necessary.'

'Sean, I can't let you take time off—'

'You can and I will. She's more important than any bloody job. Now, I'm going down to sort out your guests. Do you keep a record or an appointment book?'

She nodded. 'It's in the drawer of the dresser.'

'Good. I'll send a telegram to them all.'

'That will cost a small fortune.'

'Does that matter?'

'No. No amount of money can make her better.'

He was back in half an hour and she was grateful. He poured more water from the big enamel jug into the pan. 'Go and get something to eat, I'll watch her.'

'I couldn't. I couldn't eat a thing.'

'Well, wet the tea.' He saw the protest forming. 'And, Katherine, I'm dying for a cup myself.'

She brought the teapot, mugs, milk and sugar up on a tray, together with a couple of hastily made sandwiches for him. She'd only just set it down when Ceppi started to cough. Instantly he lifted her and they both held her as the terrifying 'whoop' echoed around the room and the childishly thin body shook as Ceppi fought for her breath.

Sean looked at Katherine with sympathy. She'd saved this child from a life of poverty, near-starvation and ignorance, was she now going to lose her? Ceppi was one of the few people, until she came to Liverpool, who had ever loved her. Not if he had to stay here day and night for a month would he lose her without a fight.

'Katherine. Katherine, look at me.'

She looked at him over Ceppi's damp, tangled curls with eyes that were full of tears.

He caught her hand and held it tightly. 'Katherine, we aren't going to lose her! We *won't* let her die! You've given her so much that at least she stands some class of a chance.'

'Don't leave me, Sean, please?'

'I'm not stirring from here until she's over it. That I can promise you.'

Some of her fear ebbed away. As always in a crisis, Sean was there to help her get through it, like that night on the Isle of Man ferry.

It was a night of overwhelming terror just the same. The time went so slowly, she thought, fighting to keep her eyes open for some of it. Sometimes she sat with her head on Sean's shoulder, others she leaned it on the pillow beside Ceppi. The steam did seem to ease Ceppi's breathing but the room had taken on the appearance of a nightmare where thick clouds of steam sometimes blocked out her vision, frightening her yet further until they cleared and she could see again.

By the time the grey light of dawn filtered into the room where the curtains had remained unclosed, she was asleep in Sean's arms, utterly exhausted. He too was asleep but only in a shallow doze from which he awoke the instant Ceppi moved or made a noise. He blinked as the room became lighter and looked at the child. His heart sank; a day similar to the anguish of the hours of darkness lay ahead of them. Ceppi's cheeks were still too flushed, her breathing too shallow, the fever still gripped her and soon the bouts of coughing would start again.

God, if you have any sense of fairness or justice, don't let her die. Don't put Katherine through such torment and grief. It wasn't a formal prayer, but it came from his heart.

Chapter Twenty-Five

———◆———

ALONG DAY AND an even longer night passed as Ceppi fought the illness that threatened her life. Both Katherine and Sean were exhausted but helped her in any way they could until at last, as the dawn of another day broke, so did the fever. Ceppi slept peacefully.

Tears of relief and tiredness filled Katherine's eyes and Sean held her close.

'She's over it, Katherine, we've beaten it, all of us.'

'Oh, Sean, what would I have done without you? I . . . I . . . would have been beaten down with the fear and the grief.'

'Hush now, alannah. Go and get something to eat. I'll have to report for duty when I've had a wash and got changed, but I'll ask Dr Walsh to call, just to make sure.'

As she automatically began to tidy the room he took her in his arms. 'If the doctor says it's all right, then Lizzie and Vi and Maggie can help you get back to normal. You've the rest of the week free to look after her.'

When he'd gone she sank into the chair by the kitchen fire that Sean had kept going. She'd never felt so relieved in all her life. Ceppi meant everything to her and Sean knew that. She'd never have got through it but for his strength, encouragement and love. She knew now that she really did want to spend the rest of her life with him and Ceppi. There were no more barriers. She sat staring into the fire, thanking God. If she'd lost Ceppi, a part of her would have died too.

Dr Walsh confirmed that Ceppi was over the worst and that she was no longer contagious, but that she would have to stay off school until she was really better for she was obviously very weak.

He'd only just gone when Lizzie came in.

'Oh, thank God an' all 'Is 'oly saints. I saw the doctor an' 'e told me. Vi's gone fer Maggie Boland.'

'Oh, Lizzie, it's been terrible, like a nightmare at times, and there was *nothing*, *nothing* I could do.'

'It's over now, Katherine, girl, an' yer look shockin'. Yer sit there, I'll make a pot of tea fer yer an' then I'll start cleanin' up and seein' ter the washin'.'

'Thanks, Lizzie. I haven't the energy to do anything.'

'An' no wonder. We watched that bedroom light fer 'ours, just 'opin' an' prayin'. We were right there with yer, girl, we've all known despair. It took us back ter when their ship went down. Waitin' ter be told, formal like, 'opin' against 'ope that they'd got out an' been picked up by the *Carpathia*, but they 'adn't.'

'Oh, Lizzie, when I first came here I sympathised, I thought I *knew* what you'd all been through but I didn't. I *didn't*.

But now I can say "I'm sorry for your loss" and understand just how terrible that loss really is.'

'No one really knows, Katherine, until they've faced it,' Lizzie said sadly.

By the time Maggie arrived with Vi, Katherine was feeling a bit better.

'Holy Mother of God be praised. Half the neighbour-hood have been praying for her. You look wore out and I couldn't help you. Twice I had my hat and coat on, I told them I *couldn't* leave you to cope on your own, but Frank stopped me.'

'I am so tired. Oh, Maggie.' All the waiting, watching, praying had taken their toll and she broke down. Maggie held her in her arms and rocked her as if she were a child herself.

'Come on now, drink this tea and then get some sleep, we'll take it in turns to watch her.'

'Yes, we'll all do our bit. Thank goodness there's none of those travellin' fellers due in fer the rest of the week. Next week we'll see ter them if yer don't feel up ter it. It's only plain cookin' mind, nothin' fancy.'

Katherine managed a weak smile. 'That's all they'll expect, Lizzie, and . . . and thanks.'

'Thanks, what fer? Just 'elpin' out. We all wish we could 'ave done more, like.'

'I know, but every little thing helps. I mean that. I'll go up now.'

She slept deeply and was woken late by Ceppi.

'Katherine! Katherine, are you sick? You look all pale.' The child's grey-green eyes were troubled and she was extremely pale herself.

311

'No. No, I'm just tired. What are you doing out of bed?'

'I woke up and there was no one there and I was frightened.'

'Come here to me.' She lifted the child onto the bed beside her. 'Oh, Ceppi, you gave us all a terrible fright.'

'I know, I was . . . frightened myself. I don't remember much except for the coughing and seeing you and Sean. Was he here or was it just a dream?'

'No, he was here. He stayed with us all the time.'

'Where's he gone now?'

'He had to go back to the Station House. He took a day's leave but he didn't ask them first.'

'Will he get into trouble?'

Katherine laughed. 'I don't think he'll care. Now, miss, you go back to bed. Dr Walsh said you can't go back to school for a few weeks. I'll write to Mother Superior, but don't think I'll be waiting on you hand and foot, and you'll do some work at home when you're up to it. Now I must get up and get dressed.'

'I went downstairs and everything is clean and tidy and the fire's been banked up.'

'That'll be Maggie and Lizzie and Vi.'

'Can Nancy come in to see me?'

Katherine deliberated. 'Not today. Maybe tomorrow, after she comes home from school.'

'What day is it tomorrow?'

'Thursday, why?'

'No special reason, I just don't know the days now. Was I *really* very sick?'

'You were indeed, everyone was praying for you. Whooping

cough can kill you but you're a born survivor, Ceppi Healy, so you are.'

'What's a "survivor"?'

'Now I *know* you're better. Questions, questions, questions.'

'Sister Imelda says we should ask questions or how will we know things?'

'I suppose she's right but then she doesn't have a house to run and a million other things to do with her time.'

'She does a lot of praying,' Ceppi said seriously.

'And so she should, isn't that what being a nun is all about? Now back to bed with you.'

She was still weak, Katherine realised, when she found Ceppi had fallen asleep after her lunch. Katherine was glad she'd not promised that Nancy could come in right away.

Sean called that evening as she was dozing before the fire.

'I didn't want to disturb you.'

'You haven't. I was wondering how you got on?'

'Not very well. I told them the circumstances but they fined me a pound just the same and cancelled one of my leave days.'

'They're a hard-hearted lot. Have they no compassion?'

'No. Apparently you yourself have to be at death's door before they'll pay for sick leave.'

'Is there no one you can go to? Like a union?'

'No, and I doubt there ever will be. Like the Army and Navy, you're not allowed to go on strike.'

'Well, it sounds to me as though you need some sort of union.'

'Ours is not to reason why, Katherine. We all signed on

313

knowing the conditions. You have to ask permission for everything. They demand to *know* everything, even down to who and what your friends do for a living.'

'And they don't approve of me and my boarding house, do they? But never mind that, I haven't thanked you, not properly anyway, for staying and helping me to get her through it.'

'Ah, that little rossi's got a way with her. She's tougher than you think. Didn't she bring herself up? She looks like a cherub, a bit of a skinny one, but a cherub just the same. She'll break a few hearts along the way to the altar.'

'That's a very profound class of a thing to say, but you're right. I don't envy the man that gets her, she'll lead him a fine dance.'

'And speaking of altars and the like, is there a hope in hell of you ever agreeing to become Mrs Sean McGovern?'

She laughed, but not unkindly. 'You do have a way with words, don't you? Was that a proposal of marriage?'

'It is so and don't you be giving out to me. I'll get down on bended knee if you want.'

She pealed with laughter. 'No, it's not what I want. You'd look even more of an eejit!'

'Well, will you, Katherine? You know I'm not very good with all this romanticising but I do love you.'

She took his hand and laid it on her cheek, suddenly serious. 'I don't want fancy speeches. I love you and I will marry you.'

Sean looked at her, a delighted smile slowly spreading over his kind features. Then he took her in his arms and kissed her. She clung to him and kissed him back and a feeling she'd never experienced before washed over her. It wasn't the way she'd felt when Edwin had kissed her. There was more, much more emotion in it.

'I never want to be apart from you – not even for a few days,' she whispered almost shyly.

'You won't, I promise. I'll always be with you, even if it's only in spirit.'

She looked up at him. 'Why did you say that?'

'I don't know. Perhaps just to make it more… definite. When will we tell people?'

'When will we tell that little rossi upstairs?'

'She'll have to know soon, but you know what she's like, she'll tell Nancy and then—'

'Sean, could we . . . would you mind . . .'

'What?'

'Getting engaged, otherwise before we know where we are they'll all have us walking down the aisle and . . .'

'And you want a bit of time to get used to the idea?'

'Sort of, but mainly to plan things. I haven't much saved up and when Ceppi leaves school I want her to go to a really good place to learn how to be a secretary. That way she'll never be without a skill; she can earn her own living, a decent one too, if anything went wrong for her and I . . . we . . . weren't here to help.'

'How long will that take? How much will you need?'

'I don't know. When she goes back to school I'll ask and if they can give me an address then I'll go and see. Do you mind?'

'No. I know how precious she is to you.'

'She is. She's the only one, apart from you, who has ever loved and trusted me so much.'

'And you've never let her down nor will you in the future. She once said to me, "Katherine never breaks a promise."'

'It's been hard at times, but I haven't, nor will I ever break a promise to you.'

'Then I'd better draw out my savings.'

'What for? We have a fully furnished house, we can live comfortably on your wages—'

'Not for things like that. For a ring. *My* wife will have both an engagement ring and a wedding ring. That's two you can pawn if you ever need to.'

'Oh, stop that!'

'Well, back to my original question, Miss Donovan. When do we tell people?'

'After we've got the ring.'

'Then we'll go on Saturday morning. I'm on the afternoon shift, so we can do it in style. We'll go to T. Brown at the bottom of London Road, that's where the Quality go.'

'Can we afford it?'

'We can so.'

She leaned her head against his shoulder, still encircled by his arms. Why had she ever doubted she was in love with him? They were made for each other, meant for each other. Look at how, after the terrible night they'd shared in Dublin, they'd bumped into each other here in Liverpool.

On Saturday morning Katherine left Ceppi with Nancy and Lizzie.

'I've a bit of business to see to, Lizzie, I won't be long. Could you come round and keep an eye on them for me, please?'

'Of course, luv, it'll give me a few 'ours' break from the rest of them. God, our Sally's givin' me a terrible time, me nerves are in shreds. She's just at that age when a good bawlin' out from her da would work wonders.'

Katherine gazed sympathetically at her neighbour. 'I'm sorry, Lizzie.'

'Oh, I'll cope! Get yerself off and don't be in an 'urry ter get back.' Lizzie settled herself in front of the fire. Katherine's kitchen was sheer luxury compared to her own.

Sean was waiting at the bottom of London Road and Katherine glanced at the clock suspended above the shop doorway. Half past nine. That gave them plenty of time.

'Right on the dot. Aren't you very punctual, Miss Donovan? Shall we go in?'

'Are you absolutely sure you can afford this?'

'I'm sure, now go on inside.'

He held the door open for her and a slim, elegant, blonde-haired woman came forward to greet them. 'May I help?'

'I hope so, ma'am. It's an engagement ring we want to buy.'

She smiled. 'Come with me and sit down then. It's a very important occasion and one that shouldn't be rushed.'

They both sat on the rather fragile-looking carved and gilded chairs she indicated. Sean just perched on the edge, afraid the thing would fall apart under his weight.

'May I ask how much you'd like to spend? It's always best to know that first, then there's no disappointment.'

Katherine looked at Sean.

'I've ten pounds saved.'

'So we'd like to see something for about seven please,' Katherine cut in quickly.

'I don't mind ten.'

'I don't want you spending everything.'

'Why not? It's only once you get engaged and I'll get it back. Sue you for breach of promise if you break it off.'

Katherine was mortified. 'Oh, please don't mind him,' she begged the assistant. 'He's got this desperate sense of humour.'

The woman smiled. 'Right, now that that is settled I'll bring you a tray to choose from.'

Katherine glanced around at the beautiful necklaces, bracelets, rings and earrings in their glass cases. It was a very high-class place to come and, although they were not dressed up to the nines in expensive clothes, they'd been treated with every respect and that counted for a lot.

She fell in love with a fairly plain ring: two diamonds on a twist. They sparkled under the shop lights.

'A wise choice, not too much setting. Sometimes a ring can have too much setting which detracts from the beauty of the stones.'

'They are beautiful, aren't they?' Katherine moved her fingers so the stones caught the light.

'I've been in this business all my life and to me there is no more beautiful stone than a well-cut diamond. Will I put it in a box or will you wear it?'

Katherine looked at Sean again and saw laughter, pleasure and love in his eyes. 'I think I'll wear it.'

Sean passed over the money.

'If you'll just wait a few moments I'll give you a receipt.'

'Oh, Sean, isn't it gorgeous? As soon as I set eyes on it I knew it was *the* one.'

'Here we are and this goes with it.' The woman handed over a small leather case. 'Open it.'

Katherine did so and lying on a bed of white satin was a beautiful silver teaspoon, the edge of which was patterned in a scroll design.

'We always give one to everyone who buys their engagement or wedding ring here. I wish you every happiness for the future.'

'Oh, that's so . . . so . . . kind of you. I'll treasure it,' Katherine said with feeling.

'Perhaps you would like to add to it from time to time.'

Katherine nodded but Sean looked doubtful. Not on a police constable's wage they couldn't.

She felt as though she were walking on air as they strolled to the tram stop.

'We've got plenty of time to tell everyone before you go on duty.'

'So, where do we go first?'

'Maggie's.'

'Why not send one of the kids up to her, then we can tell her and Ceppi and Lizzie and the rest all at the same time. You do realise that it will cost me a fortune in buying a drink for the fellers?' He laughed.

Katherine became serious. 'There's no men to buy drinks for in Lonely Street.'

'No, but we'll toast them that were lost just the same – "absent friends". And there's still Frank and Mick and Bernie and the lads at the station.'

'Then isn't it a good job I wouldn't let you spend everything?' she laughed.

*

When Maggie arrived the kitchen was already full. She'd been a bit concerned by the summons, she hoped nothing was wrong.

'What's this then, a mothers' meeting?'

'No. We've got something to tell you, well show you . . . well—'

'Ah, will you get on with it before they all burst with curiosity?' Sean interrupted, grinning.

Katherine held out her left hand and smiled as one by one the fact registered.

'Jesus, Mary and Joseph! They've done it!'

'They 'ave indeed an' did yer ever see such a ring?'

'Would yer look at them stones!'

Only Ceppi looked put out. 'Why are you all fussing about a ring?'

'Don't you know?' Maggie asked.

'No!'

Katherine bent down to be on her level. 'It means that Sean and I are engaged to be married.'

Ceppi looked bewildered. 'Will you still keep me . . . after . . .'

'Oh, Ceppi, nothing will change, except that Sean will come to live here and there won't be any more guests. The police authorities don't allow policemen's wives to work. They don't approve of wives working even though I don't go out. Still I doubt that that will satisfy them.'

'So, he'll be a sort of . . . uncle?'

'Not a blood relation, but you can think of it like that.'

'You can call me uncle if you like, Ceppi.'

'I think I'd sooner just call you Sean, like I've always done,' she said contentedly.

'So when will the wedding be then?' Lizzie asked.

'We haven't given that much thought yet.'

'Can Nancy and me be bridesmaids?'

'God, would yer listen to 'er. Ceppi, don't go givin' our Nancy them kind of ideas or she'll 'ave me moth-eaten fer a frock!'

'Well, it won't be for a while.'

'Autumn?' Vi pressed.

'Surely not in winter. We'd all freeze to death.' Maggie was indignant. 'There's nothing as bad as a winter wedding.'

'Maybe spring next year, nineteen fourteen, how will that suit?' Sean suggested.

'Yes, that's it. Spring next year,' Katherine agreed.

'Will you tell Frank and the others that I'll stand them a drink? My shift changes on Sunday, so I'll be up in the Red House about seven.'

'And we'll all go for a drink too,' Katherine added.

Lizzie was scandalised. 'We can't go traipsin' inter a pub, Katherine, us bein' widows an' all. What would Father Scanlan say?'

'What could be wrong with a drink or two for a little celebration? Sure, we'll all fit in the snug at the Unicorn. I'll call and see Father Scanlan to tell him about Sean and me. Haven't you all earned a bit of pleasure?'

'Thank God you're not going to the Red House,' Sean said with feeling, 'or I'd never hear the end of it. Wouldn't you all be counting the number of pints we'd had?'

'What night will we go then?' Vi asked. 'I can get our Janie to mind all the kids, she's the most sensible girl in the street even though she's only thirteen.'

'Don't forget yer "gentlemen", Katherine. It's business as usual from Monday,' Lizzie added.

'Then we'll make it next Friday night. I've no one in on Fridays.'

'I can't remember the last time I had a night out,' Vi said.

'Can any of us?' Lizzie answered.

Vi grinned. 'It'll be a real treat, won't it, Lizzie?'

Lizzie nodded and Katherine smiled. They all *did* deserve it.

Chapter Twenty-Six

Monday brought normality as first Mr Forrester and then Mr Dunne arrived.

'It's fortunate you didn't want to come last week for I'd have had to turn you away.'

'Turn us away, Katherine?' Mr Forrester asked as he hung his overcoat on the hallstand and placed his bowler hat on top of a peg.

'Yes, it's been an eventful week. Ceppi had whooping cough.'

Mr Dunne looked very concerned. 'Oh, how is she?'

'Over the worst but still very weak.'

'Are the other events as serious?'

'No, thank God. Sean and I have become engaged. Look.'

'Well, that is a nice surprise. It's a lovely ring and we both wish you every happiness.'

'Will this mean you'll close up your business? I know the police are very strict on such things.'

'I will eventually. Before we get married, they have to interview me. To see if I'm suitable.'

'That's really taking things a bit too far,' Mr Dunne said, and Mr Forrester nodded his agreement.

'If we don't see the lucky man, give him our congratulations.'

'I will, when he's able to take it in. The "lads" all went for a celebratory drink and none of them seem to have recovered from it yet.'

'That must have been some celebration,' Mr Forrester said wistfully. He was a bachelor and his occupation didn't lend itself to forming lasting friendships. He often envied Mr Dunne his happy family.

'We're having our celebration on Friday. Just the women from the street and Maggie and a couple of her neighbours and we certainly won't get into the state the lads apparently did. Maggie said she'd never seen Frank in that condition before.'

'Ah, it doesn't matter once in a while.'

'I don't suppose it does. Right, I'll put on the kettle and bring the tea into the sitting room and you can have it before you go out.'

'You are very thoughtful, Katherine,' Mr Forrester said fondly. 'Sean's a lucky man.'

By the middle of the week Ceppi was well enough to come downstairs and sit in the kitchen for a few hours. She was still washed-out-looking but she was beginning to eat again. Katherine noticed that it was after Ceppi had had Nancy round that the girl had least energy, but she didn't want to stop the visits, Ceppi was already becoming bored. She half-heartedly read her library book but she liked it best when Mr Dunne read it to her.

'Aren't you the thoughtful one, giving up your evening to read to her.'

'I like children, Katherine, and my own are nearly reared and off our hands. Just between us, I enjoy it as much as Ceppi does,' he'd answered.

Katherine thought suddenly how lucky she and Ceppi were. From having no one, they now had so many kind friends.

'Nancy and me don't like Janie Watson,' Ceppi complained as she watched Katherine get ready for the 'women's outing' as she had named it.

'Oh, Ceppi, don't start being awkward. What's the matter with Janie? She's very *sensible*.'

'*That's* what's wrong with her. She's such a misery. If anyone suggests something exciting she puts the damper on it *and* she's a tell-tale!'

'That's as may be but I know what you and Nancy call "exciting" and that makes me have more faith in Janie. Do I look all right?'

Ceppi looked at her quizzically. 'I don't like that hat. Brown doesn't suit you and it doesn't match.'

'You have no tact, Ceppi Healy.'

'Well, you did *ask* me.'

'Yes I did,' Katherine replied, removing the offending hat. 'What about this one? It's one or the other, I've only got two as well you know.'

'The other one.'

Katherine placed the navy blue hat on her head and

scrutinised herself in the mirror. She didn't go in for the large-brimmed and over-decorated hats that were so fashionable. This was small and looked like a plate with the side edges curled up. It was decorated with a white-and-navy striped ribbon bow. It did go better with her best coat.

'Right, I'm ready. Now, promise you'll behave. I won't be out all night. Janie's had her instructions regarding you two. You've to be in bed by half-past eight at the latest and if you feel tired before then, bring yourself to bed. Nancy can stay the night if she wants to but I don't want a war on my hands when I get back.'

Thus appealed to, Ceppi gave her promise that there would be no trick-acting or falling out or fighting no matter what the provocation might be.

'I'm ready, Lizzie. Have you got them all organised?' Katherine called as she heard the loud knocking on the front door. She opened it to find Lizzie, Vi and four other women, plus a number of children of assorted sizes and ages.

'Right, the lot of you, inside,' Katherine urged. She'd cut a pile of sandwiches for them as they were always hungry and it might keep them quiet for a while.

'Janie, in yer go, luv, an' remember what I told yer.'

Janie looked irritated. 'Yes, Mam. I won't let them break anythin', or go messin' about in the bathroom or the other rooms.'

'They won't get inter any mischief with 'er,' Vi said confidently.

'We won't 'ave much fun either,' Nancy muttered. 'I bet she 'as us doin' times tables. And she reads to us to keep us all quiet.'

'Oh, God, aren't we in for a desperate night *and* I've got to be in bed by half past eight,' Ceppi muttered back.

With some difficulty the women all managed to fit into the snug of the Unicorn and Katherine went and knocked on the sliding wooden panel set into the wall that separated them from the rest of the pub.

'Oh, I 'eard you lot were coming,' Harry Black the licensee said, peering into the room. 'I also 'eard it's another lamb to the slaughter or, in this case, to the altar.'

'Shurrup youse!' one of Maggie's neighbours shouted.

''E's only civil when their Martha's around,' another remarked.

'So, what's it to be then? Stout?'

'No, it's not. This is a celebration. Don't yer know nothin'?' Lizzie said scornfully.

'Jaysus! I'm glad yer don't come in ter "celebrate" very often.'

'Port and lemon all round?' Katherine asked and everyone agreed. She passed over the money and the partition was slammed shut.

'I don't like that feller one bit! Always ready with the sarcastic remarks,' Maggie said.

''E gets plenty of them from their Martha, she's gorra a tongue that would take the whitewash offen the walls,' Vi added.

After a few minutes the partition door opened and the drinks appeared. Katherine distributed them and passed more money over. 'The same again, please.'

''Ave yer robbed a bank or somethin'?'

'Don't be so 'ardfaced, youse,' Vi flashed at him.

'I'm not complainin'! If yer all want ter get paralytic it's fine by me, as long as yer cough up the money.'

'I'll swing fer youse yet, 'Arry Black,' Vi threatened.

'Oh, take no notice of him,' Maggie advised, holding up her glass. 'Here's to you and Sean. God bless the pair of you and give you an easy life.'

Everyone agreed noisily.

The laughing and joking got louder and then someone suggested they have 'a birrof a sing-song'. They all joined in with 'Nellie Dean', then progressed to 'Hang on the Bell, Nellie', which was when the wooden partition was slid back with some force and the landlord's head appeared.

'Yer can shurrup with that bloody racket, I'm not licensed fer singin'!' he bawled at the top of his voice to make himself heard.

'Ye're not licensed fer singin'? I've passed this door many's the time an' there's been fellers roarin' at the top of their voices. What do yer call that then?' Vi yelled back.

'Well, it's not singin' an' besides ye're drivin' the fellers in the bar mad, yowlin' like a tribe of alleycats. They come in 'ere fer a birrof peace an' quiet, away from the screechin' an' yellin' at 'ome!'

'Is that what they come for, Harry Black? I always thought it was for the ale,' Maggie said bitingly.

Lizzie turned to her. 'Yer see, Maggie, if we drive them all 'ome they won't be spendin' the rent money an' that'd go down very well with a lorra women around 'ere. Maybe we should come 'ere more often.'

'I'd get that idea right out of yer 'ead, missus. I'll bar yer. I'll bar the lot of youse! Now shurrup.'

'Mr Black, that was a bit of sparkling chat so it was, and before you leave us we'll have another round of drinks,' Katherine said with heavy sarcasm and a sweetly false smile on her face.

'Are yer goin' ter bar 'er then? She'd buy and sell the likes of youse!' Lizzie pressed.

The money was passed over and the partition slammed shut.

'That shut 'im up!'

'Perhaps we can keep it down a bit. Why don't we do something else?' Katherine suggested.

'Like what?' Vi asked. In her opinion Katherine had given in too easily to that toerag of a landlord.

'What do fellers do in pubs, apart from swillin' ale?' Lizzie asked.

'Play cards or dominos,' Vi answered and was up and hammering on the partition.

'Now what do yer want?' a red-faced Harry Black demanded, flinging the thin wooden panel open.

'Yer'll 'ave that off its 'inges iffen ye're not careful,' someone remarked.

'Dominos, an' don't tell me yer 'aven't gorrany. All pubs 'ave them an' iffen the fellers can play then so can we!' Vi shouted at him.

'Right! That's it! Out, the lot of youse! Ye're barred!'

'You can't throw us out for asking to play a quiet game of dominos!' Maggie protested.

'I can an' I will! My licence says so. "At my discretion", it says! So out before I call the scuffers in. Besides, 'alf of yer are so plastered yer wouldn't be able ter count the bloody spots let alone add them up!'

With curses and threats, uttered in voices shrill with indignation, they all left.

'I don't think there was any call for that,' Katherine laughed.

'I am a bit light-headed, I have to admit.' Maggie giggled. 'And after the names I called Frank when he'd been out celebrating, I'll never hear the end of it. I lost count of how many Vi had; there's going to be some headaches in the morning.'

'I know and if Father Scanlan hears there'll be hell to pay.'

'But when was the last time they had anything to celebrate? When was the last time they actually went out without the kids trailing them like kittens after a cat and with no money to spare for anything?'

'Too long ago. That's why I suggested it,' Katherine replied. 'Now, I wonder how all the kids are? Ceppi and Nancy should be in bed and I imagine Janie will have taken the rest home. They'll all be asleep.'

'Until their mams wake them by falling in at the door,' Maggie said ominously. 'But it was a good night, Katherine, one that won't be forgotten for a long time and not just because they all got paralytic. They all care about you and Ceppi.' Maggie hugged Katherine before turning the corner to walk home, hoping the fresh air might clear away some of the light-headedness.

Everything was tidy when Katherine got in, which was a surprise, and she made a mental note to buy Janie Watson some small thing in thanks. There were very few thirteen-year-olds who could keep order. She went upstairs and opened Ceppi's bedroom door. The child was sleeping but there was no sign of Nancy. She tried one of her other bedrooms and found Nancy huddled down beneath the bedclothes. She smiled. Nancy wouldn't have given up the chance of a night's sleep in a comfortable, warm bed without having to share it with her sisters. And a room of her own too, if only for a night.

She went back down, removing the pins from her hair so it fell loosely down over her shoulders. A cup of tea and then bed for herself, she thought.

The kettle had just boiled when she heard a faint knocking on the scullery door. Frowning, she went to open it. She sincerely hoped it wasn't Lizzie or Vi or any of the others. To her amazement Edwin was standing there.

'I didn't want to knock on the front door and disturb anyone.'

'Come in, there's only Ceppi and Nancy here. What's the matter? You aren't due here until next Tuesday.'

'I know, but I finished early and I had nowhere to go, apart from a gloomy cold boarding house, so here I am. Can I stay?'

'Of course you can. I've just wet the tea, you must have smelled it.'

He smiled. 'Thanks, Katherine. Just hearing you say you've "wet" the tea makes me feel better.'

Katherine gazed at him, compassion in her eyes. 'Edwin, why are you so . . . so . . . unhappy with life? Oh, I know about your mother and your sisters but . . .' She paused, waiting for him to explain, hoping she wasn't being too forward.

He frowned. 'I don't know. Well, I do but . . .' He stopped suddenly, gazing at her left hand. Katherine looked down.

The diamonds in her ring caught the orange flames of the fire and glowed with a fire of their own.

Edwin didn't speak.

'Aren't you pleased for me?'

'It's Sean, isn't it?'

'It is. While you've been away Ceppi got whooping cough and he stayed with me night and day and I realised then that I wanted to spend my life with him.'

Edwin's features were contorted, the firelight making them look more twisted.

She was surprised. 'What's the matter?'

'You're like all the rest, or you will be. A wife, then a mother.'

'I hope so. We're not getting married until next spring. But I'll have to close this place up. I won't be taking in any more gentlemen, the police won't allow it. Even fiancées are not supposed to work unless it's absolutely necessary; running a boarding house is definitely frowned on.'

'But you won't go short, will you? Not with a good, steady wage, which is more than I can offer.' His voice was bitter.

'Oh, Edwin, don't take it like that. I love Sean and he loves me.'

He got up and, turning away from her, balled his fists inside his jacket pocket. 'And I love you too, Katherine.'

She sighed; she'd seen this coming. 'No you don't, Edwin,' she said quietly. 'You think you do because here, in this house, you've found affection and trust, a family of sorts. All you crave is affection. Someone to care about you, look after you, and I understand that.'

'No you don't! You never will. How can you know what it's like to be rejected, unloved?'

'You're wrong, Edwin. I was unloved and rejected and so was Ceppi. That's why we found comfort and security in each other.'

He turned to face her. 'Can't we find that? The three of us?'

She shook her head. 'No, because it's not love, and for a marriage to work it *has* to be founded on love, not mutual unhappy memories.'

He turned away again. 'If you don't mind, Katherine, I'll go to my room.'

'Nancy's sleeping there. Have the one next door, they're all the same.'

'No, they're not. I always think of it as *my* room,' he answered peevishly.

'Go and get some rest, Edwin, please.'

He nodded and picked up his bag and case and without another word went upstairs, leaving her sitting in the kitchen, with an overwhelming sadness creeping over her.

There was no sign of him next morning. She went up and knocked lightly on his door. There was no reply and she opened it quietly. He was still in bed and why not, she thought, he'd probably had a restless night.

By the time she came down Ceppi and Nancy had finished their breakfasts; Nancy was still talking about the rarity and comfort of a room and bed all to herself.

'Nancy, you'd better go and see how your mam is. I've a feeling she won't be too grand and might need your help.'

'Why?' Nancy was mutinous.

'Because she enjoyed herself a bit too much last night.'

'You mean she was drunk?'

'Jaysus! Ceppi Healy, I despair of you at times, that I do! Well, yes, she was drunk, they all were, are you happy now?'

Ceppi was nonchalant. 'Mammy had a fierce temper on her the morning after a night out and I had to do most of the cleaning and shopping and I often got clattered if I so much as opened my mouth.'

'She won't belt me, Katherine, will she?' Nancy was fearful.

'No. Take no notice of this bold rossi here. Now off with you.'

'Don't talk at all, Nancy, then she can't clatter you!' Ceppi called after her friend as Nancy dejectedly walked down the lobby. She'd wanted to tell her mam about all the luxury Katherine had.

'Will you sit there or go back to bed while I go for the shopping?'

'I might as well go back to bed, I've no one to play with.'

'Edwin's here. He arrived last night.'

Ceppi's expression altered; she liked him. 'Where is he?'

'Still asleep. He was very tired so leave him. I'll get his breakfast when I get back. Up you go. Read your book.'

'It's a stupid book! I don't like reading but I promised.'

'Well, you won't get very far if you can't read properly, milady, and aren't I saving hard to send you to a school where you'll learn typing and the like?'

'I don't think I want to learn typing. It's just banging on a machine all day.'

'No it's not, there's more to it than that.'

'I'd sooner be a doctor. Edwin said I was clever enough.'

'And well you might but I . . . we won't have enough money for anything like that, it costs a fortune, so you can get that idea right out of your head, Ceppi Healy!'

When Katherine had gone Ceppi flicked through the pages of her book. She didn't like reading and she supposed that if you wanted to be a doctor you would have to read a mountain of books. Maybe typing wasn't so bad after all.

After half an hour she was bored and she heard Edwin go into the bathroom. She put on her dressing gown and slippers and sat on the top stair waiting for him. After ten minutes had passed she began to get impatient. Just what was he doing in there? It couldn't take that long to get ready. She got up and walked down the landing to his room. The door was open so she went in.

He wasn't very tidy, she thought, his clothes had been thrown on the floor. She wondered if he still had any medical books that might help her in some way, give her an idea of what she would have to learn. She tried the lid of his case; it wasn't locked and she opened it. She was surprised at its contents. There were a lot of thin, very sharp-looking knives and thin long-handled scissors, even a small saw. What did he need these for?

'Just what the hell are you doing?'

Ceppi turned and looked at him and surprise turned to fear. She'd never seen him look like that or speak to her in such a tone.

'I . . . I . . . was waiting for you and I came in and . . .'

He crossed the room and shut the lid of the case. 'You

were prying into my things. Do you hear me, *my* things! They are nothing at all to do with you!'

Tears pricked her eyes. 'I'm sorry, I didn't mean to make you as cross as a bag of weasels. You said I could be a doctor and I wondered if there was anything here about doctoring . . .'

His manner changed abruptly. 'Well, those are some of the instruments a doctor, or rather a surgeon would use. It's . . . it's my case of samples.'

'Oh.'

'I'm sorry, Ceppi, for shouting at you.'

She didn't answer. She was still wary of him. When he'd shouted he'd looked like a completely different person and she hadn't liked what she'd seen. For the first time she felt wary of him.

'Where's Katherine?'

'Gone to the shops; she'll be back soon. I'll have to get back to bed or she'll be giving out to me.'

'Ceppi, I won't tell her that you came in here and opened my case if you promise not to tell either?' His tone was wheedling. 'Is it a deal?'

Slowly she nodded and backed out. She knew she shouldn't have gone in there and rummaged in his case, but if he sold those scissors and things why didn't he have some medicines as well and rolls of bandages? Doctors used them all the time, she remembered that from when she'd been in hospital.

She closed the bedroom door behind her, got into bed and pulled the covers up to her chin. She heard him go down and then she heard Katherine's voice and she felt much easier. She got up and dressed, went downstairs and up to the kitchen door. Katherine sounded upset about something. Perhaps he had told her after all? Well, if he had she'd tell on him.

'I don't know what the world is coming to at all,' she heard him say. She pressed her ear to the door. He *had* told her!

'Neither do I. Who would do something like that in a well-to-do place like West Kirby? It's very select over there on the Wirral.'

'I know. I've passed through it.'

'Bert Kelly in the Maypole Dairy said she bled to death. It was all over in a matter of half an hour. Half an hour, can you believe it? And she a young healthy girl?'

'Did he say who told him that?'

'He did. His sister is in service over there but it's her weekend off so she came home. A weekend off, would you believe? Poor Tilly only got a day. Bert's sister said the police had asked her all kinds of questions before letting her come home. They're beginning to think that all these murders are connected, that it's not just abortion.'

'And they had no idea, no clues?'

'Nothing. The poor girl was nearly dead by the time someone found her. May God have pity on her. But enough of that, I'll get your breakfast.'

Ceppi crept back up the stairs with a very peculiar feeling stealing over her. Another girl dead – after an . . . an 'abortion', whatever that was. She had no idea what the word meant, but she did understand 'murder'. The police thought the dead girls had been murdered . . . and Edwin had all those awful knives and things . . . No! What on earth was she thinking? It couldn't be him. She was just being an eejit. He was a salesman, that's all. And he'd had every right to be angry with her for rooting amongst his things. Those instruments must be expensive, no wonder he'd been cross. She could have damaged them and he'd have had to replace them. No, it couldn't be him; he'd read to her, taught her things, made her laugh. Maybe she was just overtired after last night. There had been kids everywhere and Janie on top note for most of the time. She'd been glad to get to bed. She was tired, that was it.

Chapter Twenty-Seven

K ATHERINE CALLED ON the parish priest on Sunday afternoon after Benediction. The housekeeper showed her into the parlour where most of the parish business was conducted. It was a dark room; the one small window let in little light and what there was was further diffused by the lace curtains. The walls were painted dark green, which made Katherine smile. Even the priests must believe the theory about the bugs and the colour. Above the mantelpiece was a painting of the Crucifixion; on a small table stood a statue of the Infant of Prague. On the window sill was a statue of Our Lady of Lourdes and some spring flowers in a small vase. A large table, two chairs and an old and heavily carved sideboard were the only pieces of furniture.

Father Scanlan was a small, rotund man whose sharp eyes missed nothing.

'Ah, Katherine, 'tis nice to see you. Sit down, child.'

She sat on one of the chairs.

'Now what is it you've come to me for?'

'Two things really, Father.'

'Yes?'

'Well, on Friday night myself and some of the neighbours went for a little celebration drink at the Unicorn.'

'I heard you did.'

Katherine looked down at her folded hands. 'No harm was meant, Father, they've all had so much hardship in their lives.'

'They have indeed.'

'The celebration was because Sean McGovern and myself have become engaged.'

The priest's expression changed. 'Well, now, isn't that a great piece of news altogether. He's a fine young man, never misses Mass despite the peculiar hours he has to work, and yourself, a kind and generous young woman. Sure, I think we can dismiss the little episode on Friday night. So, when will you get married?'

'We . . . I . . . thought next spring, Father.'

He looked a little perplexed. 'Isn't that rather a long engagement?'

'It's my idea, Father. You see, when Ceppi finishes school I want to send her to a good Commercial School so she'll have a good job and a secure future, and I need to save up for that.'

'I can understand that, haven't you been goodness itself and she no kin at all? But what about your own children, Katherine?'

She was rather taken aback. 'My children?'

'That is what the Holy Sacrament of Marriage is about, procreation.'

'I know that, but . . . I hadn't thought about . . .'

'Children. Well, you must, and would it be fair to spend hard-earned money on Concepta and not do the same for your own flesh and blood?'

'I'd not thought about that, Father.'

'Then go home, child, and think about it and speak to your future intended and then come back to me. How is Concepta now?'

'She's on the mend, thank you, Father.'

'That's great to hear. A lot of people did a lot of praying and the Lord must have heard those prayers. Ah, yes, indeed we should never underestimate the power of prayer.'

She nodded as she rose. 'Thank you, Father, I'll speak to Sean.'

'You do that, child, and God bless you both.'

On Monday afternoon she was sitting with Maggie when Sean came in.

'How's the patient?'

'Fine. She says she's bored.'

'She probably is. Can't she go back to school?'

'Not until Dr Walsh says so but I'm thinking of asking him; she has me heart-scalded.'

'Where's meladdo?' Sean asked, putting a boot to the fire. 'You don't get as much heat out of this stuff as you do with turf. With a bit of a boot applied to it, turf's great with the heat.'

'And it's great with the dust and dirt out of it too!' Katherine said sceptically. 'He's gone out, he has appointments.'

'Isn't he the strange one,' Sean mused.

'How so?'

'No family.'

'He has,' Katherine replied.

'Ah, but they don't see him and he doesn't go to see them. He has no friends.'

'That's true, but I suppose that has something to do with the job. And don't forget that he doesn't come from Liverpool.'

'I still think there's just something about him that doesn't ring true.'

'I'd agree with you on that, Sean,' Maggie interjected. 'He's always here, saying he has nowhere else to go.'

'He hasn't. I feel sorry for him.'

'You're very good at sorting out all the waifs and strays, Katherine, but just be careful with him. I know I've only seen him a few times and he's always very polite, but I don't really like him.'

Sean was glad Maggie had backed up his feelings. It would have perhaps looked a little like his just being jealous otherwise.

'Well, I'll be off, luv. Thanks for the tea,' Maggie said.

'And I want no repeat performance of Friday night. Aren't you all the talk of the neighbourhood? Falling down drunk, the lot of you.'

'I was not!' Maggie retorted heatedly.

'Neither was I. And it was only a bit of fun.'

'I wouldn't call chucking a brick at McKenzie's window and calling him "a thieving skinflint" a bit of fun.'

'He *is* what Tessa Flanagan called him. He's one of the worst moneylenders in the entire parish.'

'She was lucky it was me caught her and not any of the

other lads. I told my superiors I didn't see who it was. You've got me lying through my teeth for you.'

'We promise not to do it again,' Maggie said primly before Sean and Katherine laughed.

Tessa Flanagan was a neighbour of Maggie's and usually a quiet woman. Why the hell she'd got fighting mad, God alone knew. It must have been the drink. It affected people differently, Maggie thought.

When Maggie had gone, Sean poured himself a cup of tea.

'Did you see Father Scanlan about us?'

'I did and he was after hinting that it was a long time to be engaged. I told him about my plans for Ceppi and he said had it not entered my head that we would have children of our own and that plans should be made for them too. It wouldn't be at all fair to spend so much on Ceppi's education and perhaps not be able to afford to do it for the others.'

'He's got a point, Katherine.'

'I know. But if we saved up we could do it for our own children.'

'True for you. We'll already have a grand home and one big enough for more than a couple of children too. We get a rent allowance and a boot allowance and I don't wear my boots down that much. The name on the rent book will have to be changed but that's no problem. I get overtime, and I'm hoping I'll pass my sergeant's exam, that'll mean a better wage so . . .'

'So what?'

'So suppose we get married earlier, in June, say. On your twenty-first birthday, if you like?'

'Sean, I'd never have enough money, it's only a few months.'

'Put your rates up.'

'I can't, I already feel I'm charging too much now.'

'For what they get here you're not charging enough.'

'Really? I suppose they do often say how well they're treated.'

He put his arms around her. 'So?'

She thought about it for a few minutes. Her visit to the priest had made her think more deeply about it.

'Yes, that's what we'll do, Sean. It's wrong of me to think only of Ceppi.'

'Are you sure now?'

'I am. June it will be and I'll put my rates up two shillings. Is there any way at all I can keep the business going?'

'Not a cat in hell's chance. As I've already told you we have to have permission for everything. They'll come and inspect the house, they always do, and they frown on "consorting" with the neighbours. If you have friends outside the force you're discouraged from seeing them.'

'It's desperate. It's worse than the Army!'

'I know but they can't have you living next door to known criminals or habitual drunkards.' He laughed. 'So that means that this street must become teetotal.'

'Oh, stop that! You know it was only the once, there's nothing "habitual" about it. Sure, the next drink they have will be at our wedding.'

'You're inviting the lot of them?'

'Why not? Will the authorities want to know all about that too?'

'Ah, I don't think so at all.'

344

'Will you be staying for your tea?'

'I will. Mrs Kincade above at the Station House manages to burn everything and I mean *everything*!'

Dr Walsh came on Wednesday and declared Ceppi fit to go back to school the following week. Katherine didn't know who was more relieved, herself or Ceppi.

'Have there been more cases?' he'd asked as he closed his bag.

'I don't think so.'

'It's just that I don't want her to become infected again.'

'I'll go up to the school, sir, and ask.'

'I think that's wise in the circumstances,' he'd replied.

As soon as he'd gone Katherine had gone up to the convent and was assured that there had been no other cases. She left feeling very relieved and with work that had been set for Ceppi to complete and take back on Monday. The child greeted that news with an outcry.

'Oh, do I *have* to do it?'

'Yes, you do. You've been complaining about being bored, now you have something to do. I don't want you getting behind with your lessons. I actually think they look on you as one of their "star" pupils, although sometimes I wonder why. You're certainly not a "star" with your behaviour!'

The following morning Edwin arrived back as expected.

'Did you have a good trip?' Katherine asked.

'I did. I even collected some of the money that was owed.'

'But you'll have to pass it on, won't you?'

'Yes, but I take my wages and expenses out of it, that's how it works.'

Katherine thought it a little odd. She'd never asked any of her gentlemen about how they were paid but Mr Dunne had said that it was usual for the company to pay you a weekly wage, plus commission. There had been no talk of taking your wage from the money collected.

'I have something to tell you, Edwin.'

'What?' He looked at her guardedly.

'Sean and I have decided to bring the wedding forward. To June this year.'

He was suspicious. 'Why?'

'I had a talk with Father Scanlan and he persuaded me to alter my views on a long engagement.'

'Those damned priests of yours! They meddle in everything and you all believe every single thing they say, without question.'

'I don't think that's a very nice thing to say. I don't think or speak like that about your religion.'

'I don't have one.'

'Well, anyone's religion. I have never discussed the subject with any of my gentlemen and I certainly won't have you giving out about mine.'

His expression changed. He was contrite. 'I'm sorry, Katherine, I spoke out of turn.'

She looked at him closely. This was a side of him she'd never seen before. The outburst of bigotry and the almost fanatical look that had come into his eyes frightened her, but she decided to pursue the matter in hand.

'So I'll be closing down the business at the end of May.

The police are very strict about these things.' He now looked so downcast that she smiled at him. 'Go into the sitting room and I'll make you a cup of tea.'

'That's the panacea for everything, isn't it?' he said with a note of bitterness in his voice.

'I'm sorry, I don't understand you.'

'Tea – it's the remedy for everything.'

'It's all we have, except for aspirin and laudanum and I don't hold with laudanum, except in real emergencies.' She changed the subject. 'Ceppi will be glad you're back. She's always complaining but the good news is that she can go to school next week and they've sent enough work to keep her both occupied and quiet.'

He didn't reply but went through into the writing room with his order book. She went to put the kettle on. Why had he suddenly become so bitter? He knew it was Sean she loved. She'd thought all his protestations of love were over and done with.

Sean came for his evening meal and he looked grim.

'What's the matter?' Katherine asked.

He looked pointedly at Ceppi.

'Ceppi,' Katherine said at once, 'take all that through into the dining room. They've all finished and I've cleared away.'

'It's cold,' Ceppi protested.

'Oh, aren't you in for a shock next week? I doubt Sister Imelda will stand for all these complaints and back chat.'

Ceppi went and Katherine took Sean's meal out of the oven and put it onto the table.

'Now, what's wrong?'

'It's getting serious, Katherine. Another girl has died, in a

347

small market town called Ormskirk, about fifteen miles away. It's Lancashire Constabulary's area but we've all been informed.'

She was horrified. 'Oh, not another one! What? How?'

'The same as the last. An abortion that went very wrong.'

'Oh, God Almighty, the poor girl.'

'And they've got nothing. No one saw anything. It's beginning to form a pattern. Miss Power here, the girl in West Kirby and now this. It's got to be the same person. And he's not just performing abortions, he intends to kill, that's the verdict of the police surgeons and the coroners.'

Katherine was seriously thoughtful. 'Do you think it was the same man who . . . who murdered poor Tilly?'

'They don't think it's connected but I have my own views. I think Tilly was murdered because she saw him.'

'But it was only a glance, she was too afraid to notice *anything* about him.'

'He probably didn't know that. He comes and then vanishes. Be careful, Katherine, and take care with Ceppi.'

She drew herself up indignantly. 'But I'm not pregnant and even if I were I'd never, never do anything to get rid of it. And Ceppi's only a child.'

'I know but just take care where you go. Who knows what kind of a maniac we're dealing with.'

Ceppi chewed the end of her pen. She was well and truly stuck. She hadn't even seen some of the words she was supposed to know how to spell, never mind what they meant. Katherine wouldn't know either, and although the two salesmen in the writing room probably would, she didn't like to ask them. They were both so quiet, she hadn't even had a proper conversation with either of them and they'd been coming for two months now. That only left Edwin because Sean had put his head around the dining-room door and said she was to work hard and behave, then he'd gone. Edwin would surely know but she was a little wary of him now. She took the pen out of her mouth and put it on the table beside the inkpot. She'd have to ask him.

He wasn't in the writing room nor in the sitting room so she went upstairs and knocked on his door.

'Who is it?' he called.

'It's me, Ceppi. I've some terrible words to learn and I don't know what they mean.'

'Come on in then, Ceppi.'

She opened the door cautiously and found him in his shirt sleeves, sitting on the bed.

'I'm sorry if I'm disturbing you. I don't really *know* the other gentlemen.'

'Let's see what's causing you so much trouble.'

She handed over the list.

'I see what you mean. What you need is a dictionary. I've a small one here somewhere, you can use that. Do you know how to use one?'

'I think so. You find the first letter of the word and look it up and you go along after that till you find the word.'

He was searching through piles of books and papers on the top of the chest of drawers.

'It's somewhere here, I know it.'

She looked closer and caught sight of some kind of appointment book, one page of which was covered by what looked like a map. Her gaze was fixed on the names and the places. He looked up and quickly covered the page up, but not before she'd seen the name, address and date of his next appointment.

'Here it is.' He drew out a small thick book from beneath the papers and handed it to her. 'If you have any trouble ask me.'

'I will and I'll bring it back as soon as I've finished.'

'There's no need for that. Leave it on the dining-room table. I'll pick it up over the weekend. So, you're back to school then?'

'On Monday and I'll be glad to go.'

He grinned at her. 'And I'm sure Katherine is glad too.'

She grinned back. 'Oh, she is that.'

After that he kept himself to himself, only appearing for breakfast and his evening meal which he ate in the dining room. The rest of the time he was either out or in his room.

Ceppi soon learned about the girl who'd died in Ormskirk. Katherine was discussing it with Lizzie and because Ceppi had her head stuck in a book both women forgot she was there.

'Sean says there's a pattern to it and that someone *must* know him even though he comes and goes.'

'Well, iffen 'e was a relative of mine, I'd bloody well shop 'im! All those poor women . . .'

Katherine nodded. 'No matter what they'd done they didn't deserve *that*. There's the police from three counties looking for him.'

'I'd like ter know just 'ow 'e manages it, not the . . .

the . . . you know what, but where 'e stays, 'ow 'e gets rid of
the stuff 'e uses. It must be covered in blood.'

'I know. What do you think he does with it, Lizzie?'

'I'd say 'e burns it or chucks it somewhere.'

'And how does he know who wants to go through that kind
of an operation? They must get in touch with him. He must
have some kind of address – must keep some kind of a record.'

'Maybe it's just pieces of paper with the name an' address
on.'

'They were all from good families, no shortage of money
apparently.'

'I bet 'e charges a fortune then. It just goes ter show
though, Katherine, it's not just girls from our class what get
inter trouble.'

Katherine nodded and then remembered Ceppi's presence.
'What are you doing, Ceppi?'

Ceppi held the book closer to her face and didn't look up.
'Reading. It's history and I *hate* history, it's full of dead people.
Who could be interested in *them*.'

Katherine raised her eyes to the ceiling. 'She hates
everything. God knows what I'm going to do with her.'

The word 'dead' was still ringing in Ceppi's ears. It all
seemed to make sense now. The book with the names and
addresses, the reasons why he came and went. He often stayed
at weekends when no one else did. She'd not seen anything
with blood on but there were those strange-looking knives he
had in his case. Whatever kind of 'operation' it was he did
they died from it and because it was discussed with caution it
was obviously illegal. Her eyes were fixed on the pages of the
book but her mind was racing. Should she tell Katherine or

Sean or both, or should she make sure before she told anyone? She could follow him on Monday morning for she'd seen where he was going: 'Eliza Ward, No 4. Court, Scotland Road. Monday 9.30 a.m.' She was supposed to go back to school so she'd have to get rid of Nancy somehow – she'd tell Katherine she hadn't felt well and had come back. This way she would be sure. She'd be absolutely certain before she told anyone else. It frightened her but she felt it was the right thing to do.

Chapter Twenty-Eight

'HAVE YOU EVERYTHING you'll need?' Katherine asked as Ceppi was packing her schoolbag. Nancy was sitting in the kitchen waiting for her friend. She wished she was as clever as Ceppi. Ceppi seemed to learn and remember things easily while she had to struggle for hours. Ceppi helped her of course and it was that which kept her going. That and the fact that her mam was so proud of her.

'Yer'll get good marks on yer Leaving Certificate. Yer da would 'ave been proud of yer, Nancy. It's not factory work yer'll be applying fer, it'll be shop work and somewhere decent too. I won't 'ave the money fer any fancy typing school, but you'll 'ave a good job, wait an' see, and yer'll be able to turn up some money ter me an' that'll be a big 'elp.'

'Katherine worked in a factory,' Nancy had stated. She didn't want her mam to get her hopes up for she wasn't at all confident that she'd get work in a class of shop better than just a grocer's.

'She worked there because she wasn't trained ter do anythin' else, except keep 'ouse, an' that doesn't count. Besides, she knew it wasn't fer life, only until she got enough money ter start up 'er boarding house. You work 'ard at yer books, Nancy.'

'Ceppi, what's the matter with you? You're a slowcoach this morning!'

'I can't find my history book.'

'You had it last night. You can't have forgotten where you left it.'

Ceppi rummaged in the bag. 'No. It's definitely not in here.'

'Nancy, you'd better go without her or you'll be late. If we have to search the house I'll have to send a note in with this one.'

Ceppi was thankful when Nancy left.

'Right, start in your bedroom and I'll look in the dining room, although I'm sure if it had been in there Edwin would have noticed it.'

Ceppi ran lightly up the stairs and into her room. She sat on the bed for a few minutes, butterflies in her stomach. Was it really worth all this pantomime? She thought of what Katherine and Nancy's mam had said and she knew she *had* to go through with it. She bent down and pulled the book from under the bed where she'd hidden it and went down.

'It was under the bed.'

'You said you'd looked under there.'

'I know but . . .'

'Right, get off with you now. If you hurry you won't be late and you might even catch up with Nancy.'

'I get puffed if I have to run.'

'I didn't say run, just hurry.'

Anxiously Katherine watched her walk up the street. She wasn't sure if the child really was fit, despite Dr Walsh's assurances. She wondered if there'd ever be a time when she could stop worrying about Ceppi.

Ceppi was glad she'd brought some money with her for it was too far to walk to Scotland Road. But she was early and she wanted to avoid getting the same tram as him. He hadn't left yet. She walked slowly up to the main road and stood in the doorway of Sullivan's until she saw him turn the corner, then she went into the shop, keeping an eye on the window.

'Are you buying or just looking, Ceppi?' Mr Sullivan asked.

'I don't know.'

'Is it your first day back at school? Won't you be late?'

'I've a note, Mr Sullivan.' Word that she was loitering in the sweetshop would get back to Katherine but by then Katherine wouldn't care.

Realising that she would have to buy something she asked for six aniseed balls. 'For my friends,' she explained. She caught sight of a tram approaching the shop and hung back.

'Now what it is? I've given you the right change.'

'I know you have, I was just wondering if I should get more. I don't want anyone to be left out.'

'Child, are you going to buy the whole class sweets?'

'No. No, I think I'll just keep these, thank you.'

She hurried out of the shop having seen that tram pull away and another approaching.

She paid her fare and sat near to the door, putting one

of the sweets into her mouth. It had suddenly become very dry.

She watched the other tram like a hawk, determined not to lose sight of it. She got up and stood on the conductor's platform.

'Don't go jumpin' off or yer'll 'urt yerself an' I'll get the blame. You kids are all the same,' the conductor grumbled.

She stood still to collect her wits. Her heart was racing as she caught sight of him walking down towards Blenheim Street. He stood out because of his appearance. Beside all the other men and boys he was well dressed and with his case he looked like a doctor. Obviously other people had the same thought and a few men raised their caps to him.

He turned down Blenheim Street and she waited for a few seconds before following. She wrinkled her nose. She'd forgotten the smells and the sounds of the worst slums. Ragged children, most of them barefoot as she had once been, sat on the kerb, their feet in the filthy gutter. Their faces were pale and pinched with the cold and lack of decent food. Women with the heavy black shawls and old-fashioned hairstyles queued with buckets and jugs at the one standpipe. All the doors were wide open, revealing peeling paint and missing floorboards that had been ripped up and burned when there was no money for coal. A couple of half-starved dogs rooted in the rubbish. She could feel all their eyes on her for she also stood out in her school coat, black stockings and high-buttoned boots. And she wore a hat, a knitted tam-o'-shanter that Katherine had made for her. She began to feel very uncomfortable, and then to panic a little as she realised she'd lost sight of him.

She asked one of the women, 'Could you tell me where number four court is, please?'

She was regarded with suspicion. 'What do yer want ter know for?'

'I . . . I . . . have to see someone . . . there.'

'An' who'd that be then, like?'

Ceppi racked her brains. What was the girl's name? She couldn't have forgotten it. The woman had been joined by two others.

'Yer don't belong around 'ere, do yer?'

'No, I . . . live in Lonely . . . Kildare Street.' Then she remembered. 'The person I'm looking for is Eliza Ward.'

They all looked at each other and then back at her. 'Listen 'ere, girl, youse don't want ter 'ave nothin' ter do with that one!'

'Why?'

'Yer come from a decent family, don't yer?'

Ceppi nodded.

'Well, I'm tellin' yer that that one is no better than a bloody tart!'

'Aye, she spends 'er time down in Cannin' Place with all them low, dirty foreign fellers from the ships in the docks.'

'I . . . I . . . have to give her a note, that's all. I can put it through the door.'

'Leave it with us, we'll see the little scrubber gets it.'

'No! No, I *have* to give it myself! Someone paid me to bring it.' Ceppi hoped they'd believe her and would let her go. She'd got this far, she was determined not to lose him in this warren of streets and courts. 'A feller it was. He gave me sixpence and I've spent his money so I'll have to do it or he'll be fierce angry.'

'Go on then, but I wouldn't be 'anging around 'ere fer long or the kids will 'ave that 'at and coat offen yer.'

Ceppi tossed her head and looked defiant. 'Sure, I can hold me own. Haven't I seven brothers and sisters at home in Dublin and didn't I have to fight for everything?'

'Ah, I see ye're not as daft as yer look! It's just up there, three 'ouses up on this side of the street. Now, gerroff with yer then.'

They lost interest and she walked slowly in the direction indicated. She nearly missed it for the entrance was little more than a doorway set between two of the terraced houses. It led into a small, dark, dirty, cobbled square made by the walls of the houses. There was a single gaslamp set high on one wall, the standpipe and two communal privies, the overflow from which trickled in a stinking and constant stream into the main gutter. There was also one large ashcan overflowing with rubbish in which a flea-bitten cat with hungry-looking eyes scratched with its front paws looking for anything edible. She fought down the bile that rose in her throat. Had she really lived in conditions like this in Dublin? She couldn't remember it being this bad but maybe she had forgotten.

She looked around. The place was deserted and no wonder, for a fine drizzle had started to fall. None of the doors had numbers so she had to pluck up courage and knock on the first and nearest door. A young woman with a screaming baby answered her knock. Her dark hair fell in greasy strands around her face and her feet were bare and dirty. The baby was wrapped in what looked like a piece of an old grey blanket.

'Can you tell me which is number four, please?'

'Over there in the corner,' came the sharp reply and then the door slammed in Ceppi's face.

Over the bottom half of the one ground-floor window of the house was a dirty grey curtain with holes in it. It had been tacked to the top of the sash and she couldn't see over it. She didn't even know if it was the right room. There was a cellar and an upstairs room that had no curtains at all. She knew from experience that there would be at least three families living there. She'd come this far; she had to go on. She went up the three worn steps and caught hold of a broken eveshute that ran beside the front door and hoped it wouldn't break under her weight. It held and she managed to get one foot onto the window sill. Cautiously she leaned towards the uncovered top half of the window and peered in. She couldn't see anything at first, it was so dirty. Then her eyes made out the shape of a brass beadstead. She could see a young woman lying on the rags that covered it and which served as bedclothes, her legs wide apart and Edwin, wearing a big, unbleached calico apron, was standing between them. Her eyes widened as she realised that he had one of those strange knives in his hand. Suddenly the girl on the bed screamed in agony and without thinking Ceppi screamed too. He looked up and saw her, just before the eveshute broke completely and she fell headlong down the steps. She picked herself up and ran, headless of all the dirt and the filthy mud that stuck to her boots and splashed her stockings. He'd seen her! He'd seen her! She'd have to get away from here and fast. She ran past the women with the buckets and the children playing in the gutter. She ran as quickly as she could along the main road towards a tram that was approaching. She was gasping for breath as she jumped onto the platform just as it pulled away.

'God, yer must be in a shockin' 'urry,' the conductor commented as he hauled her further onto his platform. 'Sit down there an' get yer breath, girl.'

When she was able to speak she asked for a ticket to the stop nearest to Warren Street. She was shaking and very nearly hysterical but she had to see Sean. She *had* to! Edwin Sackville was the murderer who had killed those other girls and poor Tilly and now she'd just seen him about to kill another one.

The police station was deserted except for a young-looking constable who was writing in a book on the counter.

Ceppi was near to tears. 'Is Sean McGovern here, please?'

'No, why?'

'Where is he? Please, please tell me where he is. I *must* know.'

'What's the matter? You look terrible – and shouldn't you be in school?' he finished on a stern note.

'No, you don't understand, I *have* to see him? *Please!*'

'Well, he's not here.' He checked another book. 'He's not on duty until four o'clock. He'll be in the Station House. Go and ask Mrs Kincade.'

She didn't even stop to thank him before she ran out. Fortunately the Station House was attached to the police station. Her hammering on the door eventually brought some response in the form of an elderly, grey-haired woman enveloped in a large floral-patterned pinafore who'd obviously been baking.

'What in God's name are you at, hammering on the door like that? You'd give a body a heart attack.'

'Is Sean McGovern in, please? It's very, very important.'

'No, he's not.' She looked at Ceppi closely. 'Are you the child that Katherine Donovan brought with her from Dublin?'

'I am so! But where's he gone, please?'

'I think he and Katherine were going to go into town.'

'Thanks.'

'Wait! Wait! They might have . . .' She frowned at Ceppi's disappearing back. 'Kids today, no manners at all!'

Ceppi raced home and fell into the kitchen. There was no one there. 'Katherine! Katherine!' she called and then 'Sean! Sean!' but there was no reply. They must have already left for town. She felt terrible. She was shaking all over, her head was pounding and she was gasping for breath. She couldn't go to school in this state and she had no note to explain her lateness. Even if she got changed, she felt too ill and she couldn't get the sight of that filthy room or the girl or that tormented scream out of her mind. Would the girl be dead now? Would he have been arrested? Those women must have seen him go in and seen her run away. Surely they would go for the police?

She dragged herself upstairs, stripped off her clothes and crawled into bed, pulling the covers over her head. If she could just sleep, only for a short time, she'd feel better and she would be able to think more clearly. Gradually, as she got warmer, the trembling stopped, her breathing became slower and she drifted into sleep. But there was no escaping the nightmare. It formed in her subconscious and then passed into her conscious mind and she was again running through those dark, dirty streets. Faceless women and kids were

361

screaming at her to stop, but she couldn't stop because *he* was running after her and he was getting closer and closer. She awoke screaming to find him bending over her. The sound was abruptly cut off as he clamped a hand over her mouth.

'Shut up! Shut up or I'll shut you up for ever!'

The face that was so close to hers wasn't his face, not the one she knew anyway. It was twisted and his eyes blazed as if there were a red lamp burning behind them.

'I saw you! Don't think you can run away from me! You followed me! You're a sneaking, nasty child! You don't deserve to live, but I'm not going to kill *you*! No, if you tell anyone, *anyone* at all, I'll kill Katherine. I can't have her. She doesn't love me so I don't care about her any longer. One word and I'll kill her! I'll slit her throat with one of my scalpels!'

The hand was removed and she was pushed back onto the pillows. She couldn't make a sound. Her throat seemed to have closed over and she'd never been so afraid in all her life. He'd kill Katherine! And he would, she could see it in his eyes. They were the Devil's eyes and she whimpered and turned her face away from him.

He threw the covers back over her and everything went dark. She hardly dared to breathe until she heard the door close behind him, then cautiously she pushed away the bedclothes.

She wondered what time it was. Katherine was always back before she got home from school. Would Nancy come knocking for her? Then Katherine would want to know why she hadn't been to school. She began to cry, but softly; she didn't want him to hear her.

She lay still in the darkness, terrified that he'd come back.

She didn't know how long she'd been in bed and then she heard the front door being opened. Katherine was back. Would Sean be with her? Should she go and see? If Sean was there he could arrest Edwin so he couldn't kill Katherine. But if he wasn't . . . All she could do was wait.

The light from the lamp flooded the room and it was with despair that she saw Katherine was alone.

'Ceppi! Ceppi, what's wrong?'

'Is . . . is Sean with you?'

'No, he had to go on duty. Edwin is back and he told me you'd come home.'

Tears welled up in Ceppi's eyes. What could she do? 'I . . . I . . . didn't get to school. I felt sick so I came home.'

'Why didn't you go to Lizzie? She would have come in. I was only out for a short while. I went to see Maggie.'

'I . . . I . . . didn't think.'

Katherine placed her hand on Ceppi's forehead. The child was very hot and she looked dreadfully pale. 'I think I should send for Dr Walsh.'

'No! No, please, Katherine, I'm not that bad, honestly. I'll be able to go to school tomorrow, I know I will!'

'We'll see how you go. Will I ask Edwin to come and read to you?'

'No!' She almost screamed the word.

'Ceppi, are you sure there's nothing wrong? You're acting very strangely.'

'I . . . I'm just tired, Katherine. Really, that's all it is. I'll go to sleep now and I'll be better in the morning.'

'I still think I should send for the doctor.'

'No, please wait, Katherine,' Ceppi begged. There was no

knowing what Edwin would do if the doctor came asking questions.

'All right then. Will I bring you a hot drink up later?'

Ceppi nodded. She couldn't trust herself to speak.

'I'll light the gas but I'll lower the flame. If you need me, just call down.'

Ceppi lay staring at the wall. Katherine was downstairs with him. She didn't know what had gone on. She was in terrible danger. Could Ceppi trust him not to say or do anything to Katherine? What if that madness came over him again? The two gentlemen weren't due in until half-past six. What if . . .? She *had* to do it. She *had* to go for help.

Slowly she pushed back the covers and got out of bed. Making as little noise as possible she put on the clothes she'd discarded, which still lay on the floor. She picked up her boots and crossed to the door. She opened it and stood listening for any noise from downstairs. There was none so she crept down the stairs. She couldn't go the back way through the kitchen; that meant the front door and it squeaked and she'd have to leave it open.

Each tiny groan from the protesting hinges sounded like thunder in her head and to get the door open the few inches she needed to squeeze through seemed to take for ever, and there was always the chance that either Katherine or Edwin would come into the hall. At last she managed it.

The cool, damp air felt good as she sat on the step to put on her boots, but she didn't dare to run until she got around the corner and out of sight of the sitting-room window.

Again she was gasping for breath as she reached the police

station. She clutched at the edge of the counter and looked up pleadingly into the face of the desk sergeant.

'What's the matter, girl?'

'Is . . . is . . . Sean here?'

'Constable McGovern, do you mean?'

She nodded.

'And who is it that wants him?'

'Me. Tell him it's me. Ceppi Healy.'

'Are you Katherine's ward?'

The word 'ward' brought back the terror of the morning. 'Please! Please, hurry . . .' She collapsed and the desk sergeant came around and picked her up.

'You're in a terrible state! What's happened?'

'Katherine! And . . . and Sean . . .!' she said between sobs.

'McGovern! Get out here at once!' he yelled and from a door behind him Sean appeared.

'Ceppi! Ceppi, what are you doing here? What's wrong?'

She couldn't speak.

'Has she said anything, sarge?'

'Nothing except Katherine and then Sean.'

They sat her on the counter. 'Now, Ceppi, calm down. I can't help until you tell us what's wrong,' Sean soothed.

She tried to pull herself together. 'Katherine is in the house with *him*.'

'You mean Edwin? Edwin Sackville?'

'Yes . . . but he . . . I saw him kill someone this morning . . . I followed him.'

'Just a minute, child.' The sergeant looked at Sean.

'She never lies. There must be something in what she's saying. Tell me, Ceppi, slowly and carefully,' Sean urged.

Between sobs and bouts of coughing she told them and as the story of her suspicions and her journey that morning unfolded they both looked very serious.

'You'd better get round there, and fast. Take Creswell with you. He's built like a barn door and you can rely on him in any emergency. I'll keep her here.'

'No! No! I want to go home!' Ceppi screamed, catching and clinging to Sean's arm.

'Is there anyone she can stay with, a neighbour?'

'Yes. Lizzie Maynard, who lives next door.'

'Take her there then but I'd sooner she stayed here.'

Ceppi screamed again. She wasn't going to stay here while Katherine was in danger.

'Creswell, here now!' the sergeant bellowed. 'Take her!' he instructed Sean as Creswell, who was six feet four with a barrel of a chest, came down the corridor.

'McGovern will fill you in on the way. I'd carry the child, she's all in.'

Ceppi was picked up by the huge man as though she were as light as a feather and then both men hastily made the short journey back to Lonely Street.

Ceppi was set down and told to go in to Lizzie.

'I'll go by the laneway. It . . . it'll be . . . safer,' she replied. She felt much better now but she wasn't going in to sit with Lizzie, she wanted to wait until she knew that Katherine was safe.

Sean nodded and they watched her as she walked a few yards and then turned into the entry that ran behind the houses.

Katherine was just taking a steak and kidney pie out of the

oven when she heard the knock on the front door. She knew Edwin was in the dining room and had probably finished his soup by now.

'Edwin! Could you do me a favour and see who's at the front door, please?' she called. 'But if it's any friends of Ceppi, don't let them upstairs! She's not well enough for visitors.' He had seemed very concerned about Ceppi when she'd come downstairs and told him the child was ill.

'Probably she isn't fit for school yet. Doctors aren't always right,' he'd said.

'Maybe you're right. I keep forgetting that you're a medical man yourself.'

'Hardly, one year's experience, that's all. But I wouldn't worry too much about her,' he'd answered and she'd felt more relieved.

When Edwin opened the front door he was confronted by two policemen, both over six feet in height. His face drained of all colour and he turned and ran down the hall.

'After him!' Creswell yelled and Sean belted after Edwin with the other constable close behind him. Sean flung open the kitchen door and at the sight that greeted him he stopped dead. Edwin Sackville was holding a carving knife to Katherine's throat and her eyes were full of terror.

'Get back, both of you. She's coming with me. One move and I'll slit her throat.'

Sean forced himself to remain still. 'Edwin, calm down. Calm down and let her go and we can talk . . .'

Edwin's laugh held an edge of madness. 'There's nothing to talk about. I warned Ceppi, this will be one death you can't blame me for. I told Ceppi what I'd do. It's her fault.'

'Katherine, keep calm, don't struggle,' Sean warned.

'What about all the others?' Creswell asked.

'They came to me. They needed *me*! None of them wanted their children. They were all like my mother but worse, they wanted their kids killed before they were born!'

'He's mad,' Creswell whispered.

'I know they were all wrong, Edwin. Their crime was heinous before God and man. Let Katherine go and we can talk about those . . . other women . . . and their children.'

'No! You can't fool me like that! I'll kill her.'

Katherine cried out as he pressed the knife closer to her throat and her eyes pleaded with Sean's.

'I've nothing to lose, McGovern. I'm going to hang anyway, but I'll not let you have her! I love her. I've always loved her. She was different to all the rest, but you came along and took her from me.'

'I didn't take her. Just let her go. Do you want me to beg? I will. I'll get down on my knees and beg.'

Edwin's wild gaze had cunning in it. 'Maybe I won't kill her. Maybe I'll take her with me and make her marry me!'

Katherine was close to fainting and Edwin felt her body going limp. The slam of a door behind him made him turn and he saw Ceppi standing in the doorway clutching the small hatchet used to chop wood to stoke the fire. She was shaking with terror but there was no doubt she would have attacked him to save Katherine.

The distraction was enough. Sean grabbed Katherine and Creswell grabbed the hand that held the knife and twisted it until Edwin yelled in pain and dropped it. He continued to shriek as Creswell twisted it harder. They all heard the bones crack and Edwin fell to the floor, rolling in agony. Creswell kicked him hard in the back with his heavy boot and suddenly Sean's anger turned to blind fury and he began to kick Edwin too.

Katherine screamed at them hysterically. 'Stop it! Stop it! I won't have her go through all this again!' she sobbed, holding Ceppi tightly, her own fear forgotten. 'Her father was kicked to death and so was mine! For the love of God, don't raise those memories again!'

Instantly Sean was at her side. He took both of them into his arms while Creswell picked up a ranting, screaming Edwin and bundled him out of the door.

'Ah, God, I'm sorry, Katherine! I . . . I . . . hated him so much that—'

'I couldn't go to Nancy's, I *couldn't*!' Ceppi sobbed. 'I would have killed him! I *would*!'

Sean was back in control now. 'You did well, Ceppi, we wouldn't have been able to touch him until you distracted him. Are you both all right?'

'Yes. Yes, thank God! Oh, Sean, I couldn't do anything. I was terrified!'

'Hush now, it's all over. We'll get Lizzie to sit with you both and send someone for Dr Walsh. He'll give both of you something to calm you down.'

'Don't leave us, Sean, please?' Ceppi sobbed.

'I promise I won't be long.'

'He *won't*, Ceppi, I promise you he won't.'

Ceppi looked up at Katherine and her sobs diminished. Katherine never broke a promise.

Chapter Twenty-Nine

———◆———

LIZZIE WAS GETTING very flummoxed. 'Iffen yer touch that 'eaddress again, Ceppi Healy, I'll belt yer!'

'It's too tight!' Ceppi complained.

'Mam, they *are* too tight and there's all those pins stickin' in me 'ead!' Nancy added.

'Well, if the pair of yer 'ad decent 'air they wouldn't need ter be tight. Now shurrup the both of yer. I've got a bangin' 'eadache already with the antics out of the lot of yer.'

Ceppi and Nancy looked mutinous. They'd both been up since six o'clock and there'd been nothing but chaos ever since. Now they'd been instructed not to move a muscle until it was time to go, and that wasn't for ages yet.

Ceppi had almost forgotten that terrible night two months ago. Edwin Sackville was in Walton Jail waiting for the death penalty to be carried out.

Katherine had closed her boarding house immediately after that dreadful week and as the weather grew warmer and the wedding approached they were all trying to block what had happened out of their minds. They'd received tremendous help from everyone they knew and now even Ceppi's nightmares had stopped.

The whole street had been invited to the wedding. Thanks to the co-operative scheme, whose members now included nearly every woman present and had in fact been taken up by women in other streets, there was just about enough for them to rig out the kids and buy a cheap dress for themselves or have Mrs Savage run one up. Even so a lot of borrowing from the better off in neighbouring streets had gone on.

Maggie had gone with Katherine to get her wedding dress and she'd fallen in love with the first one she'd tried on in Blacklers. It was plain white satin with a nipped-in waist, high neck and leg-o'-mutton sleeves. The bodice was pintucked as were the collar and cuffs and she had a short train and veil. Her own headdress was a wreath of artificial flowers and she'd bought white leather boots and would carry a huge bouquet of white lilies, yellow roses and trailing smilax.

There had been a great debate and some argument about the dresses for the bridesmaids. Nancy and Ceppi had wanted either pale blue or pale pink with lots of frills and bows and bits of lace.

'The pair of yer will look like somethin' from a flamin' May procession!' Lizzie had remarked tartly.

'You'd both be better with something you can wear again, say for your Confirmation,' had been Katherine's advice.

'But aren't you having satin and fancy stuff?' Ceppi had protested.

371

'No she isn't, an' anyway, iffen she was she's entitled ter it, she's the bride,' Lizzie had settled the matter.

So they'd had to put up with cream taffeta trimmed with peach-coloured bows of ribbon on the short puffed sleeves and a wide peach sash. They both wore cream stockings and cream kid buttoned boots and Nancy had said that after the wedding she'd keep hers for ever and ever and no one would be allowed to touch them.

'Little does she know that when times is 'ard they'll be goin' with the rest of the stuff ter the pawnshop,' Lizzie had commented to Maggie.

It was the wreaths of cream and peach wax flowers that were causing the problem now. Half a box of hair pins and elastic had been used to keep them securely in place.

Nancy had told Ceppi she was lucky to have all that curly hair; she didn't have to suffer having to sleep with a head full of twisted pipe cleaners so her straight hair would curl.

They'd both also had a lecture from Father Scanlan about 'behaviour' and Ceppi had said the whole thing was going to be desperate.

'Apart from the food,' Nancy had said.

Sean's only living relation, an old uncle, was coming over for a few days. The rest of his family were dead or had emigrated to America but at least there would be *someone* from home to share the happiest day of his life.

The wedding breakfast was to be held in Katherine's house and the bit of land at the back, laughingly called 'the Rose Garden'. Frank and some of his mates had worked like demons tidying up and whitewashing the yard, clearing the weeds and flattening the ground as the food and drink were to be laid out there on long trestle tables. The weather was good and everyone was praying it would stay that way otherwise it would be a terrible crush in the house.

'God knows where she got this bloody idea from!' Mick Irving had remarked as he leaned on the handle of the spade and surveyed their handiwork.

'There's too many to fit into the house and she's invited the whole flaming street?' Frank had replied. 'Why, I don't know, but that's Katherine.' He was still disappointed that his bit of a dream of growing things had never materialised. Life had just been too busy.

They'd finished by setting up the tables and they'd promised to come early next morning to put out the chairs. Maggie and some of the other women were there from first light to cover them with white sheets and then lay the places.

'Maggie, do yer think the cake will melt?' Lizzie had asked with concern, eyeing the three-tier cake, the like of which she'd never seen before, except in shop windows.

'It's not going to be blazing hot at ten o'clock is it, Lizzie? I'm more concerned about the flaming flies!'

'Put some butter muslin over it – over everythin',' Vi Savage suggested and the idea had been declared an inspiration.

Maggie, resplendent in a deep rose-coloured dress trimmed with bands of pale grey satin ribbon around the hem and cuffs and wearing a large-brimmed, heavily decorated grey-and-rose hat, gave the tables a last approving glance before going back indoors.

Frank, who was to give Katherine away, thought that all the men would be sweating like pigs in their serge suits, and their stiff white collars were bound to droop. He'd also expressed the opinion – *sotto voce* – to Bernard O'Brian that that stuffed bird perched on a nest of pink frills and feathers on his wife's hat was definitely going too far.

'God, our Edna's like the bloody wedding cake! I told her so and you should have heard the ear-bashing I got,' Bernard had muttered back.

Katherine stood in her bedroom before the long mirror. On no account was she to sit down and crease her dress, Maggie had instructed. She smiled at the thought that this day would be remembered for a long time in Kildare Street. She tried to be open-minded about her reflection. Was the dress too plain? Should she have had a long veil? Would Sean think she was beautiful? As Maggie bustled in she gave voice to her thoughts. Maggie dismissed them all. 'The dress is perfect and so is the veil and of course he'll think you're beautiful. You *are* and you always will be.'

Katherine was a little nervous, though quite why she didn't know. She loved him and he loved her. She couldn't have got through all the traumatic times in her life without his help and it had all started on the night she'd gone to Beresford Place to hear Mr George Bernard Shaw speak.

She turned as the bedroom door opened and Ceppi and Nancy came into the room, followed by Lizzie.

Ceppi couldn't believe her eyes. Katherine looked so different. She resembled a princess, like the one she'd seen in Lewis's grotto, only better.

Nancy was speechless.

'Ceppi, come here to me.' Katherine took the child's hand in her own. 'This is the happiest day in my life and I want you to be happy too.'

'I am, Katherine. I just wish . . .'

'What?' Katherine looked concerned: the child's expression had changed.

'That . . . that Da could see me now.'

Katherine touched her cheek gently. 'Oh, Ceppi, he *can*. He's looking down on us all today. Your da, my mam, Mary and Tilly . . .'

'And my da, too,' Nancy added.

'Yes, yours too, Nancy. And all those who are asleep under the waves.'

Both Maggie and Lizzie dabbed at their eyes.

Lizzie cleared her throat and swallowed hard. 'There's no reason why this street should be called "Lonely" any more. From the day yer set foot on that ferry in Dublin yer've changed all our lives, Katherine. May God bless you fer all yer've done fer us.'

'Are you lot going to be in there all day?' Frank's voice broke the spell and the two women ushered the bridesmaids out, leaving Frank staring in admiration.

'He's a lucky man, Katherine.'

'And I'm lucky too, Frank. For most of my life I'd been alone, with no friends or relatives, until I came here, and there's no one I'd sooner give me away than you.'

Frank suddenly felt a large lump in his throat.

'Frank, will you get a move on? Everyone's gone, I'm the last,' Maggie called up the stairs. 'And don't let those two kids start acting up or let Katherine's train be dragged in the gutter.'

Katherine laughed. It was the tradition to walk to the church, weather permitting.

Frank grinned. 'She never stops. She'll never change.'

'Would you wish it any other way?'

'Well, to be honest, luv, no. Let's get going or I'll have them all on at me.'

Ceppi and Nancy were waiting impatiently on the landing, clutching their beribboned posies.

'Come on, the pair of you, it's time to go. You walk behind her and make sure you behave and keep that hem off the floor.' They both nodded but Nancy nudged Ceppi.

'Everyone will be looking at us, too!'

'But we can't wave, we'd be killed,' Ceppi replied.

It seemed as if the whole neighbourhood had turned out to see her, Katherine thought. With mounting emotion she smiled to everyone as she progressed, clinging tightly to Frank's arm. It *was* going to be the happiest day of her life. She'd come amongst these people as a stranger and they'd taken her into their hearts and lives and she'd never felt more at home and surrounded by friends as she did now. Her eyes filled with tears.

Oh, you *can't* cry *now*, you eejit, she told herself sternly.

The church was full. There were even people standing outside and tears again threatened. Frank turned towards her.

'Are you ready, Katherine, luv?'

'I am. I really am,' she replied quietly but assuredly.

The organ thundered out the first bars of the Wedding March and she walked slowly up the aisle. Friends and neighbours turned and smiled as she passed them but her eyes were fixed on the tall figure in the navy-and-silver dress uniform of the Liverpool City Police. Sean turned and their eyes met. His were full of love, happiness and admiration.

Katherine's too were full of joy and love – and pride for, as he stepped out of the pew and held out his hand to her, the sunlight caught the three silver stripes on his sleeve. Today, on her twenty-first birthday, with everyone she held dear around her, she would promise to love, honour and obey Sergeant Sean McGovern, and Katherine Donovan never broke a promise.